"Someone tried to kill Noah?" She said the words out loud in an attempt to make them real. "Why?"

Chelle held up her hand, as if warning Wynter not to leap to conclusions. "That's one possibility."

"You think it was an accident?"

Chelle shook her head at the ridiculous suggestion. "I think he was driving *your* truck when someone took a shot at him."

It took Wynter a second to sort through her fuzzy thoughts. Of course. Noah had left his Jeep in the parking lot and taken her truck so he could collect the fertilizer and take it to her grandpa's farm. Anyone who'd seen him driving on the isolated road would naturally have assumed it was her.

Her lips were numb, making it hard to form the words. "They were trying to kill me. . . ."

Published by Kensington Publishing Corp.

FACELESS

ALEXANDRA IVY

ZEBRA BOOKS
KENSINGTON PUBLISHING CORP.
www.kensingtonbooks.com

ZEBRA BOOKS are published by

Kensington Publishing Corp.
119 West 40th Street
New York, NY 10018

All Kensington titles, imprints, and distributed lines are available at special quantity discounts for bulk purchases for sales promotion, premiums, fund-raising, educational, or institutional use.

Special book excerpts or customized printings can also be created to fit specific needs. For details, write or phone the office of the Kensington Sales Manager: Attn.: Sales Department. Kensington Publishing Corp., 119 West 40th Street, New York, NY 10018. Phone: 1-800-221-2647.

Zebra and the Z logo Reg. U.S. Pat. & TM Off.

First Printing: September 2021
ISBN-13: 978-1-4201-5144-2
ISBN-10: 1-4201-5144-4

ISBN-13: 978-1-4201-5145-9 (eBook)
ISBN-10: 1-4201-5145-2 (eBook)

10 9 8 7 6 5 4 3 2

Printed in the United States of America

Chapter 1

The second week of April was a happy time for most citizens of Larkin, Iowa. The worst of the harsh winter weather had hopefully passed and the air would soon be scented with the promise of spring.

But for Wynter Moore, the date was a painful reminder of her mother's brutal murder.

Leaving her small apartment, Wynter walked down the narrow flight of stairs that led to the recently remodeled kitchen of her farm-to-table restaurant, Wynter Garden.

Usually the scent of warm bread and fresh herbs greeted her. This morning, however, the long room with the sleek stainless-steel appliances and green-and-white mosaic tiled floor was dark, with a distinct chill in the air.

Wynter ignored the tiny shiver that raced through her. Next week the kitchen would be humming with activity. There would be two chefs and four waiters buzzing around, moving in a synchronized dance to produce the gourmet breakfast and lunch dishes that had made the restaurant a success in the past seven years.

For now, the windows and doors would stay shuttered. A silent tribute to her mother's death. And the knowledge that without the trust fund the older woman had left behind, the restaurant would have remained an impossible dream.

Using the side exit, Wynter stepped out of the three-story brick building that had once been the local mercantile store for the small farm community. It'd been abandoned decades ago, and it had taken Wynter several months and a shocking amount of money to transform it into a restaurant and a comfortable apartment for herself.

In the end, however, it had been worth every headache and every penny.

Wynter shivered as a sharp breeze hit her with unexpected force, lifting her silvery blond hair to whip and dance until it covered her slender face. She clicked her tongue, impatiently grasping the long strands and tucking them beneath the collar of her puffy parka.

When she was working she kept her hair pulled into a ponytail. Today she wanted to make an effort with her appearance, not only leaving her hair down, but adding a layer of mascara to the long lashes that framed her hazel eyes and exchanging her faded jeans and casual smock top for wool slacks and yellow sweater.

Unfortunately, the promise of spring was more of a wish and a prayer than a reality today. The temperature hovered around freezing despite the morning sunlight, and the wind was cold enough to cut through her like a knife.

Hunching her shoulders, Wynter scurried across the empty lot next to her building. Long ago it had been a bakery, but after a fire three years ago the owners had walked away. Wynter had purchased the land and turned it into a parking lot. Eventually she planned to use a portion of the space to create an outdoor eating area surrounded by a garden. For now, however, she was happy to have plenty of space for parking.

There was no better place to have a business in Larkin than on the town square, but the place had been built when people's transportation consisted of horses and buggies. During her Sunday morning brunches, her customers had been forced to park blocks away.

She was scurrying along the edge of her building in the futile hope it might block the wind when a van with a familiar logo painted on the side parked next to her battered black pickup.

Wynter watched in surprise as the woman jumped out of the vehicle and headed toward the back of the van. Tonya Knox was the owner of the gift shop that was on the other side of the parking lot and one of Wynter's best friends despite the fact she was fifteen years her senior.

It'd been Tonya who'd walked her through the nightmare of business licenses, taxes, and local zoning. She'd also had a shoulder for Wynter to cry on when the water line froze and busted, forcing her to close down the restaurant for over a week. And when a rival restaurant owner in town paid his staff to leave nasty online reviews.

Wynter halted to watch as Tonya pulled open the back of her van. The woman was several inches taller than Wynter and double her weight. Tonya wasn't fat, just solid with the muscles she acquired in the pottery studio she'd built at the back of the gift shop. She could lift and carry the heavy blocks of clay without breaking a sweat. In contrast, Wynter was reed slender. Her grandfather told her that a strong puff of wind would blow her away.

On cue, a gusty breeze tugged at Wynter's hair, urging her to head to her truck and get the engine revving. It was not only too cold to be standing outside, but time was ticking. She wanted to get on the road.

"Hey, Tonya. What are you doing up at this hour?" she called out. "I thought you said you needed your beauty sleep?"

Wynter Garden opened at six in the morning and served until two in the afternoon. That meant that Wynter was up by four to start prepping for the day. In contrast, Tonya slept until midmorning and opened her gift shop at noon. Of course, she also gave pottery lessons in the evening so it was often midnight before she was locking up.

It made them perfect neighbors.

Tonya turned, revealing the numerous piercings that studded her nose, her lip, and her ears. She had short black hair and pale eyes that she framed with black liner. Beneath her leather coat, her body was covered in tats that represented her love for art.

She didn't try to look Goth. She just was Goth.

Until her father had passed when she was twenty-one, Tonya had intended to become a famous artist in Paris. Instead, she'd come home from art school to take over the gift shop and care for her mother.

"I've decided beauty is highly overrated," Tonya told her. "At my age I'm lucky to remember to put my pants on before I leave the house."

"That has nothing to do with age. I forgot my bra yesterday." Wynter shoved her hands in the pockets of her parka. "Are you working in your studio this morning?"

"Nope. I wanted to catch you before you take off for Pike."

"Me? Do you need something?"

"Here." Tonya reached into the back of her delivery van

and pulled out a small urn with flowers and tiny berries etched into the clay and a shimmering ivory glaze.

"It's lovely." Wynter sent her friend a puzzled gaze. "Is it a new piece for your shop?"

"No. I made the urn for your mother's grave."

Gratitude raced through Wynter, warming her chilled blood. Living in a small town meant she was constantly surrounded by family and friends, but she was also alone. Her mother had been violently killed in a senseless crime. That made her different from her neighbors. Tonya was one of the few people who understood how hard this day was for Wynter. "You didn't have to do this. You already made an urn."

Tonya shrugged. "It's been a few years. I thought you might want a change."

"That's—" The words caught in Wynter's throat. She cleared away the lump. "It's perfect. Thank you."

Her friend shifted in obvious discomfort. Tonya might create amazing art, but she kept her emotions hidden beneath her brash personality. "Yeah, yeah."

"I mean it, Tonya," Wynter insisted. "Not only the urn, which is gorgeous, but for remembering. That means a lot to me."

Tonya waved her hand in an impatient motion. "Get going. It's too cold to stand out here yapping."

"I'll come by the shop tomorrow and we can chat without threat of frostbite," Wynter murmured.

Cradling the urn carefully in her arms, she headed to her truck and started the engine. Her heart felt lighter than usual as she began her yearly pilgrimage.

Precisely three hours later she reached Pike, Wisconsin, and pulled through the line of cedar trees that marked the edge of the cemetery. She parked the truck and walked to her mother's grave that was in a section reserved for the Hurst family.

Once, they'd been a prominent family in town that had earned them an impressive marble mausoleum and large trees throwing shade over the entire area. Wynter wasn't sure when the Hursts had lost their fortune, but the downward spiral was visible in the size and elegance of the various tombs scattered around the lot.

Over the years she determined that it had been her great-grandparents that had drained the last of the wealth. Their graves were marked with large marble angels that had been hand-carved, but there was no standing vault and no wrought-iron fence to protect it from vandals. Just two graves buried in the ground. Her grandparents' graves were lacking even the angels. Just plain marble headstones, and her mother's even more plain. If it wasn't the lovely urn she carefully placed on the white slab and filled with fresh flowers, the grave would appear barren. As if the person beneath the ground wasn't worth the time or expense of remembering.

When she was young, she'd asked her father why he'd chosen to bury her mother in Pike instead of Larkin where she could easily visit. He'd told her that her grandmother had insisted Laurel be placed with her family, but his words had that tight edge that revealed he wasn't telling her the truth. At least not the full truth.

Once she finished wiping the year's worth of dirt that had collected on the tombstone, Wynter spent some time telling her mother the latest events in her life. There wasn't much to share. Just an update on the restaurant and the new muffler on the pickup. Her life wasn't exactly a thrill a minute. In fact, she nearly put herself to sleep trying to find something interesting to say.

Maybe she should start thinking about adding some spice to her personal life, she ruefully acknowledged. The restaurant was stable now, and her apartment fully re-modeled. It was time to put a little effort into refurbishing herself.

How she intended to do that was a question that had no answer.

Not yet.

A gust of wind swirled through the air, tugging at her parka and spinning her hair over her face. With a resigned sigh, Wynter rose to her feet and brushed the dirt from her hands. This year was colder than usual. Plus she had another stop before she could return to the protection of her truck.

Grabbing the strands of her hair, she tucked them under her coat and walked through the narrow paths that divided the cemetery into sections. It wasn't a particularly large space, and the newer graves tended to be closer to the main road. She was hurrying toward a mound of earth that had recently been disturbed when she belatedly noticed the tall man standing next to the headstone. As she neared, he swiveled his head to study her, revealing his pale eyes that when combined with his short blond hair hinted at a Nordic ancestry. He was tall and lean and she guessed close to her own twenty-nine years of age.

"Can I help?" he inquired, his tone suggesting he was being more than polite. He prepared to offer whatever assistance she might need.

Wynter shoved her hands in the pockets of her parka, wishing she'd grabbed her gloves out of the truck.

"Sorry, I was looking for Sheriff Jansen's grave," she said.

"It's here." He nodded toward the plot that was covered with bare, frozen dirt. "I'm his son, Kir."

"I'm sorry for your loss."

He nodded, his gaze sweeping over her with blatant curiosity. "Did you know my dad?"

"Not personally. He investigated my mother's murder."

He frowned, as if trying to place her face. "Your mother was from Pike?"

"Originally. She was Laurel Hurst. At least until she married my father, Edgar Moore, and moved to Iowa."

"Laurel Moore." He repeated the name; then his eyes abruptly widened. "She was the woman shot at the old Shell station."

Wynter flinched. "Yes."

It was vaguely horrible that her mother's life was now defined by her death. No one mentioned that she'd been a trained artist with a talent for watercolors. Or that she'd given up her career to care for her husband and young daughter. It was always "the woman who was brutally murdered."

"I remember the night." Kir slowly nodded his head. "My father brought you to the house."

She glanced toward the headstone. "He was very kind. I was still in the car after . . ." The words died on her lips, but with an effort, she forced herself to continue. She couldn't tell Rudolf Jansen how much he'd helped her that night, but she could share her gratitude with his son. She sensed he would appreciate knowing that his father had touched her life. "He found me and took me to your home so my grandmother could go to the hospital. They were still hoping my mother could be revived." A sad smile touched her lips as she recalled being perched on the edge of a wooden kitchen chair with a heavy mug clutched in her tiny hands. "He gave me hot chocolate and wrapped me in a blanket until my grandmother could come to take me back to her house." She shook her head, meeting Kir's steady gaze with a rueful smile. "He stirred the hot chocolate with a peppermint stick. It's weird the things that stick in your mind. I barely recall anything of that night, but the hot chocolate and peppermint stick are as vivid as if it happened yesterday."

"You're right." The expression on his lean, handsome face was somber. "Trauma does very strange things to the mind."

His voice was raw, as if he'd recently endured a shock, and she had a vague memory of hearing there'd been trouble in Pike.

She reached to lightly touch his arm. "Sheriff Jansen was a good man."

"He was." He frowned, tilting his head as if he was struck by a sudden thought. "You know . . ."

"What?"

"I've been slowly sorting through my father's boxes. *Slowly* being the operative word," he said. "I came across an envelope with your mother's name on the front."

Wynter dropped her hand, blinking in surprise. "What's inside?"

"I don't know, but it was in with his files that he brought home from the sheriff's office after he retired so I have to assume it has something to do with the case."

"The case was closed a long time ago," she said. "It was

a random mugging that went fatally wrong. Open and shut."

Kir was shaking his head before she ever stopped talking. "If the criminal was never caught and tried, then the case was never closed, according to my father. He spent his vacations going over old reports in the hopes he might have missed something."

"A man dedicated to his job."

Kir's lips twisted. "Until the very end," he told her in pained tones. Then he gave a shake of his head, as if dismissing his bad memories. "Would you like to see the file?"

Wynter shivered as a blast of wind sent a chill down her spine. Or maybe it was the stark reminder of what had happened to her mother twenty-five years ago. After all, it was one thing to visit a grave and arrange fresh flowers. It was another to dig up the awful memories of being a terrified child in the back seat of a car as her mother was shot point-blank four times in the chest.

"I'm not sure," she whispered.

"Christ, I'm sorry." His features tightened with regret. "The last thing you probably want is to be reminded of that night."

She waved away his apology. "I don't usually spend time dwelling on the murder," she admitted. "But I do try to keep her in my thoughts. I was so young when she died, I don't have many memories. That's why I'm here. This is the anniversary of her death." She glanced back at the grave next to her feet. "And since I heard about your father, I wanted to take the opportunity to say good-bye to the sheriff."

"I'll let you think about it," he murmured. "I'll be at my dad's house all day attempting to repair a roof that decided to start leaking in the middle of the night. It's a two-storied house with green shutters a few blocks north of here. Just drive up Olson Street and make a left on Fourth. You can't miss it."

"Thanks."

She stood as still as a statue as Kir walked away, her stomach rolling with a strange unease.

This was always a difficult day, but it wasn't usually complicated.

Now it felt as if she was standing on the edge of the precipice. Did she get in her truck and return to the comfort of her familiar routine? Or make the leap into the unknown?

Chapter 2

Wynter was sound asleep when the sound of something pounding outside the door of her motel jerked her out of her restless dreams. She forced open her eyes, wondering if there was some sort of construction going on. It sounded like a jackhammer.

Shifting on the lumpy mattress, she pulled the covers over her head, but the pounding continued. In fact, it got louder.

Along with someone calling her name.

What the hell?

Rolling out of bed she stumbled the short distance to pull back the edge of the curtain. She blinked twice, clearing the blur from her eyes, and peered out.

It was late enough that the sun had risen over the horizon, spreading pale sunshine over the graveled parking lot. Wynter swiveled her head to glance at the dark form standing in front of her door.

Noah Heller.

The sight of him punched into her with stunning force. Not only because he was the last person she expected to see beating on the door of her motel room, but because he was the sort of man who commanded a punch-in-the-gut reaction from women.

It wasn't just his six-foot frame that was packed hard with muscles gained from his physical labor as a conservation officer. Or the tanned face with features that had been chiseled to stark perfection. Or the dark eyes that held an authority far beyond his thirty-one years of age.

It was in the power of his presence. As if he carried around his own personal force field that captivated and held attention. Not the shallow charisma of a movie star. Or slick charm of a salesman. It was a deep, resonating magnetism that was utterly natural, and utterly irresistible.

Shoving her tangled hair out of her face, Wynter hurriedly pulled on her slacks and sweater. She hadn't packed a bag, which meant she was forced to wear the same clothes from yesterday.

Once she was presentable, she yanked open the door to regard her friend with puzzled confusion.

"Noah?" She glanced over his shoulder, seeing his green Jeep parked next to her truck. "What happened?"

He shoved his hands in the front pockets of his jeans, his thick muscles rippling beneath the insulated flannel shirt. It had to be subzero for Noah to wear a sensible coat.

"Everything's fine. At least things are fine back home," he assured her, his dark gaze sweeping from her tangled hair down to her bare toes. "I'm more concerned what's happening here."

She released a breath she hadn't even known she was holding. Part of her was always braced for disaster. Her therapist had told her it was a reaction to being traumatized when she was such a young child. Personally Wynter thought it was simply being sensible.

Hope for the best and prepare for the worst, right?

"Why would you be concerned?"

"I stopped by your apartment and you weren't there, so I called your dad. He said you were staying in Pike."

Wynter grimaced. She'd completely forgotten that Noah would be stopping by with a bottle of her favorite wine. Along with Tonya, he was one of the few people who knew that she made an annual trip to Pike to visit her mother's grave. When her customers asked why she always shut down the restaurant the second week of April, she told them it was to make repairs and upgrade equipment. She didn't want anyone intruding into her private grief.

Noah was different.

He was not only a friend, but he'd endured his own tragedy when his parents had been killed by a drunk driver when he was just fourteen years old. They shared a loss that others couldn't truly understand.

"That doesn't explain why you're pounding on my door at . . ." She lifted her arm to glance at her watch. Her eyes widened in shock. "Crap, it's ten o'clock?"

"You've been coming here since you were sixteen years old, but you never stay," he said. "I was worried."

Wynter struggled to concentrate on his words. Her brain was still fuzzy from the long hours she'd spent tossing and turning on the lumpy mattress.

"How did you find me?"

A wry smile touched his lips. "There are precisely two motels and one B&B in Pike. It didn't take a genius to track you down."

It was the sound of tires crunching on gravel that snapped Wynter out of her sleep-deprived haze. Noah had driven three hours to check that she was okay. Which showed a hell of a lot more concern than her own father. When she'd called to say that she would be staying in Pike, he'd mumbled something vague and quickly ended the connection. He hadn't even remembered it was the anniversary of his wife's death.

The truth was, Dr. Edgar Moore wasn't interested in anything beyond teaching literature at the local college in Larkin and collecting old manuscripts.

She stepped back. "Come in."

Noah quickly entered the room, his brows lifting at the cramped space with its cheap furniture. There was a narrow bed and one dresser with a portable TV bolted to the top. The ceiling was studded with beams that looked like they'd been made out of Styrofoam, and there was psychedelic wallpaper peeling from the walls.

"Yow." He shuddered as he turned a full circle. "It clearly wasn't the fine accommodations of the Pike Inn that lured you to linger."

Wynter breathed in Noah's warm scent of pine. She didn't think it was a cologne, just the fresh scent that clung to him from spending so much time outdoors.

"I don't know, it has a kind of Brady Bunch vibe," she teased, nodding toward the orange and purple and lime-green comforter she'd thrown on the floor. "Or maybe it's more a melted crayon box style."

He returned her smile. There'd always been an easy companionship between them. Ever since they'd met in grief counseling when she was fourteen and he was sixteen. That was one of the reasons they'd never dated. Lovers were easy to find. And even easier to lose. A good friend was more difficult. And far more precious.

"It looks like my grandmother's house," he murmured.

"Yeah, mine, too. Pike must have had a sale on avocado shag carpeting in the seventies."

Noah grimaced. "I hope whoever was selling it went

bankrupt. I'd hate to think it might have a comeback as some retro chic style."

She snorted. "Not every house can be wood floors, wood walls, and a wooden beam ceiling," she said, referring to the cabin he'd built next to a lake a few miles north of Larkin.

"Why not?"

She pointed toward the edge of the bed. "Sit down."

There were no chairs in the room, and she didn't want him towering over her when she explained why she'd stayed in Pike rather than return home.

It wasn't his fault. She was just short, and the room was excessively cramped.

"Yes, ma'am." He perched on the edge of the mattress with a curious expression. "Now what?"

She hurried to grab the manila envelope that she'd dropped on the counter next to the sink in the bathroom around three in the morning. It was the only way to stop staring at it so she could try to get some sleep.

Returning to stand in front of Noah, she shoved the envelope in his hand. "Here."

His gaze remained locked on her face. Could he see the tension that made her face feel tight with strain? Probably.

"What is this?" he asked.

She licked her lips. They felt dry and chapped. "Before I left the cemetery, I decided to find Sheriff Jansen's grave."

Noah frowned, as if searching through his memory for the name. "He's the man who investigated the murder?"

Warmth flared through her. Noah had a long list of special qualities. He was smart, loyal, dedicated to his job as conservation officer and as a member of the community.

Oh, and gorgeous.

He was also the first person she'd ever had in her life

who actually listened to what she said. The fact that he recalled Sheriff Jansen proved just how closely he paid attention.

"Yeah. He died a couple months ago," she said. "While I was there I met his son, Kir."

"That's not why you stayed." His voice was oddly flat.

She shook her head. "No. He told me that his father had an envelope with my mother's name on the front. He asked me if I wanted it."

"Obviously you did."

"I wasn't sure. Even after I stopped by his house to pick it up, I sat in my truck for hours debating whether or not I wanted to see what was inside." She'd been parked in the driveway, stiff with cold and with darkness creeping through the quiet neighborhood before she'd finally opened the envelope and pulled out what was inside.

"Curiosity won out?"

"Unfortunately."

"Why do you say that?"

"See for yourself."

Slowly, Noah opened the flap and tilted the envelope. He gave it a shake to empty the 8x10 picture that had been tucked inside. She stepped to the side so she could catch a glimpse of the grainy black-and-white photo that had haunted her dreams.

It was a fuzzy image of a slender woman standing next to a white SUV with the driver's door open. She was wearing a knee-length designer coat and leather boots that had three-inch heels. Her long, glorious blond hair framed her pale face that even at a distance, and blurred by the poor quality of the photo, was stunningly beautiful. On the other side of her was the outline of a gas pump and overhead was a canopy where the fluorescent lights battled against the darkness that surrounded the filling station.

Noah lifted his head to meet her troubled gaze. "Is this from the night your mother was attacked?"

"Yes. It's a still shot from the surveillance tape."

"Christ."

The Stranger had lingered outside the motel all night. Waiting. Watching.

There was a puzzling change in the annual pilgrimage. In the past, Wynter would travel to Pike to sit beside her mother's grave. Sometimes she would linger for an hour or two. If the weather was mild she would spend the entire afternoon.

The Stranger would watch from the fringe of the cedar trees, savoring the opportunity to remember. And perhaps to gloat. No, not gloat. That was the wrong word. To . . . feel. Yes. After endless days of gray, dull nothingness, this was a rare chance to recall the buzzing excitement that had once brought vibrant life.

No one knew the truth of what happened that fateful night. No one but the Stranger. It was a secret so big it had to remain buried deep.

Six feet deep.

This year was different. Wynter had paid her respects with the new urn filled with fresh flowers. Then she'd cleaned the marble headstone before she walked across the cemetery. Was she randomly strolling to stretch her legs? No. She halted at a grave to speak with a man.

The Stranger continued to watch. And follow. And wait.

The curiosity was tainted with an unease as Wynter entered a small, shabby house just a few blocks from the cemetery and then quickly returned to her car with a manila envelope clutched tightly in her hand.

The Stranger didn't know what was inside, but it had altered Wynter's tradition, which altered the Stranger's tradition.

Change was never good.

Never.

Chapter 3

Noah didn't know exactly what he'd expected when he climbed into his Jeep to make the drive to Pike.

He'd been concerned last evening when he'd gone to Wynter's apartment and discovered everything dark and locked tight. Not just because he hated the thought of her driving so far alone and in a truck that was what she called "temperamental" and what he called "a death trap." But she knew he would be waiting for her. It was a tradition they'd established on her sixteenth birthday. She would travel to Pike to visit her mother's grave, and he would be waiting to offer her comfort.

His concern amped higher when she didn't answer his calls or texts. At last he'd been forced to contact Professor Moore. The older man said that Wynter was spending the night in Pike. He didn't know why, or even when she planned to return, but he seemed to think Wynter was fine.

Noah wasn't as certain.

The highway between Larkin and Pike was well maintained, but there was nothing but cornfields for endless miles. What if Wynter had broken down? There was always the possibility her phone was dead. Or even that she couldn't get service. Anyone who lived in the remote areas of Iowa and Wisconsin knew that cell phones weren't always reliable.

He knew he had to make sure Wynter was okay.

And even after he'd gotten to Pike and discovered Wynter's truck at the cheap motel, he hadn't been satisfied. He had to see her.

Why? Well, that was a question he hadn't bothered to ponder.

Now he gazed down at the blurred photo in confusion. "No wonder you were upset. Why would the sheriff keep this picture?"

"Look on the back," she commanded.

Noah flipped the picture over and studied the words that had been scrawled with a shaky hand.

"'He has the purse. Why kill her?'" he read out loud. He lifted his head to send Wynter a puzzled frown. "What does it mean?"

Reaching down, Wynter plucked the photo from his hands and turned it back over. Noah was instantly aware of her soft, feminine scent. He felt the familiar spark of awareness. It didn't matter that she was missing the usual aroma of warm bread and herbs that clung to her skin after a long morning in the kitchen. She was still a tasty treat. One he had to remind himself was a friend, and nothing more, on a regular basis.

"Look." She pointed toward the center of the picture, thankfully distracting his perilous thoughts. "The mugger has my mom's purse and a clear path to escape. Why would he shoot her?"

Noah shrugged. "He was probably afraid she would recognize him."

"His face is covered."

Noah looked closer. It was difficult to see the man who was standing at an angle from Wynter's mother. He was in a shadow from the pumps, but he could vaguely make out that he was a few inches taller than his victim and wearing a puffy coat that made it impossible to know if he was skinny or fat. He could also see what looked like a ski mask pulled over his head.

"That doesn't mean she couldn't identify his voice," he pointed out, trying to keep his tone reasonable. There was a knot forming in the pit of his stomach. He suddenly had a bad feeling about why Wynter had remained in Pike. "Or maybe he was high on drugs. I had a man shoot at me because he was drunk and he didn't want me to tell his wife he'd been fishing instead of being at work."

"Or maybe there was no reason," she agreed. "I understand the picture doesn't offer answers. Just more questions."

Noah slowly rose to his feet, his hand brushing the tangled blond hair from her cheek. Wynter was never a sleek, sophisticated woman. She didn't wear designer clothes or spend hours at a salon having her hair styled or her nails painted. One of his old girlfriends had called her a bohemian and he'd realized that it was a word that captured Wynter perfectly.

She was unconventional, creative, and as ephemeral as a summer mist. She was also as committed to the protection of the environment as he was. He'd been impressed by her decision to build greenhouses on her grandfather's farm and use the bounty to create her restaurant, along with a farmers' market. Others in town had mocked her "hipster" style, claiming the good, solid folks of Larkin would never enjoy cherry chutney on their sandwiches or veggie hash for breakfast.

They were wrong.

Within a year, Wynter had a booming business that other restaurants in town could only envy.

It was a success she'd worked hard to achieve. He wasn't going to let anything distract her.

"Don't do this, Wynter," he murmured softly.

"Do what?"

He cupped her cheek in the palm of his hand. It wasn't a caress. Not exactly. It was supposed to be a soothing gesture, even if he couldn't resist savoring the feel of her satin skin.

"You've accepted your mother's death. You've built a wonderful life and business," he reminded her. "And more importantly, you've become a woman who would make your mother proud."

She glanced down at the picture clutched in her hand. "You think I should toss this in the trash?"

"I spent years trying to find a reason for my parents' death. The thought it was just some random accident made me so angry."

She nodded. "I remember."

His lips twisted. She was referring to his outbursts during the grief counseling group they'd shared. That had only been the tip of the iceberg. His poor grandmother had endured years of his petulant moods and deliberate attempts to strike out at everything and everyone who tried to get close to him.

"You should also remember that it wasn't until I accepted that fate wasn't fair—that good people died and shitty people lived, and that there wasn't any rhyme or reason to it—that I could put the past behind me," he said.

"Grim."

"Actually it's freeing," he insisted. "I didn't have to spend my nights lying awake trying to figure out why I was being punished. Or fearing that if I wasn't good enough or smart enough, someone else I loved was going to be taken from me."

Her features softened with regret that she'd forced him to remember his painful past. "I get that. I truly do." She shook her head. "But this is different."

Noah battled his urge to continue the argument. Wynter was kind and gentle and stubborn as a mule. "How?"

A sadness touched her face. "I don't blame myself for my mother's death."

"But?"

"But I wonder if there was more involved than just a random mugging."

"Does it matter?"

She paused, as if truly considering his question. "Yeah," she at last said. "It matters."

Noah resisted the urge to grab the photo and flush it down the toilet. There was no way to make Wynter forget what she'd seen. He had to somehow convince her to let it go. "You know, when I first started attending group counseling, I envied you."

Wynter looked surprised. "Why?"

"Because you grieved your mother, but you'd accepted her death," he told her. "You weren't constantly seeking answers to why she was dead."

"I was four when she died. I didn't understand for a long time she wasn't coming home." She shrugged. "I was too busy learning how to grow up without a mom to wonder why she'd been taken from me."

"So why look for questions now? It won't change the past."

"No, but it might change the future."

"Not in a good way."

She heaved a sigh. "Stop being so reasonable."

His fingers drifted down her cheek, tracing the line of her jaw. "What do you want from me?"

"To listen."

Noah forced himself to nod. As much as he wanted to insist that nothing good could come from tearing scabs off old wounds, he wasn't her therapist. He was her friend. And friends listened. "I can do that."

Wynter stepped back, holding up the photo. "Sheriff Jansen kept this photo for twenty-five years. Why?"

"The criminal was never caught, was he? Maybe he thought it might help to eventually ID the perp."

She pointed toward the fuzzy outline of the mugger. "Noah, this figure in the photo is nothing more than a dark smear. There had to be better images on the video," she insisted. "And why the question on the back? He obviously believed there was something strange about the shooting."

Noah frowned. Did she have a point? This particular image captured the criminal pointing his gun at Laurel Moore, her handbag clearly clutched in his free hand. Laurel had her arms up, as if assuring the mugger that she didn't intend to cause any trouble. It would have been easy enough for him to turn around and disappear into the surrounding darkness.

"What do you intend to do?" he asked.

"I'm not sure." She chewed her lower lip. "I wish the sheriff was still here."

"Why don't we go back to Larkin and you can think about it?" he urged. Once she was home she might put the past where it belonged. In the past.

She shook her head. "First I want to talk to Tillie Lyddon."

"Who?"

"She was the cashier at the station the night my mother was shot," Wynter explained.

"Why would you want to talk to her?"

"When I read the police report—"

"Hold on," he interrupted, feeling a jolt of shock. "You read the police report?"

She nodded as if it was the most natural thing in the world for her to have seen the intimate details of her mother's murder.

"I found it in my father's office. I was curious."

He clicked his tongue. "You know what they say about curiosity."

She offered a winsome smile. "It's who I am."

It was. She was an avid reader, she traveled to historical sites whenever she had the time, and she devoted herself to treating her customers as if they were her family.

"Tell me what bothered you about the cashier."

"She claimed she was alone in the station and that she'd gone into a storage room," Wynter said. "It wasn't until she heard the shots that she realized a crime had been committed and ran outside to find my mother dead and the mugger already gone."

"And?"

She lifted the photo and pointed toward the gas station in the background. It was barely larger than a shed with a huge window painted with the words SHELL GAS STATION, and a glass door.

"Who is that looking out of the window?"

Wynter sensed Noah's tension, even if she didn't fully understand it. Okay, she was probably on a wild-goose chase. There'd never been any reason to suspect that her mother's death was anything but a statistic. Just one more victim of senseless crime.

Not until she'd opened the envelope.

Still, it wasn't like she was making wild accusations or leaping to conclusions. She agreed with Noah that there were a dozen reasons the criminal might have pulled the trigger. Fear. Drugs. Insanity . . .

But there was no way she could return to Larkin without asking a few questions. Sheriff Jansen had been a trained lawman. If he was troubled by something in the photo, then she owed it to her mother to at least *try* to discover more about what happened that night.

Stopping by the motel office to check out, Wynter asked directions to Tillie Lyddon's house. The middle-aged woman didn't hesitate to offer a detailed map along with a pleasant smile, despite the murders that had recently devastated Pike. Small towns never changed.

Ten minutes later she was pulling her truck to a halt in front of a small, prefab house with a narrow porch and a side deck that was sagging beneath the weight of boxes, plastic containers, and at least two moldy mattresses.

"This must be it," Noah murmured, leaning forward to peer out the front windshield.

Wynter wrinkled her nose. Even with the morning

sunlight she felt a small shiver race through her. "It's sad, isn't it?"

Noah sent her a puzzled glance. "The house?"

"Yes."

"I'm not sure it has emotions, but I'll admit it looks run-down."

Wynter continued to study the windows that were blocked by thick curtains and the yard that was cluttered with trash.

"Houses might not have emotions, but they reflect the people who live inside," she insisted. "This one is sad. Neglected. Unloved."

His dark gaze swept over her face, an indulgent amusement softening his features before he was out of the truck and headed toward the front porch. "Let's go see what she has to say."

Wynter had to scramble to catch up, barely reaching his side before he pounded on the door. From inside they could hear the sound of a TV turned on loud enough to leak through the thin walls, but there was no response. Noah pounded again. And again.

"Christ, keep your pants on," a voice called out before the front door was being jerked open.

A woman not much taller than Wynter stood on the threshold, wearing an old robe that fell to her knees and a pair of worn slippers. Her frizzy hair was dyed black and her thin face deeply lined, revealing years of smoking. Her eyes were gray and hard with suspicion as she took in first Noah and then Wynter.

She smelled of cigarette smoke, coffee, and stale regret.

"Yeah?" she demanded in a hoarse voice. As if she wasn't used to speaking.

"Tillie Lyddon?" Wynter asked.

"I'm Tillie." The woman who looked as if she was in her late fifties scowled. "I suppose you're from the sheriff's office?" She didn't wait for Wynter to respond. "Tell that bitch to get off my back. I'm waiting on a dumpster to start cleaning."

"I'm not from the sheriff's office," Wynter assured her.

"Oh." The woman furrowed her brow before releasing a sharp, ugly laugh. "Then I suppose you're looking to squeeze money out of me for some worthless cause. Tough luck. I ain't got nothing to squeeze."

Wynter shook her head. "I'm not here for money."

The woman's expression hardened with suspicion. "Then what do you want?"

"I was hoping I could ask you a few questions."

"Is this a survey?" The scowl was replaced with a sudden burst of greed. "Do I get paid? I won't take less than twenty-five bucks. My time's worth that."

Again Wynter shook her head. "I'm Wynter Moore."

"And?" Tillie snapped. "Is that supposed to mean something to me?"

"My mother was Laurel Moore." Tillie's eyes were blank at the mention of her mother's name and Wynter swallowed a sigh. There was one way to jog the woman's memory. "She was shot at the gas station where you were working twenty-five years ago."

Tillie flinched, as if Wynter had physically struck her. "What is this?" she hissed. "Some sort of joke?"

"No, Ms. Lyddon. I'm in Pike to visit my mother's grave—"

"Look, I'm going to tell you exactly what I told that damned sheriff the hundred times he questioned me," Tillie interrupted, her shock replaced by an ugly anger. "I saw nothing. I was in the storage room when the bastard shot your mother. I'm sorry, I can't help you."

Wynter didn't know what she'd expected. Perhaps confused memories after so much time had passed. Or even a reluctance to discuss an event that must have been traumatic for everyone involved.

But not this fury.

Did Tillie fear that Wynter blamed her for not having done more to protect her mother?

Wynter pulled the photo out of the envelope she clutched in her hand. "I have a picture."

"Whoopie doo for you." Tillie stepped back, her face red and her eyes dark with an emotion that Wynter couldn't read. "I got a door. And a lock."

Wynter hastily shoved her hand out, waving the photo beneath the woman's nose. "This was just before my mother was shot. There's a person standing in the window, watching it happen."

Tillie stiffened, her gaze instinctively lowering to the photo that was nearly touching her nose.

"I don't see anything," she muttered.

Wynter reached to point at the gas station. "Right there."

"It's a shadow."

"It's you," Wynter insisted.

Tillie roughly shoved Wynter's hand away. "You can't prove that."

"I can't, but the photo can. All I have to do is have it enlarged and then cleaned up. There's software now that can do miracles with old pictures." She made the claim with more bravado than facts. She'd read an article about apps capable of fixing blurry pictures, but she had no idea how they worked or exactly how good they were.

Tillie licked her lips, her hand going to the pocket of her

robe to pull out a pack of cigarettes. "Someone must have come into the station while I was in the storage room."

"Who?" Wynter pressed. "You surely saw them when you heard the shots and came out to discover what had happened."

"Go away," Tillie snapped, stepping back.

"But—"

The door slammed in Wynter's face. Next to her, Noah muttered a low curse, grabbing her hand to pull her back toward the truck.

"She's lying," Wynter said, her tone challenging him to deny the obvious truth.

Noah grimaced, glancing back at the cluttered house. "Yes. She's lying."

Chapter 4

Tillie lit her cigarette, taking nervous drags as she paced between the stacks of magazines and empty pizza boxes. She shouldn't have answered the door.

It was ironic, really.

After quitting her job at the gas station twenty-five years ago, she'd gone on disability and hidden herself in this house. She'd refused every effort from her friends and family to convince her to leave unless it was the most dire circumstances. That was also when she'd lost interest in housekeeping.

She'd always been messy. She worked long hours on her feet; who could blame her if the last thing she wanted to do was mop the floors or clean toilets? But it wasn't until after the shooting that shit really went downhill. She had all the time in the world to clean, but the thought of tackling the growing piles of trash was exhausting. Plus there was an odd sense of safety as the magazines towered higher and higher, and the bags stuffed with garbage blocked the windows. Eventually she was confined to one small spot on her couch where she could see her TV. And a narrow path that led to her bathroom.

She was hidden. Protected from the memories of what had happened that night.

And so she'd clung to her crap until the damned sheriff had arrived and pounded on her door.

It hadn't been the old sheriff. Not the one who'd hounded her with questions about the killing. It had been a younger woman with a sour temper who threatened to have her evicted if she didn't clean up the property.

The woman claimed the neighbors were complaining about rats and the smell of rotting garbage.

Tillie had been furious.

This was her house. She'd inherited it after her parents died. She could do what the hell she wanted with it. This was America, wasn't it? Land of the free?

Except the sheriff had started throwing around words like "city fines" and "fire marshals" and "condemning" her home.

The thought of being forced out of her fortress and left exposed . . . It horrified her.

So when the knock had come on the door a few minutes ago she'd forced herself to answer it. She couldn't afford to piss off the authorities. Her fingers were shaking as she took a deep drag off the cigarette, filling her lungs with hot smoke and a sense of calm.

"Everything's going to be okay," she muttered, her voice rusty as an unused hinge. She winced, taking another drag. "Just fine."

The Stranger watched the truck pull away before slipping past the piles of junk that guarded the side door.

This hadn't been on the agenda. Tillie Lyddon had been satisfactorily silenced years ago. But things had changed.

The secrets that had been buried were stirring, the festering shadows threatening to crawl out of the grave.

How could the Stranger trust Tillie?

The denials he'd overheard just minutes ago seemed genuine, but there was fear in her voice.

With the right pressure she would crack.

A risk that had to be eliminated.

The Stranger refused to admit to the tingle of anticipation. Or the eager pleasure that banished the gray dullness.

Business was business.

The diner wasn't retro. It was just old. And dingy.

The dining area was a long, narrow room with booths on one side and tables next to the windows. The tiled floor had faded to a weird shade of pumpkin and the walls were covered by bumper stickers that had been collected over the past fifty years: DON'T POKE THE BEAR. SMILE. BE HAPPY. MY OTHER CAR IS A FERRARI. The front register was set on top of a glass cooler filled with meringue-topped pies and lemon bars, and the kitchen smelled of grease.

Still, it was reasonably clean, Wynter grudgingly conceded, and there were several customers gathered around the tables despite the fact that it was just eleven A.M.

Seated at a table near the back window, she watched as Noah wrinkled his nose and pushed away his half-eaten hamburger.

"Inferior to the lunches you serve," he murmured. "It's dry as cardboard."

She rolled her eyes, but inside she felt a smug pleasure at his words. Her restaurant was her baby. Her pride and joy.

"Not every place can be a Wynter Garden."

"Sadly true. But they could make an effort." He held up a french fry, shaking his head as it dangled limply from his fingers.

Wynter pushed away her own plate. The grilled cheese hadn't been bad. But it hadn't been good.

Serviceable. That's what her father would call it. In his world things were functional, efficient, and adequate. For an English professor he was surprisingly pedantic. Shades of gray.

Wynter, on the other hand, saw the world in vivid greens and yellows and splashes of blue. "Why do you think she lied?"

Noah drummed his fingers on the table. He didn't pretend he didn't understand her abrupt question. "My first guess is that she's scared."

Wynter agreed. Tillie tried to act tough, but it didn't take a genius to detect, beneath the brittle brashness, a woman who was terrified. Of what? That was the question.

"I could understand when the shooting first happened. I'd be scared too if there was a mugger out there who was randomly killing women. But after twenty-five years, why wouldn't she tell the truth?"

"Because she might know something that is still a threat to the perp."

"You mean that she recognized him?"

Noah shrugged. "It's one theory."

Wynter studied Noah's tanned, sculpted features that had already attracted the attention of every woman in the diner. When they talked about his work it was usually about his conservation efforts, and the community outreach programs. He never discussed the law enforcement side of his job. Now she realized that he would instinctively think like an investigator.

Exactly what she needed.

"Maybe if I offered her a reward she might be willing to tell me what she knows," Wynter suggested.

"The woman is obviously desperate for money," Noah agreed. "But would you really trust anything she had to say?"

Wynter thought back to her brief conversation with Tillie. As a rule she tried not judge people until she had a chance to get to know them; it was all too easy to jump to wrong conclusions. But there'd been a hard, cynical glint in the older woman's eyes. Wynter suspected she would say anything for some easy cash.

"Probably not."

"Besides, there's more than one possibility for why she lied. It might be because she was doing something she wasn't supposed to."

Wynter arched a brow. "Like what?"

"She could have had a friend watching the place so she could take a break or have a smoke." He shrugged. "Maybe she was in the storage room having sex."

She heaved a sigh. Noah was right. There were dozens or even hundreds more possibilities. "Meaning we'll never know?"

Without warning, he reached across the table to grab her hand. His skin was warm and his palms callused from physical labor. Something inside her relaxed at his touch.

"Wynter . . ."

His soothing words trailed away at the sharp screech of sirens. Like a flock of geese sensing danger, the entire diner craned their heads to watch the fire truck zoom down the narrow street with its lights flashing. A minute later the sheriff's SUV flew past.

Voices buzzed as customers speculated on what had

happened, then a man at the booth next to them pulled his phone from his pocket and lifted it to his ear. He shared a brief conversation with the caller then abruptly rose to his feet.

"Gotta go," he announced in a terse voice. "Have Suzy put the bill on my account."

His companion eyed him with a curious expression. "What's happening?"

"Fire at the Lyddon place," the man said. "They're calling in the volunteers."

"Tillie Lyddon?" the companion demanded.

"Yep. I warned the sheriff that place was a death trap." The man reached to grab his coat and pulled it over his flannel shirt. "It was only a matter of time until she poisoned herself with toxic waste or burned herself to the ground."

"Is Tillie okay?" someone asked from another booth.

The man looked grim. "Right now it looks as if she's trapped inside."

Wynter listened to the exchange in stunned disbelief.

"Shit," Noah muttered, tightening his grip on her hand to urge her out of her seat. Then, tossing a twenty-dollar bill on the table, he tugged her out of the diner.

Wynter headed to her truck parked at the side of the building, taking her seat behind the steering wheel as Noah climbed in beside her. For several minutes they sat in silence as they considered the awful possibility.

Wynter was the first to say the words out loud. "Is this our fault?"

Noah turned in his seat to directly meet her worried gaze. "How could it be our fault?"

She grimaced as the sirens continued to echo through

the street. "It's no coincidence that Tillie's house caught fire an hour after we spoke to her."

"You heard them in the restaurant. They've been expecting her place to go up in flames—"

"Noah," she interrupted.

He heaved a sigh, scrubbing his fingers through the dark mahogany strands of his hair.

"Okay, it does seem like more than a coincidence," he grudgingly conceded.

Wynter clutched the steering wheel until her knuckles turned white. "There's someone who didn't want Tillie to talk to us."

Noah's expression was grim. "All the more reason to return to Larkin. This has gone beyond being unhealthy. It's dangerous."

Wynter considered his words. She wasn't stupid. Or eager to attract the attention of someone who might have burned down Tillie's house. Or worse, shot her mother in cold blood. But if there was a killer out there trying to protect his secrets, then would she really be safe sticking her head in the sand? "You think going home will protect me?"

"Yes."

The word was said with blunt certainty, but there was an unease in his eyes that told Wynter he wasn't as confident as he wanted her to believe. "I can't just leave. I need answers."

He heaved a harsh sigh. "Do you have any relatives in town?"

Wynter shook her head. "My grandpa died when my mother was a senior in high school and my grandma passed away ten years ago."

"No aunts or uncles?"

"My grandma had a couple miscarriages after my mom so they stopped trying."

Noah glanced out the side window of the truck, as if considering their limited possibilities. They couldn't go door to door asking if anyone knew who might have set fire to Tillie's house. Or if they remembered the shooting at the Shell station from twenty-five years ago.

"What happened to your grandmother's house after she died?" he finally asked.

"My father sold it. I used part of the money to build my greenhouses." Wynter had been sad but resigned when her father had told her they had a buyer for the house. It had felt as if she was losing a part of the older woman who'd lived there for over forty years. Still, she didn't want to see it decay like . . . "Oh, of course."

"What?" Noah demanded as she dug her keys out of her purse and started the engine. "Where are we going?"

"To my mother's cabin," she told him, turning out of the lot and headed toward Park Street, the main street out of town.

"Where is it?"

"Just a few miles north of Pike. We can be there in less than half an hour," she assured him.

He pulled on his seat belt even as he sent her a mystified glance. "Why are we going to the cabin?"

Wynter didn't have a great answer. The truth was, she didn't have any better ideas.

"The weekend my mother died, she brought me to Pike to visit my grandmother and she stayed there," she murmured, picking up speed as they reached the main road.

"At the cabin?"

Wynter nodded. "It gave her the chance to work on her paintings without a child interrupting her muse."

"Was it something she did on a regular basis?"

It wasn't just a casual question. Wynter frowned, then belatedly realized he was wondering if someone might have known her routine and followed her. Maybe from Larkin. "We came to Pike at least one or two weekends every month."

"And your mother always went to the cabin?"

"Yes, as far as I can remember." Wynter furrowed her brow, trying to dredge up the ancient memories. "Usually she dropped me off at Grandma's on Friday afternoon and picked me up Sunday," she said. The precise details were fuzzy, but she never forgot how excited she was when her mother would pull out her Rugrats suitcase and start packing her clothes. She adored spending time with her grandma. No one would tell her to sit up straight or put on her shoes. Her nose would be dusted with flour and the air would smell like yeast and butter and warm cinnamon. "On that Sunday she was later than usual. I was already asleep when she put me in the car. That's why I was lying in the back seat when . . ." Her words trailed away and she grimly pressed on the gas pedal as they reached the edge of town.

"Did your father sell the cabin?" Noah asked, thankfully not pressing for details of that night.

"No. My grandfather left it in a trust-fund for me. Until I turned eighteen it couldn't be sold. By then we both rarely remembered I own it."

Wynter veered onto an access road, forced to slow to a near crawl as her truck bounced over the potholes. Wisconsin winters had a habit of chewing up pavement and turning it into an obstacle course.

"When was the last time you were up here?"

Wynter leaned forward, concentrating on the trees that lined one side of the road. She didn't want to miss the turnoff. "I haven't been to the cabin since my mother died."

"It hasn't been used?"

Her lips twisted at his surprise. Noah was addicted to nature, to the point where he'd built his home in the middle of a patch of land ten miles from the nearest town. It would take half a day to walk to his nearest neighbor. It would be unthinkable for him to own a property in prime hunting and fishing territory and not spend every minute possible there.

"No. My grandmother had the windows shuttered after Mom's funeral and posted NO TRESPASSING signs, but no one has been inside."

Noah fell silent as she reached the turn that was marked with an old billboard that advertised a nearby lodge and water resort. Thank God it was still there. It was the only way she could remember which road to take.

She turned onto the narrow path before taking the first left and then another right and another left. She remembered the few times her grandma had driven her to the cabin, to take a picnic basket filled with lunch for her mother, that she would always sing a little song. *Left, right, left. It's easy as can be. Left, right, left. Don't forget, sweet sweetie.* Wynter had no idea if she'd sung the song to remind herself how to get to the cabin, or in case Wynter happened to wander away, so she might be able to find her way back.

The path wound upward at a steep angle, and the dirt softened to a soggy mud. Worse, as she rounded a corner she discovered a large tree had toppled to land directly in their path.

"I'm afraid we'll have to walk."

Noah shoved open his door and jumped out of the truck without hesitation. By the time she joined him, he'd tilted his head back to admire the towering red pine trees that surrounded them. "It's a beautiful location."

Wynter nodded, heading up the road to climb over the tree trunk. The cabin wasn't far. "My grandma told me that my mother loved being here. It was a special place she came with my grandfather. Just the two of them. They'd fish and cook over a campfire and my mother would paint while my grandpa would read a book."

Noah kept step beside her, his large body moving with a loose ease that came from years spent hiking through the woods. Wynter instinctively moved closer. She wasn't afraid. The sun was shining and the sound of birds chirping added a song to the air, but the trees were so densely packed they made her feel claustrophobic. As if they were closing in around her.

She'd felt the same when she was just a little girl.

"Your mom never brought you up here to spend the night?" Noah asked, almost as if he sensed she needed a distraction.

"No." She picked up the pace. The lake was over the small ridge just ahead. "I didn't care. I loved spending time with my grandma," she assured Noah. "I would sit on the kitchen floor and watch her cook. Even after my mother died, I would come to spend time with her." A smile curved her lips. "She's the inspiration for my restaurant. I'm pretty sure heaven must smell like her cinnamon rolls."

"I hope you're right," Noah murmured, releasing a low

whistle as the trees at last thinned to reveal a wooden cabin perched next to the lake. "Is this it?"

"Yes."

Wynter stepped into the clearing, taking in the picturesque sight. The lake wasn't large, but it had been well-stocked by her grandfather and the banks were seeded with wildflowers that provided a sweet perfume during the summer months. The cabin was built of weathered wood with a tin roof and a chimney that was beginning to crumble. There was a shallow porch where a rocking chair used to sit along with a wooden rack for her grandpa's fishing poles. Both were gone now, and heavy wooden shutters had been fastened over the windows.

It made the place look gloomy. As if it had shut itself away to mourn the loss of her mother. Or maybe it was sulking at being abandoned.

Wynter felt an unexpected pang of guilt.

"How are you going to get in?"

She jingled the key chain she held in her hand. "I've carried the key for years. I keep telling myself that I needed to come up here and check on things. If nothing else, I needed to make sure there was no squatter. I've just never had the courage."

"You shouldn't have to do it on your own." Noah glanced around, as if emphasizing the isolation of the cabin.

She turned her head to send him a grateful smile. "I'm not on my own."

Chapter 5

There was a high-pitched screech as Wynter forced open the stiff door. A chill crawled down her spine. It felt like the cabin was battling to keep her out. As if it held secrets it wasn't prepared to give up.

Wynter shook off her ridiculous reluctance to step over the threshold. Her raw nerves were making her jumpy. The hinges squeaked because they were rusty. Nothing sinister about that.

Entering the cabin, she was instantly swallowed by the gloom. She halted to reach into her purse and pull out her cell phone. Then, pressing the flashlight on, she turned in a slow circle.

The room was small, with a low ceiling and a few pieces of faded furniture. The walls were covered with paneling, but the floor was plain wood planks. It looked like every other fishing cabin in this area, except for the fact that it was littered with the supplies of an artist.

Near the window was an easel holding a rectangular canvas. There was a tall stool that was half-hidden by the stained smock that had been carelessly tossed on it. Around the stool were piles of paints and brushes and half-empty jars scattered in random patterns. And in the far corner was a stack of finished oil paintings waiting to be framed.

"It's like a time capsule," she murmured, imagining her mother seated on the stool, her smock pulled over her clothes as she released her creative soul on the canvas.

A sharp sense of loss cut through her. Not only had the world lost a gifted artist, but she'd been robbed of a mother. It was tragically unfair.

Easily sensing her unexpected burst of grief, Noah headed back to the door. "I'll open a couple shutters so we can have some light."

She nodded, appreciating the moment of privacy. This was why she'd waited so long to come to the cabin. She'd always suspected the ghost of her mother would be strongest here.

Drifting toward the painting left unfinished on the easel, she studied the sweeping lines of vibrant color. There was something so . . . boldly alive about the strokes. As if the artist was perfectly confident that she was creating a masterpiece.

Lost in admiration, Wynter didn't hear Noah returning. It wasn't until he released a low whistle that she realized he was standing in front of the canvases piled in the corner.

"Your mother was talented."

Wynter glanced around the room that was now filled with sunlight. It didn't dispel the ghosts, but it lightened the heavy sense of sorrow.

"I've always regretted the fact I didn't inherit her artistic ability," she told Noah. "My grandmother said she knew my mom was going to be a painter when she found her in the dining room coloring a mural on the wall when she was just five. By the time she graduated high school she had her paintings displayed in the state capitol building and a dozen scholarships to the finest art schools in the country."

Noah turned, his brows raised as if confused by her words. "You did inherit her talent."

"I can't draw a stick figure."

"You create art on each plate that comes out of your kitchen."

"That's . . ." Words failed as his praise settled in the center of her heart. Noah wasn't a charmer. He didn't flatter women or feel compelled to constantly flirt. He was direct, honest, and sometimes painfully blunt. Which made his compliment all the more precious. "Thank you."

Noah stepped forward. "Are you sure you want to do this today? I can bring you back next week. Or later this summer when it's warmer."

Wynter wavered. A part of her wanted to turn around and walk away. Not because of the layers of dust, or stale air, or lingering ghosts. But she was tired from her long, stressful day, and not sure her emotions were entirely stable. Then again, would she be able to sleep if she returned to Larkin?

Not a chance.

Meeting Noah's worried gaze, she forced a teasing smile to her lips. "You just want to come when the fish are biting."

He glanced toward the window that offered a view of the lake. "I wouldn't mind testing the waters."

"We'll come back. But first I want to look around."

"For what?"

"I'm not sure." Wynter crossed to peek through the

opening into the tiny bathroom. There was a toilet, a bare sink with the plumbing exposed, and a handheld shower-head attached to the wall. Sparse. "This was the last place she stayed before she died. We might find something that will tell us if—"

"If she was alone," Noah interrupted.

Wynter whirled around, scowling at Noah who was standing across the cabin. "Of course she was alone. I was staying with my grandma and Dad was in Larkin."

Noah nodded toward the doorway to the bedroom. "Take a look."

Wynter walked the short distance to step into the room that was dark from the heavy shutters still across the window. She could make out a double bed in the middle of the floor that was piled with tangled sheets and a quilt. On the far wall was a built-in bookshelf and a dresser. Closer to the door was a trash can filled with old takeout boxes from a local restaurant.

"It's a mess," she murmured. "But I have a vague memory of our house being littered with stacks of painting supplies and toys scattered across the floor. After my mom died, my dad hired a maid to keep it spotless. It always felt empty." She grimaced. "Even more empty."

Noah pressed past her to walk to the center of the room. He pointed toward the tray at the foot of the bed.

"No matter how messy your mom might be there's no need for two wineglasses if she was here alone." He used the tip of his boot to point to an object on the floor. "Or that."

It took a second for Wynter's eyes to adjust enough to make out the empty condom wrapper. A strange queasiness

swirled through her. Just like the time Stevie Ellington
dared her to ride the Tilt-A-Whirl ten times in a row.

Why would there be wine and a condom wrapper if her
mother was here painting?

"Someone must have broken in," she burst out. Her
voice sounded too loud as it echoed eerily through the
room. "It's a perfect place if you're trying to avoid prying
eyes."

"True," he agreed, but there was something that might
have been sympathy in his eyes.

Wynter cleared her throat. "Let's look around."

Noah moved to the dresser, pulling open the drawers.
Wynter stiffened her spine and headed to the bed. Ignoring
the tangled bedclothes, she lowered herself to her knees to
peer beneath the mattress.

It was dark, but she could tell there was nothing stuffed
under there. Not unless twenty-five years of dust bunnies
counted. She coughed, starting to straighten. Then the dull
gleam of metal caught her eye. Reaching out, she grasped
the slender golden chain that was nearly hidden in a layer
of grime.

With a small sound of distress, she wrapped her fingers
around the jewelry and sat back.

"What's wrong?" Noah was quickly kneeling beside
her, a steadying arm wrapping around her shoulders.

She held up her hand, opening her fingers to reveal the
bracelet that was studded with small but perfect emeralds.
"This belonged to my mom."

"You're sure?"

"Yes." She stroked her thumb over one of the emeralds.
"I've seen her wearing it in old pictures. It was a wedding
gift from my father."

Noah's arm tightened around her shoulders. "We should go, Wynter."

He was right. There was nothing to discover here but hollow memories.

She'd reached to grab the edge of the bed to help pull herself to her feet when she caught sight of an envelope sticking out from between the mattress and the box springs. Without thought, she grabbed it and pulled it out to discover her mother's name scrawled on the front.

"Wait, Wynter."

Wynter ignored the warning, opening the envelope to pull out a sheet of paper. Quickly scanning the letter, she dropped it on the floor then reached beneath the mattress to pull out a dozen more envelopes. She read two more before she dropped them in revulsion.

"Ugh."

"Wynter?"

"I need a minute," she muttered, trying to absorb what she'd discovered. There was an old saying about having the rug pulled out from beneath your feet. That's what it felt like. Or maybe it was closer to having the blinders torn away from her eyes.

In either case, Wynter knew she would never be quite the same.

"Are you okay?" Noah finally intruded into her dark thoughts.

With slow, methodical movements, Wynter forced herself to fold the letters and return them to the envelopes.

"The letters are to my mother." She stopped, clearing her throat. "They're . . . I don't know, I suppose they're love letters."

"What do you mean, you 'suppose'?"

"They're a description of my mother's various body parts and what he intends to do to each one of them."

Noah stiffened. "Are they threats?"

She shook her head. She almost wished they were, but the letters had obviously been from a lover who not only had an intimate knowledge of her mother, but an ongoing relationship. There'd been graphic details of their previous sexual encounters along with promises for future escapades. And worse, there was a mention of her mother's visit to the Art Institute in Chicago. She'd spoken at a seminar for young artists. Just two weeks before she died.

Which meant the affair wasn't ancient history. It'd been going on for months. Her gaze shifted to the tray with wine and two glasses. And probably until the night she died.

"They're signed 'Drake,'" she managed to mutter.

"Does the name mean anything to you?" Noah asked.

"No." She clenched the letters tight in her hands, climbing to her feet. Then a misty memory teased at the edge of her mind. "Oh wait."

"You remember something?"

"I think my grandma's neighbor was called Drake." She furrowed her brow, struggling to pin down the name. It'd been ten years since she'd visited her grandma's old house. "Yes. Drake Shelton."

"Is he a friend of the family?" Noah rose to his feet, his warm body pressed against her. As if he wanted to be close in case she collapsed.

She might have been annoyed if her knees didn't feel precariously weak.

"Not that I remember." She dredged up an image of a large man who had pulled into his driveway when Wynter had been helping her grandmother unload groceries from the back of her car. He'd politely inquired if he could assist, only to be sent away with a firm no. "In fact, I don't think my grandma liked him very much."

"Why do you say that?"

"Just her attitude when their paths crossed. My grandma was the sweetest woman, but her voice was . . ." Wynter didn't have the right word. It hadn't been angry. Or afraid. It'd been oddly disdainful. "Sharp when she spoke to Drake," she finally finished.

"Did you ever ask her why?"

"No." Wynter shrugged. She'd been a child and then a self-absorbed teenager when she'd been visiting Pike. She spent her time in the kitchen with her grandma or on the phone with her friends. "I wasn't really interested."

"Do you know anything about him?"

"I remember seeing him driving a truck that had some sort of advertising on the side. I think it was a construction company." She could recall that the decal had the name of a company and a hammer. Or was it a wrench? "Maybe a plumber."

"We should see if he still lives in the same house."

She jerked, horrified at the mere thought of confronting her mother's lover. "Why?"

"It's possible that he was one of the last people to have spoken with your mother before she died," he pointed out in gentle tones. "If she was being followed or being harassed, she might have said something."

She glanced down at the letters. "What if it's not the same Drake?"

"Then he'll tell us he doesn't know what we're talking about."

The queasiness returned. She didn't really doubt that it was the same man. The name Drake wasn't that common.

Especially not in this area. Which only made the thought of confronting him more difficult. "I'm not sure I can."

Noah moved to stand directly in front of her, his hands lightly grasping her shoulders. "Wynter, you don't have to do anything you don't want to do. Not ever."

She released a shaky sigh. "I want to. But the thought of confronting my mother's lover makes me feel sick to my stomach."

"I'll do it," he assured her without hesitation. "Unless you would prefer to go home and put this out of your mind."

She genuinely considered his offer. A part of her was fully prepared to walk out of the cabin and drive away. She could return to Larkin and pretend the past two days had been nothing more than a bad dream. God knew she was used to nightmares. They'd haunted her for years.

But a larger part refused to stick her head in the sand. If something happened twenty-five years ago, she wanted to know the truth.

She owed it to her mother.

"No." She met his searching gaze. "We need to find out what he has to say about the night Mom died. She might have told him if she was being harassed. Or shared a description of a vehicle following her. If I was afraid, I would want to tell someone."

Noah brushed his lips over her forehead before he stepped back. "Are you ready?"

Wynter absently lifted a hand to touch the spot that was still warm from his lips as he wrapped an arm around her shoulders and steered her into the main room.

The sight of the canvas near the window sent a fresh wave of pain crashing over her.

"I thought she came here to paint. I used to lie in bed and think of how she spent the last hours of her life in this world. It made me happy to think she was doing what she loved." Wynter shook her head in disgust. "Instead she was here, cheating on my father. No wonder she never wanted me around."

Noah tugged her tightly against his side, firmly urging her toward the door. "We don't know what happened. Not for certain. Let's go talk to Drake."

She turned her gaze away from the painting layered in a coat of dust. "Okay."

Chapter 6

Noah didn't protest when Wynter climbed into the driver's seat. She was in shock, but she obviously needed the distraction of negotiating the truck down the narrow path that led back to the main highway and then through the city streets of Pike. Still, he breathed a small sigh of relief when she pulled to a halt in front of a ranch-style house with white siding and black shutters.

Switching off the engine, Wynter pointed toward the house next door. It looked exactly the same as her grandmother's old home, only with green shutters instead of black.

Actually, the whole block looked the same, Noah realized. As if there was a decision in the late sixties to create a subdivision of matching houses.

"That's where Drake used to live," Wynter said, her voice steady although her face was pale and tight with strain.

Noah's instinct was to reach out and gather her into his arms. She was hurt and confused and more than a little frightened. He urgently wanted to do whatever necessary to protect her from further harm. But he resisted the urge.

Not only would it be better for Wynter to get this encounter over with as quickly as possible, but he was beginning to suspect that his impulse to pull Wynter close wasn't entirely out of a selfless need to shield her from pain.

He'd always enjoyed Wynter's company. And any man alive would think she was a beautiful, desirable woman. But the past few hours had revealed that he was more invested in Wynter Moore and her happiness than he'd ever suspected.

Or maybe he had suspected and just ignored the danger.

"There's a truck in the driveway," he said, eager to distract himself from his disturbing thoughts. "Does it look familiar?"

She leaned forward, her hands clutching the steering wheel in a death grip. "The truck is different, but the decal on the side is the same." She wrinkled her nose. "I think."

"I'm going to see if he's home." Noah shoved open his door, letting in a blast of icy air. He shivered. After sixteen years living in the north, he should be accustomed to the cold weather, but his blood still longed for heat of his childhood home in Miami. "If you want to stay here—"

"No." She shoved open her own door. "I want to hear what he has to say."

Rounding the hood of the truck, Noah reached to grab Wynter's hand as they crossed the yard and stepped onto the small cement porch. She squeezed his fingers, standing close to his side as he rapped his knuckles against the aluminum screen door. A warmth raced through him at the knowledge that she was willing to accept his strength when she was feeling vulnerable.

There was a long, tense minute before the front door was pulled open and a man peered through the screen.

"Yeah?"

Noah studied the stranger. He was at least an inch taller than Noah's six feet, but wider, with the beginnings of a paunch that pressed against his white T-shirt and threatened to roll over the waistband of his brown work pants. His dark hair was cut short and thinning in the middle. His face was what his grandmother would call "beefy" and was chapped from spending long hours outside. Perhaps at one time he might have been handsome, but the years hadn't been kind, ravaging his features until he looked like a worn tire.

"Drake Shelton?" he asked.

The man pushed open the screen door to reveal his bleary gray eyes and the faint hint of stale alcohol that clung to his breath. This man had recently been on a bender.

"Who's asking?"

"I'm Noah Heller and this is Wynter Moore."

The man jerked at the name, his hands clenching into white-knuckled fists as he intently studied Wynter from head to toe.

"Laurel's daughter?"

Wynter nodded, her lips flattening. She'd obviously realized this had to be the man who wrote the letters to her mom. His reaction to Wynter's sudden appearance was blatant shock, not the vague curiosity of an old acquaintance.

Drake cleared his throat. "I haven't seen you since your grandmother died. How are you?"

Wynter managed a strained smile. "I'm fine. Thanks."

"What brings you to Pike?"

"I come every year to visit my mother's grave."

Drake grunted, as if he'd taken a blow to the gut. "Yeah. I noticed the fresh flowers."

Noah exchanged a quick glance with Wynter. Had the man been to the graveyard yesterday? Had he remembered it was the anniversary of Laurel's death?

After twenty-five years, surely only a family member or a lover would recall the exact date.

Or a killer . . .

"That's why we're here," Noah said, taking command of the conversation.

Drake frowned. "I don't understand."

"Wynter has a few questions about the night her mother died," Noah clarified.

"Oh." Drake sent Wynter a baffled frown. "Your grandmother never discussed the shooting with me, if that's what you're hoping. To be honest, we didn't talk about anything. She could be a difficult woman."

Wynter's brows snapped together at the insult to her beloved grandmother. Noah quickly directed the attention back to himself.

"We were interested in events that happened a few hours before she died."

The man managed to look even more baffled. "What events?"

"Her weekend spent in the cabin."

Drake froze, his eyes still bloodshot but no longer bleary. In fact, there was tension humming around him that assured Noah his words had hit a raw nerve.

"A cabin?" The man darted a glance over his shoulder before returning his attention to Noah. "What cabin?"

Noah folded his arms over his chest. As a conservation officer, he'd been trained to interview witnesses as well as potential suspects, but he didn't need to be an expert to detect that Drake Shelton was lying. He hoped the man never played poker. "The one you visited the night she died," he said.

"I don't know what you're talking about."

"You were there with my mother," Wynter said, her voice hard with accusation.

Drake muttered a curse. "Whoever told you that is a liar."

"We have proof." Wynter reached into the pocket of her coat to pull out the letters she'd found in the cabin.

Drake stared at the folded envelopes, almost as if he didn't recognize them. Then the color drained from his face and he stepped out of the house to glare down at Wynter. "What the hell is wrong with you?" he snapped. "My wife is inside."

Wynter tilted her chin. It didn't matter that the guy was towering over her. Or that he doubled her in weight. She faced him without flinching.

"I'm not here to judge you. All we want to know is what you remember about my mother. Did she mention being angry with anyone? Or was someone harassing her? Was there anyone who frightened her?"

The gray eyes were hard with a bitterness that went beyond being accused of an affair. It was a soul-deep resentment. "I barely knew Laurel. We went to school together, but that's it. If there was some man with her at the cabin that night, it wasn't me."

Wynter calmly pulled out one of the letters and began to read out loud. "'To my heart and soul, Laurel. I've been dreaming of you again. Of your soft breasts, and the taste of your sweet, sweet—'"

"Stop!" Drake flushed an ugly red, shoving out his hand

that was large and calloused from years of manual labor. "Give them to me."

Noah knocked Drake's hand aside, angling his body to make sure the man couldn't reach Wynter without going through him. "Tell us about the last night you shared with Laurel," he commanded.

Drake sent him a fierce scowl. "I'm not telling you shit. And if you come back here again, I'll have you arrested for trespassing."

Without warning, the man turned around to stomp back into the house. A second later, the front door was slammed shut.

Noah grimaced as he glanced toward Wynter. "That didn't go as well as I'd hoped."

She shrugged. "We know one thing."

"What?"

"He was with my mother the night she died."

Noah nodded. Drake's denial had been too violent to be real. He'd been with Laurel that night. So why deny it? Because of his wife? Or did he have another reason for hiding the affair?

Questions without answers.

"Now what?" he asked his companion.

Wynter shivered, her face pale in the fading afternoon sunlight. "Let's go home."

Noah kept the bumper of his Jeep directly behind Wynter's truck on the journey back to Larkin. She'd insisted she was fine to drive home, refusing his offer to take her home and return to pick up her vehicle. He believed she was physically capable, but he also knew she was emotionally exhausted. He had no intention of leaving her on her own until he was sure she wasn't going to have a meltdown.

Three hours later they pulled into the parking lot next to Wynter Garden and Noah rolled down his window.

"Get in," he called as Wynter climbed out of her truck and locked the door.

She sent him a puzzled glance. "What?"

"The best restaurant in town is closed, but we can still find something to eat," he told her.

"I'm not hungry."

"Then you can watch me eat."

Her lips parted, as if she was intending to say no, then, glancing toward the brick building that was shrouded in darkness, she abruptly moved to climb into the Jeep. "Yeah. Let's go," she muttered.

Noah pulled out of the lot and headed two blocks north to the old diner, parking in front of a low, stone building with large windows and wooden shingles. It was after seven P.M., but there were several cars lining the street. The gathered crowd was no indication of the quality of the diner food. The majority of the customers were in the back, in the barroom, enjoying the fine selection of microbrews.

They entered the empty dining room, setting off the tinkle of a bell, and took a seat at one of the tables with a Formica top and chrome legs. At the front of the long room was a counter with a few stools and the old-fashioned register. Beyond that was a kitchen where a lone man in an apron leaned against the sink with his attention glued to the phone in his hand. Overhead, the flickering fluorescent lights cast a greenish glow that did nothing to add to the ambiance.

Neither Noah or Wynter bothered to grab one of the

greasy plastic menus stuck between the ketchup and mustard bottles. The diner had never been famous for its delicious food. It was quick, cheap, and occasionally edible. The only reason it'd managed to stay open was because Wynter Garden was closed during the dinner hours.

A bored waitress wandered over to take their order, and ten minutes later returned to place the plates in front of them. Waiting until the older woman returned to the counter at the back, Wynter leaned across the table to study his large wedge of apple pie topped with vanilla ice cream and whipped cream.

"How old are you?" she chided.

He smiled, grabbing his spoon to dig in. The diner food was sketchy, but they bought their pies from a local bakery. Delicious.

"Thirty-one," he murmured, licking the whipped cream from his lips. "About the same age as you."

"No way." She settled back in her seat, plucking a carrot stick from her salad. "I'm still in my twenties."

"For what? Three more months?"

She crunched her carrot between her teeth. "Still in my twenties, old man."

He scooped up another large spoonful. "That's why I have to savor each day."

"That sounds like something we learned in therapy," she teased. She wasn't eating as much as he'd hoped, but a bit of color was returning to her cheeks.

"Probably." He swallowed the pie and ate some of the ice cream. "I liked therapy," he said, his lips twisting as Wynter snorted at his claim. She obviously remembered the angry, sullen teenager who'd first joined the group. He'd done everything in his power to disrupt the sessions, hoping to get kicked out. "I'll admit it took a while, but after a few months I stopped being an angry jerk long enough to start listening. It didn't stop me from missing my parents, but at least I wasn't constantly punishing my grandmother for being the poor fool to take me into her home."

"Yeah." She picked a slice of cucumber out of the salad. "It was nice to know I wasn't alone."

"Plus I got to spend time with you," he murmured. "Bonus."

Her smile was faint, but it had never looked more beautiful to Noah. "That was a bonus."

Noah polished off the last of the pie and shoved aside the plate so he could rest his arms on the table. "I've always wondered why you dropped out."

"My dad didn't want me going anymore."

Noah arched a brow. He'd assumed that Wynter stopped attending therapy because she'd just gotten her driver's license. Why go to grief counseling when she could run around with her friends? At the time he'd been disappointed with the thought she'd no longer be a part of the group, but happy she felt ready to move on.

"Why would your dad want you to stop?" he demanded. "Wasn't he the one who insisted you go to counseling?"

She tossed aside her cucumber, wiping her fingers on a paper napkin. "Erika suggested that I start seeing a hypnotherapist," she explained, referring to Dr. Tomalin who'd been the therapist who'd organized the grief counseling sessions. "She thought my nightmares might be caused by suppressed memories from the night my mother was killed."

Noah nodded. Wynter never described her nightmares in detail, but she did share that there was rarely a night when she didn't wake at precisely 11:11 P.M., screaming in terror. Once she'd left therapy, he'd never talked to her about why she'd stopped showing up, or if her nightmares had disappeared.

The first thing you learned in therapy was that it was like *Fight Club*. What happened in that room never left. Period.

Now, however, Noah was willing to break the rules. The past hours had shaken Wynter and stirred an unease in the pit of his stomach. What happened twenty-five years ago wasn't just the stuff of nightmares. It might very well have cost Tillie Lyddon her life.

"He didn't want you to be hypnotized?"

"No. He thought if I did have memories, it would be more upsetting for me to have them retrieved." She rolled her eyes. "And my grandpa was furious. He thought hypnosis was some sort of scam. In fact, he thought any sort of therapy was a scam."

"Your grandfather is a . . . um . . ."

Noah didn't have to imagine Sander Moore's reaction to the suggestion of hypnotherapy. The older man owned a farm just a few miles from Larkin and was a well-known pain in the ass. He was gruff, opinionated, and ready to point his rifle at anyone stupid enough to step foot on his land. He also unashamedly adored his only granddaughter.

"Yeah." She chuckled. "He is."

Her smile faded, her brow furrowing as if she'd been struck by a painful thought.

"What's wrong?"

"I wonder . . ."

"Wonder what?"

She met his questioning gaze, her expression troubled. "I wonder if my dad refused to send me to the hypnotist because he suspected my mom was having an affair. Maybe he was afraid that's what I would remember."

Noah slowly nodded. "Not a bad theory."

Drake retreated to the garage, opening the fridge he kept out there to pull out a beer. His head still throbbed from his night of heavy drinking after he'd visited Laurel's grave, but he needed something to steady his nerves. A damned shame he gave up cigarettes. But Laurel hadn't liked the smell that clung to his clothes and . . .

"Do you think I didn't know?"

The shrill voice pierced into his aching skull like a drill. He slouched lower in the lawn chair that he'd set next to the workbench. Dammit, this was his private space. The only spot in this godforsaken house that he could have a bit of peace. Now even that was being ruined.

"Not now, Mona," he growled, his gaze locked on the bead of moisture dripping down his beer bottle.

A short, thin woman with faded blond hair and even more faded blue eyes stepped around the riding lawn-mower to stand in front of him. She was wearing a waitress uniform from the truck stop outside town. The same place she'd been working since she graduated from high school thirty-five years ago. She smelled of fried hamburgers and diesel fuel.

"Why?" she demanded. "Because you're mourning the loss of your lover?"

Drake pressed a finger to the center of his forehead. "Because I have a headache and your yakking is making it worse."

He expected his wife to blink as if she was about to cry

and scurry back into the house. It was her usual habit. No doubt she thought she was making him feel guilty. Nothing could be further from the truth. He didn't care enough to feel guilt.

"Tough. You've been giving me a headache for years."

Drake frowned. "What are you talking about?"

Her face that had once been pretty was now lined with wrinkles and was hard with an ugly emotion.

"It was one thing to suspect you were having sex with those skanks at the local bar," she ground out. "They were nobodies that you used and discarded. But Laurel Moore—" Her voice cracked with pain.

Drake surged to his feet, the lawn chair scraping against the cement floor. "Don't say her name."

Mona flinched, but wrapping her arms around her too-thin waist, she stood her ground. "That year you spent sneaking off to that cabin to spend your weekends with her destroyed me." She regarded him with accusing eyes. "Did you love her?"

"Shut up."

"Did you?"

"Yes. Satisfied?" Drake took a deep swig of his beer, lowering the bottle to glare at the woman who'd become little more than an unwanted squatter over the years. "I loved her since high school."

Mona flinched, as if his words had caused her a physical wound. And maybe they had. "Then why didn't you marry her?"

Drake clenched his teeth. He'd been pissed as hell when Laurel had left town to attend college in Madison. He had known deep in his heart that she would never return. She was too beautiful. Too talented. Too . . . everything, to settle for a man like him.

"Because she wanted more than a small-town construction worker." He didn't try to disguise his bitterness. "She thought that professor of hers was going to take her places. Instead she was stuck in another small town with a man who had no appreciation for the fact he possessed an extraordinary woman." He swallowed the last swig of beer. "That's why she came back to me in the end."

"And what was I?" Mona demanded. "Second best?"

Drake shrugged. At one time he'd thought this woman was pretty enough. And his ego had been soothed by the knowledge that she loved him to the point she would endure any insult or betrayal. Who could have suspected that her fawning adoration would be so annoying?

"You were convenient."

Mona made a strangled sound, her face flushing to a weird shade of purple. It wasn't pain. Or betrayal. For the first time in their marriage she was truly furious.

"I followed you."

"What?"

"That last night you spent with Laurel," she said, white flecks of spittle forming on the corner of her mouth. She looked rabid as her eyes smoldered with emotion. "I followed you to the cabin."

Drake glared at his wife. Laurel was the only good thing in his miserable life. How dare this bitch try to taint his memory with thoughts of her creeping around, peering in windows, like some sort of perv?

"Why?" he growled.

"I was going to confront the two of you. I was tired of being treated like I was too stupid to know my husband was having an affair."

"So you spied on us?"

She paused, almost as if she intended to lie. Then she shook her head. "I didn't get out of my car. I didn't have the nerve."

Drake's anger didn't ease at her confession. Just the opposite.

"Of course you didn't. You're as timid as a mouse. I barely notice you skulking around this house," he taunted. "If it had been Laurel, she would have crashed in and stuck a knife in my heart. She was a woman with courage. A woman who knew how to capture a man's passion."

A strange expression settled on Mona's flushed face. "You want a woman with courage? Fine. How is this?" She sent him a tight, humorless smile. "I think Laurel's daughter will be very interested in what I saw that night."

Spinning on her heel, she turned to march out of the garage, her back stiff.

Drake watched her leave, his protest jammed in his throat. Had the world gone mad? First Wynter showing up on his doorstep with his private letters, and now Mona acting as if someone had shoved a backbone up her ass.

A darkness clouded his mind, his gaze shifting toward the shotgun he kept on a wooden rack nailed to the wall.

Chapter 7

Wynter had expected another sleepless night after Noah dropped her off at her apartment. She had enough to keep her awake. Starting with the photo left behind by Sheriff Jansen and then the fire at Tillie's house just after they'd questioned her, and discovering her mom had been having an affair with Drake Shelton.

But exhaustion had crashed over her just minutes after crawling into her bed. The only time she'd awakened was at 11:11 P.M. The exact moment her mother had died. She always woke at that time, and often she spent the rest of the night plagued with nightmares. Last night, however, a blessed darkness had claimed her around midnight, not releasing her from its clutches until nearly seven this morning.

When she finished her shower and dressed in jeans and a casual sweater, it was after eight. She ate a quick break-fast before leaving the house and driving to Grant College on the west side of Larkin. Parking in the private lot, she climbed out of her truck. The sun was shining, and the wind had settled to a light breeze, making it feel almost warm.

She told herself that was why her steps slowed as she strolled toward the domed administration building in the center of the small campus. Beautiful days in Larkin had to be savored.

Deep inside, however, she knew it was her reluctance to confront her father that was causing her feet to drag. It was one thing to bravely decide she was going to demand answers from her dad. And another to waltz into his office and dredge up the memories they both had avoided for years.

Entering the redbrick building that hadn't been changed since it was built in the 1800s, Wynter strolled down the wide hallway lined with glass cases displaying trophies and old pictures. There was a distant hum of voices from behind the closed doors, but there wasn't the frenetic energy that filled the lecture halls or dormitories. This was the stiff hush of bureaucrats who liked to pretend they were too dignified to raise their voices.

Wynter grimaced. Although she had attended school at Grant College and her dad had taught there for thirty years, she rarely visited his office. Not only did he spend most of his time in the classroom or library, but he'd never encouraged her to interrupt him while he was at work.

In the past few years, however, he'd taken over as head of the English department, which meant he spent less time teaching and more time dealing with administrative duties. At this hour he should be behind his desk.

Taking the steps to the second floor, Wynter paused outside the door at the end of the hall. Pressing a hand to her stomach, she sucked in a deep breath. Noah had offered to come with her, but she'd refused. It wasn't that she had any secrets to keep from him. Or that her pride in being independent kept her from leaning on another. Having Noah at her side was the only reason she'd been able to survive yesterday. He was precisely the friend she'd needed.

But Professor Edgar Moore was a fiercely private man. He rarely discussed his past relationship with his dead wife—not even with Wynter—and he never, ever revealed his emotions. If Noah was there, wild horses couldn't pry the truth from his lips.

Pushing open the door, Wynter stepped into the reception room that was decorated in muted colors. There was a long desk stacked with precisely arranged files and a sophisticated computer. Behind the desk was a middle-aged woman with blond hair pulled into a smooth knot at the nape and her pale face lightly coated with makeup. Her eyes were a cold, arctic blue and her clothes chosen from the power-suits section of the store. She oddly always reminded Wynter of a reptile.

Linda Baker had been her father's secretary for as long as Wynter could remember. She'd started as a receptionist for the humanities department, and as Edgar had moved up the professional ladder, she tagged along. Now, Edgar was dean of the English department, and Linda was an administrative assistant.

"Wynter, this is a surprise." The older woman blinked before she pasted a smile on her thin lips. She had a condescending manner that set Wynter's teeth on edge. She didn't know if it was just the woman's personality to be a patronizing bitch, or if it was directed specifically at her, but Wynter did her best to avoid the woman. She didn't need the bad vibes in her life.

"Is Dad in his office?"

"Yes, but I'm afraid he's preparing for a budget meeting."

"I need to have a quick word."

The secretary's smile remained as she reached toward

the intercom on her desk. "I really should check with Dr. Moore. You know how he hates to be interrupted when he's busy."

Wynter frowned. Linda had a habit of trying to prevent Wynter from spending time with her dad. She might have thought the woman was jealous, if it wasn't so ridiculous.

"I'm his daughter." Wynter firmly headed toward the door. "He's never too busy for me."

"Wait."

Ignoring the secretary who'd jumped to her feet and was hurrying to catch up to her, Wynter crossed the ivory carpet to push open the door to the inner office. She peeked her head in, locating her father seated behind his desk near the open window. "Am I interrupting?"

Edgar glanced up in surprise. "Wynter. Of course not. Come in."

She stepped into the office, hiding her annoyance when Linda bustled in behind her.

"Can I get you anything?" the secretary demanded, staking her claim as hostess. "Coffee? Tea?"

Edgar sent his secretary a warm smile. "Nothing for me. Thank you, Linda. Wynter?"

"I'm fine."

Wynter dismissed the woman from her mind as she moved to the center of the room.

"We didn't arrange to meet today, did we?" her father asked, his tone polite but distracted.

Nothing new in that. Edgar Moore hadn't known what to do with a young daughter after the death of his wife. He'd tried his best to give her a good home with everything her heart could desire. And Wynter never doubted that he loved her. But his focus would always be on his career. She'd accepted that truth a long time ago.

"No."

"Oh good." He lifted a hand to remove his glasses and polished them with a handkerchief he took from the pocket of his shirt. Her dad was a slightly built man with gray hair he combed from his narrow face. His green eyes were piercing, hinting at his impressive intelligence. His nose was prominent, and his skin pale from long hours spent inside. As always, he was neatly attired in a white dress shirt with a black tie and black slacks with leather shoes that shined from his morning buffing. "My mind is scattered with this budget report," he told her in rueful tones. "I can recite Shakespeare's sonnets, but I can't remember if the new chairs we purchased for the writing lab should be taken out of grant money or the endowment fund."

"Aren't all professors supposed to have their heads in the clouds?"

"'A fool thinks himself to be wise, but a wise man knows himself to be a fool,'" her father quoted in dry tones. "Now, what can I do for you?"

"I just want to ask a couple questions."

"Of course." He waved a hand in a vague gesture. "Sit down."

Wynter took a seat across the cluttered desk, her gaze turning from her dad to the paneled walls that were lined with oil paintings and the sort of heavy wood furniture usually found in English country manors. Wynter furrowed her brow. Where were the lovely landscape watercolors her mom had painted? And what happened to the soft peach-and-cream curtains that added a much-needed splash of color to the dull space?

Now it was all dark and stiff and . . . different.

"When did you change your office?"

"Oh. Yes." Edgar shrugged, his expression preoccupied. "Linda insisted that it was looking a little shabby so she spruced it up a few months ago."

"You let your secretary redecorate?" Wynter demanded, not sure why she felt offended by the thought. Probably because she didn't want Linda manhandling her mother's paintings. Or shoving them in some dark closet as if they were trash.

Her dad was suddenly defensive, belatedly realizing that Wynter wasn't pleased. "You know me. My taste in fashion is worse than my math skills. Your mother used to complain that I must be color-blind."

It was the opening Wynter was wanting. With an effort, she shoved aside her annoyance toward Linda Baker and concentrated on steering the conversation in the direction she needed it to go.

"I visited Mom's grave yesterday."

Edgar nodded, his face stiffening in a familiar manner. Her dad hated discussing his wife. Wynter had always assumed it was because it was still too painful. This morning, however, she wondered if there was another reason he didn't want to dig through his memories.

"Yes, so you said when you called," he murmured, slipping on the black-rimmed glasses and returning the handkerchief to his pocket.

"I also visited the cabin," Wynter continued.

Edgar looked confused. "Your grandfather's cabin?"

"Technically it's my cabin now."

"Yes, yes. Of course." His confusion remained. "Why would you go there?"

Wynter shrugged. "Someone needs to check on the property. My visit was long overdue."

"I suppose you're right," Edgar conceded. "Have you considered contracting a real estate agent?"

Wynter sucked in a shocked breath. "To sell the cabin?"

"You never use it and it's eventually going to deteriorate to the point it has to be torn down."

He was right. And if she was honest, she'd admit that when she bothered to remember she owned the cabin, it had seemed more a liability than an inheritance. It wasn't like she had any use for it. Not when she worked 24/7. But to hear her father say the words out loud hurt like a physical blow.

"It's the only thing I have left that belonged to Mom."

"I understand, but I think it's best for you to concentrate on the future rather than dwell on the past."

"Wanting to keep a part of my mom isn't dwelling on the past."

Edgar's lips thinned. "I don't want to argue. You should do what makes you happy." He glanced toward the grandfather clock set in the corner of the office. A less than subtle indication he was done with the conversation. "Did you have a reason for stopping by this morning?"

Wynter sucked in a slow, deep breath, giving herself an opportunity to consider what she was about to do. She wasn't as close to her dad as she wanted to be, but she loved him. The last thing she wanted to do was hurt him.

Unfortunately, asking painful questions was the only way she knew how to discover if her mother had been deliberately shot or if it'd been a random crime.

"I found something while I was at the cabin." She at last forced the words past her stiff lips.

"What?"

Wynter reached into her purse, pulling out the folded

envelopes. She held them up so her dad could see them. "This."

"Letters?"

"Love letters."

"I don't understand." He regarded the envelopes with barely concealed revulsion. "You want me to read your old love letters?"

"They're not mine."

"Oh."

Wynter leaned forward, dropping the letters on the desk. "Did you know that Mom was having an affair with Drake Shelton?"

"What?" Edgar jerked in shock.

"I said that Mom was having an affair with a man named Drake Shelton. He was a neighbor to Grandmother Hurst."

His face drained of color. "I heard what you said."

"Did you know?"

Edgar clenched his jaw, deliberately refusing to glance at the envelopes. "I'm not going to discuss this with you." He did know. She could read the truth etched on his face. "Yes, you are."

"Wynter."

There was an edge in his voice that usually made her back down. Wynter hated arguments. It wasn't that she was a doormat, but she preferred to avoid disputes whenever possible. This time, she stiffened her spine and plowed forward. "For years you've refused to talk about Mom. I think I deserve answers."

A nerve twitched at the corner of his mouth. "She's buried. Can't she be allowed to rest in peace?"

The photo revealing her mom's last moments seared through Wynter's mind. Had she sensed that the mugger was about to pull the trigger? Had she recognized who was standing in front of her? Had she pleaded for mercy?

The questions battered at her with agonizing insistence.

"Is she resting in peace?" Wynter muttered. "I don't think so."

Edgar heaved a loud, exasperated sigh. "I know this is hard, Wynter. Losing your mother at such a young age—"

"Exactly. My memories have faded until I can barely picture her face. I need to know who she was."

"Fine. We'll have dinner next week." Edgar reached for his pen. His hints that he wanted her to leave were becoming more obvious. "We can talk then."

Wynter shook her head. She knew this man. He suggested dinner at least a few times a month. Dinners that were forgotten or canceled or rescheduled for a later date.

She squared her shoulders. "Did you know about the affair?"

He clutched the pen so tight, it snapped in half. "Wynter. Stop this."

"Did you?"

With a muttered curse, Edgar dropped the pen and reached for his handkerchief. He carefully wiped the drops of ink from the tips of his fingers.

"Yes." The word sounded as if it was wrenched from his tight lips. "I knew. We'd been going through a difficult time. I was working long hours, and being the wife of a professor wasn't as glamorous or as exciting as Laurel thought it would be."

Wynter sat back in her chair, feeling oddly deflated. Had she nursed a secret hope that this was all a mistake? That her mother hadn't been using the cabin as some sort of sordid love shack?

She swallowed the lump that threatened to form in her throat. "Are you saying that she was bored?"

"Frustrated," Edgar corrected.

"With what?"

"With me. With her art. With this town."

Wynter gripped the arms of her chair as a distant memory teased at the edge of her mind. The sound of her mom shouting before she was slamming out of the house.

"Frustrated with me?" she asked in a soft voice.

"Yes, with you." Edgar tossed the handkerchief in the trash can beside his desk. It was a rare display of anger. "I think she was hoping an affair would make her feel like she did when she was still a teenager. It's not uncommon. Marriages are never smooth sailing. There're always troubled seas."

"An affair is more than troubled seas."

"Perhaps." He glanced away, his jaw clenching as if he was battling back an emotion he didn't want to share. "But we were working on our relationship. She swore she was ending the affair the weekend she . . ."

"Was murdered?" she finished for him.

"Died," he snapped. He always refused to use the word *murdered*. Or even *shot*.

Wynter assumed it was to protect her from the violence that ended her mom's life. Or because he couldn't bear to use the words.

"And you believed her?" she demanded.

"Yes." Edgar shoved himself upright, his face clenched as tight as a fist. "And that's the end of it, Wynter. My meeting is in ten minutes."

Wynter slowly rose to her feet, absently grabbing the letters off the desk and shoving them back into her purse.

There was a tension humming around her dad's slender body that she'd never seen before. He was truly upset. But why?

Because she'd brought up the painful memory of his wife's infidelity? Or because he was embarrassed that Wynter had discovered the truth? Or maybe he was upset with the knowledge his wife had been taken from him just when they were getting their marriage back together.

Whatever the answer, she wasn't going to get any additional information from her dad. Not today.

Walking out of the office, she was halfway across the reception room when she felt fingers close around her arm.

"Wynter." Linda Baker's cold voice sliced into Wynter's scrambled thoughts. "Can I have a word?"

Forced to a halt, she glanced over her shoulder. "What?"

"I overheard your conversation with your father."

Wynter glanced toward the connecting door. She'd been so distracted she hadn't realized the secretary had deliberately left it open.

"You were eavesdropping." She glared at the older woman. "That was a private conversation between me and my dad."

Linda didn't bother to apologize. They both knew she wasn't sorry. Instead she offered what she no doubt hoped was a sympathetic smile.

Crocodile. The word whispered through the back of Wynter's mind.

"I know you're upset. It must be a shock."

Wynter jerked her arm free. "As I said, it's private."

She was heading toward the outer door when Linda's soft words brought her to a halt.

"Did you come here to discover the truth or not?"

Wynter slowly turned. "Excuse me?"

Linda slithered forward, her features pinched into a sour

expression. "Your father will never reveal what he endured during his marriage."

Wynter narrowed her eyes. She'd always sensed that the woman was possessive of her dad. And reluctant to share him with anyone, including his own daughter.

Now she could clearly see that the woman was bitterly jealous of Edgar's dead wife.

"But you'll tell me?"

Linda leaned forward, drenching Wynter in the cloying scent of her expensive perfume.

"The man in Pike wasn't Laurel's first lover."

Wynter gasped at the ugly accusation. "How would you know?"

Linda shrugged. "It was common knowledge in town."

The words slammed into Wynter. "I don't believe you."

"I'm sorry, Wynter. I'm not trying to be unkind, but I won't have you thinking ill of your father." There was no mistaking the admonition in the woman's cold voice. "He tried to keep his family together despite the fact your mother was constantly unfaithful."

Wynter told herself to leave. She hadn't come here to listen to a woman she didn't even like talk trash about her dead mother. But her feet refused to budge. If Linda was telling the truth, then Wynter needed to hear what she had to say. "Who?"

The secretary blinked at Wynter's abrupt question. "What?"

"You said my mother's affairs were common knowledge. Who else did she sleep with?"

"Oh." Linda shrugged. "Dr. Peyton, the art professor."

Wynter jerked before she grimly controlled her expression. She didn't want to give Linda the satisfaction of seeing her shock.

It wasn't that it was hard to imagine Dr. Peyton indulging in an affair. He was exactly what you would think a professor of art should be. A handsome hipster with a careless charm and air of a free spirit. Every woman on campus found him attractive.

"Who else?" she demanded.

"Max Jenkins."

Wynter shook her head. "I've never heard that name."

Linda puckered her lips into a moue of disapproval. "He was a delivery driver. He committed suicide shortly after your mother revealed she was pregnant with you." She paused, presumably for dramatic affect. "There were whispers that he died of a broken heart."

The icy words pierced Wynter like a dagger. Whirling away from the secretary, she hurried out of the office. Ten minutes later, she was in her truck driving back home.

She tried to concentrate on her father's admission that he knew about his wife's infidelity. And that she'd intended to end things with Drake Shelton. Was it possible that Drake had been infuriated when her mother had told him the affair was over? He'd certainly looked like a man who was deeply mourning the woman he loved when they'd seen him yesterday.

Wynter clenched the steering wheel, struggling to keep her concentration on the road.

If her mother could drive one man to suicide, could she drive another to murder?

Chapter 8

Wynter intended to drive straight home. She was tired and in desperate need of coffee, but somehow she found herself heading toward the far side of Larkin where a small cemetery was hidden behind a border of old oak trees. Pulling to a halt near the front gate, she stepped out of the truck to wander among the graves.

She didn't really expect to find anything. Even if Max Jenkins had killed himself, there was no guarantee he would be buried here. Or that she'd been able to locate his grave. Larkin was a small town, but it'd been around since the early 1800s. A lot of people had died over the years.

She was rounding the massive, gothic-inspired mausoleum that had been built by one of the town founders when her eye was caught by a simple headstone next to the pathway. *Maxwell Jenkins.*

Was this it?

Wynter crouched down to brush away the thick layer of dust.

Maxwell Jenkins
Beloved son and brother

RIP
December 22, 1991

Wynter's mouth went dry, and with a muffled curse, she scurried back to her car. Why had she come? Just to prove that a man named Max Jenkins existed? And that he'd died around the time her mother would have discovered she was pregnant? Or because she desperately hoped Linda had been lying?

Back in her truck, she drove straight to the center of town. No more detours, she sternly told herself. They only caused more headaches.

Pulling into the lot, she caught sight of a silver van. She didn't need to see the sign on the side of the vehicle that advertised Wheeler Repair Services to recognize the owner.

She'd known Oliver Wheeler, or Ollie as she called him, her whole life. When she was a young girl, he'd worked as a farmhand for her grandfather. Originally, Ollie's father had been hired, but he'd taken off when Ollie was a teenager, leaving the young man stuck doing his job to keep a roof over his mother's head.

Over the years Ollie made extra money doing odd jobs around town. Now he ran his own business and was in constant demand by the locals. It was only his loyalty to Wynter's grandfather that ensured he continued to keep her restaurant a top priority.

Pulling next to his van, Wynter jumped out of her truck. By the time she rounded the hood, Ollie was joining her.

He was short for a man, and with skin that was pale despite the time he spent in the sun. His dark blond hair was cut short, his eyes hovered somewhere between blue and gray. He was in his early forties, but looked younger.

Maybe it was his shy smile, or just an air of innocence that never changed.

This morning he was wearing his usual coveralls with his name stitched on the pocket.

"Ollie." She sent him a smile, more than happy to have a distraction from her troubled thoughts. "I didn't know you were coming by this morning."

"I found a replacement handle for your walk-in freezer. I thought you would want me to take care of it while you had the restaurant closed."

"That would be perfect, thanks," she said. The freezer still worked, but the inside handle was broken. She was terrified someone might get locked in. "And if you have time, I'd like to discuss removing the cement at the back of the lot for the extension to the restaurant. I want to have the garden laid out before we start work on the patio."

Ollie nodded. "Do you want to wait until your visitor leaves?"

"Excuse me?"

"I saw someone leaving out the side door when I pulled into the lot."

She stared at him in confusion, a part of her hoping he was joking. Ollie was a great guy, but he'd always been socially awkward. Sometimes it was hard to know when he was teasing. When he simply waited for her response, she glanced toward the brick building. There were three entrances. A main door in the front for the customers. A side door that led into the back of the dining room and into the kitchen. That was the entrance her staff used. It also served as an emergency exit for her restaurant and the door she usually used. She liked walking through the restaurant before heading into her apartment. Not only to check on her business, but to simply savor what she'd created. The door at the back of the building was wooden and rarely used.

"The old service door?" she demanded.

"Yeah."

"Did you get a look at them?"

"Not really." He shrugged. "I wasn't really paying attention. I just assumed it was a friend who was staying with you."

"Was it a guy?"

"I only caught a glimpse."

"What was he driving?"

"I didn't see. Whoever it was disappeared behind the building." Belatedly sensing the tension humming around Wynter, Ollie frowned. "Should I call nine-one-one?"

Wynter hesitated. It was possible that Ollie had made a mistake. If he only caught a glimpse of someone, they might have been coming out of the employee door. The restaurant was closed, but one of her staff might have forgotten something.

Then again, did she really want to take the chance? Yeah, it was probably nothing, but what if someone had followed her from Pike?

She was still wavering between caution and courage when a familiar Jeep pulled into the lot.

Noah.

Relief crashed over her. It wasn't that she needed a man to take care of her, but there was something about having Noah around that made her feel as if she could face any problem. It was like that from the beginning. He'd been the one she'd called to take her to her first high school dance after the boy who'd asked her to go had stood her up. And towed her out when she'd driven her car into a ditch in the middle of the night. And stood at her side when she'd gone to the city council to get the zoning she needed to open her restaurant.

Realizing that Ollie was waiting for her response, she shook her head. "No, thanks. I'm sure it must be one of my employees." She forced the smile back to her lips. "Maybe you could return later to work on the freezer?"

"No problem." He paused, regarding her with obvious concern. "Is everything okay, Wynter?"

Wynter swallowed a hysterical laugh. Everything was absolutely not okay. It hadn't been okay since she'd opened that damned envelope.

"I'm fine," she managed to mutter.

Ollie frowned, but he didn't press her. Instead, he reached out to lightly touch her arm.

"Okay. You know where to find me."

Turning away, Ollie headed for his van, waving a hand at Noah who was walking toward Wynter with his long, easy strides. There was the sound of an engine starting and Ollie driving away, but Wynter was focused on the man who was standing directly in front of her.

This morning he was wearing his uniform. The tan button-down shirt and dark slacks were crisply pressed and molded to his muscular body. His boots were polished and he had a weapon strapped around his lean waist.

He always had an air of authority, but the uniform emphasized it.

"Are you having work done?" he asked as he studied her with a searching gaze.

Wynter absently reached up to grab the long strands of her hair. The breeze was picking up, bringing with it a chill that easily cut through her sweater. So much for spring.

"He came to replace a part on the freezer but . . ." Her words died on her lips as a shiver shook her body.

Noah stepped toward her, easily sensing her anxiety. "What?"

"He said he saw someone leaving my restaurant by the back door when he pulled in."

"Who?"

"He said he only caught a glimpse."

"Stay here."

Wynter didn't argue. Noah had the training to deal with potential danger. Not to mention he was carrying a loaded gun. Jogging across the lot, Noah easily pulled open the service door and disappeared from view.

Damn, that door should have been locked.

Wynter retrieved her phone from her purse as she nervously paced the lot. She would give Noah five minutes to do a quick search of her apartment, then she was calling for backup.

Her thumb was on the screen, preparing to press 911, when the door opened and Noah was retracing his steps to stand next to her. His pace was steady, indicating that there hadn't been anyone hiding inside, but there was a grim tightness to his face. Something was bothering him.

"Well?" she demanded.

"The door was unlocked." He sent her a stern frown.

"Don't give me that look," she protested. "I always keep it locked, but it's an old door. It wouldn't take much to force it open." She glanced toward her building. From the outside it looked the same as always. "Was anything disturbed?"

"No, but I still think you should call the police."

Her heart missed a beat at his stark tone. "Why?"

"There was a note left on your bed."

"What does it say?"

"Let the dead rest in peace."

Wynter grunted, feeling as if she'd just been punched in the gut. She'd been hoping this was all a big mistake. That Ollie had seen one of her employees leaving the restaurant. Or maybe just a friend who was knocking on the door to see if she was home.

Now she had to face the reality that someone had broken in and snuck through her private space. They'd entered her bedroom. Another shiver raced through her. And they'd left behind a warning that was clearly connected to her mother's death.

"Yeah," she muttered, pressing her thumb against the screen of her phone. "Let's call the police."

The Stranger watched from the alley as the police car drove away. Such a fuss over a tiny note. That hadn't been expected. Then again, it wasn't a disappointment. Not while watching the flashing lights and worried expressions. Excitement pulsed in the air. Just like all those years ago.

A craving for more crawled through the Stranger. This was just a pale imitation of what had happened in Pike. That had been up close and personal. And intoxicating. What could be more thrilling than the pleading tears, the desperate screams, and finally the thunderous crack of a gunshot? And threaded through it all, the hysterical sobs of a child.

The Stranger relived the memories over and over during the past twenty-five years.

Now the familiar pleasure was threaded with an aching for more.

Perhaps . . .

No. There were more important matters. The interruption this morning had revealed there were still loose ends that needed attention.

Personal attention.

Noah walked Chelle Simpson to her patrol car that was parked along the curb in front of Wynter's restaurant to keep from being blocked in by the crowd of gawkers. The cop was around the same age as Noah, and they'd gone to college together at Iowa State. They'd also dated on and off. Chelle was nearly as tall as Noah, with black hair she kept short and velvet dark eyes. Her body had the solid muscles of an athlete and her features were more striking than pretty.

Noah had always been confused why they couldn't go beyond the casual dates. They were both in law enforcement. They both loved the outdoors. They both played basketball on the weekends and often jogged the same routes in the morning.

It seemed a perfect match.

But neither one of them had ever pressed to make their relationship formal. And eventually they'd drifted apart.

Chelle had been the responding officer to the call that there'd been a break-in at Wynter Garden. Luckily. She might be one of Larkin's youngest cops, but she was by far the best. Plus he knew she would listen. Not only to the facts of the break-in, but to what they'd discovered during their short visit to Pike.

That didn't mean to say she would believe there was

anything funky going on with Laurel's death, but she wouldn't dismiss them as crazy conspiracy theorists. Or insist that he keep his nose out of police business. Some of the older cops were fiercely territorial.

She listened in silence as he described the photo that had been left behind by Sheriff Jansen and the fire at Tillie Lyddon's house, and the love letters that had led them to Drake Shelton's house. Once he was done, she nodded and pulled open the door of her cruiser. Chelle wasn't the sort of person who chattered. If she had something to say, she'd say it. Otherwise, she liked the power of silence.

"Is there any hope of discovering who broke in?"

"We've dusted for prints and I'll send the note to the lab to see if they can give us any clues. I'll have a chat with Oliver Wheeler to see if he can describe who he witnessed leaving the building." She glanced around to the stores that lined Cedar Avenue. "I'll also check to see if anyone has a camera that points in this direction." Her tone indicated she wasn't expecting to find anything that might be helpful. Noah didn't blame her. Larkin didn't have much crime and there was no need to have surveillance on an empty lot. "To be honest, there's not much more I can do," she admitted.

Noah nodded. It was what he'd been expecting. "Can you do any investigating into Laurel Moore's death?"

She paused, as if considering his request. Chelle wasn't the sort of woman who made empty promises. It was one of the things he liked best about her.

"I think there's an interim sheriff in Pike," she finally said. "I'll contact the office and see if they'll send the old files." She raised her hand as his lips parted. "But there's a possibility they won't like having outsiders poking their noses into their jurisdiction. And it's even more possible that if they do send the files, I won't discover anything new."

"I'd just appreciate you taking a look," Noah told her.

"I'll make sure a squad car does an extra drive-by to keep an eye on things."

Noah smiled with genuine relief. He didn't know what was going on. During the night he'd almost managed to convince himself they were overreacting. After all, they didn't have any actual proof that her mother's death had been anything but a tragic case of being at the wrong place at the wrong time. This morning had destroyed that vague hope.

Whoever had left that note was warning Wynter to stop digging into the past. Whether it was because Laurel's death hadn't been a random crime, or because there was something else in the past they didn't want discovered. He wasn't going to leap to conclusions.

"Thanks, Chelle," he murmured.

Chelle started to climb into the car, then, pausing, she glanced over her shoulder. "Wynter is pretty rattled. I'm not sure she should stay here alone."

Noah agreed. Wynter was a sensible woman who was more than capable of taking care of herself. But the past couple of days had taken their toll. And now someone had broken into her home and left a threatening note. Even if she wanted to stay in the apartment, he would have done his best to change her mind.

"She's packing a bag," he said.

Chelle arched a brow. "Is she staying with you?"

"Her grandfather."

"Ah."

Noah studied his friend. "Ah?"

Her lips twitched. "Did you want her to stay with you?"

Yes. The word formed in his mind with shocking clarity. He'd hoped that she would suggest moving into his cabin so he could protect her. Not only because she trusted him as a friend, but because . . .

Because she wanted to be near him.

Noah swallowed a resigned sigh. The past couple of days had smashed through his stubborn pretense that Wynter was just a friend. In fact, he suspected there'd always been a part of him that knew he was just waiting for the right time to admit it, both to himself and Wynter.

Now was not the right time.

"I don't want her to be on her own," he told Chelle.

"That isn't an answer."

"It's the only one you're going to get."

"Fair enough." Chelle slid behind the wheel of her cruiser. "Let me know if Wynter has any more unwanted visitors."

Chapter 9

Wynter spent the afternoon scrubbing the rain barrels she used to water the vegetable beds in the greenhouses, along with repainting the compost container that held the fertilizer. She needed hard physical labor to keep herself from dwelling on the thought of someone creeping through her home. Perhaps the same person who killed her mother.

The mere possibility made her skin crawl.

It wasn't until the shadows began to spread over the field where she'd built her greenhouses that she headed up the hill to the small white farmhouse with a slanted roof and a wraparound porch. Over the past hour the breeze had picked up, and with the dropping temperature it had gone from chilly to downright frigid.

Picking up her pace, Wynter scurried past the milk barn and detached garage. She paused long enough to wash her hands beneath the outside water pump before she climbed the steps to the porch.

Her grandpa lifted himself out of the wooden rocking chair where he'd been waiting for her, eying her with approval. "Well, at least you have some color in your cheeks," he said.

Wynter grimaced. She'd grabbed a jacket and stocking hat before heading down to the field, but neither had been enough by the end of the day.

"I think it's called frostbite."

The older man snorted. Sander Moore was a short, reed-slender man who still had a thick mane of silver hair despite his seventy-nine years of age. His eyes were a piercing blue and his skin was perpetually ruddy. It was past five o'clock so he'd changed out of his overalls into a pair of slacks and button-down shirt. It was a ritual he performed every evening even though he'd lived alone since his wife died thirty years ago. He told Wynter that changing clothes was the only way a farmer knew the workday was over.

"Nonsense," he chided. "Air isn't good for you unless it's brisk."

She shivered. "Tell that to the people happily basking on the beaches in Florida."

"Don't tell me you're getting soft, are ya?"

Wynter turned to gaze at the rolling pastures that surrounded the farm. She loved the view. The house was built on the highest point of land, allowing her to see for miles despite the shadows that were creeping over empty fields and paddocks. Once this had been a bustling dairy farm, but over the years her grandpa had been forced to cut back. Not only because of finances, but without an heir who was willing to take over the bulk of the work, he'd grown too old and frail to continue.

"Maybe," she murmured.

Sander moved to pull open the nearby door. "Come in. I have stew and hot rolls on the table."

"Sounds good."

They walked into the kitchen that hadn't been renovated

since the late fifties. The cabinets were painted lime green and hung at wonky angles as the house settled on the sagging foundation. There was a dip in the middle of the floor and the appliances had yellowed from white to a weird beige. Still, there was a homey comfort to the house that had been built by her great-great-grandfather.

They settled at the card table next to the fridge. He had a formal dining room, but the wooden table was buried beneath boxes of receipts, tax documents, and old magazines. Sander wasn't a hoarder, but he found it hard to throw away anything he thought he might use later. Besides, when he was here alone he usually ate on a TV tray in the living room.

Wynter was buttering a hot roll when her grandpa asked the question that had no doubt been on his lips since she arrived at the farm.

"Are you going to tell me what's happened?"

She took a bite of the stew, ignoring the tough meat and potatoes that weren't quite cooked through. Her grandpa had many fine qualities. Cooking wasn't one of them.

"I'm not really sure," she muttered.

Sander cracked open his beer. It didn't matter if it was eighty degrees or eighty below zero. Her grandpa always had a beer with dinner.

"Man trouble?"

Wynter's lips twisted. If only it was that simple. "Who has time for a man?"

"Good for you." Sander lifted his bottle in a toast to her good sense. "A smart woman takes care of herself. No need to throw yourself away on some loser."

Wynter chuckled. This man had been warning her since she was a young girl to avoid boys. "You never change."

"Why would I change? I've muddled along just fine for seventy-nine years." He put down the beer bottle and began to demolish his stew. Sander could eat more than a man twice his size. "Now tell me what's on your mind."

Wynter pushed away her bowl and absently nibbled on the hot roll. "First I have a few questions for you."

"About what?"

"About my mother."

Sander sent her a startled glance. Then he slowly lowered his spoon. "I'm not sure I'm the right person to ask."

Wynter wasn't sure either, but she had to ask someone. "Why not?"

"I've told you that me and Laurel didn't often see eye to eye."

That wasn't exactly what he'd said. In fact, he'd flatly refused to discuss his daughter-in-law.

"You never said what the problem was," she murmured, crumbling the roll in her fingers. Her appetite had evaporated.

Sander sat back, as if his own appetite had disappeared. "She was a restless sort of woman."

"Restless?"

"She was never satisfied being a wife or mother. She was always . . ."

"What?"

"Looking for more."

The simple words struck a chord inside Wynter. Not a memory. Or at least not precisely. But a feeling. As if she'd sensed that agitation when she was just a baby.

"Did you know she was having affairs?"

Sander arched his silver brows at the abrupt question. Then, grabbing his beer, he took a deep swig.

"Honey, I'm not stupid," he said in blunt tones. "Besides, Laurel didn't make much of an effort to keep them secret. I think she wanted the entire town to know."

Wynter released a shaky breath. Obviously she'd been the only one in Larkin not to realize her mom's infidelity.

"Is that why the two of you didn't get along?"

Sander snorted. "The cheating I could understand."

Wynter eyed him in disbelief. "Seriously?"

"I know it ain't politically correct to talk bad about your own kid, but Edgar wasn't much of a husband. He spent all of his time with his head stuck in a book." Her grandpa clicked his tongue. "I blame your grandma. She was the one who insisted on calling him Edgar Allan after that weirdo writer."

Wynter frowned. She didn't like the edge of scorn in her grandpa's voice when he spoke of Edgar. Obviously he was disappointed that his only child wasn't going to follow in his footsteps and work on the family farm, but most men would be proud to have a child who'd earned a PhD and was now teaching at a college level.

"Of course he spent time with books," she said. "He's an English professor."

Sander shrugged. "Those fancy degrees don't mean he can spend his life caring more about characters in some old story than his own family. His wife was bound to get bored."

Wynter squashed the urge to continue defending her father. This wasn't about her parents' marriage, or if her dad had been a neglectful husband. She was interested in her mom, and if there'd been anything in her life that might have motivated the shooting in Pike.

"If it wasn't her affairs that bothered you, then what did?"

Sander drained his beer and set aside the bottle. "I don't think we should be talking about this—"

"Please, Grandpa. It's important," she pleaded.

The older man heaved a deep sigh. "Fine. She was always leaving you with babysitters or dropping you off here. I loved having you, of course, but a child needs to be with her momma." His voice was gruff as he glanced away, perhaps recalling an unpleasant memory. "Plus, she spent money like it was growing on trees. She had to have the latest fashions and trips to New York or Chicago to visit the museums. Hell, she drove a car worth more than most people's home. I had to loan them money over and over so they could pay the bills, but it was never enough. Your father eventually asked me to sell part of the farm to settle his debts."

Wynter's breath tangled in her throat. She couldn't imagine her grandpa giving up his land. It would be like selling a piece of his soul.

"Did you?"

Sander jutted out his jaw, his expression hard. "Of course not. I warned Edgar when he got married that he was making a mistake. I'd helped enough, he could deal with his own mess. This land has been in the family for two hundred years, I wasn't going to throw it away on a . . ." The angry words trailed away and a flush touched the older man's face. Wynter didn't know what he'd been about to call her mom, but it wasn't nice. "Anyway, I left him to deal with the problem."

Wynter grimaced. It was easy to imagine her grandpa tossing her dad off the farm without a penny. She adored the gruff old man, but he could be brutal. Like many men his age, he had a belief that he was always right.

"What did Dad do?"

"Sold off some old books." Sander rolled his eyes. "Honestly, he cried like a baby when he boxed them up to send to the auction. I've never been so embarrassed."

"That's not nice, Grandpa. Dad's book collection is very important to him."

"I'll never know how he could be my own flesh and blood."

Wynter ignored her grandpa's grousing. Sander might be disappointed in his son, but he loved him. And if push came to shove, he would do whatever necessary to provide for him.

Instead, her thoughts were focused on the newest revelations about her mom.

She pressed a hand to her stomach, feeling vaguely ill. It wasn't bad enough that Laurel had been sleeping around, but she'd also driven her father to selling his precious books to pay the bills. Was it because she was bored? Lonely? Regretting her life choices?

Or was it something else? Something inside her that drove her to make bad decisions? During the time that Wynter had been in therapy, she'd met numerous kids who'd been traumatized. They often acted out for any variety of reasons.

Wynter slumped back in her chair, a weariness pressing against her with a physical weight.

"I thought I knew Mom," she muttered. "I mean, not in the way normal girls know their mother. It wasn't like we got to share our lives." She shook her head. "But now it all feels like lies."

Sander studied her with obvious concern, his thin face softening with regret. "Don't trouble your head about it, girl."

"You don't understand."

"'Course I do," he insisted. "People are never willing to speak ill of the dead. You grew up seeing your mom as some sort of saint. No woman could live up to that standard."

He had a point. She hadn't thought of her mom as a saint, but she'd certainly put her on a pedestal. And her grandma Hurst had added to the myth that was Laurel Moore.

Since her mom had died when Wynter was so young, they'd never gone through the rebellious teen years, or battled over whom she could date or where she could go to college. Instead, Laurel Moore had been a beautiful woman in a photo who never aged or disappointed Wynter. Her paintings hung in Wynter's restaurant, but she'd never overshadowed her daughter with her talent. And while Wynter had regularly visited her mom's grave, they'd never had a relationship that might have been fraught with hurt feelings and regret.

"That's true," she agreed in a soft voice.

"We all have our faults. Including Laurel." Sander leaned his forearms on the table, his piercing gaze sweeping over her face. "Is that all that's troubling you?"

"No."

"Wynter?"

"I think my mom was murdered."

The words landed like a bomb and Wynter clenched her hands as a shocked silence filled the kitchen. She hadn't intended to discuss her suspicions with the older man. He would be worried enough when she told him that someone had broken into her apartment. The last thing he needed to think about was some crazed killer returning from the past. But as he said, he wasn't stupid. He was bound to wonder why she was suddenly asking questions about her mother. And why the intruder would leave a note about the dead.

Sander scowled. "We know that she was murdered."

"Deliberately," Wynter clarified. Now that she'd revealed her fears, she might as well get her grandpa's opinion. He would surely have known if her mother had any enemies.

Without warning, Sander slammed his flat palm onto the card table, rattling the dishes. "Who put that fool thought in your head?"

"Rudolf Jansen."

"The sheriff from Pike?"

"Yes."

"I thought the man was dead?"

"He is, but he left behind a photo of the night my mother was shot," she told him.

Sander froze, as if he was struggling to process her words. Wynter grimaced. She'd been too blunt. After all, Laurel had been this man's daughter-in-law, even if they hadn't been close. They were family.

"I don't understand," he finally ground out. "Is there new evidence?"

Wynter shook her head. "No, but the sheriff wasn't convinced it was a random crime."

"Why not?"

"Because my mom had already handed over her purse when she was shot."

He blinked. "That's it?"

"Don't you see? The sheriff was convinced there was no reason to shoot her."

"And he had a suspect?"

"No, but—"

"Was the case reopened?"

"No."

"Then let it go, Wynter," the older man pleaded. "I don't like seeing you upset."

She lowered her gaze to her hands tightly clenched in her lap. She had no intention of telling him that she'd confronted one of her mother's lovers, or that Linda Baker had implied that her mom had driven a man to suicide, but she had to reveal why she'd come to stay at the farm.

"I can't," she muttered.

"Why not?"

"Someone broke into the restaurant."

Sander sucked in a sharp breath, his annoyance instantly replaced with concern. "When?"

"This morning."

"Were you there? Did you see the intruder?"

"No, I was at the college talking to Dad."

"Thank God." Sander breathed a deep sigh. "How much was taken? Do you need money?"

"They didn't take anything."

"Nothing?"

"Nothing."

Sander looked confused. "Was it vandals? Did they do any damage?"

"No. Whoever broke in wasn't looking for money or to do any damage. They left a note."

"Note?" The older man was even more confused. Wynter didn't blame him. None of this made any sense. "What sort of note?"

"One that warned me to let the dead rest in peace." A

shudder raced through her body. "That's why I came here to stay for a few days."

Sander's ruddy face flushed a dark red. His ready temper was instantly inflamed by her revelation there'd been an intruder. He was the sort of man who kept a loaded rifle by the door with the theory of shooting first and asking questions later.

"Did you call the cops?"

"Yes." Wynter had been relieved when Chelle Simpson had arrived on the scene. Chelle was a couple years older, but they'd known each other in high school. Plus, Noah clearly trusted her. She had no doubt Chelle would do everything possible to track down the criminal. Still, there wasn't much to go on. A vague glimpse of the intruder by Ollie, and the hope there might be fingerprints. "They're investigating, but until they catch who did it, I wasn't comfortable staying on my own."

"Damn right, you ain't staying there," her grandpa growled, his face still flushed. "I'll go there tomorrow and change the locks."

"That's not necessary," she assured him. "I've already called Jeremy at the lumberyard. I'm having the whole door replaced."

"Good."

Wynter didn't know if it was good or not, but it was all she could do. At least for the moment.

Wiping her hands on her napkin, she tossed it aside and rose to her feet. After her stressful day, she felt like she was drowning in weariness. "I'm tired. I'm going up to bed."

Sander remained seated, his face still flushed. "Don't worry about a thing, my girl. I'll take care of you."

"I know you will, Grandpa."

* * *

Wynter slept surprisingly well. She didn't know if it was being at the farm or out of sheer exhaustion, but whatever the reason, she was up early and had breakfast ready by the time her grandpa returned from his morning chores. Then, pulling on an old pair of coveralls she kept in the coat closet, she headed to her greenhouses.

Nothing in the world was more soothing than getting her hands dirty in the long vegetable beds, and filling baskets with ripe tomatoes, cucumbers, lettuce, and peppers. The moist, warm air clung to her skin and the scent of fertilizer perfumed the air. Not a smell everyone would appreciate, but it satisfied something deep inside her.

The sound of an automobile could be heard echoing through the shallow valley. Moving cautiously toward the open flaps of the greenhouse, Wynter peered out to watch the Jeep pull to a halt in front of the farmhouse.

Noah.

Releasing a breath of relief, she placed two fingers between her lips to emit a sharp whistle. Noah waved his arm to indicate he'd heard her, and Wynter watched him jog down the pathway.

As always, she was struck by his graceful motions. He should have been a dancer. Next, her gaze moved to appreciate the faded jeans and flannel shirt. She enjoyed seeing him in uniform, but she preferred him when he was in his casual clothes, with his dark hair ruffled from the breeze and the shadow of whiskers softening the hard planes of his face.

Stepping into the greenhouse, he glanced over her shoulder as if searching for a companion. "Are you down here alone?"

"My grandpa had to go to town to pick up a few groceries. Or at least that was his excuse," she said. The older man had wolfed down his breakfast and headed toward the door before Wynter had finished her first cup of coffee. "I would guess he's at the restaurant supervising the installation of my new door." She pointed toward the loaded rifle that was propped in a nearby corner. "And I'm not alone."

Noah studied the weapon before returning his attention to her. "Do you know how to use it?"

She nodded. Her grandpa had insisted she learn how to shoot from the time she was just a child. Not just as a way to protect herself, but to keep critters out of her gardens.

"I can hit a target," she assured her companion, then she wrinkled her nose. She hadn't actually practiced shooting in years. "Most of the time."

His gaze moved from the rifle to the raised beds that were overflowing with vegetables. "So this is where the magic happens," he murmured.

She smiled with pleasure. She wasn't a vain person. At least not about her physical appearance or bank account. But she took great pride in her greenhouses.

"If you consider magic rich earth, sunshine, and plenty of TLC," she murmured.

Without warning, Noah stepped close enough for her to be wrapped in the warm aroma of pine. He always smelled as if he'd just stepped out of the forest. She loved when he stopped by her apartment and left behind the crisp scent. At the same time, he lifted his hand to brush a strand of blond hair that had escaped her braid.

"That's exactly what I consider magic," he assured her, his gaze sweeping over her upturned face with a strange intensity.

She shivered as his fingers continued to lightly brush

over her cheek. It wasn't the first time he'd touched her. But there was something different about his soft caress this morning. Something that made her think about stripping off the flannel shirt and exploring the hard muscles of his chest. With her tongue.

"Noah," she rasped.

"You have flecks of gold in your eyes." His fingers cupped her chin, his thumb tracing the curve of her lower lip. "Why have I never noticed before?"

She tried to chuckle, but it came out as a husky chuff of air. "Probably because you don't usually stand on top of me."

"Why not?"

He took another step, pressing against her body. His heat managed to penetrate the thick layers of her coveralls. Or maybe it was her imagination. Maybe the heat was coming from her racing pulse. Whichever was responsible, she had a fierce urge to press against his hard muscles.

"Because we're friends."

Her words were more an effort to remind herself of why they'd ignored the physical attraction that had hummed between them since they were both still in high school.

It'd been their therapist who'd pointed out that people who attended group together often formed intimate relationships that ended up a toxic mess. Each of them had baggage they were trying to work through, and it was too easy to mistake empathy for something deeper.

"Yes, we are," he agreed, his head slowly lowering.

"*Just* friends."

"Hmm."

His mouth touched hers, and any thought of protest shattered into a million pieces. It was the pine, she fuzzily told herself. The scent was intoxicating. Or maybe it was his taste. The lingering sweetness of the cinnamon roll he'd no doubt been eating on his drive to the farm. Or maybe it was the fingers that skimmed up and down the curve of her throat. His touch was so light she could barely feel it, but each brush sent sparks of desire sizzling through her.

Wynter allowed her lips to part in invitation, and with a low growl Noah deepened the kiss. Their tongues touched as his strong arms wrapped around her waist. A dizzying pleasure swept through her, banishing the dark heaviness that had been following her like a cloud.

She hadn't been expecting this, but suddenly she realized it was exactly what she needed. The warmth of Noah's body, the nerve-tingling jolts of excitement, the glorious reminder there was something in this world beyond dread and suspicion.

Impatiently tugging off her gardening gloves, she allowed them to drop to the ground as she rammed her fingers into his hair. The short strands were just as silky soft as she'd always imagined—

She hastily shut down the thought. This was all about delicious distraction. The heat of the moment. If she acknowledged that she'd fantasized about the texture of his hair, or the erotic sensation of his whiskers scratching against her cheek, or the muscled perfection of his chest as she pressed against his body, then she couldn't pretend this was a temporary madness.

Absorbed in the heady rapture of Noah's kiss, Wynter might have missed a vehicle approaching the house. Thankfully, Sander Moore's car was thirty years old with an exhaust system that backfired every few miles. He announced his approach from a mile away.

Untangling her fingers from Noah's hair, she leaned back. "Grandpa's back."

Noah kept his arms tightly wrapped around her waist, staring down at her with a somber expression. "Are we okay?"

She paused, truly considering his question. If he was another guy, she would have nodded and later decided how she felt about their kiss. She couldn't do that with Noah. His friendship was too important. There would be a huge hole in her life if he was no longer a part of her world.

Meeting his steady gaze, Wynter gave a slow nod of her head. Nothing had changed. Had it? This was still the person who she wanted to spend an evening drinking wine with and watching bad movies. And the person who she wanted to call when she had exciting news, or was worried, or bored . . .

She reached out to grab his hand. "Yeah, we're okay."

He squeezed her fingers. "Good."

Wynter turned to walk out of the greenhouse, waiting for Noah to join her before she closed the flaps. Together they climbed the dirt path that led to her grandpa's house.

"Is there a reason you stopped by this morning?" she asked.

"Yes."

Silence. She turned her head to study him with a frown. "Are you going to tell me why?"

His lips twisted into a wry smile. "I can't remember."

Wynter flushed, feeling oddly vulnerable. Picking up her pace, she watched her grandpa pull his car to a halt in front of the porch. She'd offered to help put a down payment on a new vehicle a few years ago, but he'd gruffly refused. He had several tractors and an ATV that he used around the farm, and since he rarely went into town, he didn't see the need for a new car.

She hadn't pressed. Sander would do whatever Sander wanted to do. End of story.

"Don't you have to work today?" She pointedly glanced toward his casual clothes.

"Nope. I'm officially off-duty for today, this weekend, and through next week."

She sent him a startled glance. "I thought you always took your vacation in the summer so you could go deep-sea fishing in Florida?"

He shrugged. "I had some personal time coming to me so I decided to take it."

A suspicion formed as he deliberately turned his head to study Sander who was getting out of his car. Was he trying to hide his expression?

"Are you going on a trip?" she demanded.

"Nope. I have some long-overdue repairs around the cabin."

She made a sound of annoyance. She didn't doubt he had repairs that needed to be made at his cabin, but Noah never took off work. Not unless it was to travel to Florida to go fishing and visit his cousins who still lived in Miami.

"You took off because of me, didn't you?"

"Does it matter?"

They reached the top of the hill and Wynter pulled her companion to a halt. The last thing she wanted was for him to waste his time off on her. It wasn't like she needed a babysitter. "Noah—"

"Your grandpa's glaring at me," he interrupted with a lift of his brows. "I think it's time for me to leave."

"My grandpa glares at everyone."

"True, but he scares the hell out of me."

On cue, Sander stomped his way across the driveway to stare at the younger man with a jaundiced frown. "Noah."

"Hello, Sander," Noah murmured.

"It's kinda early for a visit, ain't it?"

"Grandpa," Wynter chided. She wasn't sure the older man realized that she was twenty-nine, not sixteen.

"It's okay." Noah shrugged, heading toward his nearby Jeep.

"I'll see you later," Wynter called out.

Noah glanced over his shoulder to send her a smile. "Count on it."

He was turning back when Wynter saw him come to a sharp halt. Almost as if he'd been frozen in place. Then, with a raw shout of alarm, he spun on his heel and lunged back toward her.

"Get down!" he bellowed, slamming into her with shocking force.

Wynter cried out as she hit the ground, banging her head with enough force to make pain explode through her brain. And that wasn't the only explosion.

She was still flat on the ground with Noah perched on top of her when the concussive blast echoed through the dell below. It sounded like her grandpa's rusty old car backfiring, but she knew it wasn't.

Only a rifle could reverberate that loudly.

Had the weapon fallen over? How else would it fire? Struggling to think through the pain, Wynter glanced up in confusion. She expected Noah to be staring down at her. He had, after all, just tackled her like a linebacker. Her ribs were throbbing from the impact. Instead he was glancing to the side, his face tight with an intense emotion.

Ignoring the dull ache at the back of her skull, Wynter

forced herself to turn her head to see what had captured his attention.

"No!" The word was a broken cry of disbelief as Wynter caught sight of her grandpa's slender body crumpled on the driveway, the side of his face stained a brilliant red.

Chapter 10

The waiting room in the small hospital north of Larkin was an exact replica of every other hospital waiting room, Noah decided with a grimace.

A narrow space lined with sofas and chairs built for durability not comfort. A few windows that were covered with blinds. A worn carpet that muffled sound. And a low ceiling with muted lighting that was no doubt expected to offer a sense of calm.

Noah was standing in a corner, silently watching Wynter pace from one end of the long room to the other. It'd been eight hours since they'd rushed behind the ambulance to this hospital. Sander had been treated for the gaping wound where the bullet had grazed the side of his head, along with his busted skull from smacking it against the hard ground. Now he was resting in the ICU.

The doctors assured Wynter and her father that the older man was stable, but Wynter continued to pace. He understood. Her tension wasn't just concern for her grandfather. And the worst part was that there was nothing he could do. Nothing but stay close and make sure she was safe.

A movement near the entrance to the waiting room

captured Noah's attention, and, shoving away from the wall, he crossed the short distance to stand next to Chelle Simpson. He'd called the policewoman after they'd arrived at the hospital and explained what'd happened. She'd promised she'd head over to the farm to investigate.

"Any word on Sander?" she asked, her expression coolly composed. As if they were strangers, not long time friends.

Noah fully approved of her professional demeanor. He often had to deal with people he'd known for years. When he was in his uniform, he was a conservation officer. That was clearly Chelle's attitude as well.

"He's out of surgery, but the doctors have him in an induced coma to prevent his brain from swelling."

"Do they think he's going to make it?"

He nodded. The doctor had been in to speak with Wynter and her father less than an hour ago.

"He has as good a chance as any seventy-nine-year-old man who was shot," he said. "Thankfully he is in reasonably good health and the bullet just scraped the side of his head. He has blood loss from the wound, of course, but most of the damage happened when he fell and hit his head against a rock in the driveway. It cracked his skull."

"What about Wynter?"

Noah glanced over his shoulder. Wynter was staring in his direction, as if waiting to see if she was needed. Noah gave a small shake of his head. She had enough on her mind right now. He could deal with the police.

He turned back to Chelle. "She's tired. Terrified for her grandfather. And blaming herself."

"Blaming herself for what?"

"She's convinced that she put her grandfather in danger," he said, his jaw clenching with frustration. He'd done his best to reassure Wynter, but he couldn't deny a mounting suspicion that Sander wouldn't be in the hospital fighting for his life if there hadn't been some lunatic trying to stop Wynter from poking into the past. "Have you been to the farm?"

"Yeah. The rifle was still in the greenhouse," Chelle told him. "I have it at the lab."

"Can you tell if it was the weapon used to shoot Sander?"

She shrugged. "It's impossible to know without having it tested."

Noah didn't need any lab results. What were the odds that there'd been a rifle left in the greenhouse and less than ten minutes later Sander had been shot by someone using a rifle from that precise location? "Was there anything that might give a clue to who was responsible?"

"It's too remote for any security cameras and the roads are all gravel. There's no way to pull a single tire track."

Chelle's expression never changed, but Noah noticed her jaw tightening. She was a good cop, but this area made any investigation difficult. The very lack of crime meant that people didn't take the same precautions as those in big cities.

"They do it on TV all the time," he teased, hoping to lighten her mood.

She didn't smile, but her lips twitched. "Yeah, they do a lot of stuff on TV," she admitted. She tilted her head to the side, studying him with a searching gaze. "You didn't see anything?"

Noah shook his head. He'd been over those brief seconds a hundred times, desperately hoping that he could recall some clue, no matter how minuscule, that might help reveal who'd been in that greenhouse.

"No. I was headed toward my Jeep when the sunlight

glinted off the barrel of the rifle sticking out of the side of the greenhouse. Otherwise . . ." His words died on his lips.

He still hadn't allowed himself to consider what might have happened if he hadn't glanced back at that precise moment. If he hadn't managed to knock Wynter to the ground before the bullet whizzed past to hit Sander.

It was too unbearable.

"There wasn't a vehicle?" Chelle asked.

"I didn't see one." Noah was trained to notice his surroundings, especially when he was under stress. There hadn't been a vehicle in view, but that didn't mean there hadn't been one nearby. "There's a wooded area behind the barns where someone might have parked. If they had been watching Wynter, they could easily have circled down to the greenhouse while we climbed the hill to the house."

Chelle looked resigned. As if his answer was exactly what she'd been expecting to hear.

"We're interviewing the neighbors. They're too far away to be witnesses to the shooting, but they might have noticed a vehicle driving past around the time of the crime," she said. "And once Sander is able to speak, he might be able to tell us where he spent the morning and if he noticed anyone following him home."

Noah frowned at her words. "Have you considered the possibility it has something to do with her mother's death?"

Chelle planted her hands on her hips, as if preparing for a fight. "I'm not ready to jump to conclusions."

Logical advice. The sort of advice he was struggling to follow. "No one tried to kill Wynter before she started asking questions about the night Laurel was murdered," he ground out. "Not to mention the fact she'd just received a threatening note."

"Exactly. Why risk breaking into her apartment to leave a note if the suspect was going to try to kill her hours later? Wouldn't it make more sense to wait and see if the threat succeeded?" Chelle demanded. "Besides, Wynter wasn't alone this morning."

"What do you mean?"

"You're assuming the shooter was aiming at Wynter."

Noah frowned in confusion. "Who else? It couldn't have been Sander," he said. "Or me."

Chelle arched a brow. "You don't have any enemies?"

Noah snorted. He'd been a conservation officer for almost nine years in an area where ninety percent of the population hunted, fished, or drove ATVs for sport. He'd pissed off most of them at one time or another. "Plenty, but they wouldn't follow me to the Moore farm to shoot me," he pointed out in dry tones. "How often am I alone in the woods? There would be endless opportunities to bump me off without risk of being noticed."

Chelle rolled her eyes. "Like I said, I don't want to jump to conclusions. All possibilities are on the table until I have evidence to take them off." She held up her hand as his lips parted. "Including someone trying to keep Wynter from prying into the past."

Dammit. She was right. Following the facts was the only way to discover the truth. But that didn't make it any easier to accept. He hated the feeling they were stumbling in the dark. Noah wanted answers, and he wanted them now.

"We need to narrow down the possibilities ASAP," he growled.

"I'm working on it."

There was a tense silence as Noah glanced toward Wynter who continued her pacing, her face as pale as the Easter lilies that used to grow in his grandma's backyard.

"Did you get the file from the sheriff in Pike?" he abruptly demanded, turning his attention back to Chelle.

He couldn't do anything to ease Wynter's fears until they discovered who and why she was being threatened.

"No, but I made the request. I should hear something in the next day or two," she assured him. She hesitated before adding, "I found out that Tillie Lyddon died shortly after she arrived at the hospital."

"Damn." Noah shook his head in regret. "What can I do to help?"

Chelle nodded toward the end of the bustling hallway. "The hospital has a guard on duty here, and as long as Sander is in intensive care, they'll limit visitors. But I can't keep a constant eye on Wynter."

"I can do that," Noah said without hesitation.

"You'll take her to the cabin?"

"Yeah." He'd already warned Wynter she wasn't returning to the farm or her apartment.

Thankfully she was too shocked to argue.

Chelle's expression softened. "I assume you still have your mangy pack of mongrels?"

Noah smiled at the mention of the rescue dogs who he'd acquired over the years. They roamed his property and provided more protection than any alarm system he could buy.

"I've added two," he admitted.

Chelle chuckled. Although she was an outdoorsy sort of woman, she'd been less than fond of his dogs. Probably because they tended to swarm any visitor with an over-abundance of enthusiasm.

"Of course you have." She looked like she was going to say more when her phone pinged and she pulled it out to read a message. "I need to head out," she said.

"Can I go to the farm?"

She sent him a startled glance. "The area where Sander was shot is marked off as a crime scene, along with the greenhouse."

"I just want to get Wynter's bag."

Chelle nodded. "Yeah, you can go in the house. Just avoid the driveway. And bring Wynter by the station tomorrow. I'll need a formal statement."

"Thanks, Chelle."

Wynter was aware of Chelle and Noah near the entrance to the waiting room, but she couldn't force herself to join the conversation. Not only was she too distracted with worry for her grandpa, but she knew the policewoman would have insisted on speaking with her if they'd discovered any new information.

The fact that she'd turned to leave with nothing more than a distracted nod meant there was nothing to report.

She swallowed an urge to scream in frustration.

Less than a week ago she'd been going about her business with nothing more to worry about than getting her freezer repaired and replanting the heirloom tomatoes that had early blight. Her life had been predictable to the point of sheer boredom. Now she felt as if the ground was crumbling beneath her feet.

Nothing was as she believed it to be. Her mom wasn't the woman she had imagined. And the mugging that had taken her away was no longer a tragic accident. Worse, there was some crazy person who had broken into Wynter's apartment to leave a threatening note before potentially trying to kill her.

At the very least, they'd fired a warning shot.

One that had nearly killed her grandpa.

Pain stabbed through Wynter, but before she could relive that god-awful moment she'd seen Sander lying on the ground with blood covering his face, Noah was thankfully stepping in front of her.

Coming to a halt, she sucked in a slow, deep breath and forced herself to meet his searching gaze with a faint smile. She knew he'd stuck around because he was worried about her, and if she was honest, just knowing he was close by had eased the panic that threatened to overwhelm her. And his offer to allow her to stay at his cabin meant she didn't have to fret about spending the night alone.

Still, she couldn't reasonably expect him to be with her 24/7.

"Are you taking off?" she asked, her voice artificially bright.

"I'm going to get your bag from the farm," he told her. "Is there someone I can call to take care of the chores? I'd offer, but I have no idea what needs to be done."

"Ollie said he would take care of them," she said. The older man had stopped by a few hours ago, staying until Sander had been out of surgery and on his way to the ICU. "At least for the next few days."

"That was generous," Noah murmured.

Wynter hadn't been surprised. During high school Ollie spent the majority of his time at the farm, working side by side with Sander. They were as close as any father and son.

"He worked for Grandpa for years. To be honest, he was more a part of our family than his own."

Noah nodded, obviously relieved he wasn't going to be spending the next several hours hauling around feed and mucking stalls. Wynter didn't blame him. As much as she loved spending time at the farm, she hated dealing with the tedious everyday tasks it demanded.

"Is there anything else you need?" Noah asked.

"No."

Stepping close enough to surround her in his rich pine scent, Noah brushed his fingers over her shoulder and down the length of her arm.

"I'll be back to take you to the cabin. Don't leave this waiting room." He grasped her fingers, giving them a squeeze. "Promise?"

She didn't hesitate. She had no intention of going anywhere until she was convinced her grandpa was in stable condition. Plus, she wasn't an idiot. Wandering around alone after someone had just taken a shot at her wasn't in the foreseeable future.

"Yeah, I promise."

"Good." Noah brushed his lips lightly over her forehead before he turned to stride out of the room.

Bemused by his casual intimacy, Wynter lifted a hand to touch the skin that tingled from his touch. When had they started kissing good-bye? Not that she was complaining. It felt . . . right. As if the friend zone she'd placed around Noah had been shattered. He wasn't just a comfortable companion, but a sexy, gloriously perfect man that any woman would be eager to have as a lover.

Still grappling with the implications of her changing relationship with the man who'd been a part of her life for so long, Wynter nearly jumped out of her skin when her father spoke directly in her ear.

"What did the police have to say?"

Whirling around, Wynter discovered her dad and the ever-present Linda Baker standing at his side. They'd arrived together at the hospital, and Wynter had been forced to bite her tongue more than once when she'd caught sight of the secretary fussing over her dad as if he was a child, not a grown man with a PhD.

"I think they're still investigating," she said. "But I'm not sure how they can discover who pulled the trigger."

"What is there to investigate?" Linda demanded, her reptile gaze flicking over Wynter's rumpled T-shirt and jeans. As if silently chastising Wynter for not taking the time to change her clothes before rushing to the hospital. Wynter had wondered what the woman would say if she could have seen Wynter's coveralls that had been covered in blood after cradling her grandpa's head in her lap, waiting for the ambulance to arrive. "It was obviously a hunter who accidentally shot your grandfather."

Wynter scowled. "This was no accident."

Edgar cleared his throat. "We don't know what happened, Wynter."

She jerked her head to glare at her dad. The older man was in his usual white shirt and black slacks, although he'd taken off his tie and stuffed it in his pocket.

"You don't find it strange that someone broke into my apartment to leave a threatening note and then the next day I'm nearly shot?"

"You weren't shot. Your grandfather was," Linda pointed out in tart tones.

Wynter blinked. Was the woman disappointed Wynter wasn't the one lying in the hospital bed?

"Linda," Edgar's voice was unusually stern. "Wait for me in the car."

"But—"

"Please."

"Very well." With pursed lips, the woman turned to grab her jacket off one of the sofas and headed out the door.

The second she'd disappeared, Wynter narrowed her eyes. "Are you going to take her side?" she demanded.

Edgar pulled off his glasses and started to polish them with a handkerchief he carried in his pocket. "I'm not taking anyone's side," he gently corrected her. "We don't know what happened, but I think you should consider the fact that your grandfather was complaining that he'd caught a group of hunters trespassing on his land just last week. They shot two turkeys before he could run them off."

Wynter blinked in surprise. Her grandpa never said anything about trouble with poachers.

"You're sure?"

"Yes. I told him to call the cops, but he said he'd taken care of them. You know how he is."

"Stubborn," she muttered.

"Exactly." Her dad replaced his glasses and tucked away the handkerchief. "It's just something to keep in mind."

Wynter nodded, but Edgar had already turned to grab his trench coat that was folded on a coffee table.

"Are you leaving?" she asked.

Edgar pulled on his coat. "The doctor said that Dad is as comfortable as possible for now. They'll call if anything changes."

Her lips parted to argue, but he had a point. It wasn't like Sander would know if they were pacing the waiting room or in the comfort of their home. And the doctor had been quite adamant that no one would be going in to see the older man tonight.

"Are you riding with Linda?" she instead asked.

Edgar flushed, his expression defensive. "We're going back to the office. I still have to schedule the summer classes."

"Of course."

Pulling on his coat, Edgar awkwardly shifted from foot to foot. "Did you want to stay with me? At least for tonight."

"I'm staying with Noah."

"Oh." He couldn't fully disguise his relief. "Good. I'm . . ." With a vague lift of his hand, her dad bolted toward the door. "I'll see you tomorrow."

"Yeah."

Wynter shook her head, not quite sure when her relationship with her dad had become so strained. They'd never been best buds, but they'd enjoyed each other's company. Maybe it was because she'd been so busy with the restaurant. She couldn't remember the last time they'd shared dinner or spent the day together. It was too easy to grow apart.

Telling herself she would try to do better, she turned her thoughts to her dad's claim that there'd been poachers on the farm. She wasn't a hunter, but she knew that it was turkey season in Iowa. It wouldn't be the first time people from out of town wandered onto her grandpa's land.

Still, what were the odds . . . ?

She was trying to wrap her mind around the possibility that the shooting had been nothing more than a terrible accident when a woman in a tailored pantsuit with her dark hair pulled into a knot at the back of her head and striking features set in lines of sympathy crossed the waiting room to pull Wynter into her arms.

"Wynter, I'm so sorry."

"Erika," Wynter breathed in surprise.

Then she promptly burst into tears.

Chapter 11

Wynter wasn't sure how long she sobbed. It was probably only a couple of minutes, but it was enough to give her the cathartic release that she needed.

At last she pulled back and wiped the tears from her face. "Sorry. I don't know what happened."

Erika offered a gentle smile, her dark eyes filled with a compassion that Wynter remembered during the year she'd spent in group therapy. She'd always insisted that the kids call her Erika instead of Dr. Tomalin. Not to try to be their friend, but to be more approachable. Then she'd built a sense of trust that let the group know it was a safe place to express any emotion without fear of being told that it was wrong to feel that way. Overall, she had a unique ability to offer a sense of calm acceptance no matter how out of control the situation might be.

"I'm going to guess that you've been under stress and needed a shoulder to cry on," she murmured.

"Something like that." Wynter sniffed and cleared the lump from her throat. "I'm better now. Feel free to return to your regularly scheduled programming."

The smile remained. "I'm exactly where I planned to

be," she assured Wynter. "I was visiting a friend who is having surgery and I heard that Sander had been brought to the hospital. I know how close you are to your grandfather and I wanted to see how you're doing."

Wynter didn't try to put on a brave face. Not with this woman. She'd see through any pretense.

"I'm a mess," she bluntly admitted.

"Understandable. You're worried about your grandfather. You're supposed to be a mess."

Wynter glanced away. Her emotions were raw and unstable, and a part of her longed to share the fear that was gnawing at her like a cancer. But was it fair? Dr. Tomalin had only stopped by to offer her sympathy, not to deal with Wynter's current disasters.

"It's not just concern for my grandpa." The words were out before Wynter could halt them.

"Wynter. I might not be your therapist anymore, but you can always talk to me," Erika murmured softly.

"I would like that."

"Okay." The older woman steered her toward a nearby sofa and they both sat on the hard cushions. Visiting hours for the ICU were over, giving them privacy despite the public setting. Turning so she could study Wynter's face, Erika reached out to pat her knee. "What's on your mind?"

Wynter took a minute to gather her scattered thoughts. She didn't want to discuss the shooting. Or the note left in her apartment. This woman couldn't help with those troubles. But she did have a unique insight that Wynter desperately needed.

"When I was in group, you said you knew Mom, but you couldn't discuss her."

The older woman didn't actually flinch, but there was no mistaking her surprise at Wynter's words. "The therapy was about your healing and accepting your mother's death," she said, her words carefully chosen.

"But you were friends?" Wynter pressed.

"Yes." Erika tilted her head to the side. "Is there a particular reason you're asking?"

"It was the anniversary of Mom's death this week."

The therapist's pale face tightened, as if Wynter's words touched a sensitive nerve. "Twenty-five years."

"Yes." Wynter blinked. It seemed a little odd that the therapist had known the exact year her mother died. Unless the two had been closer than Wynter suspected. There was an uncomfortable silence before Wynter forced herself to continue. "I visited her grave."

"Good." A wistful smile touched Erika's lips. "It often brings us comfort to visit the resting place of a loved one."

"Not this time."

"Why not?"

"While I was in Pike I discovered that my mom wasn't the woman I believed her to be." The words came out in a staccato burst, as if speaking them quickly would ease the discomfort. Like ripping off a bandage. Fast and clean.

Erika studied Wynter with a hint of confusion. "I'm not sure what you mean. Are you suggesting that Laurel wasn't your biological mother?"

Wynter shook her head. It'd never occurred to her that her mother might not be her mother. Or her father, her father . . .

With a grimace she slammed a mental door on the possibility. She had enough problems without inventing more.

"She cheated on Dad," she bluntly clarified. "More than once."

Erika released a sigh, something that might be regret in her dark eyes. "Ah."

"And that wasn't all." Now that Wynter had started, she couldn't stop. As if she'd just been waiting for the opportunity to purge the noxious emotions that had been brewing inside her since learning of her mom's past. "She spent money she didn't have. My dad had to sell his book collection to pay her bills."

Something flickered in the dark eyes. "Anything else?"

"She didn't want me."

The older woman gasped, as if genuinely shocked by Wynter's abrupt claim. "That's not true," she rasped. "Your mother loved you. Very much."

"How do you know?"

"She told me."

"All mothers claim to love their children, don't they?"

"Listen to me, Wynter," the woman insisted, grabbing Wynter's hand in a tight grip. "Your mom didn't just claim to love you. She talked about you all the time."

A tightness she didn't even realize was clenching her muscles eased at Erika's fierce insistence. She'd obviously been more worried by the fear she'd been an unwanted burden than she wanted to admit. Even to herself.

"Were the two of you close?" she asked her companion.

A nostalgic expression settled on Erika's face. "When I came to Larkin I was hired as a counselor at Grant College. I was the first therapist they'd ever had and there were several professors who considered my position a waste of resources. It didn't help that I looked like I was sixteen and was obviously overwhelmed by my first professional position." She shrugged away the memories of dealing with the arrogant jerks who no doubt treated her with a barely concealed disdain. Wynter had grown up surrounded by academia and those stodgy professors who detested any change. Even if it was obviously for the better. "It was your mother who chatted with me at those dull academic parties and started inviting me to lunch. Even an occasional night out. She was the only one who cared that I was lonely and tried to make me feel welcomed."

Wynter eagerly absorbed the picture Erika was painting of Laurel Moore. The past few days had deeply tarnished the memory of her mom. Laurel had been transformed from a loving parent to a selfish, pettily cruel woman who didn't care about anyone's happiness but her own. But now it was obvious that she had a kind heart. At least when she wanted.

"Did you know about the affairs?" Wynter asked. She didn't have a perverted interest in her mom's lovers. She wished she could scrub the thought from her mind. But if one of them was responsible for Laurel's death, then Wynter needed to be able to protect herself.

"I suspected, but it wasn't something we discussed," Erika murmured.

"Did you hear any rumors?"

The older woman frowned, obviously uneasy. She'd been Wynter's therapist for over a year. Long enough to develop an urge to protect her.

At last she shrugged in resignation. "There were always rumors swirling around Laurel. They claimed she was having a relationship with the art professor—"

"Dr. Peyton?"

"Yes. Along with her next-door neighbor when your parents moved from an apartment to their house, her deliveryman, and even one of the students she taught at the summer art camp." Erika shook her head in disgust. "Most of those spreading the gossip were jealous and eager to make themselves feel better by trying to smear her reputation."

Wynter made a mental note to check out Dr. Peyton. She already knew the deliveryman, Max, was dead. She'd have to do some investigation on who her parents' next-door neighbor might have been, along with the student.

A shiver shook through her body. She didn't want to try and figure out who could be cold-blooded enough to stand in front of her mother and shoot her in the chest. But what choice did she have?

"My grandpa said she was restless," she said, trying to suppress the memory of the night her mom was murdered. It made the nightmares worse.

Erika considered her response. "Laurel was exuberantly emotional," she finally said.

"What's that mean?"

"Laurel lived with a passion that sometimes led her to extremes," the older woman clarified. "She could be wildly happy one moment and then so furious, she would start throwing whatever she could get her hands on the next. She was charming and unpredictable and a hopeless romantic." Erika lowered her lashes, but not before Wynter caught sight of the pain in the woman's eyes. She truly mourned for her friend. "I'm not sure your father understood why she couldn't be satisfied like the other professors' wives. Or why she constantly craved excitement."

"Larkin isn't exactly a hot spot of thrills," Wynter said dryly.

"No, but that didn't mean she didn't love her husband. And she adored you," Erika was quick to reassure Wynter. "She just needed . . ."

"More."

Erika leaned forward, her face softening. "Wynter, I'm not sure who you've been talking to, but your mother had many wonderful qualities. She was kind and funny and the very first person to offer help to anyone who needed it. She was an astonishingly talented artist and the most generous person I've ever known. Probably too generous."

"Why would you say that?"

"Every hopeful artist in the area would ask for her to be a patron. I think she even left money in her will for local artists."

Wynter made a sound of surprise. She'd known that her mother left money in a trust that she'd used to start the restaurant, but it hadn't occurred to her that there would have been other beneficiaries. "What artists?"

"There was a painter who had a local gallery. It closed a few years after your mom died. Then there were scholarships given to the local high school to be used for art students to attend the summer art camp at the college," Erika said. "I think Dr. Peyton is in charge of it."

Wynter jerked. Dr. Peyton, the art professor. *Again*. Did that mean anything? Maybe, but how did she find out?

She shook her head in frustration.

"Any others?" she asked.

"I can't remember." Erika paused, her lips pursed as if she was reaching for a distant thought. "Wait. There was another one. Something to do with pottery."

"Tonya Knox?" Wynter demanded.

"That sounds right," Erika agreed. "She left money to build a workshop or something."

Tonya had gotten an inheritance from Laurel Moore? And she'd never said anything?

Wynter didn't know how to process the information, so she didn't even try. "I had no idea."

Erika reached to give Wynter's fingers a light squeeze. "Laurel was complicated, but never doubt she was a good person who loved you."

* * *

It was a little after eleven P.M. when Noah entered his kitchen. It wasn't a large space, but it was designed to be functional. The handcrafted wooden cabinets were taller and deeper than most prefab models, the island doubled as a table, and the stainless-steel appliances had been chosen by Wynter. They were small and sleek enough to fit in the space, but still restaurant grade.

He wasn't an accomplished chef like Wynter, but he did eat at home most nights. Learning to feed himself decent meals had become a necessity, not a luxury.

Putting a small pan on the stove, Noah measured out cocoa, sugar, milk, and a pinch of salt. The hot chocolate had just reached the perfect temperature when he heard the soft pad of approaching footsteps. Turning his head, he watched Wynter enter the kitchen, his lips twitching.

After they'd left the hospital and arrived at his secluded cabin, Noah had convinced Wynter to eat the omelet and English muffin he'd made before tucking her in the guest bedroom. Now her hair was tangled around her sleep-flushed face and her slender body was faithfully outlined by her tiny muscle shirt and skimpy shorts.

A heat that had nothing to do with the nearby stove swirled through him. Noah swallowed a growl, although he did nothing to quash the desire that clenched his muscles. That horse was already out of the barn . . . or whatever ridiculous metaphor his grandmother used to quote. He wanted Wynter. It was as simple and complex as that.

And he fully hoped that Wynter was interested in a romantic relationship.

"Noah." Blinking as her eyes adjusted to the soft glow from the overhead lights, Wynter took a slow inventory of his bare chest and the jogging shorts that hung low on his hips. "What are you doing up?"

Noah poured the steaming liquid in two mugs. Then, stepping toward the center of the tiled floor, he placed them on the island.

"Making us hot chocolate."

She shuffled toward the island, grabbing the nearest mug. "I've been asleep since nine o'clock. Why would you make me hot chocolate?"

"You told me that you always wake at eleven-eleven," he reminded her. It'd been years ago, but he'd remembered her complaint that she could never sleep through the night. In fact, he remembered a lot of things about this woman. Something that should have warned him that she wasn't just another friend. "I thought something warm and sweet would help you relax."

Her lips parted as she studied him with an expression he couldn't read. "You are . . ."

"Sexy?" he offered.

She sipped her hot chocolate. "That goes without saying."

"No, let's not let it go without saying."

She lowered her gaze to his bare chest and down to his hard abs. "Fine. You're insanely, ridiculously sexy."

He grabbed his mug. "Better."

"You're also the most thoughtful man I've ever known." She took a sip. "Why aren't you married?"

It was a question he'd never been able to answer. He blamed his career and the crazy hours he worked. He blamed his past and his difficulty in trusting that happiness wasn't going to be snatched away from him. He blamed everything except for the blindingly obvious explanation.

He'd chosen his wife a long time ago.

Leaning his hip against the island, he studied her over the rim of his mug. "You tell me. I think I'm an incredible catch, but I keep getting thrown back in the pond."

She snorted at his teasing words. "You don't fool me, Noah Heller. You're too picky."

"True. Only the best will do." He held her gaze. "I'm not going to settle for less than true love."

They stared at each other, a glorious awareness sizzling between them. Noah's heart thundered in his chest, stealing his breath. He could see the desire darkening her eyes. A hunger that echoed inside him. Then, with a tiny shiver, Wynter turned her head to glance around the kitchen.

"I love this cabin," she murmured in soft tones. "You've made it into a home."

Noah dismissed his pang of disappointment. They had all the time in the world. Instead, he smiled with unabashed pride. Most of the cabin he'd built with his bare hands.

"It's getting there."

"I need to think about selling my mom's cabin." She wrinkled her nose. "It should be owned by someone who can give it the loving care that it needs."

"You could fix it up and use it as a rental," he suggested, wise enough not to mention his fear she wasn't in the best emotional state to make major decisions. "It would be a nice extra income."

She nodded. "Something to think about."

They both sipped their hot chocolate, a comfortable silence settled between them. It'd always been that way. They fit together with an ease he'd never experienced with anyone else.

Finally he set aside his empty mug. "Was it a nightmare that woke you?"

Wynter shook her head. "No. It's just an inner alarm

that goes off at the same time each night. Erika had a fancy name for it." She grimaced. "I just call it a pain in the ass."

"Trauma has a way of hanging around long after the actual event."

She pushed aside her mug, her gaze locked on him. "What about you?"

"I wasn't with my parents when they crashed so I don't have the same horrifying memories, but I had my share of nightmares."

"How did you get rid of them?"

"I haven't," he confessed. There were still nights he jerked awake, convinced he could hear his parents screaming in pain. "Not entirely. But I no longer wake in a cold sweat."

"What's your secret?"

Noah paused, then he shared the secret that he'd kept to himself for years. "I went to the jail to talk to Manny Adkins, the guy who crashed into my parents."

Her eyes widened in shock. "When?"

"Just after my eighteenth birthday."

"What happened?"

Noah folded his arms over his chest. He didn't have any memory of the long drive to Florida. And just a vague impression of the large, oppressive stone prison that had been surrounded by layers of fences and armed guards.

He did, however, have an acute recollection of the man who'd smashed into his parents' car. Adkins was tall and gaunt beneath his prison uniform with a pasty white skin and hair the color of mud. His features looked too big to fit on his narrow face, giving him the appearance of a rat.

Or maybe that had been his own imagination, Noah conceded.

"We met in one of those cramped prison cubicles where

you have to speak through plexiglass sheet," he said. "I expected . . ."

"Noah?" Wynter prompted when his words faded.

He sharply shook his head. "I don't know what I expected. Regret for the devastation he'd caused. Not only to my family, but to his own. Or maybe a defensive refusal to admit that he had done anything wrong."

"That wasn't what you found?"

"He was just . . . pathetic." Noah released a harsh sigh. "I was only eighteen, but I was more an adult than he was at forty. He whined about his sentence, he begged me to write to the parole board to get his sentence reduced, and when I refused, he asked for money." Noah made a sound of disgust. At the time he'd stared at Adkins in disbelief. What kind of creep asked the son of the couple he'd murdered for cash? He forced himself to continue. "He claimed the crash had ruined his life and it was somehow my parents' fault for dying."

"What a jerk," Wynter muttered.

"Yes, and not worthy of the years I spent hating him." Noah shrugged. "Instead of wasting my emotions on the man responsible for killing my parents, I tried to cling to the good memories of my childhood."

A faint smile curved her lips. "Tell me."

"Okay." Noah was willing to do anything to keep her distracted. When he'd come to pick her up from the hospital, she'd looked so fragile that he feared she might shatter. The stress was taking a heavy toll, but for now there was nothing he could do but stay near and offer her comfort. "As you know, my parents moved to Miami along with my aunt and uncle to open a Thai restaurant." His father's parents had immigrated from Thailand when they were newlyweds, and his family had celebrated their culture.

"My kind of people," she murmured.

"Yes. You would have loved them. They had the same gift as you do."

"Working endless hours for little pay?" she asked dryly.

"Certainly that," he agreed. His parents, along with his aunt and uncle, had lived above the restaurant and were on constant duty. "But I was referring to their amazing ability to make their customers feel as if they were a part of the family. We had to hold their funeral at one of the mega-churches to accommodate the crowd."

Noah shook his head at the memory of the vast funeral. It hadn't seemed real to a fourteen-year-old boy who hadn't accepted his parents were gone forever. Easily sensing his stab of pain, Wynter reached across the island to brush her fingers over his bare arm.

"What is your favorite memory of them?"

That was easy to answer. "No matter how crazy business might be, they always took me to the beach on Saturday morning. We built sand castles and ate ice cream and my dog would splash in the waves." A familiar warmth settled in the center of his heart. Adkins had stolen many things, but he could never take away those sun-filled hours that he'd spent laughing and playing with his parents. "Even when I got older we would go so I could flex my muscles for the local girls and work on my tan. It was our family time and nothing was more important."

She gave his arm a squeeze. "You were lucky to have them."

"I was. But after they died I allowed my fury of what I lost to blind me to the appreciation of what I'd been given."

"And now?"

"I still get angry," he conceded. "It's such a senseless loss. But I do know I was luckier than many people. I had my parents' love for fourteen years. And when they were taken, I was given the security of my grandmother's home."

Amusement sparked in Wynter's hazel eyes. "She was a wonderful woman, but she scared the hell out of me."

"Nana was a fireball." He laughed. His grandmother had barely topped five foot and weighed less than a hundred pounds, but the entire town was terrified of her. "I watched her take a broom to the neighbor when he drove over her prized rosebush." His smile faded. "I miss her every day."

She glanced away, no doubt reminded that her own grandfather was currently clinging to life by a mere thread.

"I think I'll go back to bed," she murmured.

"Okay. Don't hesitate to call out if you need anything." He reached to comb his fingers through her tousled hair. "Or if you just get lonely."

She flushed, turning to head for the doorway. "Thanks for the hot chocolate."

"Anytime." He watched her disappear, his body hard and aching to follow her to her bed. "Any. Time."

Chapter 12

From the protection of the thick woods, the Stranger watched the light switch off and the cabin plunge into the darkness. It was impossible to get closer without sending the pack of mutts into a barking frenzy.

It was annoying.

The Stranger wanted to see Wynter's face.

Was she crying? She had been earlier. Back at the farm when she'd been covered in her grandfather's blood.

A shudder of bliss raced through the Stranger.

It hadn't worked out as planned. Once again there'd been a moment of distraction and it had ruined everything.

Well, not everything.

There'd been screams. Delicious screams that had echoed through the air and ricocheted through the shallow dells. And then the ambulance and police cars had arrived with sirens blazing and lights flashing and more shouting. The melee had thundered through the Stranger.

Yes, a productive day, if not how it was meant to end.

Perhaps the next task would provide a better outcome.

Or at least more screaming.

"Alive at last," the Stranger whispered.

* * *

The text pinged at 3:30 A.M.

Grabbing her phone off the nightstand, Mona Shelton fumbled for her glasses. Over the past few years her eyesight had faded. Kind of like the rest of her body. She'd never been a beauty queen. Not like Laurel Moore. But the last decade had stolen what prettiness she could once claim.

Her hair had thinned until it laid flat and dull against her head. Her skin was wrinkled and her shoulders slumped from the years of carrying heavy trays of food at the truck stop. Even her small boobs that had once been firm and high were now drooping in defeat.

It was true. Life was a bitch and then you died.

With a harsh sigh, Mona shoved on her glasses and read the text:

> Your husband is passed out on the corner of Sixth and State. Come and get him before the cops are called.

"Shit." Mona dropped the phone and flopped back on the pillow.

She wanted to roll over and go back to sleep. Let Drake be hauled off to jail. What did she care? It wasn't like he gave a damn about her.

Ever since precious Laurel's daughter had appeared on the doorstep, Drake had been spending his nights in the bar. And when he did bother to come home, he slept in the guest bedroom. As if he couldn't bear to be next to her.

Pain of rejection sliced through Mona.

Christ, she was a fool.

No, she was a coward, she silently corrected herself. Drake was right about that. Hadn't she driven three hours to Larkin to speak to Wynter Moore, only to scuttle away with her tail between her legs?

She had everything planned. She'd Googled Wynter and discovered the young woman had one of those fancy restaurants that served the sort of food usually found in California. Everything was homemade and locally sourced and non-modified. Whatever that meant. Give her meat loaf and mashed potatoes any day over that snobby crap.

The fact that Laurel's daughter was obviously a successful businesswoman had only rubbed salt into Mona's open wounds. It was a stark reminder that she'd never followed her own dreams. She was a crappy waitress at a crappy truck stop with a crappy husband. She didn't even have an extra hundred in her bank account to take a few days off work.

That was when she'd gotten the brilliant idea to ask Wynter for money.

Why not?

From what Mona could overhear, the younger woman was looking for information about the night her mother died. Mona had information.

They could both get what they wanted.

But while Mona spent the three-hour drive to Larkin imagining a lavish vacation in Vegas, once she reached the small town she started to lose her nerve. And by the time she'd actually arrived at the restaurant, she'd had to force herself to leave her car parked in a back alley to knock on the back door. It was frankly a relief when no one answered. She didn't want a vacation in Vegas, she'd abruptly realized. Not if it meant going alone. What she wanted was for her husband to forget the past and realize that he loved her.

And what was her reward for generously deciding to return to Pike without stirring up trouble?

Endless nights in a cold bed.

"Idiot."

Tossing back the covers, Mona forced herself out of bed. Even now, she couldn't let Drake suffer the consequences of his decisions. It took her half an hour to get dressed and drive her POS car across town. Then, turning the corner on Sixth, she pulled into the parking lot.

Glancing around, she couldn't see anyone. Pike was a small town, but there were areas that had been hit hard by the recession. This street was one of them. The businesses that had once thrived were now shuttered, with plyboard over the windows, and painted with half-assed attempts at vandalism.

With a frown, Mona dug out her phone. Had she come to the wrong address? Nope. Corner of Sixth and State.

So where was Drake?

Mona's gaze landed on the nearest brick building where the front door was propped open. It'd once been a pizza joint, but it'd closed a couple years ago. Drake had loved the place despite the greasy floors and stench of stale beer.

Could he have stumbled here in a drunken haze? It would be a place that would be on his mind if he had the munchies.

Yeah, it was more than possible.

But where was the person who'd sent the text? In fact, *who* had sent the text?

She hadn't recognized the number. So how had they known to contact her?

Oh. She rolled her eyes as she latched on to the most obvious explanation. Drake insisted on listing her number for his construction business, along with his own. Just for emergencies, he'd promised, although she was the one who got the angry calls when he was late for a job, or when he conveniently forgot to pay a bill.

With a resigned sigh, she shoved the gearshift into park and climbed out. The sooner she found her useless husband, the sooner she could be back in bed.

She paused at the opening to the building. It was too dark to see anything inside. Except . . .

Was that a body on the floor?

Yes.

Muttering a curse, Mona scurried into the building. Even after being abandoned for years the place still smelled like stale beer. The perfect place for Drake to pass out.

Wishing she possessed the backbone to leave him on the grimy tiles, Mona knelt down.

"Drake." She reached out to shake him awake.

It wasn't until the head lifted off the floor that she realized her mistake.

This wasn't her husband. It was—

Explosive pain shattered her thoughts as a hard object smashed against her skull.

A trap.

Not knowing whether to laugh or cry, Mona collapsed flat on her face.

She'd always known Drake Shelton was going to be the death of her.

Chapter 13

After returning to bed, Wynter managed to get a few hours of sleep, but by five A.M. she was wide-awake. No matter what was happening, she couldn't break the habits of a lifetime.

Tossing aside the sheets, she grabbed a pair of jeans and a sweatshirt out of her suitcase and headed for the bathroom. The hot shower did more to refresh her than her restless sleep, and pulling her wet hair into a ponytail, she went to the kitchen to make breakfast.

Less than an hour later she had homemade biscuits with sausage and gravy waiting on the island. Strolling into the kitchen, Noah sucked in a deep, appreciative breath.

"Yum," he murmured, moving toward the counter to pour two mugs of coffee.

Wynter hid her smile, astonished by how comfortable it felt to be pottering around Noah's kitchen. As if she was home. Of course, when she was home she didn't have a gorgeous male wandering around, filling the air with the warm scent of pine.

Settling on a stool next to the island, Wynter allowed her gaze to skim over the man who'd been her friend for years. She'd always known he was attractive. Even if she hadn't noticed, her girlfriends' constant sighs and fluttering eyes when he passed in the school hallways would have alerted her. But she'd never taken a thorough inventory of just how fine his ass fit in a pair of worn jeans, or the hard strength of his legs, or the broad width of his shoulders beneath his khaki Henley. His dark hair was wet and there were small curls at the nape of his neck.

Her fingers suddenly itched to run through those curls. . . .

She abruptly dropped her gaze as Noah turned to walk toward the island and set down the mugs. It wasn't that she was trying to hide her appreciation of his male assets, but ogling a man before breakfast just seemed rude.

They ate in a companionable silence, Noah demolishing a second helping of biscuits with the sort of gusto that made a chef's heart sing with delight. They were both sipping their coffee when an explosion of barking destroyed the silence.

Wynter had caught sight of the numerous dogs dancing around Noah's feet when they'd arrived at the cabin last night, whining for his attention. Now they sounded as if an army was invading.

"What's going on with the Hounds of the Baskervilles out there?"

Noah rose to his feet to peer out the window over the sink. "It's my early warning system."

"Warning of what? The apocalypse?"

"That someone pulled onto the private road that leads to this cabin."

"It's . . ." She winced as the beagle howled like it was being tortured. "Hard to miss."

"I'll be right back."

He disappeared from the kitchen, but before she could follow and ask what he was doing, he returned with his gun casually clutched in his hand. Crossing to the kitchen door, he pulled it open to step onto the porch.

Wynter was quickly standing next to him, ignoring the crisp chill in the air. They watched in silence as a vehicle turned into the short drive at the side of Noah's cabin.

Wynter's breath caught as she realized it was a police car. "Grandpa."

Noah reached to give her fingers a squeeze. "It's Chelle. I'm sure she's here to check that you're okay. If something had happened to your grandfather, the hospital would have called."

Wynter stiffened at his words. Not because she didn't agree that it would be the hospital to contact her if something had happened to her grandpa, but because she didn't even know where she'd left her phone.

Unlike most people of her generation, Wynter wasn't obsessed with social media or electronically chatting with her friends. She was forever forgetting where she put it.

"My phone," she muttered in disgust. "I left it at Grandpa's house."

Noah shrugged. "I grabbed your purse and put it in the suitcase with your clothes. Is it in there?"

"I don't remember." She muttered a curse. "What if someone was trying to get ahold of me?"

"I left my number with the hospital and your father knows you're staying here," he reassured her. "If they needed to get ahold of you, they would have called me."

Wynter slowly nodded. He was right. Forcing her tense

muscles to relax, Wynter turned her attention toward the car that was now surrounded by yapping dogs ranging in size from a German Shepherd to a pug. The driver's side window slid down to reveal Chelle.

"Are you going to leash these hounds?"

Wynter snorted, glancing toward Noah. "See? I told you it was like the Hounds of the Baskervilles around here."

Noah placed two fingers in his mouth and released a whistle loud enough to make Wynter's ears ring. The dogs instantly turned to run toward the barn where they settled in the piles of hay that Noah had spread on the floor.

He turned back to the police car. "It's safe," he assured Chelle, waiting for the woman to join them on the porch before he spoke again. "A little early for a house call, isn't it?"

Chelle managed a tight smile. "Can we go inside?"

Wynter's heart squeezed, her thoughts once again returning to her greatest fear. "Grandpa?"

Chelle shook her head. "He's fine, as far as I know."

Wynter breathed a sigh of relief, only then realizing that Noah had wrapped a protective arm around her shoulders. Was he there to catch her if there was bad news?

The thought was oddly heartwarming. She'd always been surrounded by love, from her father and grandpa, as well as her grandmother in Pike, but in many ways she'd had to take care of herself from a very young age. She wasn't used to having someone standing at her side. Literally and figuratively.

It was nice. Maybe more than nice.

The strange thoughts floated through her mind as Noah steered her back into the kitchen. She instinctively settled on one of the stools next to Chelle. Noah moved toward the counter.

"Coffee?"

"Hot, black, and as strong as you can make it," the policewoman requested.

Wynter studied Chelle, noting the circles beneath her dark eyes and lines that bracketed her mouth.

"Something's happened," Wynter said, her words a statement not a question.

"Yes," Chelle admitted, waiting until Noah had handed her a mug of steaming coffee before continuing. "Do you know Mona Shelton?"

That wasn't what Wynter had been expecting. She shook her head. "No. Should I?"

"She's the wife of Drake Shelton."

"Oh." Wynter struggled to remember the woman, but she was drawing a blank. "Drake lived next door to my grandmother in Pike. I'm sure I probably saw her in the yard or on her porch, but I don't remember ever speaking with her. In fact, I don't even remember seeing her."

Noah leaned against the island next to Wynter. "Why are you asking?"

"I got a call an hour ago from the sheriff in Pike who said they'd discovered Mona's body."

Body. There would only be one reason that Chelle would describe Mona as a body. Still, Wynter was compelled to ask the obvious. "She's dead?"

"Yes."

Noah folded his arms on the table, his expression grim. "How?"

"Her head was bashed in."

Wynter jerked in shock. There was no good way to die.

But there were some awful ways. And that was one of them. "Oh my God," she breathed.

Noah's jaw tightened, but his expression wasn't horrified. Instead he looked wary. "That's a tragedy, but I'm not sure why the sheriff would call you."

Chelle took a sip of her coffee, briefly closing her eyes as if savoring the taste. Or maybe she was just trying to gather her thoughts. She looked as if she'd already had a long morning.

"Because I asked for the records on Laurel Moore's death."

Wynter jerked. She should have suspected that there was a reason for Chelle to arrive at this hour. It wasn't like Mona was an old friend.

"This has something to do with my mom?" she demanded.

Chelle took another sip of the coffee. "Mona's body was discovered at the same Shell station where your mother was shot."

Wynter clenched her teeth as the words hit her like a physical blow. Mona's death couldn't be a coincidence. Not when her body was found in the same location.

Noah narrowed his eyes. "Her body was *found* there? Does that mean she was killed somewhere else?"

Chelle grimaced, as if she hadn't meant to give away that particular detail. "I don't have all the specifics, but apparently she was murdered at an abandoned pizza parlor and her body moved to the station."

"When did it happen?" Wynter asked.

"Sometime between three A.M. and five-thirty A.M.," Chelle said. "That's when the body was found."

Wynter's thoughts returned to her brief visit to Drake's

home. Drake had mentioned his wife was there at the time.

"What was she doing out at that time?" Wynter frowned in confusion. "Does Drake know?"

Chelle set down her mug, as if accepting the coffee—no matter how strong—wasn't going to give her the energy she needed to face the day. "They haven't asked him."

"Why not?" Noah demanded.

"He's missing."

Wynter struggled to follow Chelle's words. It wasn't easy. Her brain felt like it was stuffed with fog. No doubt the result of the shock that reverberated through her.

"Drake is missing?" Wynter repeated.

Chelle shrugged. "All they would say was that they haven't been able to locate him."

Wynter furrowed her brow, futilely trying to piece together what had happened. "I don't understand," she muttered, speaking her thoughts out loud. "Was Drake with Mona when she was killed? And who would want Mona dead? Was she like poor Tillie? Did she have information about Mom's murder?"

Noah grabbed her fingers and gave them a light squeeze. "Wynter, we don't even know if this is connected to your mother. It could be a domestic fight that got out of hand. It happens all the time, unfortunately."

She grimaced. He was right, of course, but she didn't want to think this could be a case of domestic violence. Partially because she feared her arrival at Drake's house to discuss his affair with her mother might have caused the argument that led to Mona's death. That would be unbearable.

"Why would they call Chelle?" she challenged him before glancing toward the policewoman. "It has to be more than the fact that Mona was discovered at the old station, right?"

Chelle hesitated before giving a slow nod. "There is something else."

Wynter didn't know whether to be pleased or terrified that she'd guessed there was more. "What?"

Chelle tapped the tip of her fingers on the kitchen table. "Mona received a text around three A.M. telling her that her husband was passed out on the street. The sheriff assumes she drove to pick him up and was killed after she arrived at the location."

Wynter arched her brows. She had the answer to why Mona had been out and about at three in the morning.

"A trap," Wynter breathed.

"Yes," Chelle agreed.

Noah leaned forward, his expression tight. "Did Drake send the text?"

"No." Chelle paused again. This one longer. And filled with an odd tension. "It came from another phone."

"What phone?" Wynter asked in confusion.

"Yours."

Noah grunted, as if he'd been sucker punched. In fact, it felt like he'd taken a direct hit.

He'd been so focused on why Mona Shelton might have been lured to her death that he hadn't been prepared for the shocking announcement that the woman had received a text from Wynter's phone.

Equally disturbed by Chelle's accusation, Wynter jumped off the stool. "Impossible," she snapped, marching stiffly from the kitchen.

Noah watched her leave, assuming she was headed

to the spare bedroom to search for her phone. He stayed in the kitchen. Not only because he had a gut-clenching suspicion that she wasn't going to have any luck, but he wanted to speak with Chelle in private.

"What do they think happened?" he asked.

Chelle waited until Wynter was out of the kitchen before she answered. "Mona was at home, obviously alone when she got the text," she said. "She gets in her car and drives across town. From there they aren't sure, but they suspect she got out of her car and entered the restaurant. The killer was waiting or followed behind her."

Noah tried to picture what happened. Mona was alone, perhaps convinced that her husband was out drinking. She gets a text and heads out to scoop the drunken idiot off the street. Then . . . What? Was it Drake waiting for her? It was surely someone she recognized. She wouldn't have let down her guard with a stranger at that time of night.

He shook his head. There was no way to know who or what had been waiting for her. Instead he shifted his thoughts to what had happened after Mona was murdered. "You said the building was empty?"

"Yeah."

"Why move the body?"

Chelle sent him an approving glance. No doubt that had been her first thought as well.

"Exactly. And there's more." She leaned forward, her voice pitched low. Obviously she didn't want Wynter over-hearing what she had to say. "The body wasn't just dumped at the Shell station. It was arranged in the exact same spot where Laurel collapsed after she was shot."

Noah's jaw clenched. It would be easy to leap to the conclusion that it had to be the same killer for both women. But he suspected that the photo of Laurel's dead body had been splashed across more than one newspaper. Someone could remember seeing it. Or even have Googled the image. It was best to keep an open mind.

"Are there any suspects?" he asked.

Chelle's gaze dropped, shielding her eyes. "It's an ongoing investigation. Everyone is a suspect."

Noah was momentarily confused. What was she hiding? Then he muttered a curse. "Including Wynter?"

"Yes."

"She was here all night with me." His words were edged with anger. "And before you ask if she could have snuck out, just remember my pack of hounds. They would have raised hell if she stepped out of the cabin."

"That doesn't mean she didn't make the call," Chelle pointed out, lifting her hand as Noah's lips parted to continue the argument. "I'm just pointing out what the sheriff in Pike is going to say."

"I couldn't have made the call." Wynter's soft voice interrupted the tense exchange. "My phone is missing."

Chapter 14

Wynter had heard her grandma say she had the heebie-jeebies before, but she'd never known what it meant. As Noah pulled to a halt in front of the farmhouse, she suddenly understood perfectly. It felt like bugs crawling beneath her skin.

It wasn't just the sight of the police tape that flapped in the stiff breeze around the spot where her grandpa had been shot. Or the gray clouds that hung low with the threat of rain or maybe snow—they didn't look as if they'd made their decision yet. It was the brooding air of violence that lingered. As if whoever had pulled the trigger had left behind a taint of evil.

Noah switched off the engine and glanced in her direction. "Ready?"

Wynter grimaced. A heavy knot of dread was lodged in the pit of her stomach. It'd been there since she'd discovered her phone was missing.

No, that wasn't true. It'd been there for days. It was just bigger and heavier now.

"I have to make sure my phone isn't here." She forced herself to shove open the door of the Jeep.

She slid out of the vehicle, barely able to take a step toward the house before Noah was standing at her side.

"We'll do it together." He wrapped his arm around her shoulders.

Wynter readily leaned against his strength. This morning she needed Noah, and she wasn't too proud to admit it.

They moved toward the stairs that led to the wraparound porch. A sharp breeze tugged at her jacket and pulled strands of hair from her ponytail. Wynter shivered, but it wasn't from the cold.

"God," she muttered.

Noah glanced down with a frown. "Are you okay?"

"How long has it been?"

"How long has what been?"

"Since I went to Pike."

Noah took a minute to consider his answer. "Five days."

Wynter shook her head. "It feels like an eternity."

"Yeah. It does."

They climbed the wooden steps and Wynter thought of her poor grandpa lying on the hospital bed, fighting for his life, instead of home where he belonged.

"If I hadn't opened that envelope, then none of this would have happened."

Noah frowned. "You don't know that."

"I do," she responded in fierce tones. "It was Pandora's box, and if I could go back in time—"

"Secrets never stay buried," Noah sharply interrupted, his tone equally fierce. "Eventually Pandora's box would have been opened."

They crossed the porch and halted in front of the door. "Do you truly believe that?"

Noah turned, laying his hands lightly on her shoulders

as he gazed down at her with a somber expression. "Yeah, I truly do."

Wynter released a shaky sigh. "I'm glad you're with me."

His eyes darkened as he lowered his head. "I wouldn't be anywhere else." He touched his lips to hers in a whisper of a kiss before he was straightening. "Where should we start?"

Wynter licked her lips, tucking away the memory of the kiss to savor later. Right now she wanted to be done with her task so they could leave.

"I suppose the best thing is to try to retrace my steps from when I remember having the phone," she said. "I know I had it in the spare bedroom yesterday morning. I looked at it when I got up."

"Let's start there." Reaching out, Noah shoved open the wooden door. He glanced back at her. "I tried to lock the house before I left last night, but I couldn't find any keys."

Wynter snorted as they entered the living room that was dark from the heavy curtains and decorated with furniture that had been covered with the same crocheted blankets for as long as she could remember. There was a fireplace that was never used, and a glass cabinet that held small knickknacks that had been collected from a lifetime of county fairs, church fetes, and the occasional trip to Canada.

"I doubt my grandpa knows where the keys are," she told Noah, moving toward the stairs at the back of the room. "When I was a young girl he would leave jugs of cream in the kitchen and people would walk in to grab one and toss some money on the table."

Noah's expression tightened with disapproval, but he kept his opinion to himself as they climbed the stairs to the second floor. Although he'd moved to Larkin when he was just fourteen, his years in a big city had left their mark. He would never have the same casual disregard for safety as the locals.

They walked down the short hall to the bedroom tucked beneath the slanted ceiling. It was cramped, chilly, and the narrow bed and two nightstands were the only furniture. But it offered a stunning view of the farm and surrounding dells.

Wynter crossed the barren plank floor to touch the empty nightstand. "I left it here while I slept. When the alarm went off, I got up and took a shower and dressed." She absently headed out of the bedroom and entered the equally cramped bathroom. A quick glance revealed the phone wasn't there. "Next I went downstairs to make breakfast."

"Did you have the phone with you?"

She mentally ran through her movements from the day before. "Yes. I had it on the counter while I washed the dishes because I listened to music. That's the last time I remember having it before I went into the mudroom to put on my coveralls and headed out. I never take it with me when I'm in the greenhouses."

They headed back downstairs and entered the kitchen. "So it was lying on the counter the last time you remember having it."

"Yes."

Together they searched for the missing phone, opening cabinets and even the fridge on the off chance that she'd done something stupid. It wouldn't be the first time she'd misplaced the thing. Once she'd thrown it in the trash. No doubt a Freudian slip.

At last they conceded defeat. "It's not here," Wynter muttered. "Someone stole it."

"I agree." Noah planted his fists on his hips and glanced around the kitchen with a frustrated frown. "But why would anyone drive to this remote house hoping that you might have left your phone lying around?"

Wynter grimaced. He had a point. Although she often worked in the greenhouses, she didn't have a routine. It could be any time, any day of the week. Besides, it was a sheer fluke that her grandpa had chosen to drive into town while she was busy.

"And it's too isolated for someone to have walked by and seen it through a window," she added.

"They must have been here for some other purpose and taken advantage of the opportunity."

If it had been early that morning, she would have noticed a vehicle pulling into the driveway. That meant it had to be after her grandfather had been shot.

"There were a dozen people here with the emergency vehicles." She shuddered. She'd been consumed with her grandpa and her terror that he was about to die, but she had a vague memory of screaming sirens followed by a crowd of EMTs, cops, and volunteer firemen.

"True," Noah agreed. "Including a flock of gawkers who always follow the emergency vehicles. Any one of them could have wandered into the house without being noticed."

Wynter was struck by a sudden thought. "And I'm sure that Dad and Linda must have been here."

Noah arched a brow. "Why do you say that?"

"They went to lunch after Grandpa got out of surgery and when they came back they had a bag with Grandpa's pajamas and reading glasses."

Noah's head turned at the sound of tires crunching

against the gravel road. A few moments later a van pulled into the drive.

"Ah." Noah's eyes narrowed as the vehicle parked next to his Jeep and a man climbed out. "Here's someone else who was here yesterday."

Wynter rolled her eyes at his muttered words before walking down the steps of the porch to greet her old friend. "Ollie."

"Hey, Wynter. Noah. Sorry I'm late." He pulled a pair of heavy gloves from his back pocket as he prepared to start the morning chores. "My father made an unexpected return to town."

Wynter made a sound of shock. She'd known Ollie and his mother all her life, but they'd never once mentioned his father.

"I didn't know he ever came back to Larkin."

Ollie's jaws clenched. As if she'd hit a nerve. "Jay Wheeler is like a bad penny who shows up when he's least wanted. Usually whenever he runs out of money. After a few days of his endless whining my mother gets tired enough to hand over a few bucks to get rid of him." His lips twisted into a tight smile. "This morning he decided to try his luck with me. It took a while to convince him that I'm never going to give him a handout. Next he insisted that he needed a drink. I had to drive around town looking for a bar open at this hour. I finally dropped him off at the Pig & Whistle."

Wynter felt a pang of sympathy. However complicated her relationship with her father, he'd always been there for her.

"I'm sorry, Ollie. I can find someone to take care of

things here," Wynter assured him. "You have enough to deal with—"

"No, I want to be here," Ollie interrupted, his tone firm. "This is the one place that I feel at peace. Besides, I'm the only one who knows how Sander wants things done."

"That's the truth," Wynter agreed dryly. Her grandpa had many fine qualities, but he could be a pain in the ass. Especially when it came to his beloved farm.

"How is he?" Ollie asked.

"Stable, but still unconscious. I'm going to visit him later this morning."

Ollie nodded. "I intend to stop by after work."

"Thanks." Wynter reached out to lay her hand on her friend's arm. "Grandpa's lucky to have you as a friend."

"Without him . . ." Ollie shook his head, flushing as if embarrassed he'd revealed how much he depended on Sander Moore. "I need to get moving. I have a full schedule."

"Wait." Noah moved to stand in front of Ollie. "What time did you do the chores last night?"

The older man took a second to consider his answer. "I don't have an exact time. It was late. After dinner, so around eight or nine."

"Did you notice anyone around?" Noah pressed.

"No." Ollie's brows snapped together. "Oh, well I met Tonya in the driveway. She was pulling out when I was pulling in."

"Why would she be out here?" Wynter was confused. As far as she knew, Tonya had never been to the farm before.

"I suppose she was looking for you." Ollie stepped to the side, his expression distracted. "I need to get on with the chores. I have a lot to do today."

"Thanks, Ollie."

The older man headed toward the barn, and a new sadness settled in Wynter's heart. It should be her grandpa doing the chores this morning. If it hadn't been for her . . .

"I need to go to the hospital," she announced in raw tones.

Noah nodded. "I'll drop you off."

She frowned. "What are you going to do?"

"I want to track down Oliver's father."

It was the last thing Wynter had expected to hear. "Why?"

"He was around when your mother first arrived in town and during the early years of their marriage," Noah reminded her. "More importantly, he's someone who has no reason to sugarcoat what happened in the past. If he knows who might have wanted Laurel dead, he has no reason not to say who it was."

She considered his words before nodding in agreement. So far she'd heard the past from people who'd either loved or resented her mom. It would be nice to have an opinion from someone who had no reason to care one way or another.

"I can drive to the hospital," she said, lifting her hand as Noah's lips parted to argue. "You can follow behind. I need the truck to pick up a load of fertilizer I ordered from the co-op. They're expecting me to pick it up today."

Noah furrowed his brow. He clearly wasn't happy to have her alone, even in her truck. Finally he heaved a resigned sigh. "You can drive it to the hospital, then we'll change vehicles. I'll get the fertilizer and bring it here, then meet you for lunch."

"Okay," Wynter readily agreed. If Noah didn't mind helping, she was willing to accept his generous offer.

She wanted to spend as much time as possible with her grandpa.

The Stranger watched the couple from behind the numerous outbuildings.

There was no way to hear what they were saying. The distance was too great and their voices were kept low, as if they feared someone might overhear their conversation.

A shame.

There was a tension in their bodies that was obvious even from far away.

Was it fear? The Stranger hoped that was the answer. Fear was something to be savored. Not as good as the screams. Or the blood. Or the thrill of sirens.

Unfortunately, the tension looked more like determination. As if they were plotting a plan of action.

Dammit.

They'd been warned. First with Tillie. And then with the note. That should have been enough, but it wasn't. And worse, the shooting had been a debacle. The bullet had gone astray, and instead of this being ended, it was threatening to spin out of control.

Clearly direct action was necessary. The sort of direct action that the Stranger was ready and eager to deliver.

Chapter 15

Noah followed Wynter to the hospital parking lot before they switched vehicles and he drove back to Larkin.

With a grim effort he shoved aside his grinding fear of leaving Wynter. She would be fine as long as she stayed at the hospital. In fact, she was probably safer there than at his cabin. At the same time, he resisted the urge to dwell on Mona Shelton's death and the shocking revelation that the older woman had been lured from her home by a text sent from Wynter's phone.

Right now he needed to concentrate on tracking down Jay Wheeler. He had no idea if the older man would have any information about Laurel Moore, but Noah hoped he could get an overview of the people connected to Wynter's mother and what was happening that might have led to her death.

Reaching Larkin, he turned and drove toward the center of town. He had never met Oliver's father. Noah's nana, however, had pronounced Jay Wheeler a devil's child. She said he'd been caught growing marijuana on Sander Moore's land, and after being run out of town, he'd moved to Chicago where he'd promptly been arrested for petty theft and drugs. Of course, his nana had pronounced her neighbor a devil's child, along with her sister-in-law and the poor woman who took first prize at the garden show, stealing the title that his nana was sure should have gone to her.

Pulling into an alley three blocks east of Cedar Avenue, Noah parked the truck and headed into a dark, narrow building squeezed between a Laundromat on one side and an antiques store on the other. Halting at the door to allow his eyes to adjust to the gloom, Noah wrinkled his nose at the smell of old sawdust from the shuffleboard that ran along the back wall, and the yeasty tang of beer that had seeped into the wood paneling.

Once he could clearly make out the details of the long, open space, Noah searched for the handful of patrons who were gathered around the tables that crowded the center of the room. There were a surprising number, considering it was barely past breakfast time, but this was probably the only tavern open at this hour. That meant they had a monopoly on the local drinkers.

His gaze landed on the lone man seated at the bar, drinking a tall glass of beer. The stranger was slender with gray hair cut short and a face that was heavily lined from years of smoking. He was wearing a Chicago Bulls sweatshirt and worn jeans. From a distance he didn't particularly resemble Oliver, but since Noah recognized the other customers gathered around the tables, he was going to assume that this was his father.

Strolling forward, Noah leaned against the bar next to the man. "Jay?"

The stranger swiveled his head to reveal pale, deep-set eyes. He had a slender silver toothpick stuck in the corner of his mouth and a smirking smile.

"Who's asking?"

Noah held out his hand. "Noah Heller."

"Heller?" The man frowned, ignoring Noah's hand as he removed the toothpick from his mouth and tucked it into his pocket. "Any relation to Preeda Heller?"

Noah dropped his hand. "Grandson."

The man cast a worried glance over his shoulder. "She isn't with you, is she?"

Noah hid a smile. His grandma was striking fear into the hearts of men from her grave. She'd be so proud. "She died."

"Oh." Jay returned his attention to Noah. "Sorry."

"Can I join you?"

"Depends." Jay reached for his glass, draining the beer in one gulp. "Are you buying?"

Noah climbed onto a high stool, motioning toward the bored bartender. "The first round."

Waiting until they each had a beer fresh from the tap sitting in front of them, Jay leaned sideways to speak in a low tone. "I don't have my stash with me, but I'm sure we can negotiate a more private location to conclude our business."

Noah hid his grimace. If Jay had really spent time in jail, he hadn't bothered to be reformed. He was still peddling drugs. "The only thing I want is information," he assured his companion.

Jay moved back, his expression hard with suspicion. "You're not a cop, are you?"

"Nope."

Jay narrowed his eyes. "You swear?"

"Cross my heart."

The man reached for his beer, seemingly satisfied that he wasn't the target of some sting operation. "What information do you want?"

Noah wasn't exactly sure. It'd seemed simple when he'd considered the idea of approaching Jay Wheeler and asking him to share his opinion of Laurel Moore and who might want her dead. Now that he'd met the man, he had a feeling that he would dodge any direct questions. Not because he cared about the past, but because his default instinct was to lie.

Grabbing his beer, Noah took a sip, grimacing at the bitter aftertaste. It was way too early for alcohol. "You worked for Sander Moore?" he asked.

Jay snorted his disgust. "Thirty years ago. And I wouldn't call it work," he groused. "I was slave labor for that bastard and did he ever show any gratitude? No. Just nag, nag, nag. Nothing was ever good enough."

Noah didn't have sympathy for this man. He'd abandoned his own family. But he couldn't deny working on the farm would be hard labor for anyone. "Sander can be challenging."

"He's a shit." The pale eyes smoldered with a festering resentment. "I know for a fact he's the one who called the cops on me just because I had a few pot plants on a crappy piece of land he didn't even remember he owned." His hard tone revealed Jay's inability to accept blame for his own sins. Typical narcissist. "But that wasn't even the worst thing he did."

"No?"

"He turned my own son against me. Ollie worshipped the ground Sander walked on, while I was just . . ." He struggled for the words. "Some sort of lowlife."

Noah resisted the urge to point out the man's hypocrisy. Jay Wheeler was willing to abandon his family, but he resented the fact his son preferred another father figure.

"Did you know Sander's son?" he instead asked.

"Edgar?" The bitterness was abruptly replaced by amusement. "'Course I knew him. What a joke."

"What was the joke?"

"Big Man Sander, always bragging about his farm and how his great-great-something was the first settler in the area. And then he had a kid who couldn't tell a heifer from a steer." Jay took a gulp of beer. "It warmed my heart to hear the old man bitching and groaning that he'd been cursed with a worthless lump of an heir. Ha. That's why he had to steal mine."

Noah didn't have any trouble imagining Sander publicly venting his disappointment in Edgar. "Families are complicated, am I right?"

"No shit." Jay held up his glass in a mocking toast, then with a frown he set the glass back down with a loud bang. "Hold up. Why are you asking me these questions about Sander? Ollie told me about the shooting. Do you think I had something to do with it?"

Noah arched his brows. He hadn't. Well, not until this man just put the idea into his mind. "Why would I?" he asked, studying the older man's face. "It's not as if you had any reason to want him dead."

"I had plenty of reason, but if I wanted him dead, he'd be dead," Jay snapped.

It was a strange way of proclaiming his innocence, but Noah had more important matters on his mind. "Actually, I'm more interested in the past," he assured his companion.

Jay remained suspicious. "My past?"

"Were you working for Sander when Edgar got married?"

The older man glanced around the bar, as if regretting his decision to let Noah sit next to him. A free beer was all fine and dandy, but not if it meant incriminating himself. "Why are you asking?"

Noah reached into his pocket to pull out his wallet. Opening it, he tossed a twenty on the bar. "General interest." Jay reached for the money, but before he could grab it off the bar, Noah covered it with his hand. "First the information."

Jay hesitated. He wanted to be done with the conversation to drink in peace. Noah could see it etched on his narrow face. Then again, he was in desperate need of money. Oliver had already revealed that nugget of information.

Finally Jay gestured for another beer, waiting for the bartender to bring a fresh glass and wander back to the end of the bar before speaking. "Yeah, I was working at the farm when they got hitched."

"What did you think of Laurel?"

"Honestly?" Jay's lips twisted into a nasty smile. "I couldn't believe she'd married a pussy like Edgar. I mean, she was drop-dead gorgeous with one of the finest asses I've ever seen. Why waste herself on a man who could never appreciate her?"

Noah shuddered. The man was a grade-A jerk, but he'd had a front seat to the Moore family dramas. It was possible he had the information that Noah needed. "Besides having a fine ass. What did you think of her?"

Jay drained his first beer and reached for his second. "High-maintenance."

"Money?"

"Money. Tantrums. Constant demands for attention." He deliberately paused. "Attention she got in lots of places that weren't her husband's bedroom."

"Are you suggesting she had affairs?"

"The gossips said she had dozens, but they were always

yapping about crap they didn't know nothing about. Hell, there were rumors she was sleeping with me." He tried to look as if he was hiding some big secret, but Noah wasn't fooled. Laurel Moore would never have been interested. When Noah said nothing, Jay shrugged and continued. "She wasn't as bad as they said, but the girl did have her fun."

"Did you know of any supposed lovers?"

Jay glanced toward the money beneath Noah's hand. "It was a long time ago. Memories fade."

Noah swallowed a sigh and pulled out a ten-dollar bill. Tossing it with the twenty, he once again placed his hand on top.

"Tell me," he commanded.

Jay considered his response. "There was some professor at the college. And a guy who supposedly offed himself." He took another drink, glancing at Noah over the rim of his glass. "But what really set the gossips on fire was the rumors that sweet Laurel could swing both ways."

Noah blinked in surprise. "Both ways?"

"She had an eye for the ladies."

"I know what it means," Noah snapped, wondering if the man was trying to be shocking or if there really had been rumors that Laurel was bi. "Do you have any names?"

"Naw. Just jabber," Jay conceded, obviously disappointed by Noah's lack of reaction. "What's your interest in Laurel?"

"My interest is in Wynter."

"She was just a babe when I left town. I don't know anything about her."

"Wynter's reached an age where she's interested in knowing more about her mother," Noah said. "I'm concerned that what she discovers might cause her pain. I want to be able to protect her if possible."

"Ah." The older man nodded, as if finally understanding

why Noah was asking so many questions. "Laurel wasn't a bad person."

"Did she have any enemies?"

"Sander hated her," Jay said without hesitation. "'Course he hates everyone, including his own son."

"What was Edgar's relationship with his wife?"

"Desperation."

It was a strange word to describe a relationship. "What's that mean?"

"She knew how to press his buttons. Big-time. You should have heard the fights they had. Sometimes when they were visiting the farm Laurel would start screaming and throwing whatever she could get her hands on, while Edgar would stand there all white-faced with his lips pressed in a thin line. More than once I thought the fool was going to have heart failure. Can't keep all those emotions bottled up without something exploding." Jay shook his head as if with regret, but Noah didn't miss the malicious amusement in his eyes.

"What did they fight about?"

"Everything. Nothing." Jay shrugged. "He wanted to shove Laurel into a mold she didn't fit. It made them both miserable."

Noah arched a brow. He was shocked by the man's insight, but then again, he shouldn't be. Jay Wheeler had the heart of a con artist. It gave him a talent for reading weaknesses and how to exploit them.

"Anyone else have a problem with Laurel?" Noah asked.

"Edgar's secretary." Jay furrowed his brow. "Cindy?"

"Linda Baker?"

"Yeah, that's the one." Jay snapped his fingers. "I overheard an argument between Edgar and Laurel. She threatened to leave if he didn't fire the bitch."

"What did Edgar say?"

"I don't remember the exact words, but the implication was that he'd get rid of his wife before he'd fire his secretary."

Noah tapped the tips of his fingers on the bar. Clearly, Wynter's dislike for her father's secretary wasn't just a clash of personalities. Had she subconsciously sensed that Edgar's relationship with Linda wasn't just one of boss/employee?

A sudden urge to ensure that Wynter was okay thundered through Noah. "Is that all?"

"No. There was another woman. Can't remember her name." Jay lazily sipped his beer. "They had some sort of falling-out and Laurel took a bat to the woman's car. Smashed out the windows and everything." The older man released a sharp laugh. "The gal was feisty, no doubt about it. That's all I can remember."

"If you think of something else, let me know." Noah grabbed his wallet and tossed down another twenty along with his business card. That should cover the tab and hopefully urge Jay to reach out if he recalled any helpful information.

"You got it." Jay reached to snatch the money off the bar as Noah jumped off the high stool. "Good luck with the Moore gal. I've heard she's grown into a real beauty. Not to mention the fact Sander considers her his heir, even if people did whisper she didn't belong to Edgar. One day she'll inherit a tidy farm."

Noah headed toward the door, his steps never faltering as Jay casually dropped his bomb of an accusation.

Of course Edgar was Wynter's father. It was true she didn't look anything like him, but she'd taken after her mother. And even if he wasn't Wynter's father, what did it matter?

It didn't, of course.

Still, Noah couldn't deny an uneasy sensation as he left the bar and headed for Wynter's truck.

Chapter 16

Wynter leaned over her grandpa's hospital bed to place a soft kiss on his forehead before leaving the ICU ward. The doctors had urged her to keep her visits brief since the older man was still unconscious. Not that she needed the warning. Despite the fact he was listed as stable, it was obvious from the plethora of tubes and wires and beeping machines attached to the older man that he was struggling to cling to life.

Entering the thankfully empty waiting room, Wynter crossed to the table where a coffee machine and disposable cups had been arranged. She not only needed the caffeine, but it was freezing in the hospital. She didn't know if it was to combat the spread of germs, or just to keep people from lingering, but she'd made a mistake to think her sweatshirt would be warm enough. She needed a jacket. And a hat. And gloves . . .

At the sound of footsteps Wynter abruptly whirled to face the door, prepared to use her screaming hot coffee as a weapon. There was a guard just down the hall, but it would take him time to get to the waiting room. She had to be ready and willing to protect herself if necessary. A second later, Linda Baker appeared, her blond hair pulled into its usual knot at the nape and her slender body covered in yet another power suit, this one a cherry red.

Wynter's tension remained as the older woman strolled to join her.

"Linda. What are you doing here?"

A reptilian smile curved the woman's lips as she held up a small bouquet of flowers. "I promised your father I would check on Sander."

Wynter frowned. She'd been expecting her father to arrive any minute. No matter how difficult the relationship between the two men, they were family. And family was there for each other when the times were tough. Wasn't that how it was supposed to work?

"Why didn't he come himself?" Wynter was annoyed that she was forced to ask this woman about her father's absence, but without her phone she had no way to contact him.

"He has classes this morning and meetings this afternoon. He's a very busy man."

"Too busy to visit his critically ill father?"

Linda clicked her tongue, as if Wynter was being unreasonably demanding. "Edgar called the hospital first thing this morning and they told him that Sander isn't even conscious. What good would it do to pace the waiting room?" Her cold gaze skimmed over Wynter, her lips thinning at the oversized sweatshirt and old jeans. "He might as well be doing something productive."

"Did you convince him of that?"

"I only have his best interest at heart."

"The loyal secretary."

"At least I understand the meaning of loyalty."

Wynter narrowed her eyes. "What's that supposed to mean?"

"Don't act innocent, Wynter," Linda chided. "You know the truth now."

Wynter carefully turned to set down her cup of coffee on the table. It wasn't that she was afraid she might toss the scalding liquid in the woman's smirking face. Or at least she didn't think she would. She'd always considered herself a pacifist who would never hurt another human being. But there was no point in daring temptation.

She had no idea why she allowed this woman to rub against her nerves, but right now it felt as if steam was coming out the top of her head.

Slowly she turned back. "Are you talking about my mother?"

Linda pursed her lips, making a show of her reluctance to speak ill of the dead. "We no longer have to pretend she was a saint," she finally said in icy tones. "Laurel was jealous of your father's devotion to his work, and the demands on his time. If she'd loved him, she would have done everything in her power to support his career."

There was an ugly edge in Linda's voice whenever she mentioned Laurel's name. She obviously harbored a deep resentment, even after all this time.

"Why are you obsessed with a woman who died twenty-five years ago?" Wynter bluntly demanded. A surprising blush stained the woman's face, and Wynter was struck by a sudden realization. "Is it because my dad still loves her?"

Linda flinched, revealing that Wynter had struck a nerve. But she quickly recovered, sending Wynter a poisonous glare. "He was bewitched with her, nothing more. Eventually they would have divorced."

The words were no doubt intended to wound Wynter. Instead they just reaffirmed her certainty that Linda was still desperately jealous of Laurel Moore. "And you would have become the next Mrs. Moore?"

A dark emotion flared through the older woman's eyes. "Yes."

Wynter forced herself to consider the horrifying possibility. She had no idea if her father still harbored feelings for his dead wife. Or if he'd ever actually loved her at all. But she did know that if he wanted Linda Baker to be more than a secretary, he could have done something about it a long time ago.

"My dad has been a widower for years. Why hasn't he asked you to marry him?"

Linda's face paled at the direct hit, her eyes smoldering with fury. "Don't interfere in matters that don't concern you."

"He's my father. Everything about him concerns me."

A hard, strange smile twisted Linda's lips as she shoved the flowers into Wynter's hand. "Give these to your grandfather. I need to get back to the office."

The woman stomped out of the waiting room, leaving behind a cloud of heavy perfume and frustrated fury. With a muttered curse, Wynter childishly tossed the flowers into the nearby trash can. Over the years she'd crossed paths with Linda Baker, but they'd usually managed to remain polite. Now she prayed she never had to see the woman again.

She was glaring at the mutilated flowers when someone loudly cleared their throat behind her. With a choked sound of shock, Wynter whirled to discover Tonya Knox standing just a few feet away.

So much for being on guard, she ruefully chided her

distraction. "Hi, Tonya," she breathed, feeling a flush stain her cheeks.

"Is everything okay?" Tonya stepped closer. She was wearing a black sweater and yoga pants with chunky silver jewelry and plenty of attitude. Her hair was spiked and her eyes were heavily rimmed with black liner. She looked wildly out of place in the small, rural hospital, but Wynter felt a rush of relief at the sight of her. She could use a friend. "You look upset," Tonya murmured, her expression concerned. "Is it your grandfather?"

"No, he's still in critical condition, but the doctors say he's stable."

"Good." Tonya glanced toward the trash can filled with flowers. "Then I assume it was Linda Baker that's making you look like you want to punch something? Or someone? I saw her leaving when I was coming in."

Wynter heaved a sigh, feeling a pang of regret for the nasty encounter with the older woman. "Sorry. I usually like everyone, but for some reason that woman gets under my skin," she muttered.

"Don't apologize." Tonya snorted. "Unlike you, everyone annoys me. Especially stuck-up bitches like Linda Baker."

Wynter tried to dismiss her dark mood. She had enough worries without adding Linda Baker's obsession with her dad.

"Are you here to see Grandpa?" she asked her friend. "I'm afraid they're only letting in family."

"No, I was looking for you."

"Oh. Do you need something?"

Tonya reached into the leather satchel she had slung across her body. "I wanted to give you this."

Pulling out her hand, she held out a silver key. Wynter

wrapped her fingers around the key and frowned at Tonya in confusion.

"Am I supposed to do something with this?"

"It fits the new door you had installed."

"Oh." Wynter shook her head, feeling like an idiot. "I'd forgotten all about it."

"I figured you had. Jeremy from the lumberyard left the key in the mailbox after he was done, but I wasn't comfortable leaving it there." Tonya grimaced. "Not after someone just broke in. Besides . . ." Tonya bit her lip, looking annoyed with herself. Had she said more than she intended? "Never mind."

Wynter shoved the key into the front pocket of her jeans. "What is it?"

Tonya shook her head. "I don't want to bother you with something that's probably nothing. You should be thinking about your grandfather."

Wynter smiled wryly. She should allow the woman to keep her secrets. Hadn't she just told herself she had enough to worry about? But not knowing was going to be worse. Her imagination could invent all sorts of awful things.

"Now you have to tell me," she insisted.

Tonya grimaced, but studying Wynter's stubborn expression, she accepted defeat.

"Officer Simpson stopped by to ask if I had surveillance on the empty lot between our buildings."

Wynter sucked in a sharp breath. It'd never occurred to her that her neighbor might have video of the person who'd broken into her apartment. "Do you?"

"No." Tonya squashed Wynter's brief flare of hope. "But last night I was working late and I heard a vehicle pull into the lot."

"Oh. Did you see who it was?"

"I did better." Tonya once again reached into her satchel. This time she brought out her cell phone. "I took a picture." Moving to stand next to Wynter, the older woman turned the screen so Wynter could see the image. "Here."

The picture was dark and fuzzy, but Wynter could make out the side of her restaurant and then the vehicle that was near the back corner. "It's a pickup." She leaned closer, as if it would help her peer through the darkness that surrounded the vehicle. "Could you see who was driving?"

"No. They pulled up next to your building and started to park." Tonya made a sound of disgust. "I should have called nine-one-one, but I stepped out to take this picture and they took off. I think I must have spooked them."

Wynter didn't blame her friend. You couldn't call the cops just because a truck pulled into an empty lot. "What time?"

Tonya turned the phone back so she could touch the screen. "Ten thirty-eight."

Wynter considered the possibilities. There was no use jumping to conclusions. "I suppose they might have been there to drink or other late-night activities. It's usually pretty dead around there at that time of night. There's no way to know for certain."

"When they were pulling out, I got this." Tonya swiped the screen, pulling up a new image. Then using her fingers to enlarge the picture, she turned the phone toward Wynter.

For a second, Wynter didn't know what she was supposed to be seeing. It looked like the same truck, only zoomed in as it turned out of the lot. It wasn't until she was about to hand the phone to her companion that she noticed the decal on the side of the truck.

"Drake," she breathed in disbelief.

"You recognize who owns the truck?"

"Drake Shelton." Wynter shoved the phone back into Tonya's hand, her thoughts scrambled. Why would Drake be in Larkin? And why would he have been at her apartment? More importantly, had he returned to Pike to kill his wife? "You need to take this to the police station."

"Why?" Tonya dropped the phone into her satchel, studying Wynter with a curious gaze. "Was he the one who broke into your apartment?"

Wynter shuddered. It was horrifying to think Drake had followed her back to Larkin and then snuck into her private space to leave his warning. But once again, she reminded herself not to leap to conclusions. Not when they had nothing more than a fuzzy photo from a different night. "I'm not sure, but his wife was murdered last night."

Tonya gasped, visibly shaken by Wynter's revelation. "I didn't hear about that."

Wynter held up her hand, instantly regretting her blunt response. "It wasn't here. It happened in Pike."

"Oh." Tonya released the breath she'd been holding. "Did the guy in the truck do it?"

"No one knows for certain, but they're looking for him."

"Okay. I'll run by the station on my way back to the shop. I suppose they can download the picture from my phone." With a nod, Tonya headed toward the door of the waiting room. "Take care."

Wynter watched her leave, then with a muttered curse, she hurried behind the older woman. "Wait, Tonya."

Coming to a halt just outside the room, Tonya turned to send Wynter an impatient frown. "Can this wait? I have a pottery class in an hour and I still need to get organized."

"It will just take a second," Wynter assured her.

"Okay. What is it?"

Wynter didn't have any subtle way of asking for the information she wanted. Not when her nerves felt raw and her mind muddled with the endless shocks that battered her day after day. So she just went to the heart of her concern. "Why didn't you ever mention that my mom had left you an inheritance in her will?"

Tonya paused, her expression impossible to read. "I just assumed you knew. It wasn't a secret," she at last said.

"Did you know her?"

Tonya nodded, her eyes softening. "She volunteered at the art camp every summer. I took every single class she taught there. She had an amazing gift."

The icy dread that had encased her since seeing Drake Shelton's truck parked next to her building was forgotten as Wynter conjured the beauty of her mom's artwork.

It was a lasting legacy that would bring pleasure to Wynter for an eternity.

"Yes, she did," she agreed in soft tones.

"Once your mom realized that I was serious about my pottery, she started giving me private lessons," Tonya continued, blinking back sudden tears. "That's when I told her I hoped to get a degree in art. But my parents insisted I stay here and take over the gift shop. She promised that I would have the scholarship money I needed to go to college if that was what I wanted to do. I really never thought about it. Not until she died."

Wynter sighed. Dredging through the memories of Laurel Moore was like pulling a scab off an old wound. It was painful and messy and probably necessary if Wynter's soul was ever going to heal.

"Did you use the money for art school?" she asked her companion.

"A portion. The rest I saved to open my own studio." Tonya's lips twisted into a humorless smile. "I never expected that studio to be in Larkin." A silence descended between them as they became lost in the mutual sense of grief for the loss of a woman who'd touched both their lives. Then, Tonya shook away her grief. "Is there a problem? If you need the money—"

"No, no. Nothing like that," Wynter quickly denied.

"Your mother . . ." Tonya stopped as if she needed to collect herself. She breathed in deeply, squaring her shoulders as she held Wynter's gaze. "She saved me. I was an angry kid who never fit into this place. Art gave me the outlet I needed to focus on something positive." Her hands clenched at her side, revealing a deep, smoldering emotion. "And even now the studio is my place of zen. I need it like most people need air to survive." A tight smile twisted her lips. "She gave me that."

Wynter reached out to lightly touch Tonya's hand. Her mom might have destroyed lives, but she'd also saved at least one. "I'm glad."

Tonya stepped back. "I'll talk to you later."

"Oh." Wynter was struck by a sudden memory. "Just one more thing."

"What?"

"Why were you at Sander's farm yesterday?" Wynter demanded before Tonya could leave.

The woman frowned. "I wasn't . . . oh wait." She snapped her fingers. "I was looking for you."

"Why?"

Tonya shrugged. "Just wanted to make sure you were okay. Now, I really need to bounce."

"Thanks for bringing by the key."

"No problem."

With jerky motions, Tonya hurried down the hall, her back stiff and her head held high. Wynter reached into her pocket, grimacing when she recalled she didn't have her phone.

She really needed to talk to someone.

No . . . not just someone.

A particular someone.

Noah.

Chapter 17

Noah stacked the last bag of fertilizer on the wooden skid at the end of the greenhouse. It was a relief to discover that he wasn't expected to shovel a truckload of crap when he arrived at the farmers' co-op, but he couldn't deny a small twinge in his lower back by the time he'd finished packing and unpacking the heavy sacks.

How did tiny Wynter manage? The bags weighed as much as she did.

Shaking his head in wonderment, Noah closed up the greenhouse and climbed into the truck. His morning tasks had taken longer than expected, and now he was anxious to get to the hospital. Not just because he wanted to make sure Wynter was okay, but for the simple desire to share her company.

It wasn't the first time he'd been hit with an urge to share lunch with his friend. More than once he'd rearranged his schedule so he could stop by Wynter Garden when he knew the crowd would be thinning so she could join him for a few minutes. It'd never occurred to him that it was anything more than decompressing after a stressful morning.

Or at least he'd never allowed himself to consider it might be more.

Driving up the sloping hill, Noah passed the quiet farmhouse. He briefly considered stopping to walk the area. He wanted to know where you'd have to be standing to glance into the kitchen and see the counter where Wynter had left her phone. In the end, he drove past to turn onto the graveled road that would lead him back to town.

After Sander had been shot there'd been over twenty people strolling around the property. Some in the yard, others on the porch. He wouldn't doubt that a few had gone inside to use the bathroom or get a drink. There was no way to pinpoint who might have grabbed the phone.

Driving slow enough to dodge the tractors that puttered from one field to another, Noah allowed his thoughts to return to his conversation with Jay Wheeler. He hadn't learned much. He'd already known that Laurel's relationships with her husband and father-in-law were complicated, although Jay had implied that there'd been more than disappointment in Edgar's reaction to his wife.

Desperation . . .

Noah shook his head, trying to dismiss the niggle of suspicion. It didn't work.

Edgar appeared to be a stereotypical mild-mannered professor, but he was still a man. To have his wife publicly taking one lover after another, not to mention putting him at financial risk with her extravagant spending, had no doubt infuriated him. Add to that his frustration that she refused to be the wife he'd no doubt fantasized about. . . .

Noah had just reached the point of wondering where Edgar Moore had been when his wife was murdered when he heard the sound of a car behind him. Glancing in the rearview mirror he could see a truck zooming over the hill at a speed that sent gravel spraying behind it.

"Idiot," he muttered, slowing so he could inch to the side of the narrow road.

There were some people who had no regard for safety. Not their own or anyone else's. He didn't care if the truck ended up in the ditch, but he didn't intend to join the fool.

He continued to press on the brakes until he was at a complete halt as the truck swerved around him. Muttering a string of curses, he waited for the jerk to pass, only to realize that the vehicle had stopped. Turning his head, he could see a vague outline of someone in the driver's seat, but the angle of the sun made it impossible to determine more than the fact they were wearing a baseball hat and a thick coat with the collar turned up.

Wondering if they were lost and wanting directions to the nearest highway, Noah started to roll down the window. That's when he caught sight of the decal on the side of the truck.

Shit.

Drake Shelton. He jerked his gaze back just in time to see the driver lift a shotgun and point it in his direction.

His last thought as he tried to duck to the side was that he hadn't told Wynter how he felt about her. The regret that surged through him was as devastating as the pellets that smashed into the window, shattering it into a thousand painful projectiles.

Wynter paced from one end of the waiting room to the other. Where was Noah? He'd told her he would take her to lunch, and unlike most men in her life he always kept his promises.

Had something happened? Was he still trying to track down Oliver's father? Or had there been a snafu with her order of fertilizer? She couldn't call without her cell phone. And she'd promised she wouldn't leave the hospital without him.

She'd circled back to the coffee machine when she heard a footstep behind her.

"Noah?" Spinning around, Wynter's heart plunged at the sight of the tall, dark-haired woman wearing a crisply starched uniform. "Oh, Chelle." She struggled to hide her disappointment. "I was expecting Noah."

The woman halted near the door. "He's here."

"He is?" Wynter glanced over the woman's shoulder, expecting to see Noah in the hallway. "Where?"

"Getting stitched up in the emergency room."

"What?" Wynter blinked, taking a second to absorb what Chelle was saying. Then she swiftly charged across the room, her heart thundering in her chest. "What happened?"

Chelle took a step to the side, blocking the door so Wynter had no choice but to stop or to run her down.

"He's fine. Just a few scrapes and bruises," the woman assured her. "He wouldn't have allowed the doctors to clean and bandage them if I hadn't insisted."

Wynter frowned. Was Chelle with Noah when he was hurt? Or had she been called to an accident? "Was he in a wreck?"

"No." Chelle glanced around the waiting room as if making sure it was empty. At last she returned her attention to Wynter. "He was leaving your grandfather's farm when a truck pulled beside him and someone tried to shoot him."

"Are—" Wynter's throat threatened to squeeze shut as the image of Noah lying on the ground with blood pouring from a gunshot wound seared through her mind. "Are you serious?"

"Yes."

"Oh my God." Wynter reeled backward, collapsing on the edge of the nearest chair. Her knees suddenly refused to hold her weight. "Was he hit?"

"No. But several shards of glass hit him when the side window shattered."

Wynter's blast of relief that he wasn't seriously injured was tempered with the lingering horror that someone had shot at him.

"Someone tried to kill Noah?" She said the words out loud in an attempt to make them real. "Why?"

Chelle held up her hand, as if warning Wynter not to leap to conclusions. "That's one possibility."

"You think it was an accident?"

Chelle shook her head at the ridiculous suggestion. "I think he was driving *your* truck when someone took a shot at him."

It took Wynter a second to sort through her fuzzy thoughts. Of course. Noah had left his Jeep in the parking lot and taken her truck so he could collect the fertilizer and take it to her grandpa's farm. Anyone who'd seen him driving on the isolated road would naturally have assumed it was her.

Her lips were numb, making it hard to form the words. "They were trying to kill me."

Chelle moved to stand directly in front of her. Was she worried Wynter might pass out? It wasn't out of the question. She felt like a punching bag for a heavyweight fighter. One blow after another until her head was spinning.

"Again. It's just a possibility," Chelle murmured.

Wynter licked her lips. Why were they so dry? "Did Noah see who pulled the trigger?"

"Nothing more than a shadowed outline."

"Damn."

"He did, however, recognize the truck."

Wynter jerked. They'd had such crappy luck over the past few days it didn't seem possible they might have caught a break. "Who does it belong to?"

"Drake Shelton."

"Drake." Wynter paused, considering the information. She wasn't shocked, or even surprised. Not after his wife had been murdered. But she was confused. "Oh." She abruptly recalled her earlier conversation with Tonya. "He was at my apartment last night. Tonya Knox has the pictures."

"Yeah. She brought them by the station."

"Do you have an APB out or whatever it is the cops use to find people?"

"We're looking." Chelle's jaw tightened, revealing she wasn't as calm, cool, and collected as she was pretending. She obviously was feeling the pressure of having a potential killer loose in her town. Plus, she'd been friends with Noah for a very long time. She no doubt took it personally that he'd nearly been killed. "If he's still in the area, we'll find him."

Wynter nodded. She trusted Chelle would do everything in her power to track down the lunatic, but in such a rural area there were a thousand places he could hide.

A shiver raced through her. "Why would Drake want me dead?"

"I have a theory."

The familiar male voice came from the doorway, and with a gasp Wynter jumped to her feet. A second later she'd raced across the carpet to wrap Noah in her arms, carefully laying her head on his chest. For a long moment she simply held him, listening to the steady beat of his heart beneath her ear.

When she'd at last assured herself that he was alive and well, she tilted back her head, her eyes widening at the sight of the gashes that marred his cheek, his temple, and one that cut through his brow dangerously close to his eye. That one was held together with a butterfly bandage and an ugly bruise was forming around it.

"Your poor face," she breathed.

"It's nothing but a few scratches," he assured her, his hands rubbing up and down her back in a soothing motion. "I think they make me look dashing. Like a pirate."

If she hadn't been so upset she might have agreed with the dashing part. His hair was tousled and his cheeks rough with the whiskers he hadn't bothered to shave that morning. Combined with the scratches, he looked like a movie star in an action film.

Right now, however, she was far more focused on the realization he'd come terrifyingly close to dying.

"I'm so sorry," she murmured, reaching up to lightly touch one of the slashes.

"Why would you be sorry?"

Pain mixed with a large dash of regret swirled through her. "This is all my fault."

Noah brushed a soft kiss over her forehead. "None of this is your fault."

"But—"

"He's right." Chelle intruded into their conversation, moving to stand next to Noah. "Blaming yourself is a waste of energy. We need to focus on finding Drake Shelton, or whoever took a shot at your truck."

Wynter nodded. She wasn't offended by Chelle's stern words. The woman was right. Self-pity wasn't going to solve anything.

Her fingers moved to hover over the deepest gash on Noah's brow. "You're sure you're okay?"

"I'm fine." His lips twisted into a rueful smile. "Better than your truck."

"I don't care about that." She gazed deep into his eyes. "Just you."

"Wynter."

They were once again interrupted by Chelle as she loudly cleared her throat. "You said you had a theory?"

Noah nodded, reluctantly stepping away from Wynter. As if he was having difficulty concentrating when she was near. She sympathized. She didn't know if it was the shock of nearly losing him, or just the past week of spending day after day together, but suddenly she was acutely anxious to get Noah alone. And naked . . .

"You said that Drake was seen in the lot next to Wynter Garden, right?" Noah spoke directly to Chelle, but there was a hint of a flush on his cheeks. As if he sensed her wicked thoughts.

Chelle held up her hand. "His truck was there. The picture isn't clear enough to identify the driver."

"Point conceded," Noah murmured. "If it *was* Drake, why would he travel to Larkin after twenty-five years? It had to be something we said to him when we stopped by his house that provoked him to come after Wynter." His gaze shifted to Wynter. "Or something we had."

"What did we have?" Wynter cast her mind back to their brief conversation with Drake. She had a vivid image of Drake reaching toward her, his face twisted with fury. "The letters."

"They might have contained information he doesn't want anyone else to see."

Wynter shuddered. "They were just . . . gross."

Chelle sent her a searching gaze. "Did you read them all?"

"No. I just skimmed a couple." Wynter made a sound of exasperation. The thought of the letters was still like salt in an open wound. "What would he write in a love letter that would be worth killing someone?"

"He might have revealed a violent jealousy," Noah said. "Maybe he threatened your mother if she dared to end their relationship."

Wynter considered his words. The letters she'd read had been the usual raunchy stuff some men believed a woman enjoyed, but there'd been a hint of possession in the tone. As if Drake wanted to own her mom. And he'd obviously remembered the exact date of her death even after twenty-five years. Extreme for a casual lover. And he'd been visibly upset when he'd seen the letters in her hands . . .

"There might be something in the letters that would implicate him in my mom's murder," she murmured.

"Where are they now?" Chelle asked.

"At the apartment." Wynter wrinkled her nose. Her world was in chaos, which meant she wasn't sure of anything. "Or at least that's where I left them."

"What if Drake broke in and left the warning note?" Noah said, his voice sharp as if the thought had just occurred to him.

"Why not take the letters then?" Chelle demanded.

"Ollie must have interrupted him," Wynter said, recalling her friend's insistence that he'd seen someone leaving the building after he'd pulled into the lot. If Drake had seen Ollie's van, he might have bolted before getting caught.

Chelle nodded. "Were the letters still there?"

"Yes." Wynter's voice was firm. She wasn't certain of much right now, but she was certain of that. "I remember seeing them when I searched the apartment for anything missing after the break-in."

"So maybe Drake tried to go back and get them," Noah continued with his thought. "Only this time he was seen by Wynter's neighbor."

"So why shoot at Wynter today? Assuming Drake believed she was the one driving the truck."

"Desperation," Noah promptly retorted. "He thought his life was unraveling so he kills his wife and then comes back to get rid of Wynter. Maybe he believes he can start over with a clean slate." Noah shrugged. "Or maybe he's not thinking at all. Any man can be pushed beyond reason."

"Hmm." Chelle looked skeptical.

"Yeah." Noah heaved a harsh sigh. "It seemed more convincing in my head. Now it feels more like a wild guess."

They were all silent for a minute, trying to imagine what Drake was doing in Larkin and why it would involve shooting at Wynter. In the end, nothing made any more sense than Noah's wild theory.

"Maybe we should have a closer look at the letters," Wynter suggested.

"Let me," Chelle insisted. "We have people trained to spot clues that most of us would miss."

Wynter didn't argue. She had no idea what might or might not be a clue. Instead she reached into her pocket and pulled a key off the ring.

"Here. This is a key to the new door. The letters are on my bedroom dresser."

Chelle grabbed the key and glanced toward Noah. "I still need an official statement."

"Later." Wynter moved to wrap her arm around Noah's waist. "Right now I'm taking him home."

Noah glanced down at her, his expression softening with an emotion that melted her heart. "You heard the boss," he murmured.

"Take care of him," Chelle commanded, heading out the door.

Wynter smiled. "That's the plan."

Chapter 18

Noah did his best not to limp as they left the hospital and crossed the parking lot. Wynter was already stressed to the max. He didn't want her worrying about him. Even if he was aching from head to toe and his face burning from the antiseptic the doctor had insisted on pouring over his skin.

He must not have been fully convincing as Wynter pulled open the driver's door and settled behind the steering wheel.

"I can drive," he protested.

She blew him a kiss. "It's my turn to take care of you."

A giddy sense of anticipation jolted through Noah. As if he was a teenage boy about to go on his first date instead of a grown man. It was a weirdly wonderful sensation.

"I like the sound of that," he murmured, rounding the Jeep to crawl into the passenger seat.

Starting the engine, Wynter pulled out of the lot, her profile tense. "I can't bear to think that you might have . . ."

"I'm here." He reached over to lay his hand on her thigh, savoring the warmth he could feel through her jeans. He hadn't even realized how cold he was until that moment.

The combination of a near-death experience and the chilled air in the emergency room obviously wasn't a good one. "And I'm not going anywhere."

They were silent on the drive to his cabin, both lost in their thoughts. Noah didn't mind. He needed a few minutes to calm his shattered nerves.

After nearly having his head blown off by a shotgun, he'd had enough sense to dial 911. He'd wanted the cops tracking down Drake Shelton before he could escape. But then Chelle had arrived and she'd insisted he go to the emergency room before she would allow him to join Wynter. She'd claimed that the blood dripping from his face would terrify anyone who caught sight of him.

Now he needed some time to decompress.

As if reading his mind, Wynter parked the Jeep in the garage and then, shooing away the pack of hounds, led him into the cabin.

"I'll run you a hot bath," she said.

Noah heaved a sigh, his bruised muscles screaming for relief. "Yeah. A hot bath would be awesome."

Together they moved down the narrow hall and through his bedroom into his private bathroom. Wynter made a sound of startled appreciation as her gaze moved around the large space that was designed for a spa, not a simple cabin in the woods. The walls were painted a warm apricot shade with a window that overlooked the lake in the back. There was a double-sink vanity and a walk-in shower. And in the very center of the room a soaking tub had been built into the marble-tiled floor.

It was large enough for four people and deep enough that the water would come up to his chin when he was stretched out. For a man who often walked up to ten miles a day, plus helping dig out vehicles stuck in the snow or chasing after poachers, he needed a way to relax. This was perfect.

With a mysterious smile playing around her lips, Wynter bent down to switch on the faucet, allowing the water to fill the bath. Then, straightening, she turned to face him.

"Do you need help undressing?"

Noah hesitated. He wanted her help. Desperately. But he always wanted to wash away the day before he touched her. Not just the blood that had trickled beneath his shirt, or the dirt from his morning spent unloading bags of fertilizer. But the sense of evil that clung to him from the shocking attack.

"I think I can manage," he murmured.

"I'll make us some lunch."

Wynter left the room, and with low groans Noah managed to squirm out of his clothes. Tossing them toward the hamper in the corner, he used the shallow steps to enter the bath. Another groan was wrenched from his throat, this one of relief, as he sank into the hot water that swirled over his tense body.

Allowing the bath to fill to the edge, Noah stretched out and leaned his head against the towel that was placed against the rim. His lashes drifted downward as he floated in the steaming water. *Ah . . . heaven.*

He didn't know how much time had passed when he heard the sound of Wynter returning. Not more than ten minutes or so, since the water was still warm. Opening his eyes, a choked sound of shock fell from his parted lips as he caught sight of his guest.

Her sweatshirt and jeans were gone, and in their place

she was wearing a flimsy robe that did more to emphasize her slender curves than hide them. Her hair was pulled into a tight braid, although a few tendrils had escaped to dance around her flushed face.

"I thought you were making lunch?" he murmured. A stupid thing to say. But her unexpected appearance had shut down his brain.

"I did." With a smile, she untied the belt around her waist and allowed the robe to drop to the floor.

Noah hissed, his heart forgetting how to beat as he allowed his gaze to slide down her naked body. Christ, she was perfect. She was slender, but not skinny. There were clearly defined muscles from her hours spent in the greenhouses, and a supple grace from her years of yoga. Her breasts were small and soft and deliciously tempting. His mouth watered for a taste.

"How did you know exactly what I was hungry for?" he growled.

She moved to the edge of the bath. "A lucky guess."

Desire blasted through him. "I'm the lucky one."

She gazed down at him, lingering on the stinging scrapes on his face. "Are you sure you're okay?"

"I'm more okay than I've been in a long time," he said with a simple honesty.

"Good." She knelt beside the bath.

He motioned to the empty space next to him. "There's plenty of room."

"First I want to kiss you and make it all better." She leaned forward, brushing her lips over the bandaged cut above his eye.

"Mmm." Noah settled his neck on the rim of the bathtub, savoring the sensation of her soft caresses. Her touch was as light as a butterfly, but he hardened with painful anticipation.

"Better?" Her lips moved to the scrape on his cheek.

With an effort, Noah battled back the urge to yank her into the tub. She'd started this seduction so she got to set the pace. Even if it killed him.

Her fingers stroked through the damp strands of his hair as she nibbled a path of kisses toward the corner of his mouth and then down the line of his jaw. A blistering passion tightened his muscles until he was clenching his teeth. Slow was fine and dandy, but this was excruciating.

"I want to do some kissing," he complained.

Lifting her head, she offered a smile filled with feminine mystery. Then, reaching down, she pulled a condom from the pocket of her robe. He didn't know where she'd gotten it, and right now he didn't care.

At last she swung her legs over the edge of the tub and stretched out beside him. Warm water lapped over them as their naked flesh rubbed together, creating a delicious friction. Noah growled deep in his throat.

"Why didn't we do this sooner?" she murmured, nuzzling his shoulder.

He turned, wrapping her tightly in his arms. "I have a theory."

She tilted back her head to meet his gaze. "Another one?"

"This is a good one," he promised, his fingers sweeping down her back.

"Tell me."

"I think we both knew a long time ago that we were destined to be together."

Her eyes darkened as she draped her leg over his hip, pressing against his hard erection. "Fascinating."

Heat flared through Noah with a ruthless intensity. Like he was trying to contain a wildfire that was prepared to rage out of control. "It gets more fascinating," he murmured.

She deliberately rubbed against his cock, sending shock waves of desire through him. Noah sighed in pleasure.

"Yes, it does," she agreed in a throaty voice. "Much, much more fascinating."

He struggled to think. Something that was far more difficult than it should have been. "Where was I?"

She chuckled, clearly pleased she'd managed to scramble his brains. "You were telling me how we always knew we were destined to be together."

"Right."

"If we knew, then why weren't we together?"

"Because we needed to grow up."

"You've certainly grown." Lying face-to-face, with her leg draped over his hip, she rubbed her ankle up and down the back of his thigh, allowing the tip of his cock to slide just inside her body. "In all the right places."

He made a choked sound, his fingers tracing up the smooth curve of her waist until he could cup the soft mounds of her breasts. "So have you."

Her fingers tightened their grip on his hair, the small prick of pain oddly erotic.

"That's your theory?" she demanded, her face flushed and her hazel eyes glowing with flecks of gold. "We needed to grow up?"

"Yes. We had to sow our wild oats." Lowering his head, Noah wrapped his lips over the tip of her nipple. He heard her groan in pleasure, her fingers moving to dig into his shoulders.

"I don't think that I had any oats to sow, wild or otherwise," she protested, her voice harsh with need.

"We had to make our mistakes." He moved to taste her other nipple, using the tip of his tongue until she was arched tightly against him in an unspoken plea.

"I've made plenty of those."

Noah nibbled his way up the length of her neck, hiding his smile of agreement. Wynter hadn't dated a lot—she was too busy creating her business—but the guys she'd chosen had never been husband potential. Which was no doubt the only reason he'd never been threatened by them. "And discover what we didn't want."

"And what we wanted?"

Noah lifted his head, forcing himself to focus his words. As much as he wanted to tumble into the bliss of mindless desire, this was important. He wanted Wynter to understand that this was more than physical. What he needed from her was far more than just a warm body.

"Yeah, we had to discover what we wanted." He gazed down at her, allowing her to see his love etched on his face. "Each other."

Her expression softened, the shadows banished from her eyes as they gazed at one another. Then, with an unexpected shove, Wynter had him rolled onto his back so she could perch on top of him.

The water splashed over the sides of the bath, but Noah barely noticed. Lost in each other, Wynter reached for the condom. Noah's heart slammed against his ribs as she tore open the package and with a slow, sensuous caress slid it onto his straining cock. He tried to speak, but all that came out was a choked sound of bliss.

He was desperate to be inside her, but there was no way in hell he was going to complain about the feel of her fingers stroking his erection. Up and down, up and down. Quicker and quicker.

"Wynter," he rasped. "Please."

A smug smile curved her lips. "Does that mean you're ready?"

"Explosively ready."

"Sounds dangerous."

Holding his gaze, Wynter widened her legs to slowly sink onto his cock. Noah clenched his teeth as she took him in, inch by inch until she was fully impaled. The sensation sent frissons of ecstasy sizzling through him, wrenching a gasp from his lips.

They held perfectly still for a long moment, both adjusting to the titanic shift in their relationship. Hell, the titanic shift in their very existence. Glancing up, he caught sight of the vulnerability etched on her beautiful face. It was a vulnerability that echoed inside him.

Sex was one thing. He'd enjoyed his past lovers. But making love was something completely different. It was raw and scary and all-consuming.

Noah took a second to simply savor the sight of Wynter posed above him. The damp halo of blond curls that framed her flushed face, the bright sparkle of her eyes, the plush lips and the rosy-tipped breasts.

A huge emotion rushed through him.

Destiny . . .

It was a word that had haunted him for the past few days. Now it seared through his soul.

Wynter was his destiny.

The woman who was meant to stand at his side. To share his bed. And to fill the hole in his heart that had been empty since the death of his parents.

Noah wrapped his arms around her body, urging her downward. He wanted to taste her lips as he began to pump into her sweet warmth. With a moan, she found his mouth in a hungry kiss, meeting him thrust for thrust.

The steam cloaked them in a scented mist as their slick bodies moved in rhythm, their groans mingling as they reached for destiny together.

Chapter 19

Drake Shelton clawed his way out of his stupor. It was something he had a lot of practice at. More than one weekend had ended with him passed out in the corner of a bar. Most of the locals in Pike allowed him to sleep it off. A few even drove him to his house. Which was why he'd known from the beginning that this was no drunken bender.

How long had he been out? It felt like an eternity.

He had a vague memory of waking long enough to sense he was lying on a hard floor. Like the cement slab in a basement. He'd been bound and gagged, but his mind was too fuzzy to comprehend what was happening. Before he could clear his thoughts, he felt a pinprick of pain and the darkness rushed back.

This time, however, there was no pinprick, no drugs pumping through his veins to knock him out.

Cautiously Drake shuffled through his fragmented memories.

There was no way to determine how much time he'd lost, but he could recall being at work when he'd received a text from Wynter Moore. She'd said she had a change of heart and if he wanted the letters he'd written to her mom, he could have them. All he had to do was meet her at her restaurant in Larkin that night at 10:30 P.M.

Drake had read the text a dozen times. It'd felt like a trick, although he couldn't imagine who else would know about the letters. Well, his wife. But she was too stupid to do more than cry and pout about his obsession with Laurel Moore.

Still, he'd taken the precaution of calling the number from the text. It would be foolish not to check. A few seconds later he'd connected with Wynter's voice mail. It was her. He'd left a message that he would meet her that night.

He'd wanted those letters. Desperately. They were his only tangible connection to the woman he loved. It didn't matter that Laurel had been fickle and selfish and occasionally cruel. She had stolen his heart when they were just kids and she never returned it.

Sappy, but true.

And if he was being completely honest, he wanted to see Wynter again. Not in a weird, creepy way. But with the knowledge that she could have been his daughter.

Yes, that was what had happened, he groggily acknowledged.

Once he was off work, he'd showered and changed and then hopped in his truck to make the drive to Larkin. He'd just pulled into the lot next to the restaurant where they were supposed to meet when he'd gotten another text. This one had a new address.

Drake remembered an uneasy feeling. Especially when the GPS had led him through the back roads to an isolated farm.

It was only his fierce need to get his hands on the letters that had kept him from turning around and driving home.

That, and the knowledge that his damned wife would be waiting for him to return. Staring at him with those accusing eyes.

Parking next to the dark house, Drake had cautiously stepped out of his truck. The sooner he had the letters, the sooner he could find the nearest bar. He was just imagining the taste of a cold brew sliding down his throat, when pain exploded through the back of his skull.

That was when the hazy fog had consumed him and the hours had melted into one long blur.

Now he lifted his heavy lids. It was still dark. But this was the darkness of night, not an enclosed basement. And he was no longer lying on a cement floor. He was in a vehicle.

His vehicle, he realized with a stab of surprise.

With an effort he forced his heavy hands to grab the steering wheel. What the hell was going on?

Turning his aching head, he glanced out the side window. It was the same house. The one where he was supposed to meet Wynter.

How had he gotten back here? Or had he never left?

Was it possible he'd hit his head and this had all been some hideous nightmare? A lame explanation, but what else could have happened?

Grunting at the effort to move his stiff muscles, Drake leaned forward and reached out to touch the ignition. Yes! The keys were still there. He fumbled to start the engine.

Intent on his goal of getting the hell out of there, Drake didn't see the shadow approaching the truck, not until the passenger door was jerked open and someone was crawling in. His sluggish brain was still trying to process the realization that he was no longer alone when a metal cylinder was pressed against his temple.

A blessing probably.

He didn't have time to feel terror before there was the loud click of a trigger followed by a shattering pain that ripped through his brain. He was dead before his head hit the steering wheel.

The Stranger inspected the truck and then the dead body, ensuring that no clues had been left behind. At least no clues but the ones the cops were intended to find. There was a quick efficiency in the Stranger's movements. Later there would be time to savor the chaos of the crime scene. The sirens, the screams, the gawkers with their shocked expression that didn't disguise their lewd excitement at the splattered blood, the brains, the death . . .

Widening the search to the area surrounding the truck, the Stranger felt a smug satisfaction. Anyone could kill. It took a true artist not to get caught.

Twenty-five years ago the Stranger had been lucky. Now there was no luck involved. Just a pure skill that was being honed with each death.

The Stranger briefly faltered at the memory of the early snafu. For the second time the shot had missed the mark. Unacceptable.

But tomorrow was another day. Or to use another cliché, the third time was the charm.

Wynter slowly opened her eyes, glancing around the room.

She wasn't surprised to discover she was in Noah's bedroom. Or that their naked bodies were pressed close together beneath the light quilt. After they'd finally emerged from the bath, they'd gone to the kitchen for a late lunch. From there they'd returned to the bedroom, both eager to continue exploring the passion that had been ignited between them.

No, there was no surprise to wake in Noah's arms, but it was a surprise that she could see a glow of light around the curtains that covered the windows. Dawn was creeping over the horizon.

Which meant she'd slept the entire night.

She never did that.

Never, ever.

She woke at 11:11 P.M. since the night of her mom's murder. She'd just assumed that it was now etched into her very DNA.

The feel of warm lips pressing against her furrowed brow lured her out of her dark thoughts and, tilting back her head, she met Noah's searching gaze.

"You look troubled," he murmured, his voice raspy from sleep. "Is something wrong?"

She blinked at the ridiculous question. "Do you want a list?"

"Anything wrong between us?" he clarified.

Ah. Was he worried she might have regrets about taking their relationship to a new level? It didn't seem possible, considering the number of times she kissed him awake to sate her hunger for his touch.

Of course, Noah was that kind of guy. He would always be concerned that his partner was happy. That was only one of the reasons she loved him.

Her heart skidded and crashed against her ribs. *Oh crap.* Had she just allowed the *L* word to form in her head? She braced herself for a sense of panic. She'd never let herself become emotionally attached to her lovers. A part of her had assumed she was incapable of a lasting relationship. Not after she'd suffered such a traumatic incident in her childhood.

But even as she expected her stomach to clench and her breath to squeeze from her lungs, she felt nothing more than a sense of peace. Maybe Noah had been right, she silently acknowledged. Maybe she hadn't fallen in love with anyone because she'd always known she was destined to be with Noah.

She reached up to thread her fingers in his disheveled curls. "No, I would say everything is right."

A tension eased from his body at her teasing words, a smile playing around his lips. "Just right? You're sure it's not perfect?"

She rolled her eyes. "Overachiever."

"That's true," he readily agreed. "Erika warned me that losing both my parents at such a young age would either give me the attitude that nothing mattered or that everything mattered, and I would spend my days trying to please ghosts."

The words struck a chord in Wynter. She, better than anyone, understood the need to live up to the expectations of a phantom.

"Is that why you finished college in three years instead of four, and built this cabin with your bare hands?" she asked, genuinely interested in his answer.

He chuckled, his hands running down her back to cup her butt. "They weren't bare." He gave her a light squeeze. "This is bare."

She brushed her lips along his jaw. "You know what I mean."

"Yeah. If something's important to me, I have to do it to the very best of my ability," he admitted. "But I've managed to strike a bargain with myself."

"What kind of bargain?"

"To let the other things slide." He grimaced. "Don't peek into my laundry room. It will give you nightmares."

She nodded. It was all about balance. That was what they'd learned during group therapy.

"We were lucky to have Erika," she said, the furrow returning to her brows. She'd gone over her conversation with the older woman more than once and she couldn't deny a strange sense of frustration. As if there was something she was missing. "Although . . ."

"What?"

"When I think back to my conversation with her at the hospital, I have a feeling she wasn't telling me everything."

"Like what?"

"I don't know." She shook her head, unable to pinpoint the source of her angst. "Maybe something about one of Mom's lovers. Or her relationship with Mom. I think they were a lot closer than I ever realized."

Leaning forward, Noah grazed his lips over her cheek to nuzzle at the corner of her mouth. "It's easy to read too much into every conversation. I do it myself." He nibbled her bottom lip. "I'm just anxious to find out who the hell is threatening you."

"You're probably right." Warmth spread through her, easing the icy knot of fear in the pit of her stomach. It didn't get rid of it. Nothing would. Not until the truth of her mom's murder was revealed. But when she was in Noah's arms, she felt safe. "Besides, I don't want to discuss Erika. Or the past."

His eyes smoldered with desire. "What do you want to talk about?"

"What else do I need to know about you beyond your scary laundry room?"

"I work crazy hours," he warned.

"Good."

She could never be with a man who worked nine to five and expected dinner on the table when he walked through the door. She was obsessed with building her business and she needed a partner who had an equally intense love for his own career.

"I have a habit of taking in dogs that no one else wants."

"I'm becoming attached to the Hounds of the Baskervilles."

"I never turn on the TV and I wouldn't know a current trend if it hit me in the face," he continued.

"What do you do for entertainment?"

"Fish."

She wrinkled her nose. She possessed a full appreciation for a well-cooked trout with chive butter over fresh spinach, but she wasn't fond of sitting for hours next to a lake or river, waiting for one to grab her bait. "Hmm."

Noah pressed a line of kisses along her jaw. "I'm always open to trying new hobbies."

She wiggled closer to his hard body, smiling at his low groan of approval. "What kind of hobbies?"

It took him a second to respond, as if she'd stolen his ability to think clearly. "Gardening," he finally said. "Waiting tables. Mopping kitchen floors."

She arched a brow. "Mopping is a hobby?"

"Anything to spend time with you."

The words were simple, but they wiggled to the very center of her soul. Like a seed being planted that would bind them together for an eternity.

She reached up to lightly touch his cheek, careful to avoid the wounds that were beginning to heal. "I like the sound of that."

"Yeah, me, too," he growled, pressing the hard thrust of his erection against her lower stomach. "Now it's your turn."

"My turn for what?"

"Any secret vices?"

Wynter considered the question. It wasn't that she didn't have vices. She just didn't know where to start. "I talk to myself."

"When?"

"All the time," she admitted. He might as well get used to coming home and to find her chatting away as if she was hosting a dinner party. "I think it comes from being an only child. I didn't invent imaginary friends, I just had conversations with myself."

He smiled. "Which proves you're good company."

"I don't know about that."

"Anything else?"

"I work crazy hours."

"Good."

She pressed her lips against his chest, directly over his heart. "I have no fun hobbies."

"What about the fishing? That could be a fun hobby."

She chuckled. "You're going to insist on this, aren't you?"

"Just imagine us in the fresh air, sitting beside a lake with a pack of dogs and a cooler of cold beer." He sighed. "Heaven."

"I suppose I could develop a hankering to learn how to fish. With the proper encouragement."

"A hankering?" His voice thickened as he dug his fingers into the soft flesh of her butt. "Is that like a yearning? A longing?"

"More like a rueful acceptance," she conceded. She might not enjoy fishing, but if it meant spending time with Noah, she would pull on her waders and grab her pole any time he invited her.

"Ah."

Her lips moved to tease his flat nipple, savoring the shudder of pleasure she could feel race through his body. "This, however, is a yearning."

He sighed in pleasure. "And a longing?"

She chuckled, reaching down to wrap her fingers around his thick cock. "Lots of longing."

Chapter 20

Noah and Wynter had just finished a late lunch when a concussion of barks splintered the silence.

Wynter winced, placing the last glass in the dishwasher. "Your doorbell is howling."

"Yeah, I noticed."

Noah moved to open the back door. He didn't know who was coming, but he intended to get rid of them as quickly as possible. Yes, there was danger looming just out of sight. And a thousand questions that nagged at the back of his mind. But that could all wait.

He had big plans for the night. Plans that included a bottle of wine, a hot bath, and a naked Wynter. They most certainly didn't include any unwelcome intruder.

Stepping onto the porch, he ignored the sharp breeze that tugged at his loose running shorts. They were the only thing he was wearing and they left too much skin exposed to the late-afternoon chill.

Pursing his lips, he released a long whistle. Instantly his pack of dogs scrambled toward the nearby barn and he turned his attention toward the long drive.

"Damn." The word was wrenched from his lips.

There was a soft sound of footsteps before Wynter appeared beside him. She was wearing her short robe with her hair tumbled over her shoulders. "What's wrong?"

He nodded toward the approaching police car. "Chelle."

Wynter heaved a sigh. "I wish she wouldn't make a habit of this."

He wrapped an arm around her shoulders. "It could be good news."

"Do you think so?"

Noah grimaced. "Not really."

"Me either."

In silence they watched Chelle park the car before she was slipping out and heading up the steps of the porch. She was wearing her uniform and there was slump to her shoulders that revealed it'd already been a long day. Noah felt a strange sense of déjà vu as he caught sight of his friend's tense expression. This wasn't a social visit.

He nodded toward the door as Chelle joined them. "Do you want to come in for coffee?"

Social visit or not, his nana had instilled good manners. Usually with the whack of a ruler across his ass.

Chelle shook her head. "No, I have to get back to the station."

"What happened?" he asked.

"We found Drake Shelton."

Wynter made a sound of shock, tilting back her head to send him a startled glance. "You were right. It is good news."

Noah remained wary. The past few days had been one disturbing surprise after another. It seemed highly unlikely their luck was about to change now.

"Do you have him in custody?" he asked.

"He's dead." Chelle's voice was flat, her expression unreadable.

Wynter gasped in shock. "When?"

"Last night." Chelle held up her hand as Noah's lips parted. "I don't have an exact time."

"How?" Wynter asked.

"A bullet to the head."

Wynter leaned against Noah as if her knees had gone weak. Noah didn't blame her. They'd spent the past twenty-four hours convincing themselves that Drake Shelton had not only murdered her mother, but that he was now in Larkin, stalking Wynter with the intent to kill her.

Should they be relieved that the threat was gone? Or terrified that it was still lurking in the shadows, waiting to strike?

"He was murdered?" Noah asked the obvious question.

Surprisingly, Chelle hesitated. "At first glance it looks like suicide," she at last revealed. "The gun was pressed to his temple and there was a note beside him that said he was sorry."

Noah considered his brief meeting with Drake. The man had reminded him of a dozen other guys he'd known. Conceited, stubborn, unwilling to concede that he might be wrong about anything. If he'd killed his wife and then decided to get rid of Wynter, he wouldn't feel guilt. He'd be pissed that he hadn't managed to finish the job.

Noah studied Chelle's grim expression. "You don't believe it was a suicide." He said the words as a statement not a question. He knew this woman too well to think she could be so easily fooled.

"I'll leave that up to the experts," she said, refusing to offer her personal opinion. "But until the medical examiner tells me that it's a suicide, I'm going to assume it needs to be investigated as if it's a homicide."

There was a short silence as they each tried to wrap their brains around the fact that Drake was dead.

"Was he in Pike when he died?" Wynter finally asked.

"No. They found him in his truck—" Chelle bit off her words, as if not sure she wanted to answer the question.

Noah frowned. "Where?"

Chelle grimaced before heaving a rueful sigh. No doubt she was reminding herself it was a small town that was incapable of hiding a secret. The word of Drake's death was no doubt already circulating through Larkin.

"In your grandfather's driveway."

Noah tightened his arm around Wynter as she stiffened in horror. "He was at the farm?" she gasped.

"I'm afraid so."

Wynter shook her head. "Why would he be there? He didn't know my grandpa."

Chelle shrugged. "Just one question on a very long list."

Noah struggled to make sense of what she was saying. Why would Drake Shelton be at Sander Moore's farm? Even if he had decided to take his own life, it didn't make any sense.

Or had he been killed somewhere else and taken there? If that was the case, why dump him at that particular spot? If they were trying to frighten Wynter, or even warn her away from continuing her search for the truth of her mother's death, why not her apartment? Or even outside his cabin?

A growl rumbled in his throat. He suddenly sympathized with a hamster spinning on a wheel going nowhere.

"Who found the body?" he abruptly asked.

"Oliver Wheeler." Chelle glanced toward Wynter. "He said he was there to do the chores?"

Chelle's voice remained calm, but Noah knew her well enough to detect an edge in her tone. Was she hoping to catch the man in a lie? There was always a suspicion toward the person who discovered a body.

"Yes, he's been helping out since Grandpa was shot," Wynter said.

Chelle nodded, hiding any disappointment. Noah glanced toward the sky. It was nearly dusk. The body must have been discovered hours ago. That would explain the weariness that shadowed his friend's dark eyes. She no doubt had been called at the crack of dawn and hadn't stopped since then.

"Are you leading the investigation?" he asked.

"Unofficially. At least until the M.E. determines the cause of death." Her jaw tightened, as if she was battling a burst of irritation. "If it's suicide, I'll close the case. If it's murder, I'll call in the DCI."

"DCI?" Wynter looked confused. "What's that?"

"The Division of Criminal Investigation," Chelle explained.

Noah understood Chelle's frustration. Drake had been killed in her town. She wanted to be the one who caught and punished the person responsible. He'd feel the same if it was a poacher or a hunter using bait traps to lure in prey. If it was his case, the last thing he'd want was to hand it over to someone else. Especially a stranger who had no connection to Larkin.

He was frustrated, too. It felt as if the killer was toying with them. As if this was some sick game.

"The murderer tried to make us believe that it was Drake who killed his wife and then took a shot at me," he growled, angry he hadn't managed to get a better look at the person who'd been driving Drake's truck.

Of course, in his defense, he'd been busy dodging a spray of shotgun pellets. Besides, whoever it was had taken the precaution of wearing a heavy parka and a cap that kept his face in shadows.

Or her face . . .

"That would be my guess," Chelle agreed.

They exchanged a glance, both urgently aware that as long as the killer was still out there, Wynter was in danger.

"Was there anything that might give you a clue to who is responsible?" he asked.

"Nothing." Chelle made a sound of disgust. "And I mean nothing. In the movies the bad guy always leaves behind a stray cigarette butt or a convenient footprint. I spent hours searching, but all I got was a headache."

"What about my phone?"

Both Noah and Chelle glanced toward Wynter at the abrupt question.

"What about it?" Chelle asked.

Wynter considered her words. "Drake supposedly used my phone to lure Mona to the place she was murdered, right?"

Chelle slowly nodded. "True."

"So where is it now?"

"I'll have the truck searched as well as his house in Pike," Chelle said, her tone revealing a hint of annoyance that she hadn't thought of that herself. "Do you have a way to track it?"

"No. At the restaurant I use a landline and I haven't bothered to connect my cell phone with any other device. Most of the time I barely remember to carry it with me." Wynter leaned against Noah's side, shivering as the breeze tugged at the flimsy material of her robe. "Can you locate it?"

Chelle didn't look hopeful. "We can try, but it'll take

time. We're a small police department with a small budget, and so far this is being treated as a suicide, not a murder or a missing person. Even with your agreement, the phone company will drag their feet to hand over the records."

"What about Mona's death?" Noah asked. "That's obviously a murder."

"Yeah, but a temporary sheriff is in charge." Chelle sighed, her face pale with weariness. "I called him this morning so they could end the search for Drake. It took him time to even remember who I was talking about. He's obviously overwhelmed and undertrained. I'm afraid there might be details slipping through the cracks."

Another shiver raced through Wynter. "Great."

"Sorry." Chelle sent them both a rueful smile. "I'll let you know if I get any new information I can share."

"Thanks, Chelle," Noah murmured, watching his friend jog down the steps of the porch and slide into the car.

He wished there was a way to help ease her strain, not only because he was worried she was burning herself out, but more importantly, every second that passed meant Wynter was in danger.

On cue, Wynter pulled away from him and headed into the house. There was a rigid set to her shoulders that warned Noah she was a woman on a mission. Hurrying behind her, he reached out to grasp her arm, turning her to study her tense expression.

"Where are you going?" he demanded.

"To my dad's house."

"Why?"

"There're boxes of my mom's old belongings in the basement."

"What are you looking for?"

She glanced away, her jaw so tense it was a wonder her teeth didn't shatter from the pressure.

"Anything."

Wynter was silent on the drive into Larkin. It wasn't just from the latest shock. She was still trying to process the thought that Drake Shelton was dead. No, she was psyching herself for the inevitable argument with her dad.

When she was younger she'd begged to be allowed to open the boxes that were filled with her mother's old clothes, painting supplies, picture albums, and her private letters. She'd ached for the tangible connection to the woman who'd been stolen from her when she'd needed her the most.

But her dad had firmly refused her request, keeping them locked away in a closet. First he claimed she was too young, and later he gave vague excuses about having lost the key. It had been painfully obvious he didn't want her to disturb the items.

She'd always told herself that it was her dad's grief that made him so unreasonable. And that he considered the basement closet a shrine to protect his dead wife's possessions. Of course he didn't want anyone pawing through them, not even his own daughter.

As they drove through the nearly empty streets of Larkin, however, Wynter wasn't nearly so convinced. She didn't doubt that her dad had loved her mom. Or even that he was still mourning her. But their relationship hadn't been the stuff of legends. And she doubted he considered the closet a shrine.

So why hadn't he wanted her going through the boxes?

It was a question she intended to answer before the day was over.

She clung to her fierce decision as they pulled into the driveway of the fifties-style ranch house. The place looked exactly as it had for as long as Wynter could remember. The one-time yellow siding had faded to a pale cream and the shutters had peeled until they were bare wood. A porch had been added to the front, but it sagged in the middle and the swing was broken. Even the roof was in need of repair.

Her dad had many fine qualities. He was intelligent, impressively well-read, a successful professor, and a father who'd loved her to the best of his ability. But he had zero interest in his home. Just one of many bones of contention between him and her grandpa. She couldn't remember how many times Sander would stop by with his toolbox to fix one thing or another. He'd complained bitterly about the incompetence of his son, but he'd done what was necessary to keep things running.

Lost in her thoughts, it took Wynter a second to realize that her dad's car wasn't in the driveway. She didn't bother looking in the garage. It had been overrun with containers of books for years. Only a miraculous intervention could have cleared out the space enough for a vehicle.

So where was he at six o'clock on a Saturday night?

Wynter considered the possibilities. He could be out for dinner. Or visiting his father in the hospital. Both reasonable guesses, but she knew they were wrong.

If her dad wasn't home, then he was at work. And since the car was gone, he must intend to stay a while. The only time he drove was when he was going to be late getting home.

Noah turned to glance toward her. "I don't suppose you want to go back to the cabin?"

Wynter shook her head. "No, let's try the college."

Noah didn't point out that her mother's boxes had been in the closet for twenty-five years and would no doubt be there for another few days. Instead he reversed out of the driveway and drove the short distance to the college, pulling into the guest parking lot.

Wynter glanced around, surprised by the number of vehicles. There weren't any evening classes on Saturday, and the frat and sorority houses were on the other side of campus. So why were so many people there?

It wasn't until they were walking toward the admin building and Wynter heard the unmistakable sound of a string quartet that she realized why there was so many visitors.

"There's an art show tonight," she said, turning to follow the flagstone pathway that cut across the quad.

A scattering of students were dotted around the open lawn, tossing a Frisbee in the light of the lamps that lined the walkway. And a few ambitious joggers breezed past them, but overall it was a quiet evening.

Reaching the brownstone building that was too blocky and squat to claim architectural beauty, she pushed open the heavy door and stepped inside. Instantly they were surrounded by the sounds of Mozart that filled the air, luring them down the hallway to the glass conservatory at the far end.

"Why are we interested in an art show?" Noah demanded, walking next to her with a faint frown.

"There's a chance that's where my dad is," she told him. "Besides, I want to talk to Dr. Peyton. I'm sure he's in charge of the show."

"Why do you want to talk to him?"

"I've heard from more than one person he had an ongoing affair with my mom." She shrugged. "Plus, he received money for his summer art camp in my mom's will. He would have as much reason to want her dead as anyone else."

They halted at the double glass doors, both peering in at the conservatory that had been converted into an art gallery. It was traditional, with sleek walls that were covered with various paintings and pedestals to hold the smaller statues and pottery. In the very center of the room was a circular staircase that led to a loft. And at the back was a dais where the quartet were playing. The lighting was subdued and carpeting covered the floor to stifle the sound of footsteps.

Wynter wrinkled her nose as she caught sight of the guests drifting from one exhibit to another. They weren't there to enjoy the artwork; they were there to see and be seen. Carrying fluted glasses of champagne, they moved from one small group to another, performing a graceful dance as they laughed and chitchatted with the pampered ease of the very wealthy.

Obviously this wasn't a regular student exhibit, but one of the fancy receptions that were held to attract money from the elite. Endowments were the lifeblood of a small college.

Glancing down, she considered her loose sweatshirt and jeans. Noah was dressed just casually in a flannel shirt and jeans. Plus his face was still cut and bruised from his near-death experience.

Not exactly suitable for a black-tie event, but hopefully they would be in and out before anyone could notice.

"Let's go," she muttered, pulling open one of the glass

doors. It wasn't the best time to try and talk to Dr. Peyton, but she was afraid she would lose her nerve if she gave herself time to think about it.

Besides, if they cornered him when they were surrounded by potential donors to the art department, he couldn't throw them out.

A cool, dry air draped around her like a shroud as they entered the gallery. The temperature and humidity were precisely controlled. She briskly passed the uniformed staff who sent her a forbidding frown, heading toward the large, silver-haired man wearing a burgundy jacket and white frilled shirt. The head of the art department was always dressed in a flamboyant style, as if he possessed a need to attract attention.

Wynter had never taken a class with the man, but she'd had friends who'd told her that his teaching style was equally flamboyant.

Intent on her objective, Wynter barely noticed her path was taking her directly past the spiral staircase. Not until she caught sight of it out of the corner of her eye. Her feet stumbled, and she would have fallen if Noah hadn't reached out to grasp her arm.

"Are you okay?" he asked.

She swallowed the sudden lump in her throat. "I haven't been here for years."

Noah frowned. "Does it hold a special memory for you?"

She nodded toward the nearby stairs. "The loft displays several of my mom's paintings. I used to come here and stare at them for hours."

"Do you want to go up now?"

A shockingly fierce yearning tugged at Wynter's heart. Suddenly she was sixteen again, curled on the soft settee in the shadowed loft as she allowed her mom's creations to fill the void inside her. The brilliant splotches of color, the scent of paint, the hushed silence . . . It'd been the only tonic that could soothe the raw grief that would threaten to overwhelm her.

She slowly shook her head. "No. I want to talk to Dr. Peyton."

Noah reached to grasp her hand, giving her fingers a squeeze. "Okay."

Together they continued through the crowd that milled around the gallery, reaching the professor just as he was turning away from a group of elegant women who were giggling, as if he'd made some naughty parting joke.

Wynter moved to stand directly in his path. The man grudgingly halted, his expression tightening with annoyance as he gazed down at her.

"If you want to discuss a class, you need to make an appointment during my office hours," he rebuked her in low tones.

Up close Wynter could see the self-indulgent bloat of the man's face and the wrinkles that marred his tanned skin. Once he'd no doubt been a handsome man with bold features and brown eyes so dark they appeared to be black. She also assumed he possessed some sort of charm that would have bewitched her mom.

Or maybe the attraction had been that he was the complete opposite of her dad.

"I'm not a student," she corrected him. "At least not anymore."

He allowed his impatient gaze to skim over her face. Then without warning he jerked, his face paling beneath his fake tan. "Laurel?" He stared down at her, as if he'd seen a ghost. Then, with a blink of his eyes, he released a slow, shaky breath. "No. You must be Laurel's daughter. Wynter, isn't it?"

"Yes."

Lifting his glass, the professor took a deep drink of his champagne. The sight of Wynter had clearly rattled him. Why? Because she looked so much like his old lover? Or because he had something to hide?

"I haven't seen you for years," he muttered.

Wynter shrugged. "I don't come to the college that often since I graduated."

"No, I suppose you wouldn't. Would you like something to drink?" Dr. Peyton started to raise his hand toward a passing waiter.

"No, thanks."

The older man lowered his arm and regarded her with a wary curiosity. "If you aren't a student anymore, why are you here? Did you come to see your mother's art collection?"

Wynter hadn't considered how she intended to get the information she wanted from her mom's former lover. She didn't even know what information she wanted. But she was tired of waiting and hoping the nightmare would end. This man had obviously been a part of her mom's life. If he knew what happened to her, then she intended to find out.

"No." She closely watched his pudgy face. Although the air was cool, there was a sheen of sweat on his brow and his eyes were bloodshot. How much champagne had he had? "I recently discovered that she left you money in her will."

He seemed confused by her words. He glanced toward Noah before returning his attention to Wynter.

"Not to me. It was put into a scholarship fund for local high school students to attend the college's summer art camp." He took another drink before lifting his empty glass in a gesture of a toast. "I'll always be grateful for her generosity."

The toast scraped against Wynter's nerves. Her mom was dead, murdered by some coldhearted bastard. And now Tillie was dead. Mona was dead. And even Drake. It wasn't a joke.

"Yes, over the past days I've also learned that she was generous with more than just her money," she said in cold tones.

The professor stiffened. "Excuse me?"

"The two of you were having an affair, weren't you?"

"That's . . ." Dr. Peyton turned a strange shade of puce as his glass dropped from his nerveless fingers. Thankfully the thick carpet kept it from shattering. "Come with me," he rasped, turning to lead them toward a small office at the front of the gallery.

Wynter ignored Noah's warning gaze as they stepped into the small space that was crammed with a meeting table and several plastic chairs. At the back were racks that held the coats of the guests. Dr. Peyton closed the door and turned to glare at them.

"Why are you asking about my relationship with Laurel?" he snapped.

Noah squeezed her fingers, no doubt trying to halt her reckless approach, but she was too stressed for subtlety. Not to mention the fact that it was easy to be brave when they were surrounded by a dozen guests.

"Her death is being investigated," she bluntly informed him, not at all bothered by the fact she wasn't being entirely honest. So what if the officials hadn't officially reopened the case? *She* was investigating it.

Dr. Peyton grabbed the back of a chair, the harsh fluorescent lights making him look old and tired. "Why? I thought she was shot during a mugging?" His voice was unsteady. "Or maybe it was a carjacking. I know it was a random crime."

"That was the original theory," Wynter agreed.

"And now?"

"There's new evidence."

"What kind of evidence?"

"That the killer was intimately connected to my mom. And that the murder was personal." Wynter's bold claim reverberated through the small room like a challenge. "Maybe a jilted lover."

The dark eyes narrowed as the professor snapped his gaze toward the door, making sure it was closed. "Exactly what are you implying?" he at last demanded, returning his attention to Wynter. "Laurel and I had ended things months before she died."

Noah stepped forward, deliberately blocking any easy path to Wynter. Did he fear the professor might become violent? The older man certainly looked angry enough to throw a punch. His face had gone from ashen shock to puce to a dark red with veins popping out at his temples.

"Who ended it?" Noah demanded.

Dr. Peyton sent Noah a furious glare. "It was by mutual consent, if you must know."

Wynter didn't believe him. He was a pompous blowhard. If it'd been mutual consent, he would have claimed he was the one to end it. Which meant he'd gotten dumped.

"That's not what I heard," she taunted.

His lips pressed to a thin, sour line. "I don't know who's been gossiping to you, but they need to get their facts straight."

"They knew about the affair," Wynter pointed out. "And that you'd managed to convince my mom to name you in her will."

The professor's heavy jowls tightened, as if he intended to continue with his lie. Then he abruptly released a sharp laugh. "Laurel was never discreet. She enjoyed flaunting her affairs. And she was never faithful." He shook his head in disgust. "Not even to me."

"You sound bitter," Noah said.

Dr. Peyton squared his shoulders, his gaze locked on Wynter. "Look. The truth is that I was attracted to Laurel. She was a beautiful woman. But it was her talent that fascinated me. I'd never met anyone with such a natural gift. I used to sit for hours and watch her paint." His lips twisted into a tight smile. "If I'd had the tiniest fraction of her ability I would never have wasted my time teaching a bunch of uncouth barbarians who wouldn't know a Monet from a paint-by-numbers they saw on Instagram. I would have packed my bags and headed to New York."

"So you envied her?" Wynter demanded.

"Of course," the man admitted without hesitation. "She was blessed with the sort of talent that artists only dream of. But what did she do with it? Nothing." He clenched his jaws, his nose flaring as if he was offended by the mere thought. "It should have been shared with the world, not hidden in some cramped little loft at a second-rate college."

There was no missing the edge in his voice. Wynter suspected that his affair with her mom had more to do with his obsession with her artwork than his desire for her as a woman.

"Is that why you split up?" she asked. "Because you thought she was wasting her talent?"

"It had nothing to do with that. We had some fun and then it was time to move on. For both of us," he told her. "Was my pride hurt? Yeah. I'm usually the one who walks away. But once it was over we managed to become friends."

"Friends?" Wynter didn't bother to hide her disbelief.

The professor shrugged. "She was the only one in this godforsaken town who appreciated art. And she most certainly was the only one who I could call to help when I needed a teacher during summer camp." He paused, almost as if silently willing Wynter to believe his words. "Besides, if we'd had a nasty breakup, she would never have left money for my program."

"She might not have had time to change her will," Wynter countered, although a part of her was already accepting this man wasn't the killer. She was convinced he wasn't upset by the breakup. There was a wistful regret in the dark eyes, but he struck her as a shallow man. However angered he might have been by Laurel's rejection, he would never go to the effort of following her to Pike to kill her.

He was much more likely to seduce a new, younger woman and flaunt her in front of his previous lover.

"I don't have any information about what happened to Laurel," Dr. Peyton snapped. "So if that's all—"

"Where were you the night she was killed?" Noah abruptly demanded, catching both the professor and Wynter off guard.

Expecting a blank stare, or a defensive refusal to

answer the question, Wynter was surprised when Dr. Peyton offered his alibi without hesitation.

"I was still in my office after teaching a night class on art history."

Wynter arched her brows at the smooth words. "You have a good memory."

Dr. Peyton shook his head. "Not really. I was just leaving when the phone in the main office rang. At the time the humanities department all shared one secretary. I thought it might be . . ." His words trailed away before he waved a dismissive hand. "A friend I was supposed to meet on campus. So I answered it."

Wynter hid her grimace. The professor looked discomfited. Was he meeting another employee of the college? Or a student?

She shut down her speculation. It happened twenty-five years ago. There was nothing she could do about it now. "It wasn't your friend?" she instead asked.

"No, it was the cops asking for your dad," he said, something that might have been sympathy touching his sweat-dampened face. "I didn't learn until later that they were looking for him because Laurel had been killed. That's why I remember."

Wynter jerked. "Why wouldn't they call him at home?"

"They tried. When he didn't answer they called the office."

Wynter swayed. She felt like someone had pulled the plug on her emotions and they were draining away, like water down a bathtub drain. It was the strangest sensation.

"He wasn't there?" she asked, her lips numb.

"Nope." A malicious smile touched the professor's lips, as if realizing he'd managed to retaliate for Wynter's implication he was involved in Laurel's death. "I have no idea where he was, but I have plenty of eyewitnesses who know where I was. Is that all?"

"Yeah, that's all." Wynter whirled on her heel and rigidly headed toward the door.

She was vaguely aware of Noah following behind her, and the soft chatter of conversation combined with the strands of Mozart as she dashed through the gallery, but nothing mattered but getting out of there.

She couldn't breathe. She needed fresh air.

She needed . . .

Tears streamed down her face as she ran.

Chapter 21

Noah was freaked out. One minute Wynter had been confronting Dr. Peyton like a prizefighter hoping for a knockout punch, and the next she was darting out of the gallery as if the devil was on her heels. Keeping pace, he waited until they were out of the building and crossing the quad before he lightly touched her shoulder to gain her attention.

"Wynter. Wait," he murmured. "Your father's office is that way." He pointed toward the sidewalk that would lead to the admin building.

She continued her power walk toward the parking lot. "I can't talk to him. Not now," she muttered.

"What's going on?"

She turned her head, allowing him to catch a glimpse of her pale face in the glow of the streetlights. Her eyes were wide, as if she was struggling not to cry, and her lips trembled.

"I remember."

He frowned in confusion. "Remember what?"

"Something about that night."

They reached the Jeep and he quickly unlocked the doors. "The night your mom died?"

"Yeah."

He nodded, opening the passenger door. "We'll go back to the cabin. We can talk there."

Erika stood in the shadows, watching as the Jeep squealed out of the parking lot and disappeared from view.

For several minutes she simply stood there, uncertain what to do.

She'd come to the campus for her weekly group sessions. Despite having a private practice, she maintained a position as adjunct counselor. It not only gave her access to the college's facilities and health clinic, but she enjoyed spending time with students. Tonight she'd just been strolling toward her car when she'd seen Wynter hurrying toward the humanities building. There'd been an urgency in the younger woman's movements that had troubled her.

Before she could halt her weird impulse, Erika found herself trailing behind Wynter. She was not only curious, but she had an instinctive need to make sure the younger woman was all right. Wynter, along with her companion, Noah, had, after all, been a patient. It didn't matter how many years had passed; she would always care about their welfare.

Telling herself that it had nothing to do with Laurel, or the guilt that still haunted her, she silently followed behind the two, into the art gallery, watching from a distance as Wynter confronted Dr. Peyton. What the hell was going on? Erika stepped into a shallow alcove as Wynter, Noah, and Dr. Peyton walked past her to enter a small office.

Telling herself to leave, she instead hurried toward the

stairs that led to the upper loft. She'd spent endless hours up there, surrounded by Laurel's artwork. It was a painfully hollow reflection of the brilliant, vibrant woman who'd created the paintings, but it eased her loneliness.

That was how she knew that any conversation in the downstairs office floated through the vent to the corner of the loft. Now she hurried there, shamelessly straining to hear the muffled voices. Erika was honest enough to admit that it wasn't just her concern that compelled her to eaves-drop. She wanted to know what Wynter was asking Peyton. And why the old perv looked like he'd been punched in his fleshy gut.

What she heard left her pale and shaking.

Not because Peyton had admitted to an affair with Laurel. That had been common knowledge. Although he'd been less than honest about how it'd ended, she wryly acknowledged. The jerk had made a fool of himself trying to recapture Laurel's elusive attention. Once Erika had seen him on his knees in the middle of the grocery store, as if pleading for her to give him another chance.

Of course, Laurel had brought a lot of people to their knees. Including her.

No, Erika had been shaken by the man's last claim. That he'd been in his office on the night Laurel had died. Alone.

If that was true, then that changed everything.

Quickly jogging down the stairs, she rushed out of the gallery. When she'd arrived earlier in the evening she'd noticed a familiar car in the parking lot. Now she made a beeline out of the building and across the quad. Less than ten minutes later she'd entered the admin offices and was thrusting open the door to the office of the dean of the English department.

She frowned as she glanced around. The door had been unlocked, but the lights were off. About to back out, Erika frowned as she heard a muffled sound.

"Hello," she called out.

There was a bang, as if something had been dropped. Or maybe a chair overturned. Erika reached into her purse, fumbling for her cell phone to call for security. She was still searching for the damned thing when an inner door was pulled open and Dr. Edgar Moore stepped into the reception room.

He was wearing his usual white dress shirt and black slacks, but his tie was missing and his silver hair looked mussed. Had he fallen asleep at his desk? It wouldn't be unusual. Many professors spent crazy hours in their office. They were either obsessed with research, or writing articles in the hopes of having them published.

Publish or perish wasn't a joke in the academic world.

"Erika." Edgar blinked, reaching out to press a switch on the wall. Muted light filled the reception area. "What are you doing here?"

Erika was suddenly uneasy. Outrage had propelled her from the gallery to this office, but now that she was standing face-to-face with Edgar, she found it wasn't as easy as she'd expected to confront him with what she'd discovered.

Abruptly, she was struck by a fierce urge to retreat and leave the past where it belonged . . . in the past. Then she squared her shoulders. If they really were investigating Laurel's death, she couldn't keep silent. It would be a betrayal of the woman who'd changed her life.

"I have a few questions to ask you," she forced herself to say.

"Now?" Edgar glanced over his shoulder, as if longing to go back to the privacy of his office. "Now?"

"Yes. Now."

"I'm in the middle of—"

"I don't care," Erika snapped. "This can't wait."

Edgar sent her a chiding glare, obviously offended at being interrupted. "You always were pushy," he complained.

Pushy. It was a word used to demean ambitious women. Usually by men who were afraid their superior position was being threatened.

"I'm not pushy, I'm determined."

The man clicked his tongue. "I warned the previous dean before he ever hired you that it was a mistake. Grant College has a certain standard it expects from its staff. Even if you are just a counselor."

Erika was a trained professional. Nothing and no one should be able to rattle her composure. But this man had a rare ability to rub against her nerves. Probably because they'd always been on opposite sides of every fight. From her place at this college, to Laurel's affections, to how Wynter should deal with her grief.

And tonight was no different.

"At least I'm not a sneaky little jerk," she retorted.

"Sneaky?" Edgar scowled. "What's that supposed to mean?"

"You have everyone fooled, don't you?" Erika stepped forward, suppressed emotions welling to the surface. This battle was long overdue. "You pretend to be this mild-mannered professor who spends his life lost in his books."

He arched a brow. "Who am I supposed to be fooling?"

"Your wife, for one."

"My wife?" Edgar flinched, as if her words had caused him physical pain. "Laurel?"

Erika refused to feel bad. Not this time. "She was convinced that you were cold and incapable of deep passions. I knew better."

Edgar's face flushed, his hands clenching into tight fists. "Don't you dare talk about her."

"I warned her that you bottled up your emotions, and like anyone who repressed their feelings you were a ticking time bomb just waiting to explode," Erika ruthlessly pressed, a sickness rolling through her as she recalled her squabbles with Laurel.

Her friend was convinced that Edgar was a cold fish with a pathological inability to enjoy life. Erika had tried to warn the woman that Edgar was just the opposite. He felt so deeply it terrified him. So instead of sharing his emotions, he desperately tried to repress them. They weren't gone, they just bubbled and brewed beneath the surface, like hot lava beneath a volcano.

Edgar's features tightened with an ancient bitterness. "I'm sure you told Laurel a lot of things about me. You were desperate to break us up."

She couldn't argue. He was right. She had wanted Laurel to leave her husband. And it wasn't just because he was an unyielding prick who treated her like shit. Erika had been genuinely convinced that she could make Laurel happy. Who else understood the demons that drove the woman to her excesses? And who else possessed the patience to give her the freedom she needed when she was feeling trapped? And who else saw the person beneath the surface beauty and brittle charm?

Not that she was going to admit her belief that Laurel was her soul mate. Not to this man.

"You were toxic to her," she instead accused.

Edgar narrowed his eyes. "If anyone was toxic to Laurel, it wasn't me."

"You withheld your love to punish her for not behaving as a proper professor's wife. In response she misbehaved. The colder you treated her, the more outrageous she behaved." Erika met him glare for glare. "Toxic."

"And you were always there, whispering in her ear like the snake in the Garden of Eden," he snapped. "You were obsessed with her."

"She was my friend."

"But you wanted more."

The accusation slammed into her with the force of a sledgehammer. Of course she wanted more. She adored Laurel. And maybe she was a little obsessed with her. A part of it had been Erika's youth. She was ripe to tumble head over heels with the first person to give her the attention she craved. And Laurel had a gift for bewitching others. Unfortunately, she used that gift to manipulate and control the people who loved her.

"I only wanted what was best for her," she muttered.

"You?"

"Happiness."

Edgar shook his head, his expression peevish. He'd never liked Erika. From her first day at Grant College, he'd done his best to convince the other professors she was a waste of precious monetary resources. And when she'd become friends with Laurel, his dislike of her had warped into an ugly jealousy.

"No. You tried to convince her into believing no one cared about her except you," he insisted.

Erika's lips tightened. There might be some truth in his words. She'd hated sharing Laurel. With anyone. "At least I didn't try to smother her. Between you and your father's incessant nagging, Laurel couldn't breathe. I wanted her to be free."

"To be free of what?"

"Your expectations. They were crushing her."

Edgar waved a dismissive hand. He was a typical male, assuming his wife would conform to his expectations without him having to bother with compromises. It didn't matter if Laurel was forced to give up her desire to become an artist, as long as Edgar was thriving and succeeding in his career. Nothing else mattered.

"Is that why you tried to convince her to have an abortion?" he demanded.

Erika gasped at the blatant attack. "That's not true."

His lips twisted into a nasty smile. "I overheard her talking to you on the phone."

Erika's mouth dried to the texture of sand. She remembered the call. Laurel had been in tears when she'd revealed she was pregnant. She'd told Erika that she was terrified. She didn't want Edgar to know. Not because he wanted to be a father. He was too selfish to want his life burdened with a baby. But Edgar's father, Sander Moore, had been grousing for an heir from the day they'd gotten married. The old man had some weird obsession with passing on the family farm. As if it was a royal title, not a plot of sketchy land in the middle of nowhere. And since they were constantly in debt to Sander, Laurel was afraid that having a child was the price Edgar would force her to pay.

"I told her that it was a decision she would have to make on her own," Erika insisted, refusing to recall her private dismay at the thought of Laurel being pregnant. She'd known in that moment things would never be the same. She wasn't an awful person, but she'd been young and selfish. "No one could know how she felt about becoming a mother. Not me. Not you. Not your father."

"Then why did Laurel end your friendship?"

Erika wrapped her arms around her waist. She didn't need to be a psychologist to know she was instinctively trying to protect herself from the pain of her memories.

"I ended it when it became obvious I was doing more harm than good," she admitted. It hadn't been one flaming argument that had created the rift. Instead, it'd been a slow, steady decay of their relationship over the course of Laurel's pregnancy. The abrupt demands for attention when Laurel had time, followed by weeks of silence when she had something or someone more interesting to occupy her. The midnight phone calls when she cried over her latest argument with Edgar, and then seeing the two of them at a college event, arm in arm with smiles on their faces. "She was addicted to her manic spirals and I couldn't watch her self-destruct."

Edgar arched a brow. "Why did she attack your car with a baseball bat?"

Erika shrugged. A part of her had been exultant when Laurel had lost control. It'd revealed that she actually cared. Another part had been horrified by the violence. Laurel was pregnant. She needed peace and calm. It was obvious that ending the relationship was for the best.

"She was angry I wouldn't return her calls," she murmured.

A sly expression settled on his narrow face. "So you withdrew your love to punish her?"

"No, I was hoping that she could find some peace in her marriage to protect her unborn child." She gave a sad shake of her head. "The only thing we could all agree on was that Wynter was more important than our petty squabbles."

Edgar's sneer faded, his shoulders slumping. "Wynter."

Erika studied the man who'd been a thorn in her side since she arrived in Larkin, abruptly realizing this was a perfect time to ask the question that had haunted her for years.

"Why did you send Wynter to my therapy group?" she asked. "You never liked me."

"No, I didn't like you," he readily agreed. "But you were the best, and more importantly, I knew you'd do everything in your power to ensure that Wynter overcame her grief. That's what I wanted for my daughter."

Erika believed him. When Laurel had been pregnant, she'd doubted Edgar would be a good father. But Erika had to admit that she'd been impressed when he'd stepped in to take care of Wynter after Laurel's death. He wasn't the most attentive dad, but he'd given her a stable home and unconditional love.

"So why did you insist that she leave the group?" she asked. "Wynter loved being there with the other kids. It made her realize she wasn't alone in losing a parent."

Edgar looked away. "I didn't want her hypnotized."

"Why not? It's an important part of therapy for patients who struggle with traumatic memories."

"If you must know, my father was convinced that you intended to screw with her memories to punish me," he muttered, almost as if he was embarrassed to reveal the truth. "And since he was paying the bills, I had no choice but to end her sessions."

Erika blinked in confusion. "How could I screw with her memories?"

He made a sound of impatience. "My father was suspicious of any sort of therapy. He thought you would try to convince Wynter that I had something to do with her mom's death."

Erika narrowed her eyes. Had Sander Moore suspected his son was involved? And that the hypnosis sessions would uncover memories that Wynter was unconsciously trying to suppress?

The dangerous train of thoughts circled Erika back to the reason she was currently standing in the lobby of the dean's office instead of headed home for a late dinner and a well-deserved bottle of wine.

"I want to know why you lied to me about the night Laurel died."

Edgar stared at her in confusion, looking puzzled by the unexpected question. "I don't know what you're talking about."

"After Laurel had been killed I came to you," she reminded him. It'd been during the wake he'd organized a week after the funeral. The gathering had felt more like a social event with chattering guests who sipped cocktails and discussed the latest gossip from the college. She'd been grief-stricken and angry, longing to lash out at someone. No, not someone. *This* man. If he hadn't constantly pushed Laurel away, she wouldn't have been in Pike that night. She wouldn't have been dead. And so she'd cornered him in the kitchen and bluntly demanded to know if he was responsible for killing his wife. "I wanted to know where you'd been that night."

Edgar's confusion was replaced with the annoying

expression of the absentminded professor. "I told you I was in my office."

"Yeah, that's what you said. You also said you had proof if I needed it. I let it go at the time."

Edgar reached up, as if he intended to smooth the tie that wasn't there. "Why are you bringing this up now?"

"Because the police are investigating her death," Erika said.

Edgar didn't blink. Obviously he'd already suspected that there was something going on with the case. "It's a waste of time. Laurel was killed by a deranged mugger," he said in clipped tones. "End of story."

She shook her head. "If you truly believed that, then why did you lie to me?"

"I didn't—"

"Dr. Peyton just claimed that he was in his office when the cops called, looking for you," she sharply interrupted. "You were nowhere to be found."

The color slowly leached from his face. He was obviously shocked to discover his alibi was in shreds. So why had he lied? Because he'd been in Pike, killing his wife? Or because he was up to something else he didn't want exposed?

"Dr. Peyton has to be mistaken," he finally managed to croak.

"No mistake," Erika insisted. "You weren't here."

His lips pressed together, his chin tilting to a stubborn angle. "I'm not going to discuss this with you."

"Fine. Then I'll discuss it with the cops," Erika bluffed.

She didn't know what Edgar was hiding, but she'd be damned if she would allow him to continue with his lie.

Concentrating on the man who was glaring at her with blatant fury, Erika hadn't noticed the movement in the inner office. Not until a woman appeared to stand next to Edgar, her shirt half-unbuttoned and her hair tousled.

Linda Baker.

"That won't be necessary," the secretary said, her smile as cold as the glitter in her pale eyes. "He was with me."

Erika jerked in shock as she realized why Edgar looked so uncharacteristically mussed. Glancing from the professor to his secretary, Erika felt a sudden heat crawling beneath her cheeks. Why was she the one embarrassed? She hadn't been caught having sex with a staff member in her office.

Still, she discovered herself whirling to hurry out of the reception area. She'd come there for answers, and she had them. There was no point in lingering for the awkward conversation of whether or not she was going to report Edgar to the Board of Regents for his inappropriate affair. That was something that would have to be dealt with next week.

It wasn't until she was home, polishing off her second glass of wine, that she considered the notion that maybe she didn't have the answers she'd thought she had.

Erika had known that Linda Baker was besotted with Edgar for years. And now she had proof they were lovers. If the woman believed that Edgar was in danger, what was the likelihood that she would step in to protect him? One hundred percent.

That explained why she would reveal an illicit relationship that would no doubt be the end of her career at the college. Along with Edgar's.

So, if she was willing to risk her career for her lover, what was to say she wasn't willing to lie for him?

What if they hadn't been together that night?

It wasn't until Erika reached the bottom of the wine bottle

that she gained the courage to reach for her phone. Dialing Wynter's number, she waited for the younger woman to answer. One ring. Two rings. Three rings. At last she was dumped into voice mail. Erika sucked in a deep breath before she spoke.

"Hi, Wynter. This is Erika Tomalin. I have some information about the night your mom died that I think you should know. Give me a call."

Chapter 22

After they returned to the cabin, Noah seemed to sense Wynter's reluctance to discuss the memories that were returning with strange flashes. Like a movie that was coming in and out of focus. Instead, he insisted on grilling a couple of salmon steaks that he served with a fresh salad and sliced fruit.

They ate in a comfortable silence before they headed into the living room where Noah tossed a log into the fireplace to ward off the chilled night air. Then, snuggled on the couch, Noah dropped a light kiss on the top of her head.

"Wynter?"

"Mmm?"

"Are you ready to talk to me?"

Was she? Yeah. The memories hadn't completely returned, but she had a vague recollection of what had happened the night her mom had died.

"Dr. Tomalin was certain that I had a memory I was repressing."

"Was she right?"

Wynter shuddered. "Yes."

Noah tightened his arms around Wynter. "I've got you."

Wynter nestled closer. She'd spent so long depending on herself. There'd never been anyone whom she could turn to in troubled times. It was remarkably glorious to know that she could lean on Noah.

It wasn't a weakness. It made her stronger.

"I told you that I was asleep the night my mom picked me up." She waited for his nod, then she reluctantly sorted through the memories that had risen from the protective fog that her mind had instinctively wrapped around them. "I was still asleep when she put me in the back seat of her car and then stopped to get gas before our drive back to Larkin. I didn't wake up until I heard the shots." She grimaced at the vague recollection of being jerked awake to discover the driver's door open. Puzzled, she'd sat up, peering out the back window to see her mother lying on the ground. "I remember screaming when I saw my mom was covered with blood, and I think there was someone else screaming in the background." In her nightmares there was more than one scream.

"Tillie?" Noah guessed.

"It must have been." She'd never seen the woman, but she assumed that she'd been the one screaming. Who else could it be? "A few minutes later there were sirens and flashing lights and people shouting."

Noah rubbed his hand up and down her back in a comforting caress. "You must have been terrified."

"I was." She'd been curled in a small ball in the back seat as the emergency workers had scurried around the car. None of them seemed to realize she was there. Not until an older man with a cowboy hat had leaned into the car and held out his hand. "Then Sheriff Jansen took me to his house. He gave me hot chocolate and told me I was safe. Until tonight, everything after that was a blur."

"And now?"

"Now I remember sitting in the sheriff's kitchen," she said slowly, once again the vulnerable four-year-old who'd just seen her mother lying on the ground in a pool of blood. "He gave me a peppermint stick to stir it with and then he told me to wait there because he had to make some calls."

Noah shifted so he could study her face with a searching gaze. "That's what troubled you?"

Wynter took a second, allowing the distant images to sharpen into focus. She remembered sitting at the wooden table. Her feet had dangled above the floor and she'd been swinging them because she was nervous. The sheriff had been loud and cheerful and he never stopped talking while he'd moved around the kitchen. Looking back, she could see he'd been doing his best to distract her. Once he was sure that she was comfortably settled with her hot chocolate he'd promised her that he would be close by and left the kitchen.

"He was using a landline, so he was in the living room next to the kitchen," she explained. "I could hear everything he said."

"Who was he calling?"

"He was trying to find my dad."

Noah arched his brows. "Trying?"

"I was drinking my chocolate and hearing him make call after call." A shiver raced through Wynter, cold chills inching down her spine. What had her grandma said . . . *like someone walking over her grave?* "I heard the sheriff ask whoever answered the phone where he could find Edgar Moore, leaving messages to call him back ASAP.

I started crying because I was suddenly certain that the same person who'd hurt my mom had done the same thing to my dad. I was convinced I was all alone in the world and that I would never again have a home or family."

Noah's expression was oddly emotionless, as if he didn't want her to know what he was thinking. "Where did they find him?" he asked.

"I don't know." She heaved a sigh. "Eventually my grandma came to pick me up and take me back to her house. I'd never been so relieved in all my life. After that I must have fallen asleep again because when I woke up, my dad was carrying me into my bedroom in our house in Larkin."

"Do you know what time it was?"

"No, but it was daylight because my dad went to the window to pull closed the curtain to keep out the sunshine before he left the room."

"Is there anything else?"

Wynter tried to recall anything after her grandma had entered the kitchen. It was quite possible Wynter had been so exhausted that she'd collapsed the second her grandma had scooped her in her arms. And she was certain she hadn't wakened until she was back in Larkin.

There were other memories from when she was older, however, that niggled at the back of her mind. "I don't recall anything else from that night, but there are a few arguments between my grandma and my dad that make sense now," she admitted.

"What were they arguing about?"

"I could only hear bits and pieces, but my grandma was accusing him of not being there when I needed him the most. I always assumed she was referring to the hours he worked while I was home alone. But maybe she was mad because he couldn't be found the night my mom was murdered."

He held her gaze. "It could be both."

"True," Wynter agreed. In hindsight it was easy to see her grandma's barely concealed dislike for Edgar Moore. It was more difficult to guess what the root cause might have been. Did she blame Edgar for Laurel's reckless behavior? Or was it a resentment for not being the sort of doting father she thought Wynter deserved? Or was it something more nefarious? A queasiness rolled through Wynter. "Noah."

He cupped her cheek in his palm. "What is it?"

"I can't believe my dad would hurt my mom," she whispered. "I just can't."

"All we know is that he wasn't at his office that night." He bent his head down to press his lips softly against her mouth. "Anything else is just speculation."

"Why didn't he answer his phone that night?"

"We'll ask him." Another kiss. This one longer, deeper. "Tomorrow."

"Noah." She reached up to lightly brush the bruise on his temple.

Leaning forward, he pressed her onto the sofa cushions, his eyes darkening with a wicked temptation.

"We've had enough for one day."

It was just past eight A.M. when Noah pulled into the driveway in front of the faded ranch-style house. The neighborhood was swathed in the sleepy Sunday vibe that the hardworking citizens of Larkin zealously guarded. Later, they would emerge from their homes to attend church or gather together to eat brunch. For now, they savored the sense of peace.

Switching off the engine of his Jeep, he glanced toward the woman in the passenger seat.

She looked calm and composed. Her glorious hair was pulled into a smooth ponytail and she was wearing a soft pink sweater and a pair of faded jeans that hugged her legs with astonishing perfection. But in the morning light he could see the lines of strain on her pale face.

She'd slept through the night in his arms, but it hadn't been restful. She'd tossed and turned and mumbled garbled words. His first instinct had been to keep her at the cabin. He wanted her safely locked away until they discovered what the hell was going on. But she'd barely nibbled at her toast and he could tell she wasn't going to be happy until she'd reassured herself that her father wasn't involved in her mother's murder.

He'd tried to convince her that he could confront her father. There was no need to strain their relationship with ugly accusations. Not when they didn't have anything more than vague suspicions. She'd been adamant that she was going with him. But she did agree that she would search through her mother's belongings in the basement while he actually spoke with her father.

It wasn't the best compromise, but it was the only one he was going to get.

Now, he reached to touch a tendril of hair that had escaped her ponytail to lie against her throat. "Are you ready?"

She didn't hesitate. Shoving open her door, she jumped out of the Jeep. "Let's go."

She marched toward the porch at a brisk pace, and Noah had to hurry to catch up. Then, as they reached the door, her courage faltered. He watched the little color in her cheeks drain away and her lips tremble.

"Steady." He wrapped his arm around her shoulders, tugging her close to his side. "I'm here."

She tilted back her head to meet his unwavering gaze. "Always?" The color flooded back as Wynter realized what she'd just asked. "Wait. Forget I said that."

He lowered his head to press a quick kiss to her lips. "Yeah, always," he promised in a husky voice.

On the point of deepening the kiss, Noah was interrupted as the front door was pulled open. Edgar Moore had obviously heard them pull into the driveway. Straightening, Noah studied the man who was regarding them with a wary gaze.

The first thing he noticed was that the older man was wearing loose jogging pants and a casual sweatshirt. Noah had never seen the professor in anything but his crisp white shirt and black slacks. The next thing he noticed was that Edgar looked tired. His face was not only pale, but a grayish shade that emphasized the wrinkles that fanned from his bloodshot eyes. Even his hair was rumpled, as if he hadn't bothered to comb it that morning.

Noah might have suspected the man had been on a drunken bender if it hadn't been the clarity in Edgar's eyes. Not even the glasses could disguise his mind was as razor-sharp as always.

"Wynter." Edgar frowned, glancing between his daughter and Noah. "I wasn't expecting you this morning."

"Can we come in?"

"Of course." Edgar stepped back, waving them into the living room. Once they were gathered inside, he closed the door and turned to face them. "It's early for a visit."

"I'm not here for a visit," Wynter told him, her voice

tight with the tension that Noah could feel humming through her body.

Edgar looked confused. "Do you need something?"

"I want the key to the closet where you keep Mom's things."

The older man jerked at the unexpected demand. "Why?"

"Because I want to see them."

"Why?"

Wynter made a sound of frustration. Noah suspected this was an argument the two had shared in the past. Probably more than once.

"Does it matter?" she demanded.

The older man's shoulders slumped, as if he was suddenly carrying a heavy weight. Or maybe it was just gravity pulling him down. "Have you been talking to Dr. Tomalin?"

Wynter blinked at the strange question. "Erika? Not since I saw her at the hospital after Grandpa was shot."

"What does Erika have to do with Wynter?" Noah intruded into the conversation. There was obviously something going on with his and Wynter's former therapist.

"Nothing." Edgar reached up to shove his fingers through his tangled hair. "I'm not feeling well this morning."

"What's wrong?" Wynter asked, instantly concerned.

"I couldn't sleep." He nodded toward the door. "In fact, I was just about to go back to bed to get some rest. Can we do this some other time?"

Noah glanced toward Wynter, easily sensing her wavering. The older man seemed like the type of person who used guilt to manipulate others. It wasn't that uncommon in sons who had bullies as fathers. And no doubt Wynter had traditionally capitulated. She hated conflicts. This morning, however, her expression hardened and her lips flattened to a thin line.

"No."

Edgar blinked in surprise. "Wynter—"

"You might as well give her the key," Noah interrupted. Wynter found it difficult to stand up to her father. He didn't. "Once we're done we can get out of your hair and you can take a nap."

Edgar's lips snapped together as he took in Noah's stubborn expression. Muttering beneath his breath, the older man crossed toward the coffee table next to the low sofa hidden by a hand-crocheted afghan. Picking up a lamp, he grabbed the key that had been hidden under the base. "Here." Moving back to Wynter, Edgar shoved the key into her hand.

Wynter sent Noah a hesitant glance. She was having second thoughts about leaving him to deal with her father.

He nodded his head toward the opening that led to the hallway. "Go ahead. I'll be down in a few minutes," he assured her.

"Noah . . ."

"Go."

With a grudging nod, Wynter turned to head out of the living room. Noah watched her leave, hating the thought of them being separated. He wasn't a lunatic. He didn't have to keep a constant watch on the woman who owned his heart. But the thought that there was someone out there who wanted to hurt her, perhaps even wanted her dead, made him itchy whenever she was out of his sight.

"I suppose I should ask what your intentions are toward my daughter?" Edgar's low words thankfully jerked Noah out of his dark thoughts.

"I intend to marry her and devote every day of my life to making her happy," he said without hesitation.

"Does she feel the same way?"

It was a simple question, but it didn't feel simple. Noah was convinced that Wynter enjoyed spending time in his company. And that she was eager to continue sharing his bed. But did she feel the same overwhelming desire to spend the rest of her life with him?

Noah wrinkled his nose. "That's a question you'll have to ask her."

Edgar folded his arms over his narrow chest. "What is it you want from me?"

"I want to know what really happened between you and Wynter's mother."

Edgar gasped, obviously shocked by Noah's blunt confession. "My relationship with my wife is none of your business."

Noah shrugged. "Wynter has questions and she's not going to be satisfied until they're answered. You can tell me. Or tell your daughter. Your choice."

"Why now?"

"Because she no longer believes her mother's death was an accident. She's going to keep digging until she's certain she has the truth."

Edgar turned away, his back stiff. "I met Laurel when I was finishing my PhD. She was unlike anyone I'd ever known and I was dazzled."

"Love at first sight," Noah murmured. He'd been dazzled a time or two. Thankfully they'd quickly fizzled out and he'd realized it had been nothing more than a brief madness.

"Something like that," Edgar muttered. "We dated a few weeks and I was offered a position teaching at Grant

College. It was what I always wanted so I took the job. I also asked Laurel to marry me despite that fact we barely knew each other. We should have waited, but I was certain she would forget me if I didn't take her to Larkin." He slowly turned back to reveal his pained expression. "Within the first year we realized that we were like oil and water. Complete opposites who were destined to never find peace together."

"It's not that unusual," Noah pointed out. "Lots of people rush into marriage and then regret it. Why didn't you get divorced?"

"That would have been the simple solution. Instead we made a game of punishing each other. It was . . ." The older man released a strange laugh. "Toxic. But it was also addictive, and neither of us was willing to walk away. Especially not after we discovered that Laurel was pregnant."

"Was Laurel a good mother?"

The older man grimaced. "Having a child wasn't something that my wife ever wanted." He held up a slender hand as Noah's lips parted. "Don't get me wrong, Laurel adored Wynter. There were times I would get up in the middle of the night and she would be in the nursery rocking Wynter. Or standing beside the cradle, sketching her as she slept. But Laurel found motherhood as oppressive as being a wife. She didn't want to have to spend her days at home with a baby, or worse, devote endless hours to playdates, dance lessons, and birthday parties."

Noah could hear the bitterness in Edgar's voice. He resented the fact that Laurel hadn't been a motherly type of woman.

"Did you want to be a father?"

Edgar's lips twisted. "Touché. I was equally unwilling

to sacrifice for my daughter. I was ambitious, and I devoted my time and attention to the college. I didn't even realize how selfish I had been until the past few days. Now . . ." He allowed his words to trail away with a regretful shake of his head.

Noah didn't press the issue. Edgar might not have been the most attentive father, but he hadn't been abusive. And Wynter had never feared she wouldn't have a stable home with food on the table. Plenty of kids had it worse.

"You told Wynter that her mother was intending to end her relationship with Drake Shelton the weekend she was killed," Noah said, homing in on the information that mattered most to Wynter. "Was that true?"

Edgar took a second to answer. It was obviously a touchy subject, but at last he gave a restless lift of his shoulder. "Yes, but it was a promise she'd made a dozen different times with her various lovers."

Noah arched a brow. He tried to imagine how he would feel if he knew that Wynter was leaving his bed to seek the arms of another man. It was impossible. Wynter wouldn't cheat. She might tell him to his face that it was over and walk away, but she didn't know how to play games. "And that didn't bother you?" he asked.

Edgar narrowed his eyes. "Not enough to kill her, if that's what you're trying to imply."

Noah lifted his hands. "I'm not implying anything, but it does seem unlikely you wouldn't care that your wife was sleeping with another man."

"By the time Laurel died, we led separate lives. We stayed together for Wynter, but she had her amusements." He deliberately paused. "And I had mine."

Ah. Noah felt a sharp stab of dislike. This man had

allowed his wife's flashy infidelity to obscure his own sins. She was labeled a whore, while he could play the long-suffering victim. And all the while he was just as guilty.

"You were having an affair."

Edgar's lips pinched, as if he could sense Noah's loathing. "It wasn't just an affair. I was in a relationship." He glanced toward the mantel over the faux fireplace, unwilling to meet Noah's condemning gaze. "We were together the night Laurel died."

Well, that cleared up one mystery, Noah acknowledged. "That's why the sheriff couldn't track you down."

A hint of color touched Edgar's gray face. "We were at a hotel out of town."

Noah frowned. If his wife was out of town, why would he go to the trouble of spending money on a hotel? Unless she was married and he was worried her husband might come looking for her. Or . . .

Glancing toward the mantel where Edgar had been looking when he mentioned the affair, Noah took in the framed pictures. A couple were of Wynter at various school events. And then there was one larger than the others of Edgar standing in a dark-paneled office, being handed a scroll by a bald-headed man. Both men were in full academic regalia, with wide smiles. Noah assumed it was the day Edgar was named dean of the English department. His attention settled on the woman standing next to Edgar, gazing at him with open adoration.

Linda Baker.

"The secretary?"

Edgar clicked his tongue in reproach. "She's much more than just a secretary."

Noah arched a brow. There was a fierce edge in the man's

voice that warned his feelings weren't all in the past. "You're still together?"

"Yes."

Noah silently wondered if Wynter had somehow suspected the two were in a relationship. It might explain her instinctive dislike of the older woman. "Why keep it a secret?"

"She works for me."

"That's simple enough," Noah said. "Marry her."

Edgar flinched, as if Noah had suggested he leap off a cliff. "I made that mistake once. I'm never making it again."

Noah stared at him in disbelief. He wasn't sure he'd ever encountered a more selfish bastard. He'd been willing to have sex with Linda Baker, but he wasn't willing to make their relationship official. He'd kept the poor woman trapped in a sleazy affair for over twenty-five years.

It wasn't just an abuse of power, it was an abuse of human decency.

With an effort, Noah swallowed the words that hung on his lips. He planned to make this man his father-in-law in the very near future. It didn't seem the best choice to start off their relationship by calling him a humongous dick.

"So it was just fear of marriage that kept you from making your secretary your wife?"

"No." Edgar bent his head, his eyes locked on the wedding band still wrapped around his finger. "I'll always love Laurel. No matter how many times she broke my heart."

Wynter had braced herself for the pain of sorting through her mom's belongings. It didn't matter how many years passed, the trauma of losing a parent never eased.

And the fact that she'd been taken away in such a senseless act of violence only made it worse.

But Wynter hadn't expected the bittersweet joy that cascaded through her as she unloaded box after box. She'd heard story after story about her mom. Some good, some bad, some jealous, and some glossed with obsessive love. But the bits and bobs in the boxes were her mom speaking directly to Wynter.

The old yearbooks showed a vividly happy teenager with a contagious smile and talent for commanding attention. In each picture she was the obvious center of attention, the queen bee of the small hive. She was a cheerleader, a class president, on the homecoming court, and of course, her art was splashed in every corner of the high school. There were also pictures of Drake Shelton. He was young and handsome and without the petulant bitterness that had marred his expression when she'd seen him just a few days ago. As if he was looking forward to a brilliant future.

Wynter had touched the pictures, unable to believe that two such promising souls were dead.

She turned her attention to the scrapbooks, her heart melting as she realized they were filled with her baby years. There were clips of her fuzzy white hair, and ink prints of her tiny feet. There were also endless pictures of her pasted onto the pages, but it was the sketches at the back that captured Wynter's attention.

They were simple charcoal outlines, but each one captured the very essence of Wynter in that precise moment. The soft curve of her baby cheeks. The inquisitive tilt of her head. The outstretched arms and swirl of her dress as she danced to music only she could hear.

It wasn't just the magnificent talent that her mother

shared on the page. It was her unmistakable love for her daughter.

Tears trailed down Wynter's face as she packed away the boxes. She hadn't found what she was searching for. There were no old diaries, or letters from mysterious lovers who might want her dead. No debts to shady loan sharks, or jealous wives who might want her out of the way.

No, she didn't find what she wanted, but she did find what she needed.

Shoving the last box back into the closet, Wynter was about to shut the door when she noticed a small metal container on a high shelf. It was the sort of thing that was used for important papers.

Wynter hesitated. She was looking for personal items, not business stuff. But then again, she might not ever get a chance to search through the closet again. Might as well take a quick peek.

Grabbing the box, she flipped open the lid and grabbed the thick stack of papers that was folded inside.

A quick glance was enough to tell her that it was some sort of official document. There was the name of a law office printed at the top and below that a bunch of overly complicated words and mumbo jumbo that cost 125 dollars an hour to have written.

A will.

Her mom's will.

Skimming through the pages, she managed to decipher enough of the legalese to determine that most of what she'd been told about the will was true. Laurel had set up a trust fund for Wynter. She'd given money to the college for an art scholarship, a few other small donations to local artists. Wynter was startled, however, by the size of the bequest given to Tonya Knox. Fifteen thousand dollars was more than just helping a struggling student through college. It was no wonder the woman had hoped to open her own studio with the funds. And then there was the inheritance for her dad.

One hundred thousand dollars.

It wasn't that unusual for a young woman to have a large life insurance policy. Two hundred thousand dollars was only a fraction of what she could be expected to make if she'd worked full-time for thirty years, or the cost of being a caregiver to her children and husband. What surprised Wynter was the fact that her dad had spent the years she'd been at home barely scraping by.

They hadn't been poor. Her dad had made a decent, if not fabulous, salary. And there'd never been any question that there would be food on the table, and that Wynter could have nice clothes as well as take up any hobby she wanted. She had piano lessons, dance lessons, and a week at drama camp each summer. But her dad wore clothing off the rack, they never took vacations, and when she'd turned sixteen, Wynter had known she would have to buy her own vehicle. Plus, her dad had made it clear that if she wanted to go to college, it would have to be at Grant where her tuition would be free.

So where did the money go?

Replacing the will in the box, Wynter closed the closet and made her way back upstairs. She didn't know if she felt better or worse now that she'd peeked into the mysterious boxes, but she felt more . . . complete. As if a hole in her heart had been filled.

Those sketches were physical proof that her mom had cared about her daughter. And that she'd spent endless hours watching Wynter as she'd grown from a baby to a young girl.

Entering the living room, Wynter discovered the two men standing a few feet apart, the air sizzling with tension. Predictable, considering that Noah was trying to find out if her dad was somehow involved in the murder of his wife.

As she walked to stand beside Noah, her dad sent her a weary glance. She'd never seen him look so tired.

"Did you find what you were looking for?" he asked.

"In some ways." Wynter released a soft sigh as Noah wrapped an arm around her shoulders. It was a silent promise that she didn't have to do this alone. Exactly what she needed. "I do have a question."

Edgar frowned. "About your mother?"

"About her will."

"Oh." The older man looked oddly relieved. "It was fairly straightforward. Your inheritance was put into a trust until you reached the age of eighteen, and you were to be given any proceeds from the sale of your mother's art. I preferred to keep her collection at the college instead of trying to sell it. I assumed you would want to keep it in the family."

Wynter was deeply relieved her mom's collection hadn't been broken up and sold. She had no idea what it might be worth, but she wasn't ready to part with any of it.

"It's not about my inheritance," she said, her gaze locked on her dad. "It's about yours."

She'd clearly caught him off guard. "What about mine?"

"You received one hundred thousand dollars."

"Yes." He nodded, looking confused. "It was what the

life insurance salesman suggested. I have the same amount in my policy."

"That's a lot of money." She pointedly glanced around the room that had gone past comfortable to shabby. The carpet was worn, the furniture was sagging, and the wallpaper beginning to peel. "What happened to it?"

Edgar shrugged. "I donated to several charities, and I paid off this house to make sure you would never have to worry about having a home. Your mom would have wanted that for you."

That still had to leave at least fifty thousand dollars, Wynter silently calculated. "And the rest?"

"I gave it to your grandfather."

His tone was matter-of-fact, as if Wynter should have known that the money would go to the older man.

"Why?"

"He'd been forced to give us money on several occasions during our marriage," he told her. "He even took out a loan to pay off the creditors who threatened to take your mother to court. I wanted to make sure he didn't have to worry about his debts."

Wynter grimaced. It wasn't shocking that her mom had delinquent credit cards, or that her grandpa had paid the bill, but it was confusing to think that the thrifty, hardworking Sander Moore could have needed such a large sum of money. After all, he'd inherited his land from his father, and until he'd been shot, he'd never had any long-term illness. She would have assumed he was comfortably settled.

"He must have had a lot of debts," she muttered, horrified by the thought it might have been the need to constantly bail her mom out of debt that had put him in financial troubles.

As if sensing her fear, her dad sent her a reassuring smile.

"Small farms in this area stopped being profitable years ago. Something your grandfather refused to accept," he told her. "I told him a dozen times over the years that he needed to sell the place while he could still make a profit, but he nearly bit off my head at the mere suggestion. He was determined to hold on to that farm even if it meant drowning in debt." His lips twisted. "Like a captain going down with his ship, I suppose."

Wynter slowly nodded. Sander Moore was nothing if not stubborn. She remembered a feud he'd had with one of his neighbors. He claimed the plot of pasture the man was using to graze his sheep was on his property. It didn't matter that he never used the land. One night he went down with a tractor and plowed the pasture until there wasn't one blade of grass to be found. "Problem solved," he'd told her, a grin of satisfaction on his wrinkled face.

Shaking her head, Wynter returned her attention to her original question. "Why not keep at least some of the money? Just enough to buy a new car or update the house?"

Edgar looked genuinely shocked. "I wasn't going to profit from your mother's death," he snapped. "I might not have been the best husband, but I was devastated when she was killed. I'm not sure I've ever accepted her death. Not in my heart."

The words echoed through the air, bouncing off the walls with a defiant anger. Wynter released a harsh sigh. She believed him. Not only that he wasn't going to profit from his wife's death. But the fact that he still loved his dead wife.

Did that prove he hadn't been involved in her murder? Love was just as dangerous as hate, wasn't it? Maybe more dangerous. But for now she was going to cling to the belief that he had no idea what had happened that awful night.

"I'm going to the hospital to visit Grandpa," she said, her voice softened. "Do you want to go with us?"

Edgar reached up to run his fingers through his hair, his shoulders once again slumping. "No, I have to prepare for tomorrow."

"What's happening tomorrow?" she asked.

"I'm going to announce my retirement."

Chapter 23

Dr. Erika Tomalin placed her empty mug in the sink and grabbed her handbag off the kitchen table. She wanted another cup of coffee. It'd been a restless night, and the urge to sit at the table, reading the morning paper as she allowed another dose of caffeine to seep into her bloodstream, was tempting.

It was only the knowledge that her mother would be waiting for her Sunday visit that propelled her toward the door that opened into the connected garage. She'd placed her mother in a nursing home three years ago after a nasty stroke that had left the older woman partially paralyzed. It was a two-hour drive, but while it would be more convenient to have her mother closer, she had enough training as a counselor to know that her relationship with the older woman was better when they had space between them.

What was the old saying? Distance makes the heart fonder? Something like that.

She paused to pull on a jacket over the ivory sweater she'd matched with a pair of black slacks, and smoothed her hair that she'd tugged into a tight bun at the nape of her neck.

Her mother insisted that Erika be impeccably dressed whenever she visited. Her clothes, her makeup, and her hair would be inspected by the older woman's eagle gaze. Then her mother would spend the next hour telling Erika exactly what was wrong with her outfit, or her lipstick, or style of hair. And the next hour would be devoted to why Erika couldn't find a decent man to marry.

It didn't matter that Erika had no interest in men. Or marriage for that matter.

Swallowing a sigh, she shoved open the door and stepped into the shadowed garage. Erika understood that love and concern could be expressed in different ways. Her mother just happened to choose constant criticism. And if she was honest, it had been that gnawing disparagement that had honed Erika into a perfect therapist. She'd learned from a young age how to adapt and create whatever façade was needed to pacify her nagging parent.

Now she could be whatever the patient seated across from her needed. A stern taskmaster, a compassionate listener, a friend who was there to cheer them on.

Erika was busy digging her keys out of her purse when there was a faint sound behind her. On the point of turning to discover what had made the noise, Erika was blindsided by a tire iron to the side of her face. Or was it a baseball bat? It didn't really matter.

The end result was a blast of agony that sent her to her knees, swiftly followed by a tidal wave of darkness that thankfully washed away the pain.

Lying snuggled in bed, Noah held Wynter close as she skimmed her fingers over his bare chest. They'd just made love and Noah was hovering on the edge of sleep. It'd been a long day. Not only the unpleasant encounter with Edgar, but the hours of pacing the waiting room. Sander was holding his own, but he was still unconscious in the ICU. He knew it pained Wynter to see the old man so frail.

Once visiting hours were over, he'd insisted she return to the cabin for dinner. And a bottle of wine. They'd deliberately avoided any talk of murder or death or sick relatives. It felt good to just enjoy being together.

It'd been Wynter who'd suggested an early night. Not that Noah had protested. He'd nearly broken the land speed record scooping her off the couch and into the bedroom. Now all he wanted to do was close his eyes and drift into sleep.

It was only the tension he could feel humming through Wynter that kept him awake. She was clearly struggling to put the events of the day behind her.

"I don't understand," she at last muttered.

He pressed his lips to the top of her head, savoring the herbal scent of her curls. "That covers a lot of territory."

"Why would my dad retire?" she clarified. "He devoted his life to achieving his position as dean."

Noah didn't have to give the question much thought. There were only a handful of reasons an overly ambitious man who'd devoted years to his career would be willing to walk away. Ill health . . . or scandal.

"I would guess it has something to do with his secretary," he said. He'd revealed her father's confession to being with Linda Baker the night her mother had died. And that they'd been in a hotel when the sheriff was trying to get ahold of him.

"Because he's sleeping with her?" Noah could see her jaw tighten in the muted light of the bedside lamp. "He's obviously been doing it for years. Why quit his job now?"

Noah had wondered the same thing. There was only one explanation.

"There might not be an official investigation into your mother's death, but eventually people are going to start asking uncomfortable questions," he reminded her. "It's better he's no longer connected to the college before he has to answer those questions."

She shivered, pressing closer to his naked body. "It's all so horrible."

"Your father's relationship with Linda?"

"Well, that. She's such a bitch," she agreed, her voice uncharacteristically catty. "But I mean everything."

He skimmed his lips over her temple. "Again, that covers a lot of territory."

"After I opened the envelope left by Sheriff Jansen, I was supposed to discover the truth." She paused, no doubt imagining her life if she'd never crossed paths with Kir Jansen, and never considered the possibility her mother's death was anything but a tragic fluke of being in the wrong place at the wrong time. "Now I still don't know who shot my mom, while three people are dead, my grandpa is fighting for his life, and my father's career is shattered." She heaved a harsh sigh. "I told you it was Pandora's box."

"And I told you that the past never stays buried," he murmured, tightening his arms around Wynter. None of this was her fault and he'd be damned if he let her waste one second blaming herself. "We're going to find who's behind this madness."

"How?"

Noah shrugged. He didn't have a great answer, but he was a realist. They'd somehow triggered a chain of events into motion, like dominoes falling. But like dominoes, one fraction of a miscalculation would bring everything to an end.

"So far, the killer has been lucky. Eventually he's going to make a mistake," he reassured her.

"You're sure it's a he?"

Noah blinked. He hadn't considered the possibility it might be a woman. Sexist, of course. A female was just as likely as a male to be the killer. Gazing down at her pale face, he intended to continue reassuring her that the nightmare would end, but it was suddenly difficult to concentrate on anything but the feel of her nestled against him.

"The only thing I'm sure about is you," he confessed, cupping her cheek in his palm. "And how very right it feels to have you sharing this cabin with me."

He could feel Wynter's tension easing as she melted against him. Was she as ready as he was to change the conversation?

"Not just right, but *very* right?"

"Very, very right."

"That's a lot of right."

"I hope so." He held her gaze, the sensation of butterflies dancing in his stomach. As if he was once again seventeen, asking a girl to the prom. Only, this was even bigger, and far, far more important to his long-term happiness. "Will you stay?"

She tilted back her head, her expression unreadable. "Are you sure you want to make the offer now?"

"Why wouldn't I be sure?"

"There's a lot going on." She paused, as if considering her words. "It might have intensified your emotions."

"All it did was clarify them," he insisted.

"What did it clarify?"

Noah smiled, the butterflies banished as the sense of utter rightness settled in the center of his soul. He wasn't nervous, he was resolute. "Just how special our relationship has been."

Her hand brushed over his chest, her touch tentative. "Because we were friends first?"

"Because it's always been exactly what we needed," he said. "When we were young we bonded over our shared sense of loss. Then we supported each other while we concentrated on our careers, constantly there without demands that neither of us were prepared to give."

"And now?"

"Lovers who will fight to the death to protect each other."

She considered his words, a small smile at last curving her lips. "It doesn't sound like the most romantic love story."

He wasn't insulted. His parents had shared a peaceful kind of love. There were never fiery arguments followed by passionate hours behind a closed door. They didn't throw things at each other or storm away, threatening never to return.

Once his father had told him to never marry a woman who drove him crazy, no matter how exciting the relationship might feel at the time. Fireworks and rages soon lost their entertainment value.

"A man needs a soft place to land at the end of a day," his dad had said. "Find that soft place. . . ."

"You lived through the fallout when emotions are out of control," he reminded her. "Grand passions and obsession and tragic endings are great at the opera. I prefer a steady, loyal, I-got-your-back sort of love."

Her brilliant eyes darkened with an emotion that was

echoed inside Noah. A huge, constantly expanding emotion that was bigger than his heart. Or his soul. It was . . . immeasurable.

"Me, too," she whispered.

"So you'll stay?"

"You're very persistent."

"It's part of my charm."

She arched her brows. "Being stubborn is part of your charm?"

"I'm resolute in my determination. That's completely different than being stubborn."

She snorted in amusement. "Ah. I'm glad you cleared up my confusion."

He rolled onto his side, settling on his pillow until they were nose to nose. "Are you ever going to answer my question? Will you stay?"

Her hand slid up his chest and behind his neck, pulling him forward. Their lips met.

"Just try to get rid of me."

"Never." He kissed her lips before moving down her body. "Never, never, never . . ."

Chapter 24

Erika woke with an aching head and a dry mouth. For a minute she held herself perfectly still. Like an animal curled in the brush, afraid any movement might attract the attention of a predator. She wasn't sure where she was or what had happened, but she instinctively understood that she was in danger.

Forcing herself to take slow, deep breaths, she absorbed her surroundings.

She was lying on something hard and cold. It didn't feel like cement, or wood. She didn't know what it was. The air was musty and stale, with no hint of a breeze. Was she inside? Yes. Even with her eyes closed she could sense a roof over her head.

Next she concentrated on any sounds.

There was nothing. Not unless you counted her tortured breaths and the thunder of her heartbeat that echoed in her ears. It was the absolute silence that came from being in an enclosed space. A basement. A cellar. A vault. A prison . . .

Fear blasted through Erika, but she grimly battled back

her panic. Right now she needed a clear mind and a plan of action.

Cautiously she opened her eyes, slightly relieved to discover she wasn't trapped in the trunk of her car.

That was the last fuzzy memory she had—she'd just stepped out of her house and was crossing the garage to her car when she'd been hit from behind.

How long ago?

Her gaze moved toward the small rectangular window near the low ceiling. It was night outside. That explained the smothering darkness pressing against her. And why her mouth was so dry. She'd been knocked out for hours.

The next question was: Where was she?

Her gaze moved over the wooden shelves that lined brick walls, and an old-fashioned coal chute that was barely visible in the gloom. It reminded her of the basements beneath the local farmhouses. A place to store extra food for the winter along with coal and firewood, plus a safe place to ride out a storm. But not a comfortable room to spend time in.

Erika rolled slowly onto her back. Her head throbbed and her stiff muscles protested, but no crazed killer leaped out of the shadows. She was going to take that as a win.

Counting to ten, Erika pushed herself into a seated position. She still had a headache, but the fog was beginning to dissipate.

So, it was night and she was in a basement. She already suspected that she'd been brought there by the person who'd been hiding in her garage. What she didn't know was who it was or what they wanted from her.

Steeling her courage, Erika grimly rose to her feet. Her knees were weak and her balance was dubious, but she didn't collapse. Yet another win.

Once convinced she wasn't going to fall flat on her face, she turned in a slow circle. There was nothing to see beyond the dusty shelves and a short wooden staircase across the narrow space.

She wasn't sure why she'd been left on her own. Or how long she would have before her captor returned. But she suspected any hope of escape was now or never. She took a step, then halted, her heart lodged in her throat. Nothing. She took another step. And then another. The open-beamed ceiling was low enough that it brushed the top of her head and cobwebs clung to her face. Erika shuddered, but she kept creeping forward.

Now or never, she reminded herself.

She reached the steps and climbed them with the same slow, methodical speed, refusing to consider that where she was going might be worse than where she was.

When she'd been a grad student at Iowa State University, she'd been riding home from a party with a friend. The roads had been icy and they'd swerved into a ditch. At that time very few people had cell phones and they'd had to make the decision of staying in the car and waiting for someone to drive past or walking through the freezing night to find help.

Erika had chosen to walk, unable to bear the thought of sitting and hoping they would be rescued instead of taking control of the situation. She'd finally found a farmhouse, to call for help, but by the time the wrecker had arrived to pull out the car, her friend was dead. The poor girl had no idea that the snow had clogged her tailpipes and she'd died of carbon monoxide poisoning when she kept the car running to stay warm.

It had been a powerful lesson for Erika.

Take command of the situation or become a victim.

Once she was standing on the top step, she reached out. Her hand touched the smooth wood of a door. The darkness was thicker in this corner and she fumbled to find the knob. At last her fingers wrapped around the rusty metal latch and she pushed it down.

Frustration ripped through her when it refused to budge. Locked.

Throwing caution to the wind, she slammed her hand against the door.

"Hello! Is anyone there?" *Bang, bang, bang.* "Hello."

She paused, listening for any response. Silence. Erika swallowed a hysterical sob.

Had someone locked her down here to rot in this basement?

Who would do such a thing?

Edgar Moore.

The name whispered through her mind.

He had plenty of motive to want her to disappear. Not only had she threatened to go to the police to reveal the fact he hadn't been at the office as he'd told everyone the night his wife had been murdered, but she held the fate of his precious career in her hands.

No one else would have a reason to hurt her.

So what was his plan?

To frighten her into keeping her mouth shut? Or something worse? Did he intend to leave her here? *No.* Terror exploded through her, crashing through the barriers she kept her panic locked behind.

Nothing would be worse than being buried alive. Nothing.

Frantically she pounded her hands against the door. Almost as if she thought she could blast through it with the sheer force of her fear. The last thing she expected was for it to abruptly swing open.

With a low cry, Erika soared through the empty air and into a small kitchen, landing painfully on her hands and knees. Frantically she cranked her head around to discover someone standing over her. The dim light was behind the figure, so all she could determine was the outline of a smallish man who was holding something in his hand.

A gun?

Christ. Why the hell had she ever come to Larkin?

Her mother had been right about one thing. She should have found a nice man and settled down. She might have been miserable, but she would have been alive.

Now . . .

She heard the shot, but she didn't have time to be afraid. She was dead before she ever felt the bullet enter her brain.

It was still dark as Noah watched Wynter climb out of bed and grab her robe. He hadn't looked at a clock, but he was betting that it wasn't yet five o'clock. So much for sleeping in on his day off.

Not that he cared about the early hour. He'd be happy to be awake if it meant continuing his exploration of Wynter's delectable body. Or even heading to a nearby lake to try his luck with the local fish.

But he wasn't overjoyed to get up before the sun to drive her to her grandfather's farm. A place that was certain to upset her.

"I don't want you going out there," he stubbornly insisted. No, he wasn't stubborn, he silently reminded himself. He was resolute in his intentions.

Wynter shoved her silvery curls away from her face. "I have to take care of my plants. If they die, I'll be out several thousand dollars, I also need to stock up Wynter Garden's pantry."

Noah jerked in shock. With everything going on he'd forgotten that she was due to re-open her restaurant any day. "You're going to open?"

"I am."

"When?"

"Tomorrow." She held up her hand as his lips parted to protest. "Noah, I have staff who depend on a steady paycheck. I can't stay closed."

He couldn't argue. Wynter's employees had been with her from the beginning. They were all loyal and hardworking. It wouldn't be fair to ask them to wait around for days, maybe weeks, to get back to work.

That didn't make him any more eager to head out to Sander's farm.

"Call Oliver and have him deal with the greenhouses," he urged.

She shook her head. "He has enough to do taking care of the chores. It's not fair to ask him to do more. Besides, I don't trust anyone with my precious plants."

Noah climbed out of bed. He knew a brick wall when he ran headfirst into one. "You're going to insist on this, aren't you?"

"Yep."

"Okay. I'll get dressed and drive you there."

Her brow furrowed at his words. "You know, I should probably borrow my grandpa's truck."

"Why?"

"Mine's out of commission for at least a few days, and

I'll need transportation once the restaurant is open and you go back to work," she pointed out, her tone so reasonable it was impossible to argue. "As much as I enjoy having my own private chauffeur, I'll need to be able to get around."

Noah had a horrifying flashback to the moment the truck had pulled next to him and he'd caught sight of the gun pointed at his head. What if Wynter had been driving? Would she have recognized the danger in time? And if she had, would the killer have stayed to finish the job?

The mere thought was enough to make his blood run cold.

But then again, Wynter had a point. She couldn't stop living her life.

"I don't like it," he groused, strolling around the edge of the bed to pull her into his arms.

She tilted back her head to reveal her rueful smile. "Yeah, I get that."

"We should take a nice, long vacation."

"Where?"

"We could soak up the heat in Miami." A pang of longing tugged at Noah's heart. He'd made his home in Iowa and he loved being here, but there was a part of him that would always crave the sun and fun that filled his childhood days. "I know the best beaches, plus a fabulous Taiwanese restaurant. We'd even get a family discount."

"That sounds nice," she murmured.

"Or we could take a cruise to the Bahamas," he suggested.

"I've never stayed on an island."

During college Noah had spent his summers working on a chartered yacht that traveled from Miami to the Bahamas. The experience could have soured him; the vacation spots were overcrowded with noisy tourists and cheap trinkets.

But beyond the glitzy holiday towns he'd discovered few secluded coves that were stunningly beautiful.

"White beaches, blue skies, and fruity drinks," he murmured.

"Glorious."

Noah studied her delicate features. There was a smile on her lips that didn't reach her eyes. "But?"

"But I can't leave Larkin while my grandpa is fighting for his life."

"I suppose not," he reluctantly agreed. In the back of his mind, however, he pledged to sweep Wynter off to a romantic vacation as soon as the madness ended.

Going onto her tippy-toes, Wynter pressed a kiss to his jaw. "I'm going to shower."

"Do you need help scrubbing your back?"

"No, we'll never get out of here."

He lowered his head, capturing her soft lips in a kiss that lingered longer than he'd intended. "That's the plan."

She pressed her hands against his chest and stepped back. "Go make some coffee or feed your hounds," she commanded, her cheeks flushed with desire.

Noah reluctantly pulled on his clothes and took care of his morning chores. Once they'd checked on the plants and stopped by the hospital, he hoped to lure Wynter to a nearby town for a nice dinner with wine and a decadent dessert. She deserved a couple hours to forget and just relax.

They headed out of the house and drove to Sander's farm in comfortable silence. He liked that they didn't need to fill the air with constant sound. It indicated an ease that was rare between people. Pulling into the drive, he parked in front of the house. There was no easy way to get to the greenhouses. The hill was too steep to drive, and Sander was too cheap to have an access road built through the dell.

Switching off the engine, they climbed out of the Jeep and Noah headed toward the narrow pathway.

"Wait." Wynter reached out to grasp his arm. "There's someone here."

He halted, glancing over his shoulder. Belatedly he noticed the black Volvo parked on the other side of the house. It was a sleek, glossy sort of vehicle that looked sharply out of place among the shabby buildings and rusting farm equipment. "Do you recognize the car?"

"No."

"I'm going to check it out." Returning to the Jeep, he pulled his service handgun out of the locked glove compartment. "You stay here."

She leaned into the Jeep behind him, grabbing the hunting knife that was also in the glove compartment. Stepping back, she eyed him with a defiant expression. "No way. I'm going with you."

"Wynter."

She pointed the heavy knife toward the nearby house. "It's my grandpa's property. Besides, I don't want you accidentally shooting some poor neighbor who stopped by to put a casserole in the freezer or to clean the house while he's in the hospital."

He rolled his eyes, heading across the yard. "I promise not to kill any do-gooders. But if there's a threat to you, I'm shooting first and asking questions later."

She sent him a chiding gaze, but she didn't argue. Instead she climbed the steps and rounded the porch toward the side of the house.

"Noah."

Coming to a halt, she nodded toward the door. The dawn

was just starting to crest the horizon, allowing him to see that it wasn't fully closed. Together they stepped forward and Noah pushed the door wide enough to peer into the shadowed kitchen. At first there was nothing to see. No movement, nothing seemingly out of place. Then he heard Wynter's soft gasp.

His gaze lowered to the floor. Next to the wall was a slender figure sprawled on the floor, a pool of blood surrounding her head like a gruesome halo. The face was turned toward them with the eyes wide-open. It gave the corpse a look of surprise that only heightened the horror of the grisly discovery.

"Erika," he breathed.

"Oh my God," Wynter burst out, taking a step forward. As if she intended to rush toward the woman.

He reached out to grasp her arm. "No, Wynter, stay here."

"But—"

"This is a crime scene."

Wynter stilled, the color draining from her face as she accepted what her eyes were telling her. "She's dead."

Noah studied the blood that leaked from the wound in the center of her forehead. It was dried to a dark, sickly brown.

"Probably for several hours," he said.

"She was shot, wasn't she?"

"I'm no expert, but that's what it looks like."

In silence they both absorbed the fact that the woman who they'd known since they were teenagers was lying dead on the floor. Years ago she'd been his lifeline. A steadying force in a world that was churning out of control. It seemed impossible to accept that anyone would extinguish such a gentle, caring soul.

As his disbelief fogged his brain, Noah still absently noted bits and details. He was weirdly struck by the fact that her hair was half-pulled into a tidy knot and half tumbled down her back. She was dressed as if she was headed to the office—or perhaps church—but there were smudges on her cheek. Had she been in a struggle? And there was something beside her. A small silver object. Was it a needle?

Bizarre.

"Why would she be here?" Wynter broke into his distracted thoughts.

With an effort, Noah forced himself to battle through the shock humming through him like a low-level pulse of electricity. Pulling his phone from his pocket he dialed 911 and reported the body. Then, satisfied that help was on the way, he glanced toward Wynter.

"Did she know Sander?"

"I'm sure they met, but my grandpa was embarrassingly blunt about his opinion of therapists," she reminded him. "He never wanted me in the grief counseling group in the first place."

Noah frowned, trying to imagine what could have drawn the woman to this location. "Could she have been looking for you?"

Wynter hesitated, as if trying to dredge up a memory. Finally she shrugged her shoulders. "I suppose it's possible. I can't remember if I told her that I would be staying with you or not when she stopped by the hospital. She might have assumed I would be here to take care of the livestock."

Noah glanced back into the kitchen, noticing a narrow door that was open. "Where does that door go?"

Wynter followed his gaze, making a small, startled

sound. "I'd forgotten that it was even there. It leads to the basement."

"What's down there?"

"Nothing." Her tone was adamant. "My grandma used it as a root cellar for the veggies and fruit she canned every summer, but after she passed it was overtaken with dust and cobwebs. I suppose my grandpa would use it during a tornado warning, but as far as I know it's empty."

By the position of her body it looked as if Erika had been stepping out of the basement when she'd been shot. Or maybe she'd been opening the door and someone coming up from the basement had pulled the trigger. He could inspect an animal and establish the cause of death and the basics of what had happened. He could determine if a deer had been shot illegally from the road, or if the animal had been lured into position by bait traps. But this was a person. He was completely out of his depths.

Still, there had to be a reason the door was open. "Is there any other way in and out of the basement beyond the kitchen?"

"There's a small window. It would be a tight squeeze." She paused. "And an old coal chute. Grandpa's had trouble with animals crawling through that so I think he nailed it shut." She sent him a baffled frown, tears flooding her eyes as if she was just now realizing this was more than a nightmare. "Why would anyone sneak into what's nothing more than a barren cellar?"

Noah tried and failed to imagine Dr. Erika Tomalin creeping into a dirty basement in the middle of nowhere.

"I have no idea," he admitted.

Wynter shuddered, wiping the tears from her cheeks. "This is . . ."

"Madness," he finished for her.

"Yes," she agreed, another shudder shaking her slender body. "I feel like we've dropped into some dark Wonderland where nothing makes sense."

The sound of distant sirens carved through the chill morning air. Wrapping his arm around Wynter's shoulders, he tugged her back.

"Let's get out of here."

Chapter 25

The Stranger lurked in the woods to savor the plethora of emergency vehicles gathered around the farmhouse. Despite the distance, the scream of sirens echoed through the dells. The Stranger shuddered in bliss. It wasn't sexual. Only a pervert would be aroused by death. But there was magic in the frantic chaos.

Lights flashed from a dozen vehicles. Red and white and blue. So bright they threatened to blind the gathered gawkers. A thrilling sight, even if the Stranger was too far away to truly appreciate the full impact.

It wasn't as the Stranger had planned. None of it.

Dr. Erika Tomalin wasn't supposed to be involved. But she'd stuck her nose into business that didn't concern her and then she'd made that fatal call. It had sealed her fate.

There'd been no time for adequate planning. The stupid woman had to be silenced before she could speak with Wynter. His only choice was to hold her captive until there was an opportunity to consider the various options. There was too much to lose to make a mistake.

Not now.

After hours of debating one outlandish plot after another, the decision had been made. The bitch had to disappear. The cops might be suspicious, but with no body there could be no way to determine if she'd been murdered or simply decided to walk away from her old life. People did it all the time.

Waiting until the cover of darkness, the Stranger returned to the farm, intending to collect the woman and drive her far away from Larkin. Who could have suspected she was already awake? Yanking open the door, the Stranger had panicked when the meddling therapist had lunged forward.

It was too risky to try and get close enough to knock her out. Last time she'd been taken by surprise. This time she would no doubt fight back.

There was nothing to do but pull the trigger.

Now the Stranger accepted that the botched plan did at least have some benefits.

A smile appeared as the chaos filled the emptiness inside.

An hour later, Wynter finished watering her plants and picked the ripe tomatoes, lettuce, and cucumbers she needed. Some would be used in her restaurant and the rest would be sold in her stall at the farmers' market.

Noah was helping her load the crates into the back of the Jeep when a familiar woman dressed in a uniform jogged down the stairs from the house and crossed toward them.

Wynter had been reeling from a combination of shock and grief when the first wave of emergency responders had arrived. She'd watched from the shelter of Noah's arms as they'd rushed into the kitchen, vaguely relieved when she caught sight of Chelle. She didn't know if the woman had been on duty or if she'd come because she suspected the death was related to her ongoing investigations.

It'd been Noah who'd suggested she complete the tasks she'd come there to do. No doubt he'd hoped the distraction would help her recover from the horror of finding Erika Tomalin's dead body in her grandpa's kitchen.

She wasn't sure it'd worked. Granted, she was no longer battling the urge to vomit, but she'd gone from too many emotions to not enough. As if everything had shut down in an effort to protect her from the shock.

"Thanks for hanging around," Chelle murmured. "I know this wasn't easy."

"I'm almost numb," Wynter confessed.

Chelle heaved a weary sigh. "Yeah, I get that."

"Are you in charge?" Noah asked, standing just behind Wynter.

"For now. Agents from DCI will be here tomorrow." Chelle's voice was carefully bland, making it impossible to know if she was relieved or pissed that the case was being taken off her hands. She reached into her pocket to pull out an electronic pad and stylus. "But I still need to take your statements."

"Does it have to be now?" Noah demanded.

Wynter glanced over her shoulder, sending him a reassuring smile. He'd been a steady presence as she'd mindlessly moved through the greenhouses. What was that song her grandma used to sing? Something about a safe harbor. That was what Noah had become. No, what he'd been from the day they'd first met all those years ago.

"It's okay, Noah," she assured him before returning her attention to Chelle. "We came here this morning because I wanted to check on my greenhouses. The watering system isn't set up on timers so I have to do it manually. Plus I needed some produce for the restaurant. I'm opening it tomorrow and I always make vegetable soup on Tuesdays—" Wynter cut off her words, realizing she was babbling.

Chelle scribbled something on the pad. "What time did you get here?"

"Early," Noah answered. "Just past six."

Chelle touched the pad, scrolling through her notes. "The call came in at six-fifteen. So you went to the house before going down to the greenhouses?"

Wynter nodded. "We pulled into the drive and when we got out of the Jeep we noticed the car. It obviously didn't belong to my grandpa so we decided to see who was here."

"And that was when you discovered Dr. Tomalin?"

"Yes." It was oddly difficult to form the word as the image of Erika's bloody face and blank stare seared through her mind.

"Did you go into the house?"

Perhaps sensing Wynter's sudden distress, Noah smoothed his hand down the curve of her back.

"We stepped inside the door," he told Chelle. "Once we saw Erika we stopped and called nine-one-one."

"Did you see anyone else?"

Noah shook his head. "No."

Chelle glanced up, her gaze taking in the sheer isolation of the farm. It was a double-edged sword. On one hand, it would be easy to sneak around without being noticed. Then again, if someone happened to be driving past or working in one of the distant fields, they would have remembered seeing an unknown car parked at Sander's house.

"You didn't meet anyone on the drive out here?" Chelle pressed.

"Not after we turned onto the gravel road," Noah told her.

Chelle glanced back at Wynter. "Dr. Tomalin didn't say anything about coming out here?"

"No. She stopped by the hospital after my grandpa was shot, but that was the only time I've talked to her in months. She certainly never mentioned that she intended to visit the farm."

Chelle frowned. "Did she have a connection with Sander?"

Wynter tried to think of any plausible reason Erika and her grandpa would cross paths. There was nothing. "Not that I know of."

"You're sure he wasn't in therapy?"

A harsh laugh was wrenched from Wynter's throat. "Positive. He would rather chew glass than have some quack digging around his brain. That's a direct quote."

"That sounds like Sander," Chelle agreed in dry tones.

Wynter turned her attention toward the house where the coroner was preparing to at last haul away the body. For the past hour the local police had been busy taking photos and scanning the property for any traces of evidence that might lead to the killer. She pressed a hand against her stomach, battling back another wave of nausea. "I truly can't imagine why she would be out here."

Chelle wrote something on the pad before she was scrolling back through her notes. "What can you tell me about your grandfather's safe?" she abruptly asked Wynter.

"His safe?"

"Didn't you know he had one?"

It took a second for Wynter to recall the small portable safe that her grandfather had bought to protect his important documents in case of a fire.

"Oh yes. It's in the dining room next to the china cabinet," she said.

"What did he keep in there?"

"I think he had the deed to the farm and his birth certificate in there. Probably a few other papers."

"Anything else?"

Wynter started to shake her head, then she stiffened. "He liked to keep cash on hand. That's how he paid his cleaning lady that came in once a week, and the occasional farmhand who helped out."

Chelle arched a brow. "How much money did he keep in there?"

"Anywhere between a hundred bucks and a thousand," Wynter admitted.

"Did a lot of people know about the safe?"

"He didn't keep it a secret." Wynter grimaced. "I warned Grandpa not to have that kind of money lying around the house. It was an unnecessary temptation. But he insisted that his rifle kept away intruders."

"Why are you asking about the safe?" Noah asked.

Chelle paused, as if considering whether or not to answer the question. Then, perhaps realizing she would soon be taken off the case, she shrugged. "It was open and the documents were scattered on the floor."

"No money?" Wynter asked.

"Nope."

The ground seemed to shift beneath Wynter's feet. She'd just assumed that Erika's death had something to do with the horrible things that had been happening since she started asking questions about the past. But if someone had been at the farm to steal money, then maybe it didn't have any connection.

Unless . . .

"You can't suspect that Dr. Tomalin was here to rob my grandpa?" Wynter demanded.

"No, but she might have interrupted the thief," Chelle pointed out.

Wynter wrapped her arms around her waist. She should have thought of that herself. Then again, her brain wasn't functioning at optimum level. There'd been one shock too many. Or maybe a dozen shocks too many. "But it doesn't explain what Erika was doing in the house in the first place."

Beside her, Noah suddenly stiffened, his breath hissing between his clenched teeth.

"Shit. That's it," he muttered.

Wynter turned to study his tightly clenched expression. "That's what?"

"When we first stepped into the kitchen I noticed something silver on the floor next to Erika's body. I thought it was a needle." He glanced toward Chelle. "But it was a silver toothpick, wasn't it?"

The policewoman nodded. "I assumed that belonged to Sander."

"No way." Wynter's tone was adamant. "My grandpa never used a toothpick. Certainly he wouldn't waste money on a silver one."

Chelle's attention was locked on Noah. "Did you recognize it?"

"I joined Jay Wheeler for a drink the other day at the Pig & Whistle," Noah told her. "He had one just like that."

Chelle wrote the information on her pad. "That's Oliver Wheeler's father?"

Noah answered. "Yes."

Chelle's expression was distracted as she tucked away the pad and stylus. No doubt she was processing the new wrinkle in an already strange morning.

"He would know Sander was in the hospital," she said, the words slow, as if she was speaking her thoughts out loud.

Wynter nodded. "And he worked on the farm long enough to know my grandpa kept cash in the safe. He probably even knew that my grandpa kept the key to the safe in the silverware drawer."

Chelle's features tightened. "I think I'll have a word with Jay Wheeler."

"He was staying with Ollie's mother." Wynter had barely finished speaking when a familiar van pulled into the drive.

"Speak of the devil," Noah muttered as Ollie climbed out of the vehicle and crossed to the Jeep.

The man was wearing the usual coveralls with his name stitched on the pocket and a cap on his head. He was gazing toward the house where the EMTs were carrying a sheet-draped gurney down the steps of the porch.

"What's going on? What's happened?"

Chelle stepped toward the man, her hands on her hips. "Can I ask what you're doing here?"

"I came to do the chores," he said in shaken tones, his hands clenched at his side. "Is it Sander?"

"No, he's still in the hospital," Wynter assured him.

Ollie released a slow, trembling breath. "Thank God."

Wynter resisted the urge to reach out and touch her friend. Ollie had been like a son to her grandpa. Actually closer than Sander's own son. It was nice to see someone actually cared about the old man. But now wasn't the time. Chelle was obviously in a hurry to get information from him.

"Can you tell me where your father is?"

Ollie stared at the policewoman, his brow furrowed as if struggling to process the question. "My father?"

"Yes."

"He left town."

"When?"

Ollie shrugged. "Yesterday afternoon."

Chelle didn't pull out her pad, but Wynter assumed she was taking mental notes.

"Do you know where he was going?" Chelle asked.

"No. Our parting wasn't very friendly."

"Why not?"

Ollie flushed, shifting from foot to foot. It was obviously a question he didn't want to answer. "I came home early from work and caught him loading his car with my electronics." The man's flush darkened from embarrassment to anger. "I assume he intended to pawn them. I told him he could leave town or I would call the cops and have him arrested."

Noah and Wynter exchanged a glance. Ollie just confirmed that his father was desperate for money. And willing to do whatever necessary to get his hands on it.

"And that's the last time you spoke with him?" Chelle continued her interrogation.

"Yes." A strange emotion rippled over the man's face. "Wait. Is my dad hurt? Did something happen to him?"

Chelle lifted her hand. "Not that we know of."

"Then why are you asking about him?"

"Someone broke into Sander's house and opened the safe."

"Oh." Ollie glanced toward Wynter, as if she was somehow responsible for the intrusive questions. Then, slowly, he turned back to Chelle. "Why would you think it was my father?"

Chelle offered a meaningless smile. "Just considering all the possibilities. If you hear from your father, let me know." Reaching into the pocket of her jacket, she pulled out a small business card.

Handing Ollie the card, she turned and headed toward the ambulance where they were loading Erika's body.

"I don't understand," Ollie muttered.

Wynter shuddered, feeling a creepy tingle inch down her spine. She felt as if a thunderstorm was gathering, looming just above her head.

"Join the club," she whispered.

Chapter 26

Noah turned on the main road heading back to Larkin. Next to him Wynter sat in dazed silence, her face pale and her eyes shadowed with sadness. His own mourning for Erika would have to wait. As much as he would always appreciate the therapist's ability to pull him out of the quagmire of self-pity that had threatened to drown him, his concern right now was for Wynter.

She was still in danger, and now she was going to have to deal with the sight of Erika's dead body lying on her grandfather's kitchen floor. There was a point where a person couldn't handle any more stress. They either snapped or shut down.

He was betting that Wynter was the type who shut down.

"Do you want to go back to the cabin?" he asked. "You can soak in the tub while I make us lunch."

She glanced over her shoulder at the crates that were loaded into the back of his Jeep. "I need to take the produce to the restaurant."

"I can run them by later," he assured her.

"No." Her lips twisted into a humorless smile. "I want to stay busy."

"Yeah, I get that."

She made a choked sound of distress. "How many are going to die? Tillie. Mona. Drake. Erika." Her voice broke before she forced herself to continue. "My grandpa."

Noah reached out to grab her hand. "Sander is too ornery to die."

She clutched his fingers as if they were a lifeline. "I hope you're right."

"I'm always right."

A whisper of a smile touched her lips before it faded to a frown. "This has to stop, Noah."

He didn't have to ask what she meant. This madness was spreading through Larkin. Like a cancerous growth that was consuming everything and everyone in its path. It was only a matter of time before it claimed them.

"Maybe the DCI officers coming tomorrow will have more luck than Chelle. I'm sure they have more training in murder investigations and better access to crime labs. Things should at least move faster."

"Maybe." There was a silence as he slowed the Jeep and turned onto Cedar Avenue. Then Wynter made a sharp sound of frustration. "I've tried to imagine why Erika would be at the farm. She had to be looking for me."

"That's the most obvious possibility," Noah agreed.

She sent him a startled glance. "Do you have another one?"

Noah took a moment to consider whether or not to answer the question. They'd been chasing shadows and vague clues for days with nothing to show for their efforts beyond more mystery. And death. Was it going to help for him to add to the confusion?

Still, it might at least distract her from her morbid brooding.

"It's fairly far-fetched," he warned.

"Life is far-fetched right now," Wynter muttered, a shiver shaking her slender body.

"True."

She shifted in her seat so she could study him, her distracted grief replaced by an expression of curiosity. Exactly what he'd hoped for.

"Tell me."

"What if it was Jay Wheeler in your grandpa's house with Erika?"

Her brows drew together. "That's not far-fetched. Who else would have a silver toothpick? It's not something that most people in Larkin carry around," she reminded him. "And from everything I've heard about Jay Wheeler, he's a grade-A loser who abuses the generosity of both his friends and family. I'm sure he wouldn't hesitate to add petty theft to his résumé."

He drove past the dry cleaners and the small park where they held the town's annual festivals. Next to it was the farmers' market where Wynter set up her weekly booth.

"What if he's more than just a thief?"

She considered the question. "Are you talking about him killing Erika?"

Again Noah hesitated. Then he shrugged. What was the harm in tossing out a crazy theory that would no doubt turn out to be a bust? If nothing else, it might spur a more logical explanation for the reason the man had been at Sander's farm.

"I'm just thinking out loud, but there was no trouble in Larkin until Jay returned to town," he pointed out.

"He has no connection to me."

"He does to your grandfather." Noah thought back to his brief encounter with the older man. "In fact, when I spoke to him at the bar he didn't bother to hide his bitterness toward his former boss."

"And that's why he decided to rob him?"

"Let's go back to the beginning," Noah suggested.

"The beginning of what?"

"To the night your mom died."

She grunted, as if she'd taken a physical blow. "Seriously?"

Noah sent her an apologetic smile. "I'm grasping at straws," he reminded her, hating the knowledge he was stirring up painful memories. "If you'd rather discuss something else—"

"No," she interrupted in firm tones. "Grasp away."

"Okay. Do we know where Jay Wheeler went after he abandoned his family and left Larkin?"

She considered his question. "No," she finally admitted. "The few times Ollie ever mentioned his father he made it sound like Jay traveled around. I remember he called him a vagabond."

It was what Noah had been hoping to hear. "What if his travels took him through Pike?"

"Why would he go there? It's not exactly a hot spot of activity."

"Random chance. Perhaps he was passing through on his way back to Larkin to try his luck with his ex-wife."

She slowly nodded. "That's possible. If you're coming from the east, you have to take a bridge across the Missis-

sippi River to enter Larkin. The most obvious route goes
through Pike."

"Let's say he stops at the gas station to fill up or grab
some cigarettes." Noah allowed himself to imagine that
night. It was eleven P.M. Not extraordinarily late, but the
middle of Wisconsin wasn't a bustling metropolis. Anyone
traveling would make sure they kept their gas tanks full
and had whatever else they might need for their journey.
"And he sees your mom."

"He would recognize her," Wynter said, joining his
guessing game.

"Yes." Noah visualized Laurel Moore pulling next to
the pumps. She would be familiar with the station and no
doubt in a hurry to get her tank filled so she could be on
her way to Larkin. There'd be no reason to look around.
The last thing she'd expect would be trouble in her small
hometown. "Jay is either inside the store or sitting in his
vehicle. He sees your mom step out of her car to get gas
and he's hit with the memory of his former life."

"A life he walked away from," she reminded him.

"Not in his mind. Jay Wheeler is one of those sort of men
who are always a victim, and he blames Sander for everything going wrong," he told her. Noah encountered people
like Jay all the time. They poached on private land because
they felt entitled. Or they camped in protected wildlands
and destroyed the natural habitat. They thought the laws
didn't apply to them. "In the short time I talked to him, he
complained that he didn't get paid enough, he had to work
like a slave, and his son didn't respect him. And worse, he
resented the fact that your grandfather had inherited a
family farm. He was convinced that Sander looked down
on him."

She grimaced. "I believe that. Grandpa can be a snob."

Noah kept his thoughts of Sander Moore to himself. Instead, he concentrated on what might have happened that night.

"Okay, let's assume that Jay is sitting in his vehicle, maybe high or drunk, and he sees your mom. He might have decided that she would be the perfect means to punish Sander."

"Why not just rob Grandpa?" she asked, not to be argumentative. She was playing the devil's advocate. Exactly what he needed to poke any potential holes in his wacky suppositions.

"Men like Jay Wheeler aren't planners. They're opportunists." His tone was firm. He was confident that any crime by Jay would be done by the seat of his pants. "Your mom is there, seemingly alone. Why not use her to get some of what he was owed from the Moore family?"

She made a choked sound. Something between a laugh and a sob. "Especially since it was probably my grandpa's money in her wallet."

"Exactly."

Wynter took a second to regain control of her emotions. Then, clearing her throat, she continued his wild conjecture. "That doesn't explain why he killed her."

That part was easy for Noah. "She would have known Jay well enough to recognize him even with a stocking hat over his face. His eyes. Or his voice."

"And he panicked and pulled the trigger?"

Noah rolled to a halt at the four-way stop. The more he thought about the theory, the more dubious it seemed. "I warned you that it was far-fetched."

"It's as good an explanation as any other we've come up with," she protested. "And it does offer a reason why nothing happened for years. If killing Mom was a reckless accident, then Jay would do everything possible to avoid attracting attention."

Noah drove through the intersection, his imagination moving beyond Laurel's death to current events. "Now we need to figure out how he would know the sheriff had given you the picture."

"Maybe he wasn't passing through Pike. Maybe he moved there at some point," she suggested. "He could have seen me at the graveyard and followed me to the sheriff's old house."

"Why would he be at the graveyard?" Noah asked, taking over the role of devil's advocate.

She shrugged. "It was the twenty-fifth anniversary of my mom's death."

"I doubt Jay Wheeler is a sentimental kind of guy," he said in dry tones.

"True," she agreed, her expression distracted as she considered alternate theories. "What if Tillie recognized Jay that night and contacted him after we stopped by her house?" she at last offered.

Noah pulled into the empty lot and parked next to Wynter's building. Unhooking his seat belt, he swiveled to face her, thinking back to their meeting with Tillie.

"But why would she call him? Blackmail?" They'd spent less than ten minutes in the company of the former cashier, and she'd tried to angle a way to get money from them. She was obviously desperate and he didn't doubt she would stoop to blackmail if she could get a few bucks.

Wynter unhooked her own seat belt. "Or to warn him."

Noah jerked. Yes. That made sense. The woman had obviously been lying. He'd assumed it was to protect herself. Now he wondered if it was to protect someone else. "She might have worried that Jay would discover we'd been asking about your mother's death and fear he would think she revealed the truth." His lips twisted. "Ironically the call might actually have sealed her death warrant."

Wynter shivered, no doubt considering the possibility she was responsible for the woman's death. "What about the Sheltons?"

"Drake obviously spent a lot of time in bars. Maybe he overheard Jay confessing to someone." Noah tapped his fingers on the steering wheel. "Or he might have done some sort of repairs at Tillie's house and she said something."

"That could be. But why kill Mona?"

"A warning, maybe?"

They glanced at each other, both realizing that the explanations were thin. And worse, they demanded a series of coincidences that seemed unlikely. Still, they didn't have any better theories.

"Perhaps," Wynter murmured, obviously skeptical, but like him, unwilling to give up on the theory. Then she blinked, as if struck by a sudden thought. "If it was Jay, he must have been shooting at my grandpa, not me."

Noah allowed his mind to conjure the image of Jay lurking in the shadows. He would be familiar with the farm. Probably more familiar than anyone other than Sander. It wouldn't have been hard to slip past them to enter the greenhouse and grab the rifle. He would also have been able to disappear without being noticed. The one thing that nagged at Noah was Jay's own words. He'd said that he wouldn't have missed if he'd been aiming at Sander, and Noah believed him. But what if he'd been aiming at Wynter? Noah had tackled her at the same time the bullet had raced past them and hit the older man.

"Not necessarily," he murmured.

"What do you mean?"

"If I was trying to end the investigation into Laurel Moore's death, I would get rid of you, not Sander," he said.

Her eyes widened as she considered his words. "You're right. No one would bother to discover what happened to my mom if it wasn't for me. So why would he return to the farmhouse? Did he think I was staying there?"

Noah shook his head. "He might have decided things were spiraling out of control," he said. "We know he tried to get money from his ex-wife, and next his son, but that fell through. Then he might have remembered that Sander kept money in his safe."

"That explains how the toothpick ended up on Grandpa's kitchen floor." She deliberately paused. "But not how Erika got there."

Noah released his breath in a loud gush. Bits and pieces of his theory might fit the mysterious events, but the rest . . . "Let's hope that Chelle has more luck figuring it out than we have."

Climbing out of the Jeep, Noah opened the back hatch to grab the crates of vegetables. By the time he reached the brick building, Wynter had the door open and the lights switched on. He strolled into the kitchen, making a sound of pleasure. He'd grown up in a restaurant, and there was nothing better than the scent of dried herbs and a faint tang of lemon. It drove away the horrifying images of Erika and the pool of blood that leached into the tiled floor of Sander's house.

At least for the moment.

"I love the smell when I walk in here," he told Wynter. She smiled with obvious pleasure, busily stashing away the crates. "Tomorrow it will smell even better. Flossie will be in at four in the morning to start baking bread."

He leaned against the stainless-steel counter, folding his arms over his chest. "You've created a masterpiece."

"Yes, I have," she agreed without false modesty.

"Do you ever consider expanding the business?"

"Yes, I just got word from the city that they approved my plan to add on additional seating outside."

"No, I meant another restaurant."

"Oh." Wynter shook her head, effortlessly moving around the kitchen as she pulled out pots and pans from an industrial-sized dishwasher, arranging them on the stove as if preparing for an early morning rush. "Not really. Quality control is the reason Wynter Garden has been so successful. I know that every plate being served is made from the freshest ingredients and cooked by someone I trust. Even my waiters have been here from the beginning. They treat the customers like family." She sent him a smile. "Usually because they are family."

Noah felt a surge of pride rush through him. This woman had created a business that the savviest entrepreneur would envy. But she hadn't stepped on others or bullied her way to success. She'd turned her dream into reality. And more than that, she'd filled this place with love.

That was more important than anything she served on a plate.

"I like that." He moved to wrap his arms around her waist, tugging her against his body.

She tilted back her head to meet his gaze. "What?"

"A woman who knows exactly what she wants and is satisfied when she gets it."

She flushed with pleasure. "What about you?"

"Am I satisfied?" He waited for her nod. "I will be."

"When?"

He smiled down at her. "When I have the woman I love agreeing to be my wife."

Her flush deepened. "Noah—"

He didn't know what she intended to say. Even as the words formed on her lips, the sound of shattering glass split the air.

Chapter 27

Wynter darted beneath Noah's arm, avoiding his effort to keep her in the kitchen. Dashing into the dining area of the restaurant, she took in the sight of splintered glass that sparkled like diamonds scattered across the floor. Oddly, her first reaction was relief that it was one of the narrow windows that ran along the side of the building and not the large pane in front that was painted with WYNTER GARDEN in dark gold. The cost of replacing it would be considerably less. Her second reaction was a need to confront whoever was responsible.

With brisk steps she hurried to pull open the door, ignoring Noah's aggravated demand that she wait. If it was the killer, why would they throw a rock through the window and alert her to their presence? It was much more likely they would try to sneak up on them.

No, this was the work of some petty vandal. And she intended to find out exactly who was responsible. Stomping into the empty lot, Wynter expected to see a group of kids who assumed the building was empty. Instead she caught sight of an expensive black SUV parked next to Noah's Jeep and a middle-aged woman in a black pantsuit standing next to it with a rock in her hand.

Wynter halted in shock. Noah, however, stepped next to her, calmly holding his weapon in his hand.

"Put down the rock," he commanded in a voice that demanded obedience.

Linda Baker sniffed, several tendrils of blond hair escaping from her tidy bun to dance around her flushed face.

"Or what? You'll shoot me?" Linda released a hysterical laugh. "Go ahead. My life is over."

"Noah." Wynter grabbed Noah's arm as he took a step forward. She didn't think he intended to shoot the older woman, but he most certainly was going to run her off. Before he did, she wanted to know what had gotten into the normally frigid secretary. "What are you talking about? Why would your life be over?"

"Your father retired this morning."

Wynter frowned. "I know. He told me he was going to."

"And I was politely asked to clear my desk."

That caught Wynter off guard. It hadn't occurred to her that this woman would be fired at the same time. The new dean would need a secretary, wouldn't he? Or she?

Then Wynter realized that her father must have confessed why he was retiring. And the whole sordid affair would have been exposed to the powers that be, destroying Linda's career at the college.

"I'm sorry, but what does that have to do with busting my window?" Wynter demanded.

Linda's blue eyes were no longer icy. In fact, they blazed with a fierce emotion. Hate.

"It's your fault."

Wynter stared at her in confusion. "What is?"

"Everything."

"That covers a lot of territory." Noah repeated his words

from the previous night, and Wynter smiled wryly at his teasing.

Linda, however, wasn't amused. Lifting her arm, she waved the rock she still clutched in her hand. "This isn't funny."

Noah narrowed his eyes. "Throw that and I'll hog-tie you and drag you to the police station."

"If it hadn't been for you, Edgar would never have retired," Linda snarled, but she did drop the rock. Clearly she wasn't so lost in her fury that she didn't sense Noah meant every word he said.

"I wasn't the one having a secret affair with my secretary," Wynter reminded the older woman.

"No, but you were the one who was so childishly jealous you couldn't bear to see your father happy."

"That's not true," Wynter protested. "Of course I want Dad to be happy."

Linda shook her head, her hands clenching at her side. "You don't even realize what you've done, do you, you selfish bitch?"

There was a low growl from Noah as he took another step forward. Obviously his patience with Linda Baker was at an end.

"No." Wynter tightened her grip on his arm. "I want to hear what she has to say." She returned her attention to the older woman. "What have I done?"

"After your mother died you turned her into a saint." There was a shrill edge to Linda's voice. "Edgar should have told you the truth about her, but he wanted you to have your fantasies."

Wynter couldn't argue. She had put her mom on a pedestal and her dad never tried to destroy her illusions. It probably had been better for both of them to acknowledge that Laurel Moore was as human as everyone else. A woman with virtues and faults.

"That doesn't mean he couldn't have remarried," Wynter countered.

"And replace the perfect Laurel Moore?" Linda mocked. "Impossible."

Wynter shook her head. The secretary was fooling herself if she thought that it was only Edgar's dead wife who kept them apart.

"If it was impossible, then why did you continue your affair with him?" Wynter asked.

Linda wrapped her arms around her waist, suddenly looking pathetic. "Because I loved him." She sniffed back tears. "I was willing to take whatever he could offer me."

Without warning, Noah made a sound of disgust. "Including a ride up the career ladder."

Both women glanced at him in surprise.

"What?" Linda asked.

"You latched on to Dr. Edgar Moore because you sensed he was ambitious and was destined to take over the chair of the English department," Noah accused the secretary. "No doubt you assumed he would someday take over as president of the college."

The deepening flush on Linda's face proved that Noah had struck a nerve. She *had* expected Edgar to become president of Grant College with her at his side. Obviously it hadn't mattered whether it was as his administrative assistant or as his wife.

"There's nothing shameful in being ambitious," she protested, her features settling in sulky lines.

"There is if you sleep your way to the top."

Linda gasped at the direct attack. "Don't you dare judge me."

Wynter shook her head, any feelings of pity she'd felt for a woman who'd been kept as a dirty secret for over twenty-five years crushed by the realization that Noah was right.

"You know I almost felt sorry for you," she told Linda.

The older woman stiffened in outrage. "Sorry for me? Why?"

"You had to know that if my dad genuinely cared for you, he would have married you a long time ago," Wynter said. "It wouldn't have mattered what I thought about the relationship. It wouldn't have mattered what anyone thought or said." She glanced toward Noah, a lovely warmth chasing away the distress at having her restaurant vandalized by a hateful, bitter woman. "He would have done everything in his power to be with you."

"He does care about me," Linda insisted, her voice still shrill.

Wynter glanced back. "I'm sure he feels . . . something, but Dad is simply incapable of a healthy relationship. I don't know if it had something to do with how he was raised, or if it was his dysfunctional marriage to my mom, but he's too selfish to share his emotions." Her lips twisted as she thought of her own strained connection with Edgar Moore. "With anyone."

Linda took a step back, as if hoping to avoid the truth of Wynter's words. "That's ridiculous."

Wynter wasn't done. She narrowed her eyes. "But that didn't matter to you because you were using him as much as he was using you, weren't you?"

Linda tilted her chin, her expression defensive. "I loved him."

"You loved being secretary to the dean," Wynter pressed, studying the woman with a new insight into her pretense of devotion. All those years standing guard outside Edgar

Moore's office, offering him whatever he needed, including a warm body in his bed. And in return for her loyalty, Edgar had ensured that she was given the position she craved. "And now that that's gone, you're going to walk away from him, aren't you?"

Linda lifted her hand to point a finger directly at Wynter's face. "I didn't walk away. He threw me out. He said he was ashamed that you found out we were together the night your mother died."

Wynter paused. Could her father truly be ashamed? Or was it a convenient excuse to dump the woman he no longer needed in his life?

Questions that Wynter didn't really want answered.

Instead she deliberately glanced over her shoulder. "And in retaliation you decided to vandalize my property?"

"You hurt me. So I hurt you."

Wynter rolled her eyes. The woman sounded like a petulant child, not the professional assistant who'd treated Wynter with an icy contempt for years.

"Do you want me to call the police?" Noah asked.

Wynter considered the question. She wasn't in the mood for the fuss of calling the cops and filling out paperwork. Not to mention the horde of gawkers that was bound to show up. On the other hand, if she didn't report the crime, then the insurance company wouldn't pay for the repairs.

She was busy deciding which choice would cause the least amount of annoyance when Linda interrupted her thoughts.

"If you call the cops, I'll tell them the truth," she warned.

Wynter froze, already sensing she wasn't going to like what the woman had to say. "What truth?"

"Your father and I were at a hotel the night your mom died."

"I already know that."

With a defiant expression Linda headed toward her SUV. "Did you know that hotel was in Pike?"

Wynter watched Linda squeal out of the lot, her hand pressed over the unsteady beat of her heart. If the older woman had hoped for a dramatic exit, she'd been amazingly successful.

The SUV disappeared down the street as Noah wrapped a comforting arm around her shoulders. She tilted back her head to study his brooding expression.

"Dad was in Pike the night my mom died," she repeated the words, trying to make herself accept them. She couldn't. It didn't make any sense. "Do you think she's lying?"

Perhaps sensing her desperate desire to deny the idea that her dad could have been in the same location her mom had been murdered, he nodded.

"It's possible. She was obviously trying to find a way to hurt you."

Wynter clenched her teeth. Neither of them believed that Linda was lying. Not when it would be easy to discover the truth.

"Why would he be there?" she burst out. "It doesn't make any sense."

"The only way to find out is to ask him."

"Yes." The word came out as a regretful sigh.

"But not now." Noah turned her to face the building. "We have other things to worry about."

Wynter clicked her tongue as she studied the busted window. "Damn. It looks like I won't be opening tomorrow after all."

"Don't worry about it. I'll take you to the hospital so you can check on your grandfather and then run by the lumberyard to pick up some plywood to cover the broken window. Once the glass is swept away, you should be able to serve the hungry masses. I'll also order a replacement window."

Wynter shook her head. "It's my job to take care of those things."

"You have me to help. At some point I'll need you and you'll be there for me." He smiled. "That's how relationships work."

She gazed up at his face that was shockingly handsome in the late-morning sunlight. Her heart filled with a warmth that felt like sunshine. It swelled and spilled through her with a delicious surge of warmth.

Turning, she leaned against Noah, nestling her head against his chest. "I think I like this relationship thing," she murmured.

He kissed the top of her head. "Just *like?*"

She chuckled, a small portion of her tension easing. This man made everything better.

"Perhaps I *love* this relationship thing."

"Me, too."

They stood in the empty lot, leaning together for several minutes. The feel of Noah's solid muscles and the steady beat of his heart beneath her cheek gave her the strength she needed. With this man at her side, she could deal with anything.

"Okay, let's go to the hospital," she at last said.

They drove in silence, but as Noah pulled to a halt in front of the entrance he leaned across to grasp her hand.

"Don't leave this hospital until I come to pick you up," he warned.

"Honestly I'm too tired to go anywhere," Wynter retorted.

Noah lifted her hand to press her fingers against his lips. "Once you've visited your grandfather, we'll go back to the cabin and take a hot bath. I think we could both use it."

She shivered at the memory of hot water swirling around her body as Noah moved over her. . . .

"Sounds like heaven," she whispered.

She leaned forward to brush her mouth over his cheek before climbing out of the Jeep and heading into the hospital.

She wrinkled her nose as Noah's fresh pine scent was replaced by the astringent smell of bleach. She would be with him soon enough, she reminded herself, bypassing the front desk and taking the elevator to the third floor.

Her sneakers squeaked against the waxed floor, drawing unwanted attention as she walked down the hall. She flushed as the nurses at the station lifted their heads to watch her pass, but before she could enter the waiting room, a tall, slender man in a white coat hurried to stop her.

"Ah, Ms. Moore," the doctor called out. "I tried to call you earlier."

Wynter silently cursed. She had to get the stupid phone replaced. Yet another chore that needed her attention. "Has something happened?"

The doctor smiled, halting any panic before it could get started. "Mr. Moore's brain swelling has gone down and we've taken him off the medication keeping him unconscious," he told her in soothing tones that doctors no doubt practiced in med school. "It's possible he might wake this afternoon."

Relief crashed over her like a tidal wave. Until that moment she hadn't realized just how scared she was that the old man wasn't going to survive.

"Can I see him?"

"Of course. He's been moved to a private room across from the ICU. But don't push him," the doctor warned in stern tones. "If—and I stress the *if*—he does wake, he'll be weak and potentially confused. Let him take his time recalling what happened."

Wynter offered an eager nod. "I will."

"I'll stop by later this afternoon, but if you need anything before then just have the nurse page me."

"Thank you."

Hurrying down the hall, she peeked inside the shadowed room. Once she caught sight of her grandpa lying on the narrow bed, she tiptoed inside. He still looked disturbingly frail and there were a dozen different wires and tubes and IVs traveling from his body to the machines that surrounded him like an invading army. But there was color in his cheeks and his breathing was deep and steady.

She moved closer, standing next to the bed.

What was going to happen when he left the hospital? She couldn't imagine he would be strong enough to return to the farm. The sensible thing would be for him to go to one of the senior housing apartments in town. Or even to come and stay with her.

But when had Sander Moore ever been sensible?

A wry smile twisted her lips. Her grandpa wasn't the easiest man—in fact he was downright cantankerous—but she loved him.

From the time she was old enough to walk, she'd trailed

behind him, discovering the beauty of the farm. She'd chased around the chickens and splashed in mud puddles. As she grew older she helped repair fences and put up hay in the summer. There was nothing better than spending her days in the fresh air.

Her grandpa was always happy to have her company, never seeming to get tired of a young girl with her incessant questions. And it was his suggestion that she build a greenhouse where she could start a small garden. By the time she was fifteen she'd been selling her own fruits and veggies to the locals for some extra money.

It was her grandma in Pike who'd given her a love for cooking, but this man had been the driving force in her appreciation for clean, fresh-grown ingredients. She wasn't sure she'd truly realized what he'd taught her during those hot summer days.

Reaching out, she lightly touched his hand that was gnarled by age. The hands of a man who'd worked hard his entire life.

Without warning, the older man released a soft moan, turning his head from side to side. "Edgar . . ."

Wynter leaned forward. "No, it's Wynter."

"Edgar," the man repeated, his voice hoarse. "Stupid idiot. Weak. Like his mother. No spine in his back."

Wynter frowned. Was the older man having a bad dream? "Grandpa, it's Wynter."

Sander's wrinkled face softened, a small smile curving his lips. "Ah, sweet Wynter. My pride and joy. You have the Moore blood running through your veins. Strong. Brave. Too brave sometimes."

"Shh." She patted his hand. "Just relax."

He stilled, almost as if he was slipping back into sleep, and Wynter started to step back.

"Wynter." Without warning, his eyes opened and he tried to lift his hand.

"I'm here." She leaned forward so he could see her without moving.

He released a hissing breath, as if the air was being squeezed from his lungs. "I'm sorry."

"Don't say that," she breathed, guilt blasting through her. She would never, ever forgive herself for putting this man in danger. "I'm the one who's sorry. If it wasn't for me, you would never have been hurt."

"No, no." He clutched at her hand, the tubes and wires rattling. "Never you. You're the only good thing left in my miserable life."

"Please, listen to me," she urged. "You mustn't get upset."

"I want . . ." His words trailed away and his eyes fluttered closed.

"Just rest," she whispered.

Again she started to pull away, only to be halted when her grandpa's eyes snapped open. "I want the truth."

Wynter glanced toward the door. Should she get a nurse? The last thing she wanted was for her grandpa to hurt himself. But she was scared to struggle against his surprisingly tight grip.

Maybe the best thing to do would be to humor him until he dropped back to sleep. "You want the truth about what?"

"Laurel."

Wynter was caught off guard. Why would her mom be the first thing on his mind when he woke? They obviously hadn't been close when she was alive. Then again, maybe he'd realized when he'd been shot that it had something to do with the death of his daughter-in-law.

"I don't know." Wynter couldn't disguise the frustration

in her voice. "And every time I try to find out it only makes everything worse."

Sander turned his head, gazing sightlessly at the ceiling. His throat contracted, as if he was having difficulty swallowing.

"They should never have married," he muttered. "I warned Edgar, but she bewitched him."

Wynter felt a familiar pang of annoyance. Her mom wasn't a saint, but then again, neither was her dad.

"They both made mistakes," she insisted.

"Yes," Sander rasped. "Young. Selfish. Extravagant. Watching them together was like watching a raft hurtling toward the edge of a waterfall. It was obvious they were destined for disaster."

Wynter frowned. This man was plainspoken. Usually too plainspoken. It wasn't like him to use such flamboyant language. Was it his personal disappointment in his son's choice of a bride that caused such an extreme reaction? Or had her parents truly been so out of control?

"Many first marriages fail," she pointed out in reasonable tones. "People divorce and move on."

Sander made a sound of disgust. "Not those two."

"Why not?"

"Obsession."

Wynter shivered. She told herself it was the chill in the air. The hospital was rocking the AC as if it was ninety degrees outside, not barely above forty. But that wasn't it.

Obsession.

The word struck a nerve. Like a theme running through a horror flick.

There was the love/hate marriage between her parents. Drake's fixation on the woman who'd stolen his heart.

Dr. Peyton's lust for her talent. Even Tonya's desperate dream to create her pottery studio.

And a faceless monster lurking in the shadows, just waiting to pounce again.

"It doesn't matter anymore, Grandpa," she tried to re-assure him. "It's in the past."

Sander grunted. "It was. It was buried. Forgotten." He turned his head to glare at her. "Why did you dig it up again? Foolish girl."

She flinched at his harsh tone. She'd heard him use it often enough with other people, but never when he was speaking to her.

"I didn't mean to upset you," she said in soothing tones. "Just rest."

He squirmed beneath the thin blankets that were tightly tucked around him, as if he was feeling trapped. "I can't."

"Are you in pain? Do you need a nurse?"

"No." His eyes locked with her worried gaze. "I need . . ." He paused, his breath rasping loudly in the silence of the room. "Forgiveness."

Chapter 28

Wynter made soft, soothing noises. She didn't know what was causing the older man's agitation. Was it a reaction to coming out of the coma? Had the drugs given him nightmares?

"I forgive you," she assured him.

Sander gazed at her with a pleading expression. "Do you?"

"All that matters is getting you better."

His grip on her hand tightened until tiny shafts of pain darted up her arm. He was as strong as ever. A good thing, she told herself as she struggled not to yank her fingers out of his grinding grip.

"You understand that I had no choice," he implored.

"Of course."

"She was going to ruin us."

Wynter stilled, concern for her grandpa driven from her mind as a strange sensation crawled through her. Goose bumps prickled over her skin that had nothing to do with the chill in the air. "She?"

"Your mother."

She should walk away. Her grandpa was groggy from

the drugs and in no condition to make any sense. But she couldn't move. As if something had frozen her in place.

"How was she going to ruin you?" The question was out of her mouth before she could stop it.

His jaws bulged, his eyes smoldering with hatred. "She turned your father into a joke," he snarled. "Everyone in Larkin knew she was sleeping with anything that moved."

"Grandpa—"

"It wasn't bad enough that he acted like a sissy. Always prancing around with his nose stuck in a book. Now he was a man who didn't have the balls to satisfy his wife." He overrode her efforts to halt his grievances. "Pathetic."

Wynter pressed her lips together. Her grandpa might be injured, and maybe even delusional, but she felt compelled to defend her parents.

"Why are you so hard on him?"

"Because he's the last of the Moores," Sander snapped. "We come from a long line of courageous pioneers. We work with our hands and tend to the land. We don't sit on our ass in some fancy office."

Wynter swallowed a sigh. She'd heard this story a thousand times. Of how her ancestors had braved the long voyage from Ireland to settle in New York. And how they built wagons with their own hands and pawned the family silver to buy two horses to travel west. Sometimes the story included battles with Indians, other times they fought off bandits, but in the end they persevered and settled a homestead that had been in the Moore family ever since.

"It's not the eighteen hundreds," she reminded him in soft tones.

His brows snapped together. "It's a Moore tradition."

"Okay, okay. I get it," she murmured, even though she

didn't. Every family that wasn't indigenous had come from somewhere to settle. It didn't make them special.

As if sensing Wynter's lack of pioneering pride, Sander clicked his tongue. "That wasn't all."

"It wasn't?"

"No. It was the money." The older man's tone was peevish. "The school loans, the mortgage, the endless credit cards. Edgar was at my house every week with his hand out."

It took Wynter a second to realize they'd moved on from Sander's annoyance at his son's lack of manly attributes and her mom's infidelity.

"Why didn't you just say no?"

"Laurel."

Wynter waited as Sander stared at her with a mute plea in his eyes. At last she realized he was waiting for her blessing to continue. She hesitated. A whisper of warning urged her to walk away. She could get a nurse who would give the older man something that would calm him while she went to the waiting room for a cup of coffee. She was in desperate need of caffeine.

But instead, she spoke the fateful words. "What about her?"

"She discovered my one weakness."

Sander Moore was confessing to a weakness? She never thought she'd hear that come out of his mouth. "What weakness?"

"You," he whispered. "I would do anything for you."

An aching emotion tugged at her heart. This man had been the one constant in her life. A rock she could cling to no matter how stormy the seas might get.

"I know that, Grandpa."

"She threatened to take you away."

Wynter jerked. That was the last thing she expected. "Mom?"

"Yes, your mom," he snarled.

Wynter was confused. There was no way Laurel Moore would ever take her away. Not when it would make her a single mother.

"I'm sure you must have misunderstood."

"No, there was no misunderstanding," he growled. "She walked into my home, waving around her stack of bills, and said if I didn't give her money, she would leave Larkin and I would never see you again."

"Oh my God."

"I couldn't bear it." The old man blinked back tears. "I couldn't."

"Please," she whispered. "Don't say anymore."

"I had to stop her." Sander used his grip on her hand to tug her closer, nearly bending her over the steel bed rail. "You understand, don't you? I couldn't let her steal you from me. Not after she'd destroyed everything else."

"Dad would never have let her leave," she assured him, wincing at the press of hard steel against her waist.

"Bah. That moron wouldn't have the spine to stop her."

"Of course he would. You said yourself they were obsessed with one another—"

"I had to do something," he interrupted. "I had to protect you from that evil bitch. No court in the land would convict me for doing that."

Convict him? That was an odd phrase. Especially for the older man.

"What did you do?"

"What I always do. Solved the problem."

The chill in the room seeped into Wynter's skin. Remaining posed over the bed, she took in Sander's defensive expression and tear-filled eyes.

This wasn't a man confessing that he'd paid off Laurel so she wouldn't move away with his granddaughter. He'd already admitted he'd given them money.

A sense of foreboding curled through the pit of her stomach. "How? How did you solve it?"

"I couldn't go myself." Her grandpa glanced away, as if he couldn't bear to look her in the eye. "So I told him I would give him the money he needed."

Wynter shook her head. Was the older man confused? Had he forgotten what they were discussing?

"We were talking about Mom and her threatening to take me away," she reminded him.

"I know what we're talking about," Sander bit out.

"I don't understand. You said you gave him the money he needed," she repeated his words. "Needed for what?"

"Isn't it obvious? I paid him to make sure she never came back from Pike."

Wynter slowly straightened, a strangled laugh wrenched from her throat. Just for a crazy second she'd almost thought her grandpa was confessing that he'd paid someone to kill her mom.

But that couldn't be right. Could it?

"No," she breathed.

Sander muttered a curse. "I couldn't believe the idiot would do it in front of you. What sort of monster would kill a mother in front of her child?"

In front of her child . . .

Wynter stepped away from the bed, staring at Sander in numb disbelief. Eventually she would feel the sharp pain of betrayal. For now, she was too shocked to absorb what he was telling her.

"You paid someone to shoot my mom?" She had to hear the words from his lips.

"I never wanted things to go that far." His tone was pleading. "But she kept pushing and pushing. She demanded more money every week. She even suggested that I sell the farm to pay off her debts." He released a sharp, humorless laugh. "That land is my legacy. It runs in my veins and she . . ." His words trailed away as a wave of weariness appeared to wash over him. "I knew the blackmail would never end, so I did the only thing I could to protect you and your inheritance."

Wynter struggled to swallow. There was a lump stuck in her throat. "Who?" she finally managed to rasp. "Who shot my mother?"

A low, familiar voice whispered from the door behind Wynter.

"I did."

Chapter 29

Noah drove back to Larkin, intending to stop by the lumberyard to pick up a sheet of plywood and order the new window. He wanted to finish the repairs ASAP and head back to the hospital. He didn't worry Wynter was in danger, but he knew she was upset.

Hell, *he* was upset.

Each day he woke up thinking things couldn't get worse, and each day he was proven wrong. More lies were uncovered, secrets revealed, and dead bodies were turning up at an alarming rate. It was enough to make him consider packing a bag and moving Wynter to Miami. The only way she would be truly safe was to put this town and her family far behind her.

He was driving past the police station when he caught sight of Chelle standing in the parking lot. Abruptly he turned the steering wheel to pull in beside her. It was a perfect opportunity to report Linda Baker's vandalism, as well as to reveal the fact that Edgar Moore had potentially been in Pike the night his wife was murdered. He wasn't trying to point the finger at Wynter's father, but the cops needed every scrap of information if they were going to stop the madness that had infected Larkin.

Stepping out of his Jeep, he moved to stand next to Chelle. Before he could speak, she nodded toward the wrecker that was unloading an old pickup with a smashed front end, dripping water.

"I was going to say we have to stop meeting like this, but I'm not in the mood for jokes," she murmured.

Noah arched his brows as a half-dozen men in dark suits moved to stand around the pickup. His reason for pulling into the lot was forgotten as he stared at the strangers.

"Who're the men in black?" he asked.

"The DCI."

"Ah. The cavalry rides into town."

"They arrived an hour ago."

There was a sour edge in her voice. Noah sent her a knowing glance. "You don't like them." It was a statement, not a question.

Chelle grimaced. "Territorial aggression. I don't like handing over the case to a bunch of strangers. The chief, however, insists we're out of our league." She met his gaze with a wry smile. "You were the one who warned me before joining the force that I don't play well with others."

He laid his hand on her shoulder, sensing her frustration. "You're a good cop, Chelle. Don't let anyone tell you any different."

She visibly forced her stiff muscles to relax. "Good or not, I haven't had much success in finding out who is wreaking havoc in my town. Maybe the guys from Des Moines will have more luck."

Noah nodded, keeping his thoughts to himself. His friend would always struggle to accept her role as a junior officer. She wasn't arrogant, but she had a natural confidence that made it hard for her to take orders from anyone. And it didn't help that her chief had made it clear he didn't think women should wear a uniform.

"What's their interest in a wrecked car?" he instead asked.

"Their interest is in the person driving it."

Noah frowned. He didn't recognize the truck. "Who was it?"

"Jay Wheeler."

"You found him?" Noah felt a flare of hope. Had the man wrecked his truck trying to flee town? It would be their first stroke of luck since Wynter had opened that envelope in Pike.

"Yeah. He's at the morgue."

Noah grunted at Chelle's blunt retort. *Well, hell.* Of course he was at the morgue. Only a fool would expect anything else.

"What happened?"

"It looks as if he drove off the bridge and ended up in the river."

"Was he drunk or just trying to leave town in a hurry?"

Chelle glanced toward the truck, her expression hard with frustration. "The coroner is doing the autopsy now, but the men in black seem convinced he was on the run."

Noah turned to regard his friend. He knew that tone. She wasn't happy with the direction the investigation was headed. "You have a different theory?"

Chelle hesitated. Then, with a jerk of her head to follow her, she circled Noah's Jeep to make sure they were out of earshot.

"I did a search of Erika's home before the DCI showed up," she admitted, glancing around.

She didn't seem nervous, but Noah was betting she didn't want anyone to know she'd taken the initiative to continue the investigation. No doubt she'd been told to stand down as soon as the big guns arrived in Larkin.

"Did you find anything?"

"Blood on the floor of the garage."

Noah absorbed the words, suddenly feeling stupid. He'd been so focused on trying to imagine why Erika had gone to the farm, it'd never occurred to him to consider the possibility that someone had forced her out there. Of course, they still didn't know that. There were lots of reasons there could have been blood on the floor.

"Fresh?" he asked.

"Yes."

Noah frowned, trying not to jump to conclusions. "She could have tripped and hurt herself."

Chelle wasn't nearly so hesitant to make the leap. "Or been attacked and driven to the farm."

Noah leaned against the back of the Jeep, folding his arms over his chest. "Is there more?"

Chelle once again glanced over her shoulder. "I shouldn't be talking to you."

"You know you can trust me," Noah reminded her.

There was a long pause, before Chelle revealed what she'd discovered. "I found Erika's phone in the garage."

"And?"

"And her last call was Saturday night."

"Okay."

"To Wynter's number."

"Wynter lost her phone days ago," Noah reminded his companion.

"We know that, but Erika probably didn't."

"True."

"Which means she likely left a message."

Noah nodded, wondering why the therapist was calling Wynter. Had she been checking on Sander? The two women weren't that close anymore, but Erika would certainly know how worried Wynter would be about her grandpa.

It wasn't until he noticed Chelle's patient expression that he realized he was missing the relevant point. "If she left a message, then whoever stole Wynter's phone would have listened to it."

"Exactly."

"It would have been easy enough. She has an old phone and never bothered with putting in a security code." Noah narrowed his gaze. "Do you suspect Erika knew something about the mystery killer?"

"It would be the most obvious reason someone would kidnap her and haul her to a remote farm."

Noah shuffled through his thoughts, trying to arrange and rearrange them in a way that made sense.

Erika was a therapist. It was possible she'd suspected someone in town who would have the temperament to kill. She might have wanted to warn Wynter. Or maybe someone had said something that struck a memory. She'd admitted to being friends with Laurel Moore. Perhaps she'd grabbed her phone and hit Wynter's number, never suspecting that she was signing her own death warrant.

Then what?

The killer had snuck into her garage, waiting for an opportunity to strike. Last night? Maybe this morning.

He—or she—had driven her car to the farm knowing that Sander was in the hospital and that it was empty.

"The basement," he breathed.

"What?"

"We couldn't figure out why the door to the basement was open. Wynter was certain that nothing was down there. But if she'd been kidnapped . . ."

"It's a perfect place to hold a captive." Chelle completed his thought. "Or dispose of a body."

Noah nodded, his jaws clenched as he battled back the thought of Erika alone and petrified in the hands of a monster. There would be time later to grieve. For now, he had to concentrate on what had happened to her. "It makes more sense that she was forced to the farmhouse instead of having her drive there on her own."

"If Erika had found information on the killer, she might have called to warn Wynter without knowing she was putting herself in danger," Chelle murmured, going back over the time line. As if hoping to clarify what had potentially happened. "When Wynter didn't answer, she left a message."

"If she had information, why not call the police?" Noah asked the obvious question.

"She might not have been certain," Chelle retorted. "It's the trickiest part of being a cop. Some people call nine-one-one if they see a cat cross their lawn. Other people are reluctant to get involved. I'm sure a trained professional like Erika would be well aware of the danger of pointing fingers."

Noah nodded in agreement. No one wanted to get someone in trouble if they weren't one hundred percent confident of their guilt. Especially if it was someone she knew. A patient?

"Or she was protecting the someone," he suggested.

They exchanged a long glance, knowing that Erika would have gone to great lengths to shield the identity of a client. Had the news of Drake's death spurred Erika to try and do something to protect Wynter while still trying to maintain her professional ethics?

"Let's say you're right," Chelle murmured. "Erika called Wynter to warn her. Then the killer attacks her in the garage and drives her to the farm."

Noah tried to put himself in the mind of the maniac. Had he panicked when he'd gotten the call? Had he rushed to Erika's house or waited until the next morning? Had he known she would be going into the garage at that time? Maybe he'd somehow contacted the therapist to lure her from the house.

His train of thoughts were interrupted when he was struck by the difficulty of kidnapping the woman and taking her to Sander's farm. There was an easier method to silence her.

"Why not kill her at the house?" he demanded. "Erika lives alone. No one would have found her for hours. Maybe days."

Chelle grimaced. "A good question."

"And what does Jay Wheeler have to do with any of this?" Noah added.

He was willing to consider the idea that the older man had been looting Sander's safe and killed Erika when she interrupted him. But there was no way he could imagine Jay hiding in the woman's garage and then driving her to the farm to shoot her in the head.

A muscle worked in Chelle's jaw, as if she was equally confounded. "Jay Wheeler," she growled.

Noah arched a brow. "What's wrong?"

"When I was little I loved to put together jigsaw puzzles," Chelle muttered.

"That doesn't surprise me," Noah said. Since he'd known Chelle, she'd loved doing crosswords and watching mystery shows. Anything to challenge her mind.

"My younger brother used to think it was funny to slip a piece from another puzzle into the box and watch me struggle to fit it in."

"Frustrating."

Chelle snorted. "You have no idea."

"Do you have a point?" he asked. He wasn't being rude, but he had a long list of things to do before it was time to return to the hospital to pick up Wynter.

"Jay Wheeler," she repeated. "He's a piece that doesn't fit into the puzzle."

Noah nodded. "You're right."

They shared a moment of mutual aggravation. It was beginning to feel as if they would never uncover the truth.

Then Chelle heaved a deep sigh. "Did you need anything?" she asked.

"Wynter had a morning visitor at her restaurant," he told her.

"Is that a bad thing?"

"It was Linda Baker. She stopped by to throw rocks through the window."

Chelle turned to fully face him, her brows drawn together as if she suspected he was playing some sort of stupid game. "Is that a joke?"

"Nope."

Chelle planted her hands on her hips. "Why the hell

would Linda Baker throw rocks at anything, let alone through a restaurant window?"

Noah gave her a quick rundown of Edgar's decision to retire rather than have his affair with his secretary exposed, and Linda's less-than-delighted reaction to being dismissed from her job. Not to mention being dumped by her lover.

Chelle looked weary. Soul-deep weary. "Have Wynter stop by and make a formal report. And make sure you take pictures of the damage. I'm not sure when we can get an officer over there. The chief is already on a rampage about the overtime we've been putting in."

Noah lifted his hand. "I'm not sure she wants to bother. I only wanted you to know because Linda made a threat before she left."

Chelle's weariness evaporated as she stiffened, clearly ready to take action. "A physical threat?"

"No, she said she would go to the cops with information about Wynter's father."

"What was the information?"

"That Edgar had been at a hotel with her the night Wynter's mom was murdered."

Chelle narrowed her eyes. "And?"

"And that hotel was in Pike," he said.

Chelle jerked in shock. "Shit."

"Yep."

Chelle bent her head to stare at the tips of her polished shoes. Noah assumed she was trying to determine what to do with the information. Laurel Moore's death wasn't in her jurisdiction. But it was obvious she had no faith in the temporary sheriff in Pike.

She was still silently debating her choices when the

sound of her name being called echoed across the parking lot.

Chelle rolled her eyes. "I'm being summoned."

Noah reached out to pat her shoulder. "Good luck."

"I'm going to need it," she muttered, stomping toward the men gathered next to the crashed pickup.

Regretting the knowledge he'd only piled on to the pressure his friend was carrying on her shoulders, Noah climbed into his Jeep and headed toward the Wynter Garden.

Tapping his fingers on the steering wheel, he easily weaved through the light traffic. He tried to concentrate on the tasks he needed to take care of before he could return to pick up Wynter, but his thoughts kept straying back to Chelle's words.

A piece that doesn't fit into the puzzle . . .

Was Chelle right? Jay Wheeler had a connection to both Laurel Moore and Sander. And the fact that the trouble had started after he'd returned to Larkin pointed toward him very much being a part of the puzzle.

But he couldn't deny that there was something about the older man that didn't feel right. A nagging sensation that had only intensified now he knew that he was dead.

What if he'd been a convenient fall guy? After all, they didn't have any proof Jay had been to the house except for the toothpick that had been lying next to Erika's body. Anyone could have left it there.

Well, not anyone, he was forced to admit. It would have to be someone who wanted to frame the older man. And someone who would just happen to have a silver toothpick to leave at the crime scene. . . .

Muttering a curse, Noah yanked the steering wheel to the side, doing a sharp U-turn.

He knew exactly who could have access to a silver toothpick.

Wynter had heard about an "out-of-body" experience, but she had no idea what it meant. Not until she slowly turned to watch the familiar man stroll into the room, his hands shoved into his coveralls as he casually approached the bed.

It felt as if she was floating overhead, looking down at Oliver Wheeler. This was the man who'd worked for her grandpa for years. And stood side by side with her for months as they'd remodeled her restaurant. And happily volunteered at the food bank and during the yearly blood drive. Just last year he'd played Santa Claus for the school assembly.

He couldn't possibly be involved in a series of heinous crimes. It was . . . unthinkable.

"Ollie," she muttered, her lips stiff, as if they didn't want to form his name.

Ollie smiled as he halted next to her. "Hello, Wynter."

She shook her head, trying to clear away the weird sense of unreality. "I don't understand."

There was a series of beeps from the machines that surrounded her grandpa as the older man struggled to sit up.

"Careful, Sander." Ollie pulled his hand from his pocket to reveal the gun clutched in his fingers. Wynter jerked in shock, belatedly wishing the small hospital had metal detectors at the doors. Or at least a guard that didn't spend most of his time scrolling through his phone. "We don't want any unfortunate accidents."

"You bastard." Sander flopped back on the pillow, and the beeps settled into a steady rhythm.

Wynter released a shaky breath. As much as she wanted a nurse to rush in and check on her grandpa, she couldn't risk Ollie pulling the trigger.

"Isn't that calling the kettle black, partner?" Ollie drawled, sending the older man a mocking glance. "You're the one who wanted Laurel Moore dead. You came to me with the offer."

The words hammered into Wynter like spikes, injecting a toxic sense of betrayal as she turned her head to meet her grandpa's wary gaze.

"You paid Ollie to shoot my mom?"

Sander opened and shut his mouth, as if trying to decide whether to cry out for help. Then his gaze dropped to the weapon in Ollie's hand and he cleared his throat. "I paid him to make her disappear," he muttered.

The avalanche of emotions landed on top of her with a crushing force. No. She couldn't take them all in. The only way to maintain her sanity was to concentrate on something she could process.

"He was a child." The words tumbled out of her mouth in a rush.

Sander's brows snapped together. He was obviously as shocked as she was by the initial direction of her thoughts. "Bullshit. He was a few days from being eighteen." His tone was indignant. As if he was offended by Wynter's question. "Besides, he'd been taking care of himself and his mom for years."

"He's right," Ollie agreed with a shrug. "I had to grow up young."

She stubbornly shook her head. It wasn't about Ollie's age. It was about her grandfather's willingness to exploit the vulnerability of someone who trusted him.

"You took advantage of a boy who'd been abandoned

by his father and depended on you to fill that role," she grimly insisted.

Sander snorted, his face flushing with a sudden color. "If anything, he took advantage of me. He demanded twenty thousand dollars."

Wynter blinked. She hadn't expected that. Turning her head, she glanced toward the man next to her.

"I needed seed money to start my business," he told her. "I wasn't going to be a farmhand forever, but I had to go to school to get my electrician's license. After that I had to have tools and a van and eventually a shop. That all cost money."

A sound somewhere between a laugh and a sob was wrenched from her lips. "I can't believe this." She pressed a hand over her aching heart, returning her attention to Sander. "It has to be a nightmare."

His face settled in peevish lines. "I told you I had no choice. Laurel was going to take you away from me."

With an effort, Wynter forced herself to accept the appalling truth. The man she'd loved and respected had committed the ultimate sin.

"And that gave you the right to murder her?"

"I was protecting you."

"From my own mother?" Her voice was shrill with a raw pain she made no effort to hide.

Sander plucked at the sheet that was pulled up to his waist. "She'd never been a real mother to you. Never. She dumped you on whoever was willing to take you so she could hop in bed with her latest lover." His nose flared with disgust. "If she left town with you, who knows what the hell might have happened? She'd probably have left you on your own. Or dumped you with strangers."

Wynter wrapped her arms around her waist. She wasn't

going to admit that there might be some truth in his words. Dealing with her grandpa's treachery plus the realization that Ollie was a crazed madman who might shoot her was bad enough to worry about at the moment.

More than enough.

"She might not have been perfect, but she would never have put me in danger," Wynter insisted.

Sander glared at her as if willing her to believe he had no choice. "You didn't know her. Not like I did. She was a selfish witch who didn't care about anyone but herself." He stuck out his chin, like a little boy who dared to be called a liar. "I couldn't risk it."

Wynter frowned. She was willing to admit that her mom had her faults. A lot of faults. But there was a desperate edge in her grandpa's voice that suggested he wasn't just trying to convince her that he'd saved her from a fate worth than death. He was also trying to convince himself.

"No." A flood of bitterness joined the venomous brew of fear and disillusionment that churned in the pit of her stomach. "You weren't concerned about me."

"Of course I was," the older man protested.

She shook her head. "You were worried about the precious Moore name."

"Very good, Wynter," Ollie commended with a mocking smile toward the hospital bed. "She knows you better than you expected her to, eh, Sander?"

The older man kept his gaze locked on Wynter, refusing to acknowledge the man pointing a gun at his heart. "If you mean I was tired of seeing your mother turn my son into the town idiot, I'll agree."

Wynter didn't have to imagine her grandpa's fury as he watched his flamboyant daughter-in-law blaze a path of pandemonium through stodgy Larkin. Laurel obviously hadn't cared about scandal. In fact, she seemed to do everything in her power to be a constant source of gossip.

Even worse, Sander was an old-fashioned sort of man who would expect a woman to obey his commands. The fact that his own daughter-in-law wouldn't be tamed would have driven him crazy.

"You were the one embarrassed, not my dad," she insisted.

"Because the dolt doesn't have the sense that God gave a goose," he snapped. "She was destroying the family reputation."

Wynter blinked back sudden tears. How often had the world been bathed in pain and bloodshed because some stubborn man was afraid his pride had been injured?

"And she had to die for that?"

Sander lifted his hand in a pleading gesture. "I was desperate."

Wynter stepped back. Over the years she'd forgiven her grandpa for his gruff temper, his refusal to admit he might be wrong, and his habit of waving around his rifle when he was losing an argument.

But this . . .

She would never, ever absolve him for his part in her mom's death.

"You were an arrogant bastard who didn't care about anyone but yourself."

Next to her, Ollie chuckled, as if enjoying the tension between Wynter and the older man. "It gets worse, doesn't it, Sander? Tell her about the money."

Sander clenched his teeth. "Shut up."

Gets worse? Her grandpa had arranged the death of her mom. How could it get worse?

"What money?" she demanded.

Sander glanced away, refusing to meet her gaze. "I told you. She always had her hand out. Every week she needed more and more—"

"She wasn't the only one who needed more," Ollie interrupted.

Wynter turned her attention toward the man next to her. It was obvious her grandpa wasn't going to admit the truth. "What are you talking about?"

"The life insurance policy that Sander convinced your dad to buy. He wanted to make sure he had enough to pay off the debts he owed on the farm."

Wynter's heart forgot how to beat. Ollie had been right. This *was* worse. Damaged pride and embarrassment could provoke someone to strike out in anger. A momentary madness that you would later regret. But convincing her dad to purchase a life insurance policy meant that Sander had planned and plotted her mom's death in cold blood.

A calculating monster who took advantage of everyone around him.

As if sensing her surge of revulsion, Sander made a sound of despair. "Debts from your mother, Wynter," he insisted. "She had credit cards, and a new vehicle, and house payments she insisted I pay for. Of course I was in debt."

"It wasn't just her debt," Ollie taunted. "The precious Moore estate that was built by pioneers and the pride of Larkin is a money pit."

"It's a family heirloom. A legacy," the older man snarled. "Something a man like you would never understand."

Ollie laughed. "I'm not one of the idiots at the barbershop who believe your pathetic lies. It's a failing patch of land in the middle of nowhere with a few scrawny cows, a couple chickens, and a house on the point of collapse. Not much of a legacy."

Sander flushed. Obviously he was more offended to have the failure of his precious inheritance exposed than the fact he'd been willing to kill his daughter-in-law to keep his secret.

"We had a few bad years, that's all," he muttered.

Ollie sent Wynter a triumphant glance. "Without the cash from the insurance company he would have lost everything. That's why he wanted me to kill your mom."

"No," Sander rasped, once again trying to struggle to sit up. "Don't listen to him—"

The beeping from the machines sent out a shrill warning as Sander tugged at the wires, and with a speed that caught Wynter off guard, Ollie leaned forward and smashed the butt of his handgun against the side of Sander's head. He connected directly with the bandaged area where the bullet had grazed him nearly a week ago.

With a grunt of pain, Sander fell back on the pillow, his eyes closing and the beeps fading.

"What are you doing?" Wynter gasped, shocked by the unexpected attack.

She shouldn't have been. She now knew that Ollie had killed her mom, and no doubt four other people. He was a violent sociopath. But knowing the truth and accepting it were two different things.

She'd known him for so long. How was it possible she'd never suspected that behind that shy smile was a heart of evil?

"Keeping him quiet." Ollie leaned over the bed rail, studying Sander's pale face with an emotionless expression. "Hopefully he'll die. If not, I'll come back and finish him off." He straightened, turning to face her. "After I'm done with you."

"Done with me?" Her mouth was so dry it was difficult to form the words. "What's that mean?"

He stepped toward her, pressing the tip of the gun against her side. "We're going to leave the hospital. You're going to smile and nod and convince everyone you're delighted to be with me." He dug the weapon into her flesh, hard enough to leave a bruise. "Got it?"

Wynter's thoughts were racing. A part of her knew she should scream for help. It was Survival 101 not to meekly travel to some isolated spot with the crazed madman, right? Why make it easy for Ollie? But another part of her warned her not to do anything stupid. Her grandpa might wake up and alert the cops. Or Noah could come looking for her . . .

The gun dug even deeper and she winced in pain. "Yeah, I got it."

Ollie put his arm around her shoulders, keeping the gun hidden as he pulled her close to his side. Anyone glancing in their direction would assume they were a couple, supporting each other during a time of stress. It was a regular sight for people entering and leaving the ICU. Still, she hoped someone would notice that Ollie was holding her just a little too close, and that his face was flushed with something Wynter assumed was excitement. The smallest distraction would hopefully give her the nerve to try and escape.

But any chance of being noticed was dashed when he turned away from the main hallway and instead pushed through a swinging door. Moments later they were heading down the service elevator.

Chapter 30

Wynter struggled to breathe. The panic she'd been desperately trying to contain was thundering through her by the time they stepped out of the elevator. It was obvious that no one was going to rush to the rescue. She was on her own with a psychopath who had every reason to want her dead.

Reaching a narrow back door, Ollie used a key she assumed he'd been given to do maintenance work. Or maybe he'd stolen it. Either way, they avoided staff and visitors as he led her to his van that was parked only a few feet away.

Wynter released a small whimper as he opened the back of the van and shoved her into the darkness. She'd always been an optimistic person who loved life. But the thought of dying truly crystalized how urgently she wanted to survive.

She wanted to walk into her restaurant and smell the warm bread baking. She wanted to spend the evening working in her greenhouses, gathering the plump vegetables and digging her fingers in the rich earth. She wanted to fall asleep in Noah's arms, his soft breath brushing her face.

She wanted to grow old, complaining that her knees ached and that the world wasn't the same as it used to be. . . .

Ollie forced her past the neatly stacked tools and spare parts. Then, as they reached the mesh barrier that protected the driver from the cargo in the back, he forced her to sit on a narrow ledge.

"Ollie, you don't have to do this," she breathed, her eyes wide as he efficiently grabbed a roll of duct tape and bound her wrists together. Next he ripped off a piece of tape and started to place it over her mouth. Wynter jerked back, banging her head against the side of the van. "No, please, Ollie."

He scowled, but perhaps sensing her panic, balled the piece of tape and tossed it aside.

"Scream, and I'll not only kill you, but I'll hunt down your father and your precious boyfriend and destroy them." He pointed the gun directly over her galloping heart. "Do you believe me?"

"Yes." It wasn't a lie. She not only believed that he would kill everyone she loved, but that he'd take pleasure in doing it.

"Good."

Backing out of the van, he slammed the door and she heard the jangle of keys as he turned the lock. A minute later he was climbing behind the steering wheel and starting the engine to pull out of the parking lot and turn onto a side street.

For a petrifying moment, Wynter thought she might pass out. The fear was pounding through her, making her head spin and her breath come in shallow pants. It was only the knowledge that if she lost consciousness she would never wake again that gave her the courage to battle back the looming darkness.

She was going to survive, she told herself. Somehow, some way.

Grimly clearing her mind, Wynter glanced toward the equipment around her. There had to be something that could help her escape. The built-in shelves were loaded with tools. At the same time, she forced herself to lean toward the metal mesh that separated her from Ollie. She had to keep him distracted. Otherwise he was going to sense she was plotting something.

"Where are you taking me?" she demanded.

Ollie glanced in the rearview mirror, sending her a smile that chilled her to the bone. "You're about to have a horrible accident." He mockingly clicked his tongue. "Such a shame."

"Why, Ollie? I thought we were friends." She didn't have to fake the tremor in her voice.

"We are." There was a genuine surprise in his tone, as if startled by the question. "I've always considered you my little sister. That's why I agreed to get rid of your mom when Sander asked me to take care of his problem."

Wynter grimaced. She would never forgive her grandpa. Not for his part in killing her mom, or for choosing a mere boy to do his dirty work. Ollie was clearly mentally ill, but Sander was the one who'd pushed him over the edge.

"I thought it was for the money," she reminded him.

Her gaze skimmed over the gadgets and plumbing parts on the shelves. There was nothing in easy reach that she could use as a weapon. Presumably the sharper equipment was locked in the steel toolboxes that were stacked at the back.

Ollie turned onto the narrow access road that ran

parallel to the highway. Was he worried he might get stopped by a cop? Or just avoiding traffic? Whatever the reason, Wynter found herself barely able to stay on the narrow ledge as they bounced over the crumbling cement.

"If Sander was going to ask me to take out his trash, then he should have to pay for my services," Ollie told her.

An uncontrollable fury blasted through Wynter. "My mom was not trash."

She could see Ollie frown in the rearview mirror. "Sander made me believe she was. He told me over and over that she was putting you in danger and that it was only a matter of time before something awful happened to you."

Wynter swallowed her hot words. There was no point in arguing. As long as she knew in her heart that her mom had loved her, that was all that mattered. Besides, she had more important matters to concentrate on right now.

About to demand to know if they were headed to Larkin, Wynter was abruptly flying forward as they hit a deep pothole, landing on her knees. At the same time, a plastic bucket directly across from her toppled over. She'd noticed it when they'd first pulled out of the parking lot, but it was filled with brushes and masking tape and other painting supplies. Nothing that could be a weapon. It wasn't until it turned over that she could see the curved handle of a box cutter at the bottom.

It wasn't big enough to cause any damage, but it was perfect for slicing through the tape that bound her wrists together.

Still on her knees, Wynter grabbed the cutter and swiftly hid it between her palms as Ollie slowed and glanced over his shoulder.

"What are you doing?" he snapped.

"Trying to keep my balance." Wynter awkwardly pushed

herself back onto the ledge, sliding her hands between her legs. Ollie continued to slow the van, as if considering the idea of stopping to make sure she hadn't managed to get ahold of a hammer or screwdriver. "Did you follow my mom when she went to Pike that last weekend?" she hastily asked.

She sensed in the hospital that Ollie was aching to reveal how clever he'd been. There hadn't been the least amount of guilt when he'd admitted he'd been the one responsible for killing her mom. He'd gotten away with murder for years, but he hadn't been able to share his secret.

Now he was eager to display his cunning.

Ollie studied her expression, as if searching for whether she was truly interested or just trying to divert him. Then, seemingly satisfied, he returned his attention to the road and pressed down the accelerator.

"Yes, I followed her," he admitted. "And Sander was right."

Wynter breathed a silent sigh of relief, covertly turning the cutter until the blade was pressed against the edge of the tape.

"Right about what?"

"Your mom did dump you on your grandmother's porch and raced off to the cabin to be with the next-door neighbor."

Wynter didn't allow herself to think about her mom and Drake Shelton indulging their passions. It was in the past. Nothing mattered but this moment. And staying alive.

"Did you spy on them?" she asked, sawing the blade up and down with light strokes. The last thing she wanted was to slice open her wrist.

"I kept an eye on the cabin. That's where I intended to . . ." His words trailed away before he shrugged. "You know."

Wynter clenched her teeth. She had to concentrate on the blade. Up and down. Up and down. One fraction of an inch at a time.

"Why didn't you kill her there?" she forced herself to ask.

Ollie snorted. "Her lover barely left her side to take a piss the whole time they were together." He paused, tilting back his head so she could see the sly smile that curved his lips. "Plus I wasn't the only one watching."

Wynter jerked in shock, nearly dropping the cutter. The cabin was too isolated for a stray Peeping Tom to wander by.

"Are you serious?" she blurted out.

"Dead serious." He swerved to avoid something in the road, then his gaze returned to the rearview mirror. "Ask me who was there."

Wynter didn't want to. She'd been forced to see the worst in people she loved and trusted. Her mom. Her dad. Her grandpa. She didn't want to discover the dark motives of anyone else.

Unfortunately, she had to keep Ollie talking. Even if it did cause her more pain.

"Who was there?"

"A woman."

Wynter frowned, pressing the blade harder against the stubborn tape. The stuff was like slicing through steel.

"What woman?"

"I didn't know at the time, but turns out it was the lover's wife. I watched her pull into the next-door driveway while I waited for your mom to pick you up from your grandmother's house."

"Mona Shelton?"

"Yep."

Wynter shivered. She should probably have felt sad for the woman. How awful to spend your nights following a husband who was obsessed with someone else. But catching Ollie's watchful gaze in the mirror, her stomach clenched with premonition.

Mona Shelton wasn't the only one at the cabin.

"Who else?"

He chuckled, pleased with the harsh edge in her voice. "You know."

"I don't."

"Think, Wynter."

She didn't want to play his sick game. She didn't want to give him the satisfaction. But she didn't dare make him angry. There was every possibility he would simply turn around and shoot her in the head.

"My dad," she muttered.

"Good," he said in satisfaction.

"What was he doing there?" Wynter lowered her head, as if trying to hide her expression. It gave her the opportunity to see how far she'd managed to cut.

Over halfway.

"Peeking through the windows like a pervert," Ollie taunted. "I had to climb a tree to keep from being seen when he showed up. Nearly froze my balls off before he finally left."

Wynter refused to think about her dad taking his secretary to a hotel in Pike so he could spy on his wife who was in bed with another man. And Ollie lurking in the dark, like a grim reaper waiting to strike.

It was all so sad and twisted and horrible.

"You followed my mom to my grandma's house after she left the cabin?" She prompted Ollie to continue his story.

They were only a few miles from Larkin. She needed her hands free before they got there.

"Yes. I was afraid I'd missed my opportunity." He shook his head, as if disappointed in his inability to pull the trigger. "I knew Sander would be furious. But then Laurel stopped to get gas. Bingo. I was back in business."

"How could you, Ollie? She was my mother."

"I told you. I was convinced that she was a bad woman," he said, his tone devoid of emotion. He might have been discussing a bug he'd been forced to squash.

Thankfully he didn't notice her distraction as she concentrated on cutting through the last of the tape.

"Sander told me. He said she did perverted things with men and even women. And that she was drinking too much, and that he suspected she was doing drugs. He said you would turn out just like her if we didn't get rid of her." He paused, as if savoring the memory of shooting an unarmed woman who'd never done a thing to hurt him. Then he heaved a loud sigh. "Of course, I am sorry you were there, Wynter. I was sloppy. It was never my intention for you to see your mother die."

She didn't believe his pretense of regret. It might not have been his intention to kill Laurel in front of her small child, but a part of him no doubt reveled in the idea that there'd been someone to watch his moment of glory. She wasn't going to tell him that she'd been asleep until he'd fired his weapon . . .

Wait. A sudden realization slammed into her. There'd

been someone else at the gas station to observe his evil deed.

"Someone witnessed the murder, didn't they?" she abruptly asked.

"Very good, Wynter," he sounded surprised. "You always were a clever girl."

"Did Tillie recognize you?"

"No, I had enough sense not to show my face in Pike."

"Then why kill her?"

There was a long silence. As if Ollie was reluctant to admit his blunder. "Because I was stupid enough to park on the curb next to the station," he finally admitted. "A rookie mistake, but then, I was a rookie."

Wynter frowned in confusion. "That's it? You parked next to the station?"

"After I shot your mom I ran to the truck. The cashier was standing there."

"Standing where?"

"In the window of the station, staring straight at my truck."

Wynter flashed back to the picture the sheriff had saved for her. He'd obviously been troubled by the fact that there'd been no reason to kill her mother, but had he also seen the outline of the cashier in the window? A cashier who'd claimed to be in the storage room during the shooting.

"So what?" she asked. "Lots of people drive trucks in this area."

"Not like mine. I bought a clunker from the junkyard and spent months salvaging parts to get it up and running. The body was a rusted red with a yellow hood and green doors. There was also a huge dent in the bumper." He shook his head in disgust. "I couldn't let her describe it to the cops. They would have tracked me down in a heartbeat."

"Why didn't you kill her that night?" It was an awful question, but it kept him occupied as she finished cutting the tape.

"I assumed that someone had heard the earlier shots and called the cops. I couldn't risk taking time to go into the station and then hope I could get back to the truck and drive away before they showed up. Pike isn't that big of a town." Ollie slowed as they reached the edge of Larkin. "Instead, I pointed the gun straight at her. She screamed and ran toward the back of the station."

Wynter arched a brow. It didn't seem much of a threat. "That's it?"

"No. I drove several blocks and then parked so I could return to the gas station. I hid in the shadows of an alley just across the street. When the sheriff brought the cashier out of the station to question her, I stepped into the light long enough to let her see that I was watching her." He abruptly laughed, a weird sense of elation in his voice. "She fainted. I knew then that she'd keep her lips shut."

Wynter ground her teeth. Tillie Lyddon had obviously been traumatized by that night. Just another victim who'd paid the price for an old man's bloated pride.

"And that was that?" Her tone was deliberately tart. "You went back to Larkin and got your money to start your business."

"As you said, 'That was that,'" Ollie agreed, turning onto a side street that would take them through the residential section of town.

Where the hell was he going? She'd somehow assumed they'd head to her grandpa's farm. It was where all the other horrible things had been happening. But if he had a destination in town, that meant she had only minutes to get ready to make her escape.

Forcing herself to take slow, deep breaths, she pressed the blade until she reached the far edge of the tape. She didn't want to cut all the way through and risk having the binding fall away.

At the same time, she struggled to keep the conversation going. "So what changed? If you'd gotten what you wanted, then why risk killing Tillie and the others?"

"You stayed the night in Pike."

Wynter blinked, waiting for more. "What does that have to do with anything?"

"I was there."

"In Pike?"

"At the cemetery."

"Why?"

"It was a monumental moment in my life, Wynter," he chided, as offended by her question. "Like you, I felt compelled to mark the yearly anniversary with a visit to Laurel's grave."

Wynter stared at Ollie's profile through the steel mesh, struggling to accept what he was telling her.

"You've been following me to the graveyard every year?"

"I wanted to pay my respects."

A shudder raced through Wynter. While she'd been standing over her mom's grave, mourning the woman who'd been brutally taken away from her, the bastard who'd shot her was lurking in the shadows. That was just . . . sick.

"God," she muttered.

She could see Ollie's jaw tighten, as if he was resisting the urge to insist that he was there to somehow honor her dead mother. Instead, he jerked the steering wheel to turn onto Cedar Avenue.

"I saw you talking with someone at the sheriff's grave and then you went to that house a few blocks away. It seemed odd, especially when you checked into the motel," he admitted. "I knew something had happened, but it wasn't until I saw you talking to Tillie that I realized you were digging into the past." He slowed to a rolling stop at the flashing red light. "Why?"

"Sheriff Jansen had a photo of my mom. She'd already given you her purse so he wondered why you would shoot her," Wynter told him. There was no point in lying. "It obviously stayed on his mind over the years."

"Ah." Ollie clicked his tongue in regret. "I was such an amateur."

"A lethal amateur," Wynter reminded him in harsh tones. "How many people did you end up killing?"

His expression remained undisturbed. He wasn't remotely offended to have his murderous spree thrown in his face. In fact, he seemed so proud of shooting her mom.

"I didn't want to hurt anyone," he protested. "That's why I went to your apartment. To leave the note."

"That was you?"

"Who else?"

"Did you really think a note was going to stop me finding out what happened to my mom?"

"It should have. None of this would be necessary if you'd just let the past stay in the past."

He pressed on the gas, childishly swerving the van to slam her against the steel mesh barrier. Wynter smacked her head, but she wasn't worried about the sharp pain. It was the fact that the unexpected jerk had dislodged the cutter from her hand to send it skidding toward the back of the van.

For a crazed second she considered diving after it. It wasn't much of a weapon, but it was better than nothing. Then sanity returned. She couldn't risk Ollie discovering that she'd managed to cut through the tape.

She ignored his soft laugh as she struggled to straighten. "I suppose you used the key I gave you to make the repairs in the kitchen." Wynter frowned, abruptly remembering that Ollie was in her parking lot when she'd pulled in. She'd been so stupidly blind. "Christ, I should have suspected you were lying about the mystery intruder."

"Oh no. I wasn't lying about the intruder. At least, not entirely," he protested. "While I was inside your apartment there was a knock on the door. When I glanced out the window I could see someone heading back to their car that was parked behind the restaurant."

"Who was it?"

"Mona Shelton."

Wynter made a sound of shock. "Mona? What was she doing there?"

He shrugged. "At first I didn't recognize her. Then I saw the decal in the back of her window that said Shelton Construction and I realized it had to be the lover's wife." Ollie lifted his hand as he waved to someone on the street. As if it was just another day, driving through the streets of Larkin, and he wasn't holding a woman he'd known his entire life captive in the back of his van. "I intended to follow her and demand to know what she was doing there, but you showed up."

Wynter considered what had happened after she'd discovered Ollie in the lot. Noah had shown up, and then the cops. She'd been too freaked out by the break-in to stay, so she'd moved to the farm.

The next morning she'd gone to her greenhouses. Yes, that was right. And Noah had been there. A few minutes later her grandpa had returned home. . . .

She sucked in a sharp breath. "So when you realized the note wasn't going to stop me, you decided to shoot me?"

"Shoot you?" He snorted. "You've seen me fire a rifle, Wynter. You can't imagine I would miss if I was aiming at you?"

That was true. He'd always won the skeet shooting contest at the fair. "Grandpa?"

"Ding, ding," Ollie taunted. "Sander came to see me that morning. He said he was going to tell you everything. I couldn't allow that. Just because he had a crisis of conscience didn't mean I was going down with him."

Wynter didn't know what to feel. She would never forget her horror at the sight of her grandpa lying on the ground with blood coating the side of his head. But now that she knew the truth, she was no longer plagued with guilt that she was somehow responsible. Sander Moore had been shot because he'd hired a lunatic to kill her mom.

"Were you trying to frighten him into silence or did you want him dead?" she asked, her voice oddly matter-of-fact.

"Dead." Ollie sent her a glare through the rearview mirror. "But your boyfriend distracted me when he knocked you to the ground."

Wynter didn't want to think about what would have happened if Noah hadn't been there. Her emotions were complicated when it came to her grandpa, but she didn't want him dead.

It was easier to focus on Ollie and his ready willingness to play the role of Judas.

"He was like a father to you," she accused.

Ollie snorted. "Being like a father isn't a compliment to me."

"Fine, fathers can be challenging," Wynter conceded in dry tones. "But my grandpa was at least willing to hire you when your dad walked away."

"And you think I should be appreciative?" He watched her in the mirror, waiting for her to give a hesitant nod. "Let me tell you about my relationship with Sander." His voice was suddenly harsh. "He worked me like a dog and paid me off the books so he didn't have to worry about child labor laws. I had to show up no matter what the weather, or if I was sick, or if I wanted to take a day off to join my friends."

"Why did you stay?"

"I had no choice. My mother didn't make enough money to pay for rent and groceries." His shoulders lifted in a careless shrug. "I worked or I starved."

Wynter didn't feel sorry for Ollie. He was evil through and through. But she suspected he hadn't become this way on his own. There'd been a lot of hands sculpting him into the soulless monster he'd become.

"You didn't feel any guilt when you pulled the trigger?"

Ollie slowed at another intersection and Wynter glanced out the front windshield. They were reaching the center of town. The perfect place to try and attract the attention of the pedestrians who were strolling along the sidewalks. Or even one of the vehicles that flowed through the traffic next to the van.

Only the knowledge that she was trapped kept her from screaming. As long as she was locked in, it would be too dangerous to try to call for help.

"The only thing I felt was annoyance that I'd missed putting a bullet between his eyes," Ollie drawled. "Unfortunately there was nothing I could do once he was taken to the ICU. There was always someone watching him. All I could do was pray that he would die, while I tidied up the other loose ends."

The stark lack of regret in his voice assured Wynter there was no hoping that she could convince Ollie to release her. He might claim to think of her as a sister, but he was a true sociopath. He didn't have the ability to care about anyone but himself.

The only thing she could do for now was keep him talking and hope someone was searching for her.

"What loose ends?"

"Mona, for one."

Wynter was reminded that the woman had traveled to Larkin, presumably to see her. And that mystery visit had led to her death.

"You used my phone to lure her into your trap," she accused.

"Yes, I found it when I went to the farm to do the chores," he admitted without hesitation. "I didn't really know what I was going to do with it until it occurred to me that it would be a perfect way to get rid of the woman."

"How did you get her number?"

"Her husband was kind enough to have two numbers listed on his construction website. A quick computer search revealed he was a one-man business like me, so who else would the second number belong to?"

That answered one question, but not the actual reason he'd murdered the poor woman.

"Why?" Wynter made no effort to hide her revulsion.

"You had no idea what she might have wanted. *I* have no idea what she wanted."

"Why would she travel to Larkin if she didn't have something important to tell you?" Ollie retorted in defensive tones. "It was possible she'd seen me the night your mom died." He said it as if he had no part in her death. "I have no idea how long she'd been lurking in the shadows outside the cabin that night. Or if she'd seen me trail your mom out there. And even if she didn't know anything about my connection to the murder, she'd seen my van in the parking lot when she arrived at your restaurant," he reminded her. "And for all I knew she might have caught sight of me when I looked out the window. I couldn't allow her to tell you that I was the one who'd left the note."

Wynter flattened her lips. He was making excuses. He'd obviously wanted to kill Mona and had found a reason to fulfill that desire.

"And what about Drake?" she demanded.

His fingers tightened on the steering wheel. Could he hear the edge of disdain in her voice?

"It was possible she'd confessed she'd been spying on the cabin that night." She could see him grimace, as if realizing his words sounded lame. "More importantly, I'd hoped to make it look like he'd been the one to kill his wife and then committed suicide."

"How did you get him to Larkin?"

"I used your phone."

Wynter hissed in shock. "You called him?"

"No, I sent him a text."

Drake hadn't struck her as a particularly naïve man. Just the opposite. Why on earth would he answer a random text from a stranger?

"What did it say?"

"That you wanted him to have the love letters he'd sent to your mother."

"How did—" She bit off her words. There was only one way Ollie would know how to manipulate Drake Shelton. "You were spying on us when we went to talk to him."

"I had to know how much you'd managed to figure out."

Wynter shook her head in disgust. "Not nearly enough," she muttered.

"Too much," Ollie argued. "If you'd left it alone, none of this would have happened."

"Don't blame me." Wynter would be damned if she took any responsibility for Ollie's descent into madness. "I think you enjoyed hurting them."

"No." He slowed the van, as if lost in the pleasure of his memories. "I enjoyed the chaos. The lights. The sirens. The screams. They made me feel."

"Feel what?"

"*Feel,*" he repeated. "Until I was standing in that alley watching the police and ambulances and fire trucks surround the gas station, I'd never experienced excitement. There were people shouting and you were screaming." He released a shuddering sigh. "My heart was beating so hard I thought it might leap out of my chest. It was amazing."

Amazing? Her lips parted to inform him that there was nothing amazing about murder, when Ollie abruptly turned the steering wheel and cut across traffic to pull into an empty lot.

Wynter bounced against the side of the van, once again smacking her head. But that wasn't what ripped the gasp from her lips.

No, it was the realization of where they were.

Wynter Garden.

Chapter 31

Noah parked behind the white brick building that had once been an auto shop. He glanced around. No sign of Oliver's van. Perfect.

Climbing out of the Jeep, he moved to peer through the small window above the dumpster. He could see the empty bays that were now lined with floor-to-ceiling shelves packed with spare parts. There were wires, switches, PVC pipe, and a hundred other doohickeys needed by a handyman. The center of the bays were used to store the large table saw and the bulkier equipment that wouldn't fit in a tool cabinet.

The lights were off, as if Oliver didn't intend to return for a while.

Noah moved to the back door and turned the knob. No surprise that it wouldn't budge. It was a small town, but someone would walk off with the tools if they were left lying around.

The door, however, was as old as the building, and with one firm shove with his shoulder, Noah managed to bust the flimsy lock. If Oliver wanted to press charges against

him for trespassing, Noah didn't give a shit. He'd even pay
for a new door if his suspicions were wrong.

Stepping into the narrow hall, Noah passed the small
bathroom and the opening to the bays. His only interest
was in the office that was at the front of the building.

The door was closed, but thankfully it wasn't locked.
Pushing it open, he stepped into the narrow space that had
once been the reception area.

The space was remarkably tidy, with a line of filing
cabinets along one wall and a wooden desk near the large
front window. Pausing to make sure that no one was walking past the building, Noah crossed the plush carpeting to
shuffle through the files piled on the desk.

He found bills, and order forms, and bank statements,
but nothing that revealed Oliver was involved in the murders. With a frown, Noah turned to leave only to halt when
he caught sight of the door nearly hidden behind one of
the file cabinets. A private bathroom? A storage closet?

Noah hurriedly moved to pull open the door. It wouldn't
hurt to check it out while he was there.

What he found was a sharp flight of stairs that led to
the second floor.

Of course. Like Wynter, Oliver had created an apartment above his place of business.

Noah refused to consider the right or wrong of intruding into the man's private space. Nothing mattered but
protecting Wynter.

Nothing.

Jogging up the steps, Noah discovered himself in an
open loft, with a living room that flowed directly into the
small kitchen. He could see a door that led to the bathroom and on the other side an opening that revealed a
large bedroom.

Noah did a quick search of the living room and kitchen before heading into the bedroom. That seemed the logical place to hide any evidence. Stepping into the shadowed room, Noah ignored the narrow bed and the bookshelf. Instead he concentrated on the dresser, pulling open the top drawer to find neatly folded boxers and socks arranged by color. Who did that?

With a shake of his head, he pulled open a second drawer to find white T-shirts and—

A cell phone.

Noah's breath was squeezed from his lungs as he snatched the phone out of the drawer and turned it toward the light that spilled from the living room. He didn't need to turn it on to know it belonged to Wynter. He'd seen it hundreds of times over the years since she refused to upgrade to a newer model.

"Gotcha."

Pulling his own phone from his pocket he raced out of the apartment. He pressed Chelle's number, muttering a curse when it went straight to voice mail.

"Chelle, I know who the killer is," he said, taking the steps two at a time. "Don't ask how, but I found Wynter's phone in Oliver Wheeler's bedroom. I'm going to pick Wynter up from the hospital. I'll bring the phone to the station when I get back to Larkin."

Wynter watched with a sick sense of anticipation as the back doors of the van were opened. Why had Ollie brought her here? Whatever his purpose, it couldn't be good.

Then again, she felt a surge of courage at the familiar surroundings. This was the one place she might actually have a chance to escape. Right?

As if to squash any hope, Ollie pointed his gun at the center of her chest.

"Be very, very careful, Wynter," he warned. "We're going to walk across the parking lot and enter your restaurant as if we're two old friends enjoying the day. Any indication you're going to try and run away or attract the attention of anyone, I'll shoot you through the kidney. A very messy way to die."

Wynter nodded, careful to hold her hands together as if the tape was still binding them. Ollie studied her before giving a small gesture with the gun. Carefully, Wynter rose to her feet, bending low to inch her way forward.

She flinched as Ollie reached out to grasp her by the upper arm, yanking her out of the van. Her feet hit hard pavement and she stumbled forward. Only Ollie's ruthless grip kept her upright.

Once she had her balance, Ollie wrapped an arm around her shoulders and pressed the gun against her side. Urging her forward, they crossed the lot that was bathed in bright sunlight. Wynter tilted back her head, gazing at the bright blue sky. It was a beautiful day. It seemed oddly ironic. She'd waited forever for spring. Now it might foreshadow her death.

No, no, no. Wynter shoved aside the dark wave of doom, keeping her gaze locked on the building in front of them. She wasn't going to give up. Especially when she caught sight of the window out of the corner of her eye. Noah was no doubt at the hardware store. Or even on his way back to the restaurant. All she had to do was stay alive until then.

With her courage restored, Wynter asked the question that had been nagging at her. "What about Erika?"

Ollie was scanning the nearby street, obviously worried they might be noticed. "Who?"

"Dr. Tomalin."

"Oh. The shrink."

His dismissive tone ground against Wynter's raw nerves. He sounded as if she was just trash that had stuck to the sole of his shoe. Something to be scraped off and discarded.

"Why did you kill her?"

Her voice was sharper than she intended, and Ollie's fingers dug into her flesh with punishing force.

"She left a message on your phone. She said she had information about the night your mother was killed."

Wynter glanced at him in surprise. Erika wasn't connected to her family. Or the past. How could she know what happened the night her mom died? "What information?"

"It didn't matter. She was just another loose end."

Wynter didn't dwell on her former therapist's reason for calling. It was more than likely a mystery that would never be solved. Instead, she focused on the horrifying scene she'd discovered in her grandpa's kitchen. It was going to give her nightmares for years to come.

"How did you get her to the farm?"

"After I heard the message I knew I had to take care of her before she could reveal whatever she'd discovered. I waited in her garage and knocked her over the head. Then I drove her out there."

Well, that cleared up the confusion of why Erika would go to the remote farmhouse. She didn't.

"You put her in the basement?"

"Yes." They reached the side door and Wynter frowned as he reached into his pocket to pull out a key. This was a new door; how had he gotten a copy? Then she remembered Tonya saying that the original had been left in the mailbox after Jeremy had finished with the installation. Had Ollie found it and made a copy before Tonya could bring it to Wynter at the hospital? Or more likely, Jeremy had left more than one key and Ollie had simply stolen it. He unlocked the door and shoved her inside. "She was supposed to stay there until I figured out how to get rid of her. There'd been too many bodies for me to risk another one showing up. There's only so much luck before things go in the crapper."

"What happened?"

"When I got back to the farm I discovered the bitch was awake and trying to get out of the basement. I hadn't expected that. I'll admit that I panicked."

He slammed the door shut behind them, as if annoyed by the memory of Erika's refusal to remain unconscious. Or maybe it was his hasty killing.

Wynter tried to look sympathetic, as if absorbed in his story. Her attention, however, had shifted to the kitchen she'd personally designed. There were dozens of obvious weapons in here. Knives, small blowtorches, skewers. But even as she judged the distance to the counter where she kept the meat mallets, Ollie was jerking her closer to his body.

Time for another diversion.

"So your father was never at the farmhouse?"

"No." He forced her across the tiled floor. "But I didn't lie when I told you I'd caught the bastard trying to take off with my stuff. Miserable loser." He shook his head, releasing his hold on her arm to grab a heavy bottle of oil she kept next to the deep fryer. "I told him that if I saw him in town again, I'd put a bullet between his eyes. He must have believed me because he took off. I should have known he'd find an easier mark. He's nothing if not predictable."

She frowned in confusion. What was he doing with the oil?

"Then how did his toothpick get there?"

Ollie smiled with smug satisfaction. "Once I pulled the trigger, I realized it wasn't a total loss. In fact, I decided I could turn it to my advantage. What better opportunity to point the finger of blame at someone else?" He shrugged. "My dad had left one of his toothpicks in my van when I drove him to the bar. It was a simple matter of dropping it next to the body and opening the safe. Problem solved."

Wynter stared at him in disbelief. "You framed your own father for murder?"

"Why not? He's a loser. He begs, lies, cheats, and steals." Ollie shrugged. "If one of us had to go to jail, better him than me."

"I thought *my* family was screwed up," Wynter muttered.

"I knew from the time I was in second grade I would never be like my dad." Ollie tilted his chin, his expression hard. "It didn't matter what I had to do. I was going to succeed."

"Even if your climb to the top included killing people?"

He smiled, as if proud of his homicidal success. "Business is business," he informed her.

"What happened to your father?"

The smile faded, his eyes flat. He looked like a snake. "He's gone."

"Gone where?"

"To hell. Where he belongs."

Wynter shivered. She and Noah had considered several possibilities about Jay Wheeler. That he was the killer. That he'd been framed. That he'd been in the wrong place at the wrong time.

They'd never considered the possibility that he was dead.

"Ollie—"

She bit off her words as Ollie opened the bottle of oil and began splashing it over the tiles and then the heavy wooden island in the center of the room.

"I love this place. I really do," he murmured, moving to pour oil on the stacks of neatly folded tablecloths and napkins. He turned back to offer a regretful smile. "And I love you, Wynter. It's such a pity that it all has to be destroyed."

"Destroyed?" Wynter frantically shook her head as Ollie pulled a lighter from his pocket. "Please, don't do this."

"You didn't give me any choice." He glared at her, as if he genuinely thought it was her fault. "Things didn't have to change, but you couldn't stop poking your nose into the past. Now you're about to die in a terrible accident."

Holding her horrified gaze, Ollie flicked the lighter and held it toward the tablecloths. There was a spark, and then a flicker before blue flames swept over the pile. Wynter was frozen in place, watching in disbelief as the smoke filled the kitchen, stinging her eyes and clogging her throat.

The cooking oil was spreading the fire at an alarming rate. Wynter Garden was going to burn to the ground . . .

Move, Wynter, move, a voice urgently screamed in the back of her mind.

The restaurant could be repaired. She couldn't.

Stiffening her spine, she watched Ollie spreading the oil in a line toward the opening that led into the dining room. She coughed, waiting for Ollie to step out of the kitchen before she rushed forward, slamming the swinging doors behind him. Then, grabbing a wooden spoon, she slid it between the matching handles.

It wouldn't take much of a shove to break the spoon and open the doors, but it gave her a few seconds to try and make her escape.

Ignoring his shouts of annoyance and the blinding smoke, Wynter dashed toward the door to her apartment. There was no way she could make it out of the kitchen and across the parking lot before he could see her out the window. He would just shoot her in the back. And she couldn't lock herself in her apartment. Not when he had the key.

Survival depended on cunning.

Opening the door she ripped the clinging tape off her wrists and dropped it on the top step. There was the sound of wood cracking as Ollie kicked at the doors, and with a small whimper of fear, Wynter ran back across the kitchen. The heat was unexpectedly intense, but she refused to glance toward the flames that had spread over the oil on the tiled floor to reach the wooden island.

She was cunning. Cunning as a . . . fox? Wolf?

She swallowed a hysterical urge to laugh as she grabbed the handle of the walk-in freezer and pulled it open just a crack. Would he see it? She didn't dare leave it open any farther.

There was another snap and the spoon shattered. With a muffled curse, Wynter leaped toward the narrow janitorial closet beside the freezer and jammed herself next to the mops and brooms.

Barely daring to breathe, she heard Ollie enter the kitchen. "Wynter," he called out. "Why do you have to make this so difficult?"

She bit her bottom lip. The heat from the flames was becoming oppressive and tears were running down her cheeks from the combination of smoke and terror. And worse, the urge to cough was nearly overwhelming.

"Ah."

His footsteps headed toward the apartment door. Wynter braced herself, prepared to make a mad dash into the dining room if he headed upstairs. She could exit out the front door and scream for help.

Not surprisingly, he didn't fall for her ruse. She had, after all, made it fairly obvious.

"Tut, tut, Wynter," he called out in mocking tones. "Do you think I'm stupid?" The footsteps headed back to the center of the kitchen. "Come out, come out, wherever you are."

Wynter shuddered, biting her lip so hard she could taste blood. Every instinct told her to run. Like a mouse cornered by a cat. What was it called? Flight or fight? She was definitely in flight mode. Poignantly, it was Erika's training that kept her from doing something stupid. She'd given Wynter breathing techniques to overcome her occasional bouts of panic.

Breathe in, hold it, and breathe out. Breathe in, hold it, and breathe out.

She repeated the mantra in her head as the footsteps came closer. She pressed deeper into the mops, sending up a quick prayer. It was now or never.

"Clever, Wynter," Ollie murmured, so close that the hair rose on Wynter's nape. "But not clever enough."

There was a soft squeak as Ollie pulled open the door to the freezer and peered inside. He was smart enough not to step in all the way, but it didn't matter.

Fueled by a combination of fear, fury, and adrenaline, Wynter leaped out of the closet and threw her entire weight against the door. It slammed shut with a satisfying thud, locking Ollie inside.

"Bitch!" he shouted in anger. "I was going to make this as painless as possible for you. Now I intend to make you suffer."

There was the rattle as he jiggled the handle. Then there was a shocked pause before Ollie realized what she'd done.

"No!" His scream was muffled by the thick door. "Let me out."

"You should have fixed the handle, you sick bastard."

Kicking the freezer to release a portion of her avalanche of emotions, she wiped the tears from her eyes. She'd done it. She'd survived. And now Ollie was trapped in the freezer until the cops could come and haul him to jail.

She hoped they locked the cell and never, ever let him out.

Wynter turned, intending to flee from the kitchen. She wanted to be far away from this place. But she never got to take a step.

Directly in front of her was a wall of flames.

Her heart sank in dismay. She was as trapped as Ollie.

Noah squealed away from Oliver's shop, blowing through the stop signs and pretending the speed limit didn't exist as he raced through the narrow streets. He wasn't sure what was compelling his sense of urgency to get to the hospital. He was reasonably certain he'd uncovered the bad guy. Why else would Oliver have Wynter's phone hidden in his dresser? And he was equally confident Chelle would be searching Larkin for the handyman. There was no need for him to be driving like a maniac.

But telling himself that everything was okay and making himself believe it were two different things. In fact, it only made it worse. How many times had he been wrong in the past week? Although, in his defense, no one truly thought the quiet, hardworking man with the shy smile was a stone-cold killer, he wryly conceded.

Still, he wasn't going to ignore the heavy sense of dread that pulsed through him. He needed to be with Wynter. To have her wrapped in his arms so he knew beyond a shadow of a doubt that she was safe.

Tossing caution to the wind, Noah took the corner fast enough to nearly tip over his Jeep. There was a loud honk followed by a shout from the car he'd just cut off, but he didn't care. He kept his gaze forward as he raced up Cedar Avenue. There were other streets that would have less traffic, but this was the fastest route to the nearby highway.

He was a couple of blocks from Wynter Garden when he smelled smoke. At first it barely registered. There were always people who were burning leaves or trash despite the fact it was illegal in the city limits. But the closer he came to the restaurant, the thicker the smoke.

Reluctantly slowing, Noah allowed his gaze to run over the three-story brick building. At first he couldn't see anything out of the ordinary. Then he caught sight of the dark plume of smoke escaping from the broken window. A second later, he noticed the van parked next to the restaurant.

Shit. That was Oliver Wheeler's van.

Whipping the Jeep to the side, Noah jolted over the curb and into the empty lot. If he didn't know the truth about Oliver he might have thought the man was there to try and put out the fire. Now, he was certain that the lunatic was responsible for the cloud of smoke.

And worse, he had a mindless fear that Wynter might be inside.

Barely remembering to put the vehicle in park, Noah was leaping out and racing toward the side of the building. A small crowd was beginning to form and in the distance Noah could hear the sound of sirens. His pace never slowed as he smashed his shoulder into the newly installed door.

It flew open and a cloud of smoke billowed around him. There was a cry from one of the onlookers. He thought they were urging him to wait for the fire trucks. Probably a smart idea, but there was no way in hell he was waiting.

The sight of Oliver's van set off all sorts of warning bells. He was going to make damned certain that Wynter wasn't in danger.

Entering the kitchen, he was instantly blasted by a wall of heat. He lifted his arm as if it might offer protection as he studied the flames swirling in the middle of the room. They appeared to be concentrated on the wooden island while small trails of fire danced over the tiled floor. Those, however, were starting to flicker and die. As if they were running out of fuel.

Noah coughed, his eyes watering as he tried to peer through the smoke. At the same time, he reached out to search for the fire extinguisher that he'd seen hanging next to the door.

He'd just managed to wrap his fingers around the steel cylinder when he heard a voice from the other side of the flames.

"Is someone there? Help!"

Wynter.

His heart lodged in his throat, a surge of panic making

his fingers clumsy as he pulled the pin from the handle of the extinguisher and raced toward the flames.

"I'm coming, Wynter. Hang on." He sprayed the tendrils of fire that were fading, determined to get through the fiery barrier.

"Be careful," she called back, her voice surprisingly steady.

"Is Oliver here?" He continued spraying, creating a pathway.

"Yes. I locked him in the freezer."

Noah laughed, belatedly realizing the source of the banging he could hear in the background. He didn't know how Oliver had managed to get Wynter to this restaurant. Or exactly what he'd intended to do with her. But the maniac had been a fool to underestimate her.

"You, my love, are a remarkable woman."

He sprayed the last of the foam, tossing aside the canister as he prepared to charge forward. Before he could take a step, Wynter was hurtling through the narrow gap and tossing herself directly into his arms.

Noah held her close, reassuring his aching heart that she was alive.

"Are you hurt?" Reluctantly he pulled back to run a searching gaze over her slender form.

He could see soot staining her face, but no visible injuries.

"I'm fine." She glanced around, her eyes filling with tears. "But my poor restaurant."

He grabbed her hand, urgently pulling her out of the building. "The fire trucks are on the way," he assured her.

She jogged next to him, glancing over her shoulder at the fire. "What about Ollie?"

Noah didn't hesitate. "Let him burn."

Epilogue

It was a miracle that the weather decided to cooperate as Wynter stood on the hill behind her grandpa's farmhouse. The afternoon sunlight drenched the fields and shallow dells, revealing the first sprinkling of wildflowers and the green leaves beginning to unfurl on the trees.

Everything appeared fresh and new and magical.

This was why her forefathers had settled here, she suddenly realized. This view. This rich, fertile land. This opportunity to make their claim for the American dream.

A bittersweet acceptance settled in her heart, providing a layer of peace over her grief.

The past two weeks had been a bleak effort to pick up the shattered pieces of her life. Not only her restaurant that was still drying out from the overenthusiastic spray of water from the fire trucks. But the unraveling of Oliver Wheeler's secret life. He was currently sitting in jail, refusing to speak, but she was confident the police would find the evidence they needed to tie him to the crimes. Including her mom's murder.

And then there was her grandpa.

Wynter had no idea how to deal with his betrayal. She

couldn't forgive him for the damage he'd caused, but then again, she couldn't erase a lifetime of love. In the end, it didn't matter.

Two hours after Ollie had struck him on the head, Sander Moore had died. She never had a chance to speak with him, but Wynter had come to terms with the aching sense of loss.

A part of her suspected her grandpa had willed himself to death. It was easier to slip away than to face the consequences of his dreadful behavior.

The emotional toll might have been overwhelming if Wynter hadn't had Noah at her side. She'd heard about someone being a "rock," but she'd never actually had anyone in her life she could depend on. Not until Noah.

As if sensing her thoughts, Noah moved to stand next to her, wrapping his arms around her shoulders. She tilted back her head to study his face that had healed of the lingering bruises. The trauma of the past days would take longer to heal.

On the other side was her dad, providing his own surprising reassurance.

Since her grandpa's death, the two of them had gradually started to talk. Edgar had admitted that he'd followed his wife to Pike. And that he'd even gone up to the cabin with the intention of confronting the two lovers. Instead, he'd returned to the hotel, using poor Linda Baker to forget his unfaithful wife. He'd been driving back to Larkin with Linda when the cops were trying to get ahold of him to tell him of Laurel's murder.

They'd discussed the fact that he'd never gotten over the death of his wife. And their mutual trauma to discover Sander was behind her death.

Wynter had begun to hope that they might forge a new

relationship. And maybe when she had her own kids they could—

She hastily cut off the direction of her unruly thoughts, touching the bracelet she wore around her wrist. It was the bracelet that she'd found in her mom's cabin. It was an unspoken acceptance of her beautiful, loving, tragically flawed mother.

Noah was already hinting at a large brood of children. And the image of her holding their baby in her arms was enough to make Wynter melt in anticipation. But first she intended to plan a beautiful wedding, followed by an extended honeymoon at her mom's cabin and then on to Miami for some sun and fun on the beach.

"Are you ready?" Noah whispered in her ear.

Wynter hesitated. He was referring to the urn she held in her hands. But when she nodded, Wynter was thinking of much more than saying good-bye to her grandpa. She was preparing to look forward to her future.

"Ready." She opened the top of the urn and tilted it to the side, allowing the ashes to catch on the brisk breeze. They swirled and danced through the air before lightly landing in the field below. "Be at peace, Grandpa." Turning her head, she met Noah's watchful gaze. "Let's go home."

He smiled, turning to lead her toward the Jeep.

There were a thousand tasks waiting for her attention. Wynter Garden, this farm, the greenhouses. Even her truck that was still waiting at the shop.

Today, however, she was going to spend soaking in a hot tub, wrapped in the arms of a man who had taught her that true love wasn't a dark, jealous emotion. Or a cold, distant punishment.

It was two halves coming together in peaceful harmony.